PENGUIN PLAYS

BACK TO METHUSELAH

D0401637

BACK
TO METHUSELAH

A METABIOLOGICAL

PENTATEUCH

BY

BERNARD SHAW

PENGUIN BOOKS

Penguin Books Inc., 7110 Ambassador Road, Baltimore, Maryland 21207, U.S.A.
Penguin Books Australia Ltd, Ringwood, Victoria, Australia

—

First published 1921
Published in Penguin Books 1939
Reprinted 1940, 1954, 1961, 1965
Reissued 1971

—

—

Made and printed in Great Britain
by Cox & Wyman Ltd,
London, Reading and Fakenham
Set in Monotype Baskerville

Contents

PREFACE

The Infidel Half Century

THE DAWN OF DARWINISM

ONE day early in the eighteen hundred and sixties, I, being then a small boy, was with my nurse, buying something in the shop of a petty newsagent, bookseller, and stationer in Camden Street, Dublin, when there entered an elderly man, weighty and solemn, who advanced to the counter, and said pompously, 'Have you the works of the celebrated Buffoon?'

My own works were at that time unwritten, or it is possible that the shop assistant might have misunderstood me so far as to produce a copy of Man and Superman. As it was, she knew quite well what he wanted; for this was before the Education Act of 1870 had produced shop assistants who know how to read and know nothing else. The celebrated Buffoon was not a humorist, but the famous naturalist Buffon. Every literate child at that time knew Buffon's Natural History as well as Esop's Fables. And no living child had heard the name that has since obliterated Buffon's in the popular consciousness: the name of Darwin.

Ten years elapsed. The celebrated Buffoon was forgotten; I had doubled my years and my length; and I had discarded the religion of my forefathers. One day the richest and consequently most dogmatic of my uncles came into a restaurant where I was dining, and found himself, much against his will, in conversation with the most questionable of his nephews. By way of making myself agreeable, I spoke of modern thought and Darwin. He said, 'Oh, thats the fellow who wants to make out that we all have tails like monkeys.' I tried to explain that what Darwin had insisted on in this connection was that some monkeys have no tails. But my uncle was as impervious to what Darwin really said as any Neo-Darwinian nowadays. He died impenitent, and did not mention me in his will.

Twenty years elapsed. If my uncle had been alive, he would have known all about Darwin, and known it all wrong. In spite of the efforts of Grant Allen to set him right, he would have accepted Darwin as the discoverer of Evolution, of Heredity, and of modification of species by Selection. For the pre-Darwinian age had come to be regarded as a Dark Age in which men still believed that the book of Genesis was a standard scientific treatise, and that the only additions to it were Galileo's demonstration of Leonardo da Vinci's simple remark that the earth is a moon of the sun, Newton's theory of gravitation, Sir Humphry Davy's invention of the safety-lamp, the discovery of electricity, the application of steam to industrial purposes, and the penny post. It was just the same in other subjects. Thus Nietzsche, by the two or three who had come across his writings, was supposed to have been the first man to whom it occurred that mere morality and legality and urbanity lead nowhere, as if Bunyan had never written Badman. Schopenhauer was credited with inventing the distinction between the Covenant of Grace and the Covenant of Works which troubled Cromwell on his deathbed. People talked as if there had been no dramatic or descriptive music before Wagner; no impressionist painting before Whistler; whilst as to myself, I was finding that the surest way to produce an effect of daring innovation and originality was to revive the ancient attraction of long rhetorical speeches; to stick closely to the methods of Molière; and to lift characters bodily out of the pages of Charles Dickens.

THE ADVENT OF THE NEO-DARWINIANS

This particular sort of ignorance does not always or often matter. But in Darwin's case it did matter. If Darwin had really led the world at one bound from the book of Genesis to Heredity, to Modification of Species by Selection, and to Evolution, he would have been a philosopher and a prophet as well as an eminent professional naturalist, with geology as a hobby. The delusion that he had actually achieved this feat did no harm at first, because if people's views are sound, about evolution or anything else, it does not make two straws difference whether they call the revealer of their views Tom or Dick. But later on such apparently negligible errors have awkward consequences. Darwin was given an imposing reputation as not only an Evolutionist, but as the Evolutionist, with the immense majority who never read his books. The few who never read any others were led by them to concentrate exclusively on Circumstantial Selection as the explanation of all the transformations and adaptations which were the evidence for Evolution. And they presently found themselves so cut off by this specialization from the majority who knew Darwin only by his spurious reputation, that they were obliged to distinguish themselves, not as Darwinians, but as Neo-Darwinians.

Before ten more years had elapsed, the Neo-Darwinians were practically running current Science. It was 1906; I was fifty; I published my own view of evolution in a play called Man and Superman; and I found that most people were unable to understand how I could be an Evolutionist and not a Neo-Darwinian, or why I habitually derided Neo-Darwinism as a ghastly idiocy, and would fall on its professors slaughterously in public discussions. It was in the hope of making me clear the matter up that the Fabian Society, which was then organizing a series of lectures on Prophets of the Nineteenth Century, asked me to deliver a lecture on the prophet Darwin. I did so; and scraps of that lecture, which was never published, variegate these pages.

POLITICAL INADEQUACY OF THE HUMAN ANIMAL

Ten more years elapsed. Neo-Darwinism in politics had produced a European catastrophe of a magnitude so appalling, and a scope so unpredictable, that as I write these lines in 1920, it is still far from certain whether our civilization will survive it. The circumstances of this catastrophe, the boyish cinema-fed romanticism which made it possible to impose it on the people as a crusade, and especially the ignorance and errors of the victors of Western Europe when its violent phase had passed and the time for reconstruction arrived, confirmed a doubt which had grown steadily in my mind during my forty years public work as a Socialist: namely, whether the human animal, as he exists at present, is capable of solving the social problems raised by his own aggregation, or, as he calls it, his civilization.

COWARDICE OF THE IRRELIGIOUS

Another observation I had made was that goodnatured unambitious men are cowards when they have no religion. They are dominated and exploited not only by greedy and often half-witted and half-alive weaklings who will do anything for cigars, champagne, motor cars, and the more childish and selfish uses of money, but by able and sound administrators who can do nothing else with them than dominate and exploit them. Government and exploitation become synonymous under such circumstances; and the world is finally ruled by the childish, the brigands, and the blackguards. Those who refuse to stand in with them are persecuted and occasionally executed when they give any trouble to the exploiters. They fall into poverty when they lack lucrative specific talents. At the present moment one half of Europe, having knocked the other half down, is trying to kick it to death, and may succeed: a procedure which is, logically, sound Neo-Darwinism. And the goodnatured majority are looking on in helpless horror, or allowing themselves to be persuaded by the newspapers of their exploiters that the kicking is not only a sound commercial investment, but an act of divine justice of which they are the ardent instruments.

But if Man is really incapable of organizing a big civilization, and cannot organize even a village or a tribe any too well, what is the use of giving him a religion? A religion may make him hunger and thirst for righteousness; but will it endow him with the practical capacity to satisfy that appetite? Good intentions do not carry with them a grain of political science, which is a very complicated one. The most devoted and indefatigable, the most able and disinterested students of this science in England, as far as I know, are my friends Sidney and Beatrice Webb. It has taken them forty years of preliminary work, in the course of which they have published several treatises comparable to Adam Smith's Wealth of Nations, to formulate a political constitution adequate to existing needs. If this is the measure of what can be done in a lifetime by extraordinary ability, keen natural aptitude, exceptional opportunities, and freedom from the preoccupations of bread-winning, what are we to expect from the parliament man to whom political science is as remote and distasteful as the differential calculus, and to whom such an elementary but vital point as the law of economic rent is a *pons asinorum* never to be approached, much less crossed? Or from the common voter who is mostly so hard at work all day earning a living that he cannot keep awake for five minutes over a book?

IS THERE ANY HOPE IN EDUCATION?

The usual answer is that we must educate our masters: that is, ourselves. We must teach citizenship and political science at school. But must we? There is no must about it, the hard fact being that we must *not* teach political science or citizenship at school. The schoolmaster who attempted it would soon find himself penniless in the streets without pupils, if not in the dock pleading to a pompously worded indictment for sedition against the exploiters. Our schools teach the morality of feudalism corrupted by commercialism, and hold up the military conqueror, the robber baron, and the profiteer, as models of the illustrious and the successful. In vain do the prophets who see through this imposture preach and teach a better gospel: the individuals whom they convert are doomed to pass away in a few years; and the new generations are dragged back in

the schools to the morality of the fifteenth century, and think themselves Liberal when they are defending the ideas of Henry VII,
and gentlemanly when they are opposing to them the ideas of
Richard III. Thus the educated man is a greater nuisance than the
uneducated one: indeed it is the inefficiency and sham of the educational side of our schools (to which, except under compulsion,
children would not be sent by their parents at all if they did not act
as prisons in which the immature are kept from worrying the
mature) that save us from being dashed on the rocks of false doctrine
instead of drifting down the midstream of mere ignorance. There
is no way out through the schoolmaster.

HOMEOPATHIC EDUCATION

In truth, mankind cannot be saved from without, by schoolmasters
or any other sort of masters: it can only be lamed and enslaved by
them. It is said that if you wash a cat it will never again wash itself.
This may or may not be true: what is certain is that if you teach a
man anything he will never learn it; and if you cure him of a disease
he will be unable to cure himself the next time it attacks him. Therefore, if you want to see a cat clean, you throw a bucket of mud over
it, when it will immediately take extraordinary pains to lick the mud
off, and finally be cleaner than it was before. In the same way
doctors who are up-to-date (say ·00005 per cent of all the registered
practitioners, and 20 per cent of the unregistered ones), when they
want to rid you of a disease or a symptom, inoculate you with that
disease or give you a drug that produces that symptom, in order to
provoke you to resist it as the mud provokes the cat to wash itself.

Now an acute person will ask me why, if this be so, our false
education does not provoke our scholars to find out the truth. My
answer is that it sometimes does. Voltaire was a pupil of the Jesuits;
Samuel Butler was the pupil of a hopelessly conventional and
erroneous country parson. But then Voltaire was Voltaire, and
Butler was Butler: that is, their minds were so abnormally strong
that they could throw off the doses of poison that paralyse ordinary
minds. When the doctors inoculate you and the homeopathists
dose you, they give you an infinitesimally attenuated dose. If they
gave you the virus at full strength it would overcome your resistance
and produce its direct effect. The doses of false doctrine given at
public schools and universities are so big that they overwhelm the
resistance that a tiny dose would provoke. The normal student is
corrupted beyond redemption, and will drive the genius who resists

out of the country if he can. Byron and Shelley had to fly to Italy, whilst Castlereagh and Eldon ruled the roost at home. Rousseau was hunted from frontier to frontier; Karl Marx starved in exile in a Soho lodging; Ruskin's articles were refused by the magazines (he was too rich to be otherwise persecuted); whilst mindless forgotten nonentities governed the land; sent men to the prison or the gallows for blasphemy and sedition (meaning the truth about Church and State); and sedulously stored up the social disease and corruption which explode from time to time in gigantic boils that have to be lanced by a million bayonets. This is the result of allopathic education. Homeopathic education has not yet been officially tried, and would obviously be a delicate matter if it were. A body of schoolmasters inciting their pupils to infinitesimal peccadilloes with the object of provoking them to exclaim, 'Get thee behind me, Satan,' or telling them white lies about history for the sake of being contradicted, insulted, and refuted, would certainly do less harm than our present educational allopaths do; but then nobody will advocate homeopathic education. Allopathy has produced the poisonous illusion that it enlightens instead of darkening. The suggestion may, however, explain why, whilst most people's minds succumb to inculcation and environment, a few react vigorously: honest and decent people coming from thievish slums, and sceptics and realists from country parsonages.

THE DIABOLICAL EFFICIENCY OF TECHNICAL EDUCATION

But meanwhile – and here comes the horror of it – our technical instruction is honest and efficient. The public schoolboy who is carefully blinded, duped, and corrupted as to the nature of a society based on profiteering, and is taught to honor parasitic idleness and luxury, learns to shoot and ride and keep fit with all the assistance and guidance that can be procured for him by the most anxiously sincere desire that he may do these things well, and if possible superlatively well. In the army he learns to fly; to drop bombs; to use machine-guns to the utmost of his capacity. The discovery of high explosives is rewarded and dignified: instruction in the manufacture of the weapons, battleships, submarines, and land batteries by which they are applied destructively, is quite genuine: the instructors know their business, and really mean the learners to succeed. The result is that the powers of destruction that could hardly without uneasiness be entrusted to infinite wisdom and infinite benevolence are placed in the hands of romantic schoolboy patriots who, however generous by nature, are by education ignoramuses, dupes, snobs, and sportsmen to whom fighting is a religion and killing an accomplishment; whilst political power, useless under such circumstances except to militarist imperialists in chronic terror of invasion and subjugation, pompous tufthunting fools, commercial adventurers to whom the organization by the nation of its own industrial services would mean checkmate, financial parasites on the money market, and stupid people who cling to the *status quo* merely because they are used to it, is obtained by heredity, by simple purchase, by keeping newspapers and pretending that they are organs of public opinion, by the wiles of seductive women, and by prostituting ambitious talent to the service of the profiteers, who call the tune because, having secured all the spare plunder, they alone can afford to pay the piper. Neither the rulers nor the ruled understand high politics. They do not even know that there is such a branch of knowledge as political science; but between them they can coerce and enslave with the deadliest efficiency, even to the wiping out of civilization, because their education as slayers has been honestly and thoroughly carried out. Essentially the rulers are all defectives; and there is nothing worse than government by defectives who wield irresistible powers of physical coercion. The commonplace sound people submit, and compel the rest to submit, because they have been taught to do so as an article of religion and a point of honor. Those in whom natural enlightenment has reacted against artificial education submit because they are compelled; but they would resist, and finally resist effectively, if they were not cowards. And they are cowards because they have neither an officially accredited and established religion nor a generally recognized point of honor, and are all at sixes and sevens with their various private speculations, sending their children perforce to the schools where they will be corrupted for want of any other schools. The rulers are equally intimidated by the immense extension and cheapening of the means of slaughter and destruction. The British Government is more afraid of Ireland now that submarines, bombs, and poison gas are cheap and easily made than it was of the German Empire before the war; consequently the old British custom which maintained a balance of power through command of the sea is intensified into a terror that sees security in nothing short of absolute military mastery of the entire globe: that is, in an impossibility that will yet seem possible in detail to soldiers and to parochial and insular patriotic civilians.

FLIMSINESS OF CIVILIZATION

This situation has occurred so often before, always with the same result of a collapse of civilization (Professor Flinders Petrie has let out the secret of previous collapses), that the rich are instinctively crying 'Let us eat and drink; for tomorrow we die,' and the poor, 'How long, O Lord, how long?' But the pitiless reply still is that God helps those who help themselves. This does not mean that if Man cannot find the remedy no remedy will be found. The power that produced Man when the monkey was not up to the mark, can produce a higher creature than Man if Man does not come up to the mark. What it means is that if Man is to be saved, Man must save himself. There seems no compelling reason why he should be saved. He is by no means an ideal creature. At his present best many of his ways are so unpleasant that they are unmentionable in polite society, and so painful that he is compelled to pretend that pain is often a good. Nature holds no brief for the human experiment: it must stand or fall by its results. If Man will not serve, Nature will try another experiment.

What hope is there then of human improvement? According to the Neo-Darwinists, to the Mechanists, no hope whatever, because improvement can come only through some senseless accident which must, on the statistical average of accidents, be presently wiped out by some other equally senseless accident.

CREATIVE EVOLUTION

But this dismal creed does not discourage those who believe that the impulse that produces evolution is creative. They have observed the simple fact that the will to do anything can and does, at a certain pitch of intensity set up by conviction of its necessity, create and organize new tissue to do it with. To them therefore mankind is by no means played out yet. If the weight lifter, under the trivial stimulus of an athletic competition, can 'put up a muscle,' it seems reasonable to believe that an equally earnest and convinced philosopher could 'put up a brain.' Both are directions of vitality to a certain end. Evolution shews us this direction of vitality doing all sorts of things: providing the centipede with a hundred legs, and ridding the fish of any legs at all; building lungs and arms for the land and gills and fins for the sea; enabling the mammal to gestate its young inside its body, and the fowl to incubate hers outside it; offering us, we may say, our choice of any sort of bodily contrivance to maintain our activity and increase our resources.

VOLUNTARY LONGEVITY

Among other matters apparently changeable at will is the duration of individual life. Weismann, a very clever and suggestive biologist who was unhappily reduced to idiocy by Neo-Darwinism, pointed out that death is not an eternal condition of life, but an expedient introduced to provide for continual renewal without overcrowding. Now, Circumstantial Selection does not account for natural death: it accounts only for the survival of species in which the individuals have sense enough to decay and die on purpose. But the individuals do not seem to have calculated very reasonably: nobody can explain why a parrot should live ten times as long as a dog, and a turtle be almost immortal. In the case of man, the operation has overshot its mark: men do not live long enough: they are, for all the purposes of high civilization, mere children when they die; and our Prime Ministers, though rated as mature, divide their time between the golf course and the Treasury Bench in parliament. Presumably, however, the same power that made this mistake can remedy it. If on opportunist grounds Man now fixes the term of his life at three score and ten years, he can equally fix it at three hundred, or three thousand, or even at the genuine Circumstantial Selection limit, which would be until a sooner-or-later-inevitable fatal accident makes an end of the individual. All that is necessary to make him extend his present span is that tremendous catastrophes such as the late war shall convince him of the necessity of at least outliving his taste for golf and cigars if the race is to be saved. This is not fantastic speculation: it is deductive biology, if there is such a science as biology. Here, then, is a stone that we have left unturned, and that may be worth turning. To make the suggestion more entertaining than it would be to most people in the form of a biological treatise, I have written Back to Methuselah as a contribution to the modern Bible.

Many people, however, can read treatises and cannot read Bibles. Darwin could not read Shakespear. Some who can read both, like to learn the history of their ideas. Some are so entangled in the current confusion of Creative Evolution with Circumstantial Selection by their historical ignorance that they are puzzled by any distinction between the two. For all their sakes I must give here a little history of the conflict between the view of Evolution taken by the Darwinians (though not altogether by Darwin himself) and called Natural Selection, and that which is emerging, under the title of Creative Evolution, as the genuinely scientific religion for which all wise men are now anxiously looking.

THE EARLY EVOLUTIONISTS

The idea of Evolution, or Transformation as it is now sometimes called, was not first conceived by Charles Darwin, nor by Alfred Russel Wallace, who observed the operation of Circumstantial Selection simultaneously with Charles. The celebrated Buffoon was a better Evolutionist than either of them; and two thousand years before Buffon was born, the Greek philosopher Empedocles opined that all forms of life are transformations of four elements, Fire, Air, Earth, and Water, effected by the two innate forces of attraction and repulsion, or love and hate. As lately as 1860 I myself was taught as a child that everything was made out of these four elements. Both the Empedocleans and the Evolutionists were opposed to those who believed in the separate creation of all forms of life as described in the book of Genesis. This 'conflict between religion and science', as the phrase went then, did not perplex my infant mind in the least: I knew perfectly well, without knowing that I knew it, that the validity of a story is not the same as the occurrence of a fact. But as I grew up I found that I had to choose between Evolution and Genesis. If you believed that dogs and cats and snakes and birds and beetles and oysters and whales and men and women were all separately designed and made and named in Eden garden at the beginning of things, and have since survived simply by reproducing their kind, then you were not an Evolutionist. If you believed, on the contrary, that all the different species are modifications, variations, and elaborations of one primal stock, or even of a few primal stocks, then you were an Evolutionist. But you were not necessarily a Darwinian; for you might have been a modern Evolutionist twenty years before Charles Darwin was born, and a whole lifetime before he published his Origin of Species. For that matter, when Aristotle grouped animals with backbones as blood relations, he began the sort of classification which, when extended by Darwin to monkeys and men, so shocked my uncle.

Genesis had held the field until the time (1707–1778) of Linnaeus the famous botanist. In the meantime the microscope had been invented. It revealed a new world of hitherto invisible creatures called Infusorians, as common water was found to be an infusion of them. In the eighteenth century naturalists were very keen on the Infusorian Amoebas, and were much struck by the way in which the members of this old family behaved and developed. But it was still possible for Linnaeus to begin a treatise by saying 'There are just so many species as there were forms created in the beginning,' though there were hundreds of commonplace Scotch gardeners, pigeon fanciers, and stock breeders then living who knew better. Linnaeus himself knew better before he died. In the last edition of his System of Nature, he began to wonder whether the transmutation of species by variation might not be possible. Then came the great poet who jumped over the facts to the conclusion. Goethe said that all the shapes of creation were cousins; that there must be some common stock from which all the species had sprung; that it was the environment of air that had produced the eagle, of water the seal, and of earth the mole. He could not say how this happened; but he divined that it did happen. Erasmus Darwin, the grandfather of Charles, carried the environment theory much further, pointing out instance after instance of modifications made in species apparently to adapt it to circumstances and environment: for instance, that the brilliant colors of the leopard, which make it so conspicuous in Regent's Park, conceal it in a tropical jungle. Finally he wrote, as his declaration of faith, 'The world has been evolved, not created: it has arisen little by little from a small beginning, and has increased through the activity of the elemental forces embodied in itself, and so has rather grown than come into being at an almighty word. What a sublime idea of the infinite might of the great Architect, the Cause of all causes, the Father of all fathers, the Ens Entium! For if we would compare the Infinite, it would surely require a greater Infinite to cause the causes of effects than to produce the effects themselves.' In this, published in the year 1794, you have nineteenth-century Evolution precisely defined. And Erasmus Darwin was by no means its only apostle. It was in the air then. A German biologist named Treviranus, whose book was published in 1802, wrote, 'In every living being there exists a capacity for endless diversity of form. Each possesses the power of adapting its organization to the variations of the external world; and it is this power, called into activity by cosmic changes, which has enabled the simple zoophytes of the primitive world to climb to higher and higher stages of organization, and has brought endless variety into nature.' There you have your evolution of Man from the amoeba all complete whilst Nelson was still alive on the seas. And in 1809, before the battle of Waterloo, a French soldier named Lamarck, who had beaten his musket into a microscope and turned zoologist, declared that species were an illusion produced by the shortness of our individual lives, and that they were constantly changing and melting into one another and into new forms as surely as the hand of a clock is continually moving, though it moves so slowly that it looks stationary to us. We have since come to think that its industry is less continuous: that the clock stops for a long time, and then is suddenly 'put on' by a mysterious finger. But never mind that just at present.

THE ADVENT OF THE NEO-LAMARCKIANS

I call your special attention to Lamarck, because later on there were Neo-Lamarckians as well as Neo-Darwinians. I was a Neo-Lamarckian. Lamarck passed on from the conception of Evolution as a general law to Charles Darwin's department of it, which was the method of Evolution. Lamarck, whilst making many ingenious suggestions as to the reaction of external causes on life and habit, such as changes of climate, food supply, geological upheavals and so forth, really held as his fundamental proposition that living organisms changed because they wanted to. As he stated it, the great factor in Evolution is use and disuse. If you have no eyes, and want to see, and keep trying to see, you will finally get eyes. If, like a mole or a subterranean fish, you have eyes and dont want to see, you will lose your eyes. If you like eating the tender tops of trees enough to make you concentrate all your energies on the stretching of your neck, you will finally get a long neck, like the giraffe. This seems absurd to inconsiderate people at the first blush; but it is within the personal experience of all of us that it is just by this process that a child tumbling about the floor becomes a boy walking erect; and that a man sprawling on the road with a bruised chin, or supine on the ice with a bashed occiput, becomes a bicyclist and a skater. The process is not continuous, as it would be if mere practice had anything to do with it; for though you may improve at each bicycling lesson *during* the lesson, when you begin your next lesson you do not begin at the point at which you left off: you relapse apparently to the beginning. Finally, you succeed quite suddenly, and do not relapse again. More miraculous still, you at once exercise the new power unconsciously. Although you are adapting your front wheel to your balance so elaborately and actively that the accidental locking of your handle bars for a second will throw you off; though five minutes before you could not do it at all, yet now you do it as unconsciously as you grow your finger nails. You have a new faculty, and must have created some new bodily tissue as its organ. And you have done it solely by willing. For here there can be no question of Circumstantial Selection, or the survival of the fittest. The man who is learning how to ride a bicycle has no advantage over the non-cyclist in the struggle for existence: quite the contrary. He has acquired a new habit, an automatic unconscious habit, solely because he wanted to, and kept trying until it was added unto him.

HOW ACQUIREMENTS ARE INHERITED

But when your son tries to skate or bicycle in his turn, he does not pick up the accomplishment where you left it, any more than he is born six feet high with a beard and a tall hat. The set-back that occurred between your lessons occurs again. The race learns exactly as the individual learns. Your son relapses, not to the very beginning, but to a point which no mortal method of measurement can distinguish from the beginning. Now this is odd; for certain other habits of yours, equally acquired (to the Evolutionist, of course, all habits are acquired), equally unconscious, equally automatic, are transmitted without any perceptible relapse. For instance, the very first act of your son when he enters the world as a separate individual is to yell with indignation: that yell which Shakespear thought the most tragic and piteous of all sounds. In the act of yelling he begins to breathe: another habit, and not even a necessary one, as the object of breathing can be achieved in other ways, as by deep sea fishes. He circulates his blood by pumping it with his heart. He demands a meal, and proceeds at once to perform the most elaborate chemical operations on the food he swallows. He manufactures teeth; discards them; and replaces them with fresh ones. Compared to these habitual feats, walking, standing upright, and bicycling are the merest trifles; yet it is only by going through the wanting, trying process that he can stand, walk, or cycle, whereas in the other and far more difficult and complex habits he not only does not consciously want nor consciously try, but actually consciously objects very strongly. Take that early habit of cutting the teeth: would he do that if he could help it? Take that later habit of decaying and eliminating himself by death – equally an acquired habit, remember – how he abhors it! Yet the habit has become so rooted, so automatic, that he must do it in spite of himself, even to his own destruction.

We have here a routine which, given time enough for it to operate, will finally produce the most elaborate forms of organized life on Lamarckian lines without the intervention of Circumstantial Selection at all. If you can turn a pedestrian into a cyclist, and a cyclist into a pianist or violinist, without the intervention of Circumstantial Selection, you can turn an amoeba into a man, or a man into a superman, without it. All of which is rank heresy to the Neo-

Darwinian, who imagines that if you stop Circumstantial Selection, you not only stop development but inaugurate a rapid and disastrous degeneration.

Let us fix the Lamarckian evolutionary process well in our minds. You are alive; and you want to be more alive. You want an extension of consciousness and of power. You want, consequently, additional organs, or additional uses of your existing organs: that is, additional habits. You get them because you want them badly enough to keep trying for them until they come. Nobody knows how: nobody knows why: all we know is that the thing actually takes place. We relapse miserably from effort to effort until the old organ is modified or the new one created, when suddenly the impossible becomes possible and the habit is formed. The moment we form it we want to get rid of the consciousness of it so as to economize our consciousness for fresh conquests of life; as all consciousness means preoccupation and obstruction. If we had to think about breathing or digesting or circulating our blood we should have no attention to spare for anything else, as we find to our cost when anything goes wrong with these operations. We want to be unconscious of them just as we wanted to acquire them; and we finally win what we want. But we win unconsciousness of our habits at the cost of losing our control of them; and we also build one habit and its corresponding functional modification of our organs on another, and so become dependent on our old habits. Consequently we have to persist in them even when they hurt us. We cannot stop breathing to avoid an attack of asthma, or to escape drowning. We can lose a habit and discard an organ when we no longer need them, just as we acquired them; but this process is slow and broken by relapses; and relics of the organ and the habit long survive its utility. And if other and still indispensable habits and modifications have been built on the ones we wish to discard, we must provide a new foundation for them before we demolish the old one. This is also a slow process and a very curious one.

THE MIRACLE OF CONDENSED RECAPITULATION

The relapses between the efforts to acquire a habit are important because, as we have seen, they recur not only from effort to effort in the case of the individual, but from generation to generation in the case of the race. This relapsing from generation to generation is an invariable characteristic of the evolutionary process. For instance, Raphael, though descended from eight uninterrupted generations of painters, had to learn to paint apparently as if no Sanzio had ever handled a brush before. But he had also to learn to breathe, and digest, and circulate his blood. Although his father and mother were fully grown adults when he was conceived, he was not conceived or even born fully grown: he had to go back and begin as a speck of protoplasm, and to struggle through an embryonic lifetime, during part of which he was indistinguishable from an embryonic dog, and had neither a skull nor a backbone. When he at last acquired these articles, he was for some time doubtful whether he was a bird or a fish. He had to compress untold centuries of development into nine months before he was human enough to break loose as an independent being. And even then he was still so incomplete that his parents might well have exclaimed 'Good Heavens! have you learnt nothing from our experience that you come into the world in this ridiculously elementary state? Why cant you talk and walk and paint and behave decently?' To that question Baby Raphael had no answer. All he could have said was that this is how evolution or transformation happens. The time may come when the same force that compressed the development of millions of years into nine months may pack many more millions into even a shorter space; so that Raphaels may be born painters as they are now born breathers and blood circulators. But they will still begin as specks of protoplasm, and acquire the faculty of painting in their mother's womb at quite a late stage of their embryonic life. They must recapitulate the history of mankind in their own persons, however briefly they may condense it.

Nothing was so astonishing and significant in the discoveries of the embryologists, nor anything so absurdly little appreciated, as this recapitulation, as it is now called: this power of hurrying up into months a process which was once so long and tedious that the mere contemplation of it is unendurable by men whose span of life is three-score-and-ten. It widened human possibilities to the extent of enabling us to hope that the most prolonged and difficult operation of our minds may yet become instantaneous, or, as we call it, instinctive. It also directed our attention to examples of this packing up of centuries into seconds which were staring us in the face in all directions. As I write these lines the newspapers are occupied by the exploits of a child of eight, who has just defeated twenty adult chess players in twenty games played simultaneously, and has been able afterwards to reconstruct all the twenty games without any apparent effort of memory. Most people, including myself, play chess (when they play it at all) from hand to mouth, and can hardly recall the last move but one, or foresee the next but two. Also, when I have to make an arithmetical calculation, I have to do it step by step with pencil and paper, slowly, reluctantly, and with so little confidence in the result that I dare not act on it without 'proving' the sum by a further calculation involving more ciphering. But there are men who can neither read, write, nor cipher, to whom the answer to such sums as I can do is instantly obvious without any conscious calculation at all; and the result is infallible. Yet some of these natural arithmeticians have but a small vocabulary; are at a loss when they have to find words for any but the simplest everyday occasions; and cannot for the life of them describe mechanical operations which they perform daily in the course of their trade; whereas to me the whole vocabulary of English literature, from Shakespear to the latest edition of the Encyclopaedia Britannica, is so completely and instantaneously at my call that I have never had to consult even a thesaurus except once or twice when for some reason I wanted a third or fourth synonym. Again, though I have tried and failed to draw recognizable portraits of persons I have seen every day for years, Mr Bernard Partridge, having seen a man once, will, without more strain than is involved in eating a sandwich, draw him to the life. The keyboard of a piano is a device I have never been able to master; yet Mr Cyril Scott uses it exactly as I use my own fingers; and to Sir Edward Elgar an orchestral score is as instantaneously intelligible at sight as a page of Shakespear is to me. One man cannot, after trying for years, finger the flute fluently. Another will take up a flute with a newly invented arrangement of keys on it, and play it at once with hardly a mistake. We find people to whom writing is so difficult that they prefer to sign their name with a mark, and beside them men who master systems of shorthand and improvise new systems of their own as easily as they learnt the alphabet. These contrasts are to be seen on all hands, and have nothing to do with variations in general intelligence, nor even in the specialized intelligence proper to the faculty in question: for example, no composer or dramatic poet has ever pretended to be able to perform all the parts he writes for the singers, actors, and players who are his executants. One might as well expect Napoleon to be a fencer, or the Astronomer Royal to know how many beans make five any better than his bookkeeper. Even exceptional command of language does not imply the possession of ideas to express; Mezzofanti, the master of fifty-eight languages, had less to say in them than Shakespear with his little Latin and less Greek; and public life is the paradise of voluble windbags.

All these examples, which might be multiplied by millions, are cases in which a long, laborious, conscious, detailed process of acquirement has been condensed into an instinctive and unconscious inborn one. Factors which formerly had to be considered one by one in succession are integrated into what seems a single simple factor. Chains of hardly soluble problems have coalesced in one problem which solves itself the moment it is raised. What is more, they have been pushed back (or forward, if you like) from post-natal to pre-natal ones. The child in the womb may take some time over them; but it is a miraculously shortened time.

The time phenomena involved are curious, and suggest that we are either wrong about our history or else that we enormously exaggerate the periods required for the pre-natal acquirement of habits. In the nineteenth century we talked very glibly about geological periods, and flung millions of eons about in the most lordly manner in our reaction against Archbishop Ussher's chronology. We had a craze for big figures, and positively liked to believe that the progress made by the child in the womb in a month was represented in prehistoric time by ages and ages. We insisted that Evolution advanced more slowly than any snail ever crawled, and that Nature does not proceed by leaps and bounds. This was all very well as long as we were dealing with such acquired habits as breathing or digestion. It was possible to believe that dozens of epochs had gone to the slow building up of these habits. But when we have to consider the case of a man born not only as an accomplished metabolist, but with such an aptitude for shorthand and keyboard manipulation that he is a stenographer or pianist at least five sixths ready-made as soon as he can control his hands intelligently, we are forced to suspect either that keyboards and shorthand are older inventions than we suppose, or else that acquirements can be assimilated and stored as congenital qualifications in a shorter time than we think; so that, as between Lyell and Archbishop Ussher, the laugh may not be with Lyell quite so uproariously as it seemed fifty years ago.

HEREDITY AN OLD STORY

It is evident that the evolutionary process is a hereditary one, or, to put it less drily, that human life is continuous and immortal. The Evolutionists took heredity for granted. So did everybody. The human mind has been soaked in heredity as long back as we can trace its thought. Hereditary peers, hereditary monarchs, hereditary castes and trades and classes were the best known of social institutions, and in some cases of public nuisances. Pedigree men counted pedigree dogs and pedigree horses among their most cherished possessions. Far from being unconscious of heredity, or sceptical, men were insanely credulous about it: they not only believed in the transmission of qualities and habits from generation to generation, but expected the son to begin mentally where the father left off.

This belief in heredity led naturally to the practice of Intentional Selection. Good blood and breeding were eagerly sought after in human marriage. In dealing with plants and animals, selection with a view to the production of new varieties and the improvement and modification of species had been practised ever since men began to cultivate them. My pre-Darwinian uncle knew as well as Darwin that the race-horse and the dray-horse are not separate creations from the Garden of Eden, but adaptations by deliberate human selection of the medieval war-horse to modern racing and industrial haulage. He knew that there are nearly two hundred different sorts of dogs, all capable of breeding with one another and of producing cross varieties unknown to Adam. He knew that the same thing is true of pigeons. He knew that gardeners had spent their lives trying to breed black tulips and green carnations and unheard-of orchids, and had actually produced flowers just as strange to Eve. His quarrel with the Evolutionists was not a quarrel with the evidence for Evolution: he had accepted enough of it to prove Evolution ten times over before he ever heard of it. What he repudiated was cousinship with the ape, and the implied suspicion of a rudimentary tail, because it was offensive to his sense of his own dignity, and because he thought that apes were ridiculous, and tails diabolical when associated with the erect posture. Also he believed that Evolution was a heresy which involved the destruction of Christianity, of which, as a member of the Irish Church (the pseudo-Protestant one), he conceived himself a pillar. But this was only his ignorance; for man may deny his descent from an ape and be eligible as a churchwarden without being any the less a convinced Evolutionist.

DISCOVERY ANTICIPATED BY DIVINATION

What is more, the religious folk can claim to be among the pioneers of Evolutionism. Weismann, Neo-Darwinist though he was, devoted a long passage in his History of Evolution to the Nature Philosophy of Lorenz Oken, published in 1809. Oken defined natural science as 'the science of the everlasting transmutations of the Holy Ghost in the world.' His religion had started him on the right track, and not only led him to think out a whole scheme of Evolution in abstract terms, but guided his aim in a significantly good scientific shot which brought him within the scope of Weismann. He not only defined the original substance from which all forms of life have developed as protoplasm, or, as he called it, primitive slime (*Urschleim*), but actually declared that this slime took the form of vesicles out of which the universe was built. Here was the modern cell morphology guessed by a religious thinker long before the microscope and the scalpel forced it on the vision of mere laboratory workers who could not think and had no religion. They worked hard to discover the vital secrets of the glands by opening up dogs and cutting out the glands, or tying up their ducts, or severing their nerves, thereby learning, negatively, that the governors of our vital forces do not hold their incessant conversations through the nerves, and, positively, how miserably a horribly injured dog can die, leaving us to infer that we shall probably perish likewise if we grudge our guineas to Harley Street. Lorenz Oken *thought* very hard to find out what was happening to the Holy Ghost, and thereby made a contribution of extraordinary importance to our understanding of uninjured creatures. The man who was scientific enough to see that the Holy Ghost is a scientific fact got easily in front of the blockheads who could only sin against it. Hence my uncle was turning his back on very respectable company when he derided Evolution, and would probably have recanted and apologized at once had anybody pointed out to him what a solecism he was committing.

The metaphysical side of Evolution was thus no novelty when Darwin arrived. Had Oken never lived, there would still have been millions of persons trained from their childhood to believe that we are continually urged upwards by a force called the Will of God. In 1819 Schopenhauer published his treatise on The World as Will, which is the metaphysical complement to Lamarck's natural history, as it demonstrates that the driving force behind Evolution is a will-to-live, and to live, as Christ said long before, more abundantly. And the earlier philosophers, from Plato to Leibniz, had kept the human mind open for the thought of the universe as one idea behind all its physically apprehensible transformations.

CORRECTED DATES FOR THE DISCOVERY OF EVOLUTION

All this, remember, is the state of things in the pre-Darwin period, which so many of us still think of as a pre-evolutionary period. Evolutionism was the rage before Queen Victoria came to the throne. To fix this chronology, let me repeat the story told by Weismann of the July revolution in Paris in 1830, when the French got rid of Charles the Tenth. Goethe was then still living; and a French friend of his called on him and found him wildly excited. 'What do you think of the great event?' said Goethe. 'The volcano is in eruption; and all is in flames. There can no longer be discussion with closed doors.' The Frenchman replied that no doubt it was a terrible business; but what could they expect with such a ministry and such a king? 'Stuff!' said Goethe: 'I am not thinking of these people at all, but of the open rupture in the French Academy between Cuvier and St Hilaire. It is of the utmost importance to science.' The rupture Goethe meant was about Evolution, Cuvier contending that there were four species, and St Hilaire that there was only one.

From 1830, when Darwin was an apparently unpromising lad of twenty-one, until 1859, when he turned the world upside down by his Origin of Species, there was a slump in Evolutionism. The first generation of its enthusiasts was ageing and dying out; and their successors were being taught from the Book of Genesis, just as Edward VI was (and Edward VII too, for that matter). Nobody who knew the theory was adding anything to it. This slump not only heightened the impression of entire novelty when Darwin brought the subject to the front again: it probably prevented him from realizing how much had been done before, even by his own grandfather, to whom he was accused of being unjust. Besides, he was not really carrying on the family business. He was an entirely original worker; and he was on a new tack, as we shall see presently. And he would not in any case have thought much, as a practical naturalist, of the more or less mystical intellectual speculations of the Deists of 1790–1830. Scientific workers were very tired of Deism just then. They had given up the riddle of the Great First Cause as insoluble, and were calling themselves, accordingly, Agnostics. They had turned from the inscrutable question of Why things existed, to the spade work of discovering What was really occurring in the world and How it really occurred.

With all his attention bent in this new direction, Darwin soon noticed that a good deal was occurring in an entirely unmystical and even unmeaning way of which the older speculative Deist-Evolutionists had taken little or no account. Nowadays, when we are turning in weary disgust and disillusion from Neo-Darwinism and Mechanism to Vitalism and Creative Evolution, it is difficult to imagine how this new departure of Darwin's could possibly have appealed to his contemporaries as exciting, agreeable, above all as hopeful. Let me therefore try to bring back something of the atmosphere of that time by describing a scene, very characteristic of its superstitions, in which I took what was then considered an unspeakably shocking part.

DEFYING THE LIGHTNING: A FRUSTRATED EXPERIMENT

One evening in 1878 or thereabouts, I, being then in my earliest twenties, was at a bachelor party of young men of the professional class in the house of a doctor in the Kensingtonian quarter of London. They fell to talking about religious revivals; and an anecdote was related of a man who, having incautiously scoffed at the mission of Messrs Moody and Sankey, a then famous firm of American evangelists, was subsequently carried home on a shutter, slain by divine vengeance as a blasphemer. A timid minority, without quite venturing to question the truth of the incident – for they naturally did not care to run the risk of going home on shutters themselves – nevertheless shewed a certain disposition to cavil at those who exulted in it; and something approaching to an argument began. At last it was alleged by the most evangelical of the disputants that Charles Bradlaugh, the most formidable atheist on the Secularist platform, had taken out his watch publicly and challenged the Almighty to strike him dead in five minutes if he really existed and disapproved of atheism. The leader of the cavillers, with great heat, repudiated this as a gross calumny, declaring that Bradlaugh had repeatedly and indignantly contradicted it, and implying that the atheist champion was far too pious a man to commit such a blasphemy. This exquisite confusion of ideas roused my sense of comedy. It was clear to me that the challenge attributed to Charles Bradlaugh was a scientific experiment of a quite simple, straightforward, and proper kind to ascertain whether the expression of atheistic opinions really did involve any personal risk. It was certainly the method taught in the Bible, Elijah having confuted the prophets of Baal in precisely that way, with every circumstance of bitter mockery of their god when he failed to send down fire from heaven. Accordingly I said that if the question at issue were whether the penalty of questioning the theology of Messrs Moody and Sankey was to be struck dead on the spot by an incensed deity, nothing could effect a more convincing settlement of it than the very obvious experiment attributed to Mr Bradlaugh, and that consequently if he had not tried it, he ought to have tried it. The omission, I added, was one which could easily be remedied there and then, as I happened to share Mr Bradlaugh's views as to the absurdity of the belief in these violent interferences with the order of nature by a short-tempered and thin-skinned supernatural deity. Therefore – and at that point I took out my watch.

The effect was electrical. Neither sceptics nor devotees were prepared to abide the result of the experiment. In vain did I urge the pious to trust in the accuracy of their deity's aim with a thunderbolt, and the justice of his discrimination between the innocent and the guilty. In vain did I appeal to the sceptics to accept the logical outcome of their scepticism: it soon appeared that when thunderbolts were in question there were no sceptics. Our host, seeing that his guests would vanish precipitately if the impious challenge were uttered, leaving him alone with a solitary infidel under sentence of extermination in five minutes, interposed and forbade the experiment, pleading at the same time for a change of subject. I of course complied, but could not refrain from remarking that though the dreadful words had not been uttered, yet, as the thought had been formulated in my mind it was very doubtful whether the consequences could be averted by sealing my lips. However, the rest appeared to feel that the game would be played according to the rules, and that it mattered very little what I thought so long as I said nothing. Only the leader of the evangelical party, I thought, was a little preoccupied until five minutes had elapsed and the weather was still calm.

IN QUEST OF THE FIRST CAUSE

Another reminiscence. In those days we thought in terms of time and space, of cause and effect, as we still do; but we do not now demand from a religion that it shall explain the universe completely in terms of cause and effect, and present the world to us as a manufactured article and as the private property of its Manufacturer. We did then. We were invited to pity the delusion of certain heathens who held that the world is supported by an elephant who is supported by a tortoise. Mahomet decided that the mountains are great weights to keep the world from being blown away into space. But we refuted these orientals by asking triumphantly what the tortoise stands on? Freethinkers asked which came first: the owl or the egg. Nobody thought of saying that the ultimate problem of existence, being clearly insoluble and even unthinkable on causation lines, could not be a causation problem. To pious people this would have been flat atheism, because they assumed that God must be a Cause, and sometimes called him The Great First Cause, or, in still choicer language, The Primal Cause. To the Rationalists it would have been a renunciation of reason. Here and there a man would confess that he stood as with a dim lantern in a dense fog, and could see but a little way in any direction into infinity. But he did not really believe that infinity was infinite or that the eternal was also sempiternal: he assumed that all things, known and unknown, were caused.

Hence it was that I found myself one day towards the end of the eighteen-seventies in a cell in the old Brompton Oratory arguing with Father Addis, who had been called by one of his flock to attempt my conversion to Roman Catholicism. The universe exists, said the father: somebody must have made it. If that somebody exists, said I, somebody must have made him. I grant that for the sake of argument, said the Oratorian. I grant you a maker of God. I grant you a maker of the maker of God. I grant you as long a line of makers as you please; but an infinity of makers is unthinkable and extravagant: it is no harder to believe in number one than in number fifty thousand or fifty million; so why not accept number one and stop there, since no attempt to get behind him will remove your logical difficulty? By your leave, said I, it is as easy for me to believe that the universe made itself as that a maker of the universe made himself: in fact much easier; for the universe visibly exists and makes itself as it goes along, whereas a maker for it is a hypothesis. Of course we could get no further on these lines. He rose and said that we were like two men working a saw, he pushing it forward and I pushing it back, and cutting nothing; but when we had dropped the subject and were walking through the refectory, he returned to it for a moment to say that he should go mad if he lost his belief. I, glorying in the robust callousness of youth and the comedic spirit, felt quite comfortable and said so; though I was touched, too, by his evident sincerity.

These two anecdotes are superficially trivial and even comic; but there is an abyss of horror beneath them. They reveal a condition so utterly irreligious that religion means nothing but belief in a nursery bogey, and its inadequacy is demonstrated by a toy logical dilemma, neither the bogey nor the dilemma having anything to do with religion, or being serious enough to impose on or confuse any properly educated child over the age of six. One hardly knows which is the more appalling: the abjectness of the credulity or the flippancy of the scepticism. The result was inevitable. All who were strong-minded enough not to be terrified by the bogey were left stranded in empty contemptuous negation, and argued, when they argued at all, as I argued with Father Addis. But their position was not intellectually comfortable. A member of parliament expressed their

discomfort when, objecting to the admission of Charles Bradlaugh into parliament, he said 'Hang it all, a man should believe in something
or somebody.' It was easy to throw the bogey into the dustbin; but
none the less the world, our corner of the universe, did not look like
a pure accident: it presented evidences of design in every direction.
There was mind and purpose behind it. As the anti-Bradlaugh
member would have put it, there must be somebody behind the
something: no atheist could get over that.

PALEY'S WATCH

Paley had put the argument in an apparently unanswerable form.
If you found a watch, full of mechanism exquisitely adapted to produce a series of operations all leading to the fulfilment of one central
purpose of measuring for mankind the march of the day and night,
could you believe that it was not the work of a cunning artificer
who had designed and contrived it all to that end? And here was a
far more wonderful thing than a watch, a man with all his organs
ingeniously contrived, cords and levers, girders and kingposts,
circulating systems of pipes and valves, dialysing membranes, chemical retorts, carburettors, ventilators, inlets and outlets, telephone
transmitters in his ears, light recorders and lenses in his eye: was it
conceivable that this was the work of chance? that no artificer had
wrought here? that there was no purpose in this, no design, no guiding intelligence? The thing was incredible. In vain did Helmholtz
declare that 'the eye has every possible defect that can be found in
an optical instrument, and even some peculiar to itself,' and that 'if
an optician tried to sell me an instrument which had all these defects
I should think myself quite justified in blaming his carelessness in
the strongest terms, and sending him back his instrument.' To discredit the optician's skill was not to get rid of the optician. The eye
might not be so cleverly made as Paley thought, but it was made
somehow, by somebody.

And then my argument with Father Addis began all over again.
It was easy enough to say that every man makes his own eyes: indeed
the embryologists had actually caught him doing it. But what about
the very evident purpose that prompted him to do it? Why did he
want to see, if not to extend his consciousness and his knowledge and
his power? That purpose was at work everywhere, and must be
something bigger than the individual eye-making man. Only the
stupidest muckrakers could fail to see this, and even to know it as
part of their own consciousness. Yet to admit it seemed to involve

letting the bogey come back, so inextricably had we managed to mix up belief in the bogey's existence with belief in the existence of design in the universe.

THE IRRESISTIBLE CRY OF ORDER, ORDER!

Our scornful young scientific and philosophic lions of today must not blame the Church of England for this confusion of thought. In 1562 the Church, in convocation in London 'for the avoiding of diversities of opinions and for the establishment of consent touching true religion,' proclaimed in their first utterance, and as an Article of Religion, that God is 'without body, parts, or passions,' or, as we say, an *Élan Vital* or Life Force. Unfortunately neither parents, parsons, nor pedagogues could be induced to adopt that article. St John might say that 'God is spirit' as pointedly as he pleased; our Sovereign Lady Elizabeth might ratify the Article again and again; serious divines might feel as deeply as they could that a God with body, parts, and passions could be nothing but an anthropomorphic idol: no matter: people at large could not conceive a God who was not anthropomorphic: they stood by the Old Testament legends of a God whose parts had been seen by one of the patriarchs, and finally set up as against the Church a God who, far from being without body, parts, or passions, was composed of nothing else, and of very evil passions too. They imposed this idol in practice on the Church itself, in spite of the First Article, and thereby homeopathically produced the atheist, whose denial of God was simply a denial of the idol and a demonstration against an unbearable and most unchristian idolatry. The idol was, as Shelley had been expelled from Oxford for pointing out, an almighty fiend, with a petty character and unlimited power, spiteful, cruel, jealous, vindictive, and physically violent. The most villainous schoolmasters, the most tyrannical parents, fell far short in their attempts to imitate it. But it was not its social vices that brought it low. What made it scientifically intolerable was that it was ready at a moment's notice to upset the whole order of the universe on the most trumpery provocation, whether by stopping the sun in the valley of Ajalon or sending an atheist home dead on a shutter (the shutter was indispensable because it marked the utter unpreparedness of the atheist, who, unable to save himself by a deathbed repentance, was subsequently roasted through all eternity in blazing brimstone). It was this disorderliness, this refusal to obey its own laws of nature, that created a scientific need for its destruction. Science could stand a cruel and unjust god; for nature was full of suffering and injustice. But a disorderly god was impossible. In the Middle Ages a compromise had been made by which two different orders of truth, religious and scientific, had been recognized, in order that a schoolman might say that two and two make four without being burnt for heresy. But the nineteenth century, steeped in a meddling, presumptuous, reading-and-writing, socially and politically powerful ignorance inconceivable by Thomas Aquinas or even Roger Bacon, was incapable of so convenient an arrangement; and science was strangled by bigoted ignoramuses claiming infallibility for their interpretation of the Bible, which was regarded, not as a literature nor even as a book, but partly as an oracle which answered and settled all questions, and partly as a talisman to be carried by soldiers in their breast pockets or placed under the pillows of persons who were afraid of ghosts. The tract shops exhibited in their windows bullet-dinted testaments, mothers' gifts to their soldier sons whose lives had been saved by it; for the muzzle-loaders of those days could not drive a projectile through so many pages.

THE MOMENT AND THE MAN

This superstition of a continual capricious disorder in nature, of a lawgiver who was also a lawbreaker, made atheists in all directions among clever and lightminded people. But atheism did not account for Paley's watch. Atheism accounted for nothing; and it was the business of science to account for everything that was plainly accountable. Science had no use for mere negation: what was desired by it above all things just then was a demonstration that the evidences of design could be explained without resort to the hypothesis of a personal designer. If only some genius, whilst admitting Paley's facts, could knock the brains out of Paley by the discovery of a method whereby watches could happen without watchmakers, that genius was assured of such a welcome from the thought of his day as no natural philosopher had ever enjoyed before.

The time being thus ripe, the genius appeared; and his name was Charles Darwin. And now, what did Darwin really discover?

Here, I am afraid, I shall require once more the assistance of the giraffe, or, as he was called in the days of the celebrated Buffoon, the camelopard (by children, cammyleopard). I do not remember how this animal imposed himself illustratively on the Evolution controversy; but there was no getting away from him then; and I am old-fashioned enough to be unable to get away from him now. How did he come by his long neck? Lamarck would have said, by wanting to get at the tender leaves high up on the tree, and trying until he succeeded in wishing the necessary length of neck into existence. Another answer was also possible: namely, that some prehistoric stockbreeder, wishing to produce a natural curiosity, selected the longest-necked animals he could find, and bred from them until at last an animal with an abnormally long neck was evolved by intentional selection, just as the race-horse or the fantail pigeon has been evolved. Both these explanations, you will observe, involve consciousness, will, design, purpose, either on the part of the animal itself or on the part of a superior intelligence controlling its destiny. Darwin pointed out – and this and no more was Darwin's famous discovery – that a third explanation, involving neither will nor purpose nor design either in the animal or anyone else, was on the cards. If your neck is too short to reach your food, you die. That may be the simple explanation of the fact that all the surviving animals that feed on foliage have necks or trunks long enough to reach it. So bang goes your belief that the necks must have been designed to reach the food. But Lamarck did not believe that the necks were so designed in the beginning: he believed that the long necks were evolved by wanting and trying. Not necessarily, said Darwin. Consider the effect on the giraffes of the natural multiplication of their numbers, as insisted on by Malthus. Suppose the average height of the foliage-eating animals is four feet, and that they increase in numbers until a time comes when all the trees are eaten away to within four feet of the ground. Then the animals who happen to be an inch or two short of the average will die of starvation. All the animals who happen to be an inch or so above the average will be better fed and stronger than the others. They will secure the strongest and tallest mates; and their progeny will survive whilst the average ones and the sub-average ones will die out. This process, by which the species gains, say, an inch in reach, will repeat itself until the giraffe's neck is so long that he can always find food enough within his reach, at which point, of course, the selective process stops and the length of the giraffe's neck stops with it. Otherwise, he would grow until he could browse off the trees in the moon. And this, mark you, without the intervention of any stockbreeder, human or divine, and without will, purpose, design, or even consciousness beyond the blind will to satisfy hunger. It is true that this blind will, being in effect a will to live, gives away the whole case; but still, as compared to the open-eyed intelligent wanting and trying of Lamarck, the Darwinian process may be described as a chapter of accidents. As such, it seems simple, because you do not at first realize all that it involves. But when its whole significance dawns on you, your heart sinks into a heap of sand within you. There is a hideous fatalism about it, a ghastly and damnable reduction of beauty and intelligence, of strength and purpose, of honor and aspiration, to such casually picturesque changes as an avalanche may make in a mountain landscape, or a railway accident in a human figure. To call this Natural Selection is a blasphemy, possible to many for whom Nature is nothing but a casual aggregation of inert and dead matter, but eternally impossible to the spirits and souls of the righteous. If it be no blasphemy, but a truth of science, then the stars of heaven, the showers and dew, the winter and summer, the fire and heat, the mountains and hills, may no longer be called to exalt the Lord with us by praise; their work is to modify all things by blindly starving and murdering everything that is not lucky enough to survive in the universal struggle for hogwash.

THE BRINK OF THE BOTTOMLESS PIT

Thus did the neck of the giraffe reach out across the whole heavens and make men believe that what they saw there was a gloaming of the gods. For if this sort of selection could turn an antelope into a giraffe, it could conceivably turn a pond full of amoebas into the French Academy. Though Lamarck's way, the way of life, will, aspiration, and achievement, remained still possible, this newly shewn way of hunger, death, stupidity, delusion, chance, and bare survival was also possible: was indeed most certainly the way in which many apparently intelligently designed transformations had actually come to pass. Had I not preluded with the apparently idle story of my revival of the controversial methods of Elijah, I should be asked how it was that the explorer who opened up this gulf of despair, far from being stoned or crucified as the destroyer of the honor of the race and the purpose of the world, was hailed as Deliverer, Savior, Prophet, Redeemer, Enlightener, Rescuer, Hope Giver, and Epoch Maker; whilst poor Lamarck was swept aside as a crude and exploded guesser hardly worthy to be named as his erroneous forerunner. In the light of my anecdote, the explanation is obvious. The first thing the gulf did was to swallow up Paley, and the Disorderly Designer, and Shelley's Almighty Fiend, and all the rest of the pseudo-religious rubbish that had blocked every upward and onward path since the hopes of men had turned to Science as their true Savior. It seemed such a convenient grave that nobody at

first noticed that it was nothing less than the bottomless pit, now
become a very real terror. For though Darwin left a path round it
for his soul, his followers presently dug it right across the whole
width of the way. Yet for the moment, there was nothing but wild
rejoicing: a sort of scientific mafficking. We had been so oppressed
by the notion that everything that happened in the world was the
arbitrary personal act of an arbitrary personal god of dangerously
jealous and cruel personal character, so that even the relief of the
pains of childbed and the operating table by chloroform was objected to as an interference with his arrangements which he would
probably resent, that we just jumped at Darwin. When Napoleon
was asked what would happen when he died, he said that Europe
would express its intense relief with a great 'Ouf!': Well, when Darwin
killed the god who objected to chloroform, everybody who had ever
thought about it said 'Ouf!' Paley was buried fathoms deep with his
watch, now fully accounted for without any divine artificer at all.
We were so glad to be rid of both that we never gave a thought to the
consequences. When a prisoner sees the door of his dungeon open, he
dashes for it without stopping to think where he shall get his dinner
outside. The moment we found that we could do without Shelley's
almighty fiend intellectually, he went into the gulf that seemed only
a dustbin with a suddenness that made our own lives one of the most
astonishing periods in history. If I had told that uncle of mine that
within thirty years from the date of our conversation I should be
exposing myself to suspicions of the grossest superstition by questioning the sufficiency of Darwin; maintaining the reality of the Holy
Ghost; declaring that the phenomenon of the Word becoming
Flesh was occurring daily, he would have regarded me as the most
extravagant madman our family had ever produced. Yet it was so.
In 1906 I might have vituperated Jehovah more heartily than ever
Shelley did without eliciting a protest in any circle of thinkers, or
shocking any public audience accustomed to modern discussion;
but when I described Darwin as 'an intelligent and industrious
pigeon fancier,' that blasphemous levity, as it seemed, was received
with horror and indignation. The tide has now turned; and every
puny whipster may say what he likes about Darwin; but anyone
who wants to know what it was to be a Lamarckian during the last
quarter of the nineteenth century has only to read Mr Festing
Jones's memoir of Samuel Butler to learn how completely even a
man of genius could isolate himself by antagonizing Darwin on the
one hand and the Church on the other.

WHY DARWIN CONVERTED THE CROWD

I am well aware that in describing the effect of Darwin's discovery on naturalists and on persons capable of serious reflection on the nature and attributes of God, I am leaving the vast mass of the British public out of account. I have pointed out elsewhere that the British nation does not consist of atheists and Plymouth Brothers; and I am not now going to pretend that it ever consisted of Darwinians and Lamarckians. The average citizen is irreligious and unscientific: you talk to him about cricket and golf, market prices and party politics, not about evolution and relativity, transubstantiation and predestination. Nothing will knock into his head the fateful distinction between Evolution as promulgated by Erasmus Darwin, and Circumstantial (so-called Natural) Selection as revealed by his grandson. Yet the doctrine of Charles reached him, though the doctrine of Erasmus had passed over his head. Why did not Erasmus Darwin popularize the word Evolution as effectively as Charles?

The reason was, I think, that Circumstantial Selection is easier to understand, more visible and concrete, than Lamarckian evolution. Evolution as a philosophy and physiology of the will is a mystical process, which can be apprehended only by a trained, apt, and comprehensive thinker. Though the phenomena of use and disuse, of wanting and trying, of the manufacture of weight lifters and wrestlers from men of ordinary strength, are familiar enough as facts, they are extremely puzzling as subjects of thought, and lead you into metaphysics the moment you try to account for them. But pigeon fanciers, dog fanciers, gardeners, stockbreeders, or stud grooms, can understand Circumstantial Selection, because it is their business to produce transformation by imposing on flowers and animals a Selection From Without. All that Darwin had to say to them was that the mere chapter of accidents is always doing on a huge scale what they themselves are doing on a very small scale. There is hardly a laborer attached to an English country house who has not taken a litter of kittens or puppies to the bucket, and drowned all of them except the one he thinks the most promising. Such a man has nothing to learn about the survival of the fittest except that it acts in more ways than he has yet noticed; for he knows quite well, as you will find if you are not too proud to talk to him, that this sort of selection occurs naturally (in Darwin's sense) too: that, for instance, a hard winter will kill off a weakly child as the bucket kills off a weakly puppy. Then there is the farm laborer. Shakespear's Touchstone, a court-bred fool, was shocked to find in the shepherd a natural philosopher, and opined that he would be damned for the part he took in the sexual selection of sheep. As to the production of new species by the selection of variations, that is no news to your gardener. Now if you are familiar with these three processes: the survival of the fittest, sexual selection, and variation leading to new kinds, there is nothing to puzzle you in Darwinism.

That was the secret of Darwin's popularity. He never puzzled anybody. If very few of us have read The Origin of Species from end to end, it is not because it overtaxes our mind, but because we take in the whole case and are prepared to accept it long before we have come to the end of the innumerable instances and illustrations of which the book mainly consists. Darwin becomes tedious in the manner of a man who insists on continuing to prove his innocence after he has been acquitted. You assure him that there is not a stain on his character, and beg him to leave the court; but he will not be content with enough evidence: he will have you listen to all the evidence that exists in the world. Darwin's industry was enormous. His patience, his perseverance, his conscientiousness reached the human limit. But he never got deeper beneath or higher above his facts than an ordinary man could follow him. He was not conscious of having raised a stupendous issue, because, though it arose instantly, it was not his business. He was conscious of having discovered a process of transformation and modification which accounted for a great deal of natural history. But he did not put it forward as accounting for the whole of natural history. He included it under the heading of Evolution, though it was only pseudo-evolution at best; but he revealed it as *a* method of evolution, not as *the* method of evolution. He did not pretend that it excluded other methods, or that it was the chief method. Though he demonstrated that many transformations which had been taken as functional adaptations (the current phrase for Lamarckian evolution) either certainly were or conceivably might be due to Circumstantial Selection, he was careful not to claim that he had superseded Lamarck or disproved Functional Adaptation. In short, he was not a Darwinian, but an honest naturalist working away at his job with so little preoccupation with theological speculation that he never quarrelled with the theistic Unitarianism into which he was born, and remained to the end the engagingly simple and socially easy-going soul he had been in his boyhood, when his elders doubted whether he would ever be of much use in the world.

HOW WE RUSHED DOWN A STEEP PLACE

Not so the rest of us intellectuals. We all began going to the devil with the utmost cheerfulness. Everyone who had a mind to change, changed it. Only Samuel Butler, on whom Darwin had acted homeopathically, reacted against him furiously; ran up the Lamarckian flag to the top-gallant peak; declared with penetrating accuracy that Darwin had 'banished mind from the universe'; and even attacked Darwin's personal character, unable to bear the fact that the author of so abhorrent a doctrine was an amiable and upright man. Nobody would listen to him. He was so completely submerged by the flowing tide of Darwinism that when Darwin wanted to clear up the misunderstanding on which Butler was basing his personal attacks, Darwin's friends, very foolishly and snobbishly, persuaded him that Butler was too ill-conditioned and negligible to be answered. That they could not recognize in Butler a man of genius mattered little: what did matter was that they could not understand the provocation under which he was raging. They actually regarded the banishment of mind from the universe as a glorious enlightenment and emancipation for which he was ignorantly ungrateful. Even now, when Butler's eminence is unchallenged, and his biographer, Mr Festing Jones, is enjoying a vogue like that of Boswell or Lockhart, his memoirs shew him rather as a shocking example of the bad controversial manners of our country parsonages than as a prophet who tried to head us back when we were gaily dancing to our damnation across the rainbow bridge which Darwinism had thrown over the gulf which separates life and hope from death and despair. We were intellectually intoxicated with the idea that the world could make itself without design, purpose, skill, or intelligence: in short, without life. We completely overlooked the difference between the modification of species by adaptation to their environment and the appearance of new species: we just threw in the word 'variations' or the word 'sports' (fancy a man of science talking of an unknown factor as a sport instead of as x!) and left them to 'accumulate' and account for the difference between a cockatoo and a hippopotamus. Such phrases set us free to revel in demonstrating to the Vitalists and Bible worshippers that if we once admit the existence of any kind of force, however unintelligent, and stretch out the past to unlimited time for such force to operate accidentally in, that force may conceivably, by the action of Circumstantial Selection, produce a world in which every function has an organ perfectly adapted to perform it, and therefore presents every appearance of having been designed, like

Paley's watch, by a conscious and intelligent artificer for the purpose. We took a perverse pleasure in arguing, without the least suspicion that we were reducing ourselves to absurdity, that all the books in the British Museum library might have been written word for word as they stand on the shelves if no human being had ever been conscious, just as the trees stand in the forest doing wonderful things without consciousness.

And the Darwinians went far beyond denying consciousness to trees. Weismann insisted that the chick breaks out of its eggshell automatically; that the butterfly, springing into the air to avoid the pounce of the lizard, 'does not wish to avoid death; knows nothing about death,' what has happened being simply that a flight instinct evolved by Circumstantial Selection reacts promptly to a visual impression produced by the lizard's movement. His proof is that the butterfly immediately settles again on the flower, and repeats the performance every time the lizard springs, thus shewing that it learns nothing from experience, and – Weismann concludes – is not conscious of what it does.

It should hardly have escaped so curious an observer that when the cat jumps up on the dinner table, and you put it down, it instantly jumps up again, and finally establishes its right to a place on the cloth by convincing you that if you put it down a hundred times it will jump up a hundred and one times; so that if you desire its company at dinner you can have it only on its own terms. If Weismann really thought that cats act thus without any consciousness or any purpose, immediate or ulterior, he must have known very little about cats. But a thoroughgoing Weismannite, if any such still survive from those mad days, would contend that I am not at present necessarily conscious of what I am doing; that my writing of these lines, and your reading of them, are effects of Circumstantial Selection; that I need know no more about Darwinism than a butterfly knows of a lizard's appetite; and that the proof that I actually am doing it unconsciously is that as I have spent forty years in writing in this fashion without, as far as I can see, producing any visible effect on public opinion, I must be incapable of learning from experience, and am therefore a mere automaton. And the Weismannite demonstration of this would of course be an equally unconscious effect of Circumstantial Selection.

DARWINISM NOT FINALLY REFUTABLE

Do not too hastily say that this is inconceivable. To Circumstantial Selection all mechanical and chemical reactions are possible, provided you accept the geologists' estimates of the great age of the earth, and therefore allow time enough for the circumstances to operate. It is true that mere survival of the fittest in the struggle for existence plus sexual selection fail as hopelessly to account for Darwin's own life work as for my conquest of the bicycle; but who can prove that there are not other soulless factors, unnoticed or undiscovered, which only require imagination enough to fit them to the evolution of an automatic Jesus or Shakespear? When a man tells you that you are a product of Circumstantial Selection solely, you cannot finally disprove it. You can only tell him out of the depths of your inner conviction that he is a fool and a liar. But as this, though British, is uncivil, it is wiser to offer him the counter-assurance that you are the product of Lamarckian evolution, formerly called Functional Adaptation and now Creative Evolution, and challenge him to disprove *that*, which he can no more do than you can disprove Circumstantial Selection, both forces being conceivably able to produce anything if you only give them rope enough. You may also defy him to act for a single hour on the assumption that he may safely cross Oxford Street in a state of unconsciousness, trusting to his dodging reflexes to react automatically and promptly enough to the visual impression produced by a motor bus, and the audible impression produced by its hooter. But if you allow yourself to defy him to explain any particular action of yours by Circumstantial Selection, he should always be able to find some explanation that will fit the case if only he is ingenious enough and goes far enough to find it. Darwin found several such explanations in his controversies. Anybody who really wants to believe that the universe has been produced by Circumstantial Selection co-operating with a force as inhuman as we conceive magnetism to be can find a logical excuse for his belief if he tries hard enough.

THREE BLIND MICE

The stultification and damnation which ensued are illustrated by a comparison of the ease and certainty with which Butler's mind moved to humane and inspiring conclusions with the grotesque stupidities and cruelties of the idle and silly controversy which arose among the Darwinians as to whether acquired habits can be transmitted from parents to offspring. Consider, for example, how Weismann set to work on that subject. An Evolutionist with a live mind would first have dropped the popular expression 'acquired habits,' because to an Evolutionist there are no other habits and can be no others, a man being only an amoeba with acquirements. He would then have considered carefully the process by which he himself had acquired his habits. He would have assumed that the habits with which he was born must have been acquired by a similar process. He would have known what a habit is: that is, an action voluntarily attempted until it has become more or less automatic and involuntary; and it would never have occurred to him that injuries or accidents coming from external sources against the will of the victim could possibly establish a habit; that, for instance, a family could acquire a habit of being killed in railway accidents.

And yet Weismann began to investigate the point by behaving like the butcher's wife in the old catch. He got a colony of mice, and cut off their tails. Then he waited to see whether their children would be born without tails. They were not, as Butler could have told him beforehand. He then cut off the children's tails, and waited to see whether the grandchildren would be born with at least rather short tails. They were not, as I could have told him beforehand. So with the patience and industry on which men of science pride themselves, he cut off the grandchildren's tails too, and waited, full of hope, for the birth of curtailed great-grandchildren. But their tails were quite up to the mark, as any fool could have told him beforehand. Weismann then gravely drew the inference that acquired habits cannot be transmitted. And yet Weismann was not a born imbecile. He was an exceptionally clever and studious man, not without roots of imagination and philosophy in him which Darwinism killed as weeds. How was it that he did not see that he was not experimenting with habits or characteristics at all? How had he overlooked the glaring fact that his experiment had been tried for many generations in China on the feet of Chinese women without producing the smallest tendency on their part to be born with abnormally small feet? He must have known about the bound feet even if he knew nothing of the mutilations, the clipped ears and docked tails, practised by dog fanciers and horse breeders on many generations of the unfortunate animals they deal in. Such amazing blindness and stupidity on the part of a man who was naturally neither blind nor stupid is a telling illustration of what Darwin unintentionally did to the minds of his disciples by turning their attention so exclusively towards the part played in Evolution by accident and violence operating with entire callousness to suffering and sentiment.

A vital conception of Evolution would have taught Weismann that biological problems are not to be solved by assaults on mice. The scientific form of his experiment would have been something like this. First, he should have procured a colony of mice highly susceptible to hypnotic suggestion. He should then have hypnotized them into an urgent conviction that the fate of the musque world depended on the disappearance of its tail, just as some ancient and forgotten experimenter seems to have convinced the cats of the Isle of Man. Having thus made the mice desire to lose their tails with a life-or-death intensity, he would very soon have seen a few mice born with little or no tail. These would be recognized by the other mice as superior beings, and privileged in the division of food and in sexual selection. Ultimately the tailed mice would be put to death as monsters by their fellows, and the miracle of the tailless mouse completely achieved.

The objection to this experiment is not that it seems too funny to be taken seriously, and is not cruel enough to overawe the mob, but simply that it is impossible because the human experimenter cannot get at the mouse's mind. And that is what is wrong with all the barren cruelties of the laboratories. Darwin's followers did not think of this. Their only idea of investigation was to imitate 'Nature' by perpetrating violent and senseless cruelties, and watch the effect of them with a paralyzing fatalism which forbade the smallest effort to use their minds instead of their knives and eyes, and established an abominable tradition that the man who hesitates to be as cruel as Circumstantial Selection itself is a traitor to science. For Weismann's experiment upon the mice was a mere joke compared to the atrocities committed by other Darwinians in their attempts to prove that mutilations could not be transmitted. No doubt the worst of these experiments were not really experiments at all, but cruelties committed by cruel men who were attracted to the laboratory by the fact that it was a secret refuge left by law and public superstition for the amateur of passionate torture. But there is no reason to suspect Weismann of Sadism. Cutting off the tails of several generations of mice is not voluptuous enough to tempt a scientific Nero. It was a mere piece of one-eyedness; and it was Darwin who put out Weismann's humane and sensible eye. He blinded many another eye and paralyzed many another will also. Ever since he set up Circumstantial Selection as the creator and ruler of the universe, the scientific world has been the very citadel of stupidity and cruelty. Fearful as the tribal god of the Hebrews was, nobody ever shuddered as they passed even his meanest and narrowest Little Bethel or his proudest war-consecrating cathedral as we shudder now when we pass a physiological laboratory. If we dreaded and mistrusted the priest, we could at least keep him out of the house; but what of the modern Darwinist surgeon whom we dread and mistrust ten times more, but into whose hands we must all give ourselves from time to time? Miserably as religion had been debased, it did at least still proclaim that our relation to one another was that of a fellowship in which we were all equal and members one of another before the judgment-seat of our common father. Darwinism proclaimed that our true relation is that of competitors and combatants in a struggle for mere survival, and that every act of pity or loyalty to the old fellowship is a vain and mischievous attempt to lessen the severity of the struggle and preserve inferior varieties from the efforts of Nature to weed them out. Even in Socialist Societies which existed solely to substitute the law of fellowship for the law of competition, and the method of providence and wisdom for the method of rushing violently down a steep place into the sea, I found myself regarded as a blasphemer and an ignorant sentimentalist because whenever the Neo-Darwinian doctrine was preached there I made no attempt to conceal my intellectual contempt for its blind coarseness and shallow logic, or my natural abhorrence of its sickening inhumanity.

THE GREATEST OF THESE IS SELF-CONTROL

As there is no place in Darwinism for free will, or any other sort of will, the Neo-Darwinists held that there is no such thing as self-control. Yet self-control is just the one quality of survival value which Circumstantial Selection must invariably and inevitably develop in the long run. Uncontrolled qualities may be selected for survival and development for certain periods and under certain circumstances. For instance, since it is the ungovernable gluttons who strive the hardest to get food and drink, their efforts would develop their strength and cunning in a period of such scarcity that the utmost they could do would not enable them to over-eat themselves. But a change of circumstances involving a plentiful supply of food would destroy them. We see this very thing happening often enough in the case of the healthy and vigorous poor man who becomes a millionaire by one of the accidents of our competitive commerce, and immediately proceeds to dig his grave with his teeth. But the self-controlled man survives all such changes of circumstance, because he adapts himself to them, and eats neither as much as he can hold nor as little as he can scrape along on, but as much as is good for him. What *is* self-control? It is nothing but a highly developed vital sense, dominating and regulating the mere appetites. To overlook the very existence of this supreme sense; to miss the obvious inference that it is the quality that distinguishes the fittest to survive; to omit, in short, the highest moral claim of Evolutionary Selection: all this, which the Neo-Darwinians did in the name of Natural Selection, shewed the most pitiable want of mastery of their own subject, the dullest lack of observation of the forces upon which Natural Selection works.

A SAMPLE OF LAMARCKO-SHAVIAN INVECTIVE

The Vitalist philosophers made no such mistakes. Nietzsche, for example, thinking out the great central truth of the Will to Power instead of cutting off mouse-tails, had no difficulty in concluding that the final objective of this Will was power over self, and that the seekers after power over others and material possessions were on a false scent.

The stultification naturally became much worse as the first Darwinians died out. The prestige of these pioneers, who had the older evolutionary culture to build on, and were in fact no more Darwinian in the modern sense than Darwin himself, ceased to dazzle us when Huxley and Tyndall and Spencer and Darwin passed away, and we were left with the smaller people who began with Darwin and took in nothing else. Accordingly, I find that in the year 1906 I indulged my temper by hurling invectives at the Neo-Darwinians in the following terms.

'I really do not wish to be abusive; but when I think of these poor little dullards, with their precarious hold of just that corner of evolution that a blackbeetle can understand – with their retinue of twopenny-halfpenny Torquemadas wallowing in the infamies of the vivisector's laboratory, and solemnly offering us as epoch-making discoveries their demonstrations that dogs get weaker and die if you give them no food; that intense pain makes mice sweat; and that if you cut off a dog's leg the three-legged dog will have a four-legged puppy, I ask myself what spell has fallen on intelligent and humane men that they allow themselves to be imposed on by this rabble of dolts, blackguards, impostors, quacks, liars, and, worst of all, credulous conscientious fools. Better a thousand times Moses and Spurgeon [a then famous preacher] back again. After all, you cannot understand Moses without imagination nor Spurgeon without metaphysics; but you can be a thorough-going Neo-Darwinian without imagination, metaphysics, poetry, conscience, or decency. For "Natural Selection" has no moral significance: it deals with that part of evolution which has no purpose, no intelligence, and might more appropriately be called accidental selection, or better still, Unnatural Selection, since nothing is more unnatural than an accident. If it could be proved that the whole universe had been produced by such Selection, only fools and rascals could bear to live.'

THE HUMANITARIANS AND THE PROBLEM OF EVIL

Yet the humanitarians were as delighted as anybody with Darwinism at first. They had been perplexed by the Problem of Evil and the Cruelty of Nature. They were Shelleyists, but not atheists. Those who believed in God were at a terrible disadvantage with the atheist. They could not deny the existence of natural facts so cruel that to attribute them to the will of God is to make God a demon. Belief in God was impossible to any thoughtful person without belief in the Devil as well. The painted Devil, with his horns, his barbed tail, and his abode of burning brimstone, was an incredible bogey; but the evil attributed to him was real enough; and the atheists argued that the author of evil, if he exists, must be strong enough to overcome God, else God is morally responsible for everything he permits the Devil to do. Neither conclusion delivered us from the horror of attributing the cruelty of nature to the workings of an evil will, or could reconcile it with our impulses towards justice, mercy, and a higher life.

A complete deliverance was offered by the discovery of Circumstantial Selection: that is to say, of a method by which horrors having every appearance of being elaborately planned by some intelligent contriver are only accidents without any moral significance at all. Suppose a watcher from the stars saw a frightful accident produced by two crowded trains at full speed crashing into one another! How could he conceive that a catastrophe brought about by such elaborate machinery, such ingenious preparation, such skilled direction, such vigilant industry, was quite unintentional? Would he not conclude that the signal-men were devils?

Well, Circumstantial Selection is largely a theory of collisions: that is, a theory of the innocence of much apparently designed devilry. In this way Darwin brought intense relief as well as an enlarged knowledge of facts to the humanitarians. He destroyed the omnipotence of God for them; but he also exonerated God from a hideous charge of cruelty. Granted that the comfort was shallow, and that deeper reflection was bound to shew that worse than all conceivable devil-deities is a blind, deaf, dumb, heartless, senseless mob of forces that strike as a tree does when it is blown down by the wind, or as the tree itself is struck by lightning. That did not occur to the humanitarians at the moment: people do not reflect deeply when they are in the first happiness of escape from an intolerably oppressive situation. Like Bunyan's pilgrim they could not see the wicket gate, nor the Slough of Despond, nor the castle of Giant Despair; but they saw the shining light at the end of the path, and so started gaily towards it as Evolutionists.

And they were right; for the problem of evil yields very easily to Creative Evolution. If the driving power behind Evolution is omnipotent only in the sense that there seems no limit to its final achievement; and if it must meanwhile struggle with matter and circumstance by the method of trial and error, then the world must be full of its unsuccessful experiments. Christ may meet a tiger, or a High Priest arm-in-arm with a Roman Governor, and be the unfittest to survive under the circumstances. Mozart may have a genius that prevails against Emperors and Archbishops, and a lung that succumbs to some obscure and noxious property of foul air. If all our calamities are either accidents or sincerely repented mistakes, there is no malice in the Cruelty of Nature and no Problem of Evil in the Victorian sense at all. The theology of the women who told us that they became atheists when they sat by the cradles of their children and saw them strangled by the hand of God is succeeded by the theology of Blanco Posnet, with his 'It was early days when He made the croup, I guess. It was the best He could think of then; but when it turned out wrong on His hands He made you and me to fight the croup for Him.'

HOW ONE TOUCH OF DARWIN MAKES THE WHOLE WORLD KIN

Another humanitarian interest in Darwinism was that Darwin popularized Evolution generally, as well as making his own special contribution to it. Now the general conception of Evolution provides the humanitarian with a scientific basis, because it establishes the fundamental equality of all living things. It makes the killing of an animal murder in exactly the same sense as the killing of a man is murder. It is sometimes necessary to kill men as it is always necessary to kill tigers; but the old theoretic distinction between the two acts has been obliterated by Evolution. When I was a child and was told that our dog and our parrot, with whom I was on intimate terms, were not creatures like myself, but were brutal whilst I was reasonable, I not only did not believe it, but quite consciously and intellectually formed the opinion that the distinction was false; so that afterwards, when Darwin's views were first unfolded to me, I promptly said that I had found out all that for myself before I was ten years old; and I am far from sure that my youthful arrogance was not justified; for this sense of the kinship of all forms of life is all that is needed to make Evolution not only a conceivable theory, but an inspiring one. St Anthony was ripe for the Evolution theory when he preached to the fishes, and St Francis when he called the birds his little brothers. Our vanity, and our snobbish conception of Godhead as being, like earthly kingship, a supreme class distinction instead of the rock on which Equality is built, had led us to insist on God offering us special terms by placing us apart from and above all the rest of his creatures. Evolution took that conceit out of us; and now, though we may kill a flea without the smallest remorse, we at all events know that we are killing our cousin. No doubt it shocks the flea when the creature that an almighty Celestial Flea created expressly for the food of fleas, destroys the jumping lord of creation with his sharp and enormous thumbnail; but no flea will ever be so foolish as to preach that in slaying fleas Man is applying a method of Natural Selection which will finally evolve a flea so swift that no man can catch him, and so hardy of constitution that Insect Powder will have no more effect on him than strychnine on an elephant.

WHY DARWIN PLEASED THE SOCIALISTS

The Humanitarians were not alone among the agitators in their welcome to Darwin. He had the luck to please everybody who had an axe to grind. The Militarists were as enthusiastic as the Humanitarians, the Socialists as the Capitalists. The Socialists were specially encouraged by Darwin's insistence on the influence of environment. Perhaps the strongest moral bulwark of Capitalism is the belief in the efficacy of individual righteousness. Robert Owen made desperate efforts to convince England that her criminals, her drunkards, her ignorant and stupid masses, were the victims of circumstance: that if we would only establish his new moral world we should find that the masses born into an educated and moralized community would be themselves educated and moralized. The stock reply to this is to be found in Lewes's Life of Goethe. Lewes scorned the notion that circumstances govern character. He pointed to the variety of character in the governing rich class to prove the contrary. Similarity of circumstance can hardly be carried to a more desolating dead level than in the case of the individuals who are born and bred in English country houses, and sent first to Eton or Harrow, and then to Oxford or Cambridge, to have their minds and habits formed. Such a routine would destroy individuality if anything could. Yet individuals come out from it as different as Pitt from Fox, as Lord Russell from Lord Curzon, as Mr Winston Churchill from Lord Robert Cecil. This acceptance of the congenital character of the individual as the determining factor in his destiny had been reinforced by the Lamarckian view of Evolution. If the giraffe can develop his neck by wanting and trying, a man can develop his character in the same way. The old saying, 'Where there is a will, there is a way,' condenses Lamarck's theory of functional adaptation into a proverb. This felt bracingly moral to strong minds, and reassuringly pious to feeble ones. There was no more effective retort to the Socialist than to tell him to reform himself before he pretends to reform society. If you were rich, how pleasant it was to feel that you owed your riches to the superiority of your own character! The industrial revolution had turned numbers of greedy dullards into monstrously rich men. Nothing could be more humiliating and threatening to them than the view that the falling of a shower of gold into their pockets was as pure an accident as the falling of a shower of hail on their umbrellas, and happened alike to the just and unjust. Nothing could be more flattering and fortifying to them than the assumption that they were rich because they were virtuous.

Now Darwinism made a clean sweep of all such self-righteousness. It more than justified Robert Owen by discovering in the environment of an organism an influence on it more potent than Owen had ever claimed. It implied that street arabs are produced by slums and not by original sin: that prostitutes are produced by starvation wages and not by feminine concupiscence. It threw the authority of science on the side of the Socialist who said that he who would reform himself must first reform society. It suggested that if we want healthy and wealthy citizens we must have healthy and wealthy towns; and that these can exist only in healthy and wealthy countries. It could be led to the conclusion that the type of character which remains indifferent to the welfare of its neighbors as long as its own personal appetite is satisfied is the disastrous type, and the type which is deeply concerned about its environment the only possible type for a permanently prosperous community. It shewed that the surprising changes which Robert Owen had produced in factory children by a change in their circumstances which does not seem any too generous to us nowadays were as nothing to the changes – changes not only of habits but of species, not only of species but of orders – which might conceivably be the work of environment acting on individuals without any character or intellectual consciousness whatever. No wonder the Socialists received Darwin with open arms.

DARWIN AND KARL MARX

Besides, the Socialists had an evolutionary prophet of their own, who had discredited Manchester as Darwin discredited the Garden of Eden. Karl Marx had proclaimed in his Communist Manifesto of 1848 (now enjoying Scriptural authority in Russia) that civilization is an organism evolving irresistibly by circumstantial selection; and he published the first volume of his Das Kapital in 1867. The revolt against anthropomorphic idolatry, which was, as we have seen, the secret of Darwin's success, had been accompanied by a revolt against the conventional respectability which covered not only the brigandage and piracy of the feudal barons, but the hypocrisy, inhumanity, snobbery, and greed of the bourgeoisie, who were utterly corrupted by an essentially diabolical identification of success in life with big profits. The moment Marx shewed that the relation of the bourgeoisie to society was grossly immoral and disastrous, and that the whited wall of starched shirt fronts concealed and defended the most infamous of all tyrannies and the basest of all robberies, he became an inspired prophet in the mind of every generous soul whom his book reached. He had said and proved what they wanted to have proved; and they would hear nothing against him. Now Marx was by no means infallible: his economics, half borrowed, and half home-made by a literary amateur, were not, when strictly followed up, even favorable to Socialism. His theory of civilization had been promulgated already in Buckle's History of Civilization, a book as epoch-making in the minds of its readers as Das Kapital. There was nothing about Socialism in the widely read first volume of Das Kapital: every reference it made to workers and capitalists shewed that Marx had never breathed industrial air, and had dug his case out of bluebooks in the British Museum. Compared to Darwin, he seemed to have no power of observation: there was not a fact in Das Kapital that had not been taken out of a book, nor a discussion that had not been opened by somebody else's pamphlet. No matter: he exposed the bourgeoisie and made an end of its moral prestige. That

was enough: like Darwin he had for the moment the World Will by
the ear. Marx had, too, what Darwin had not: implacability and a
fine Jewish literary gift, with terrible powers of hatred, invective,
irony, and all the bitter qualities bred, first in the oppression of a
rather pampered young genius (Marx was the spoilt child of a well-
to-do family) by a social system utterly uncongenial to him, and later
on by exile and poverty. Thus Marx and Darwin between them
toppled over two closely related idols, and became the prophets of
two new creeds.

WHY DARWIN PLEASED THE PROFITEERS ALSO

But how, at this rate, did Darwin succeed with the capitalists too?
It is not easy to make the best of both worlds when one of the worlds
is preaching a Class War, and the other vigorously practising it. The
explanation is that Darwinism was so closely related to Capitalism
that Marx regarded it as an economic product rather than as a biological theory. Darwin got his main postulate, the pressure of
population on the available means of subsistence, from the treatise
of Malthus on Population, just as he got his other postulate of a
practically unlimited time for that pressure to operate from the
geologist Lyell, who made an end of Archbishop Ussher's Biblical
estimate of the age of the earth as 4004 B.C. plus A.D. The treatises of
the Ricardian economists on the Law of Diminishing Return, which
was only the Manchester School's version of the giraffe and the trees,
were all very fiercely discussed when Darwin was a young man. In
fact the discovery in the eighteenth century by the French Physio-
crats of the economic effects of Commercial Selection in soils and
sites, and by Malthus of a competition for subsistence which he
attributed to pressure of population on available subsistence, had
already brought political science into that unbreathable atmosphere
of fatalism which is the characteristic blight of Darwinism. Long
before Darwin published a line, the Ricardo-Malthusian economists
were preaching the fatalistic Wages Fund doctrine, and assuring the
workers that Trade Unionism is a vain defiance of the inexorable
laws of political economy, just as the Neo-Darwinians were presently
assuring us that Temperance Legislation is a vain defiance of
Natural Selection, and that the true way to deal with drunkenness is
to flood the country with cheap gin and let the fittest survive. Cob-
denism is, after all, nothing but the abandonment of trade to Circumstantial Selection.

It is hardly possible to exaggerate the importance of this preparation for Darwinism by a vast political and clerical propaganda of its moral atmosphere. Never in history, as far as we know, had there been such a determined, richly subsidized, politically organized attempt to persuade the human race that all progress, all prosperity, all salvation, individual and social, depend on an unrestrained conflict for food and money, on the suppression and elimination of the weak by the strong, on Free Trade, Free Contract, Free Competition, Natural Liberty, Laisser-faire: in short, on 'doing the other fellow down' with impunity, all interference by a guiding government, all organization except police organization to protect legalized fraud against fisticuffs, all attempt to introduce human purpose and design and forethought into the industrial welter, being 'contrary to the laws of political economy.' Even the proletariat sympathized, though to them Capitalist liberty meant only wage slavery without the legal safeguards of chattel slavery. People were tired of governments and kings and priests and providences, and wanted to find out how Nature would arrange matters if she were let alone. And they found it out to their cost in the days when Lancashire used up nine generations of wage slaves in one generation of their masters. But their masters, becoming richer and richer, were very well satisfied, and Bastiat proved convincingly that Nature had arranged Economic Harmonies which would settle social questions far better than theocracies or aristocracies or mobocracies, the real *deus ex machina* being unrestrained plutocracy.

THE POETRY AND PURITY OF MATERIALISM

Thus the stars in their courses fought for Darwin. Every faction drew a moral from him; every catholic hater of faction founded a hope on him; every blackguard felt justified by him; and every saint felt encouraged by him. The notion that any harm could come of so splendid an enlightenment seemed as silly as the notion that the atheists would steal all our spoons. The physicists went further than the Darwinians. Tyndall declared that he saw in Matter the promise and potency of all forms of life, and with his Irish graphic lucidity made a picture of a world of magnetic atoms, each atom with a positive and a negative pole, arranging itself by attraction and repulsion in orderly crystalline structure. Such a picture is dangerously fascinating to thinkers oppressed by the bloody disorders of the living world. Craving for purer subjects of thought, they find in the contemplation of crystals and magnets a happiness more dramatic and less childish than the happiness found by the mathematicians in

abstract numbers, because they see in the crystals beauty and movement without the corrupting appetites of fleshly vitality. In such
Materialism as that of Lucretius and Tyndall there is a nobility
which produces poetry: John Davidson found his highest inspiration in it. Even its pessimism as it faces the cooling of the sun and the
return of the ice-caps does not degrade the pessimist: for example,
the Quincy Adamses, with their insistence on modern democratic
degradation as an inevitable result of solar shrinkage, are not de-
humanized as the vivisectionists are. Perhaps nobody is at heart fool
enough to believe that life is at the mercy of temperature: Dante was
not troubled by the objection that Brunetto could not have lived in
the fire nor Ugolino in the ice.

But the physicists found their intellectual vision of the world in-
communicable to those who were not born with it. It came to the
public simply as Materialism; and Materialism lost its peculiar
purity and dignity when it entered into the Darwinian reaction
against Bible fetishism. Between the two of them religion was
knocked to pieces; and where there had been a god, a cause, a faith
that the universe was ordered however inexplicable by us its order
might be, and therefore a sense of moral responsibility as part of
that order, there was now an utter void. Chaos had come again. The
first effect was exhilarating: we had the runaway child's sense of
freedom before it gets hungry and lonely and frightened. In this
phase we did not desire our God back again. We printed the verses
in which William Blake, the most religious of our great poets, called
the anthropomorphic idol Old Nobodaddy, and gibed at him in
terms which the printer had to leave us to guess from his blank
spaces. We had heard the parson droning that God is not mocked;
and it was great fun to mock Him to our hearts' content and not be
a penny the worse. It did not occur to us that Old Nobodaddy, instead of being a ridiculous fiction, might be only an impostor, and
that the exposure of this Koepenik Captain of the heavens, far from
proving that there was no real captain, rather proved the contrary:
that, in short, Nobodaddy could not have impersonated anybody
if there had not been Somebodaddy to impersonate. We did not see
the significance of the fact that on the last occasion on which God
had been 'expelled with a pitchfork,' men so different as Voltaire
and Robespierre had said, the one that if God did not exist it would
be necessary to invent him, and the other that after an honest attempt
to dispense with a Supreme Being in practical politics, some such
hypothesis had been found quite indispensable, and could not be
replaced by a mere Goddess of Reason. If these two opinions were

quoted at all, they were quoted as jokes at the expense of Nobodaddy. We were quite sure for the moment that whatever linger-
ing superstition might have daunted these men of the eighteenth
century, we Darwinians could do without God, and had made a
good riddance of Him.

THE VICEROYS OF THE KING OF KINGS

Now in politics it is much easier to do without God than to do without his viceroys and vicars and lieutenants; and we begin to miss the
lieutenants long before we begin to miss their principal. Roman
Catholics do what their confessors advise without troubling God;
and Royalists are content to worship the King and ask the police-
man. But God's trustiest lieutenants often lack official credentials.
They may be professed atheists who are also men of honor and high
public spirit. The old belief that it matters dreadfully to God whether
a man thinks himself an atheist or not, and that the extent to which
it matters can be stated with exactness as one single damn, was an
error: for the divinity is in the honor and public spirit, not in the
mouthed *credo* or *non credo*. The consequences of this error became
grave when the fitness of a man for public trust was tested, not by his
honor and public spirit, but by asking him whether he believed in
Nobodaddy or not. If he said yes, he was held fit to be a Prime
Minister, though, as our ablest Churchman has said, the real im-
plication was that he was either a fool, a bigot, or a liar. Darwin
destroyed this test; but when it was only thoughtlessly dropped,
there was no test at all; and the door to public trust was open to the
man who had no sense of God because he had no sense of anything
beyond his own business interests and personal appetites and ambitions. As a result, the people who did not feel in the least inconvenienced by being no longer governed by Nobodaddy soon found
themselves very acutely inconvenienced by being governed by fools
and commercial adventurers. They had forgotten not only God but
Goldsmith, who had warned them that 'honor sinks where commerce long prevails.'

The lieutenants of God are not always persons: some of them are
legal and parliamentary fictions. One of them is Public Opinion.
The pre-Darwinian statesmen and publicists were not restrained
directly by God; but they restrained themselves by setting up an
image of a Public Opinion which would not tolerate any attempt to
tamper with British liberties. Their favorite way of putting it was
that any Government which proposed such and such an infringe-

ment of such and such a British liberty would be hurled from office in a week. This was not true: there was no such public opinion, no limit to what the British people would put up with in the abstract, and no hardship short of immediate and sudden starvation that it would not and did not put up with in the concrete. But this very helplessness of the people had forced their rulers to pretend that they were not helpless, and that the certainty of a sturdy and unconquerable popular resistance forbade any trifling with Magna Carta or the Petition of Rights or the authority of parliament. Now the reality behind this fiction was the divine sense that liberty is a need vital to human growth. Accordingly, though it was difficult enough to effect a political reform, yet, once parliament had passed it, its wildest opponent had no hope that the Government would cancel it, or shelve it, or be bought off from executing it. From Walpole to Campbell-Bannerman there was no Prime Minister to whom such renagueing or trafficking would ever have occurred, though there were plenty who employed corruption unsparingly to procure the votes of members of parliament for their policy.

POLITICAL OPPORTUNISM IN EXCELSIS

The moment Nobodaddy was slain by Darwin, Public Opinion, as divine deputy, lost its sanctity. Politicians no longer told themselves that the British public would never suffer this or that: they allowed themselves to know that for their own personal purposes, which are limited to their ten or twenty years on the front benches in parliament, the British public can be humbugged and coerced into believing and suffering everything that it pays to impose on them, and that any false excuse for an unpopular step will serve if it can be kept in countenance for a fortnight: that is, until the terms of the excuse are forgotten. The people, untaught or mistaught, are so ignorant and incapable politically that this in itself would not greatly matter; for a statesman who told them the truth would not be understood, and would in effect mislead them more completely than if he dealt with them according to their blindness instead of to his own wisdom. But though there is no difference in this respect between the best demagogue and the worst, both of them having to present their cases equally in terms of melodrama, there is all the difference in the world between the statesman who is humbugging the people into allowing him to do the will of God, in whatever disguise it may come to him, and one who is humbugging them into furthering his personal ambition and the commercial interests of the plutocrats who own the newspapers and support him on reciprocal terms. And there is almost as great a difference between the statesman who does this naïvely and automatically, or even does it telling himself that he is ambitious and selfish and unscrupulous, and the one who does it on principle, believing that if everyone takes the line of least material resistance the result will be the survival of the fittest in a perfectly harmonious universe. Once produce an atmosphere of fatalism on principle, and it matters little what the opinions or superstitions of the individual statesmen concerned may be. A Kaiser who is a devout reader of sermons, a Prime Minister who is an emotional singer of hymns, and a General who is a bigoted Roman Catholic may be the executants of the policy; but the policy itself will be one of un-principled opportunism; and all the Governments will be like the tramp who walks always with the wind and ends as a pauper, or the stone that rolls down the hill and ends as an avalanche: their way is the way to destruction.

THE BETRAYAL OF WESTERN CIVILIZATION

Within sixty years from the publication of Darwin's Origin of Species political opportunism had brought parliaments into contempt; created a popular demand for direct action by the organized industries ('Syndicalism'); and wrecked the centre of Europe in a paroxysm of that chronic terror of one another, that cowardice of the irreligious, which, masked in the bravado of militarist patriotism, had ridden the Powers like a nightmare since the Franco-Prussian war of 1870–71. The sturdy old cosmopolitan Liberalism vanished almost unnoticed. At the present moment all the new ordinances for the government of our Crown Colonies contain, as a matter of course, prohibitions of all criticism, spoken or written, of their ruling officials, which would have scandalized George III and elicited Liberal pamphlets from Catherine II. Statesmen are afraid of the suburbs, of the newspapers, of the profiteers, of the diplomatists, of the militarists, of the country houses, of the trade unions, of every-thing ephemeral on earth except the revolutions they are provoking; and they would be afraid of these if they were not too ignorant of society and history to appreciate the risk, and to know that a revolu-tion always seems hopeless and impossible the day before it breaks out, and indeed never does break out until it seems hopeless and impossible; for rulers who think it possible take care to insure the risk by ruling reasonably. This brings about a condition fatal to all political stability: namely, that you never know where to have the politicians. If the fear of God was in them it might be possible to come to some general understanding as to what God disapproves of; and Europe might pull together on that basis. But the present panic, in which Prime Ministers drift from election to election, either fighting or running away from everybody who shakes a fist at them, makes a European civilization impossible. Such peace and prosperity as we enjoyed before the war depended on the loyalty of the Western States to their own civilization. That loyalty could find practical expression only in an alliance of the highly civilized Western Powers against the primitive tyrannies of the East. Britain, Germany, France, and the United States of America could have imposed peace on the world, and nursed modern civilization in Russia, Turkey, and the Balkans. Every meaner consideration should have given way to this need for the solidarity of the higher civilization. What actually happened was that France and England, through their clerks the diplomatists, made an alliance with Russia to defend themselves against Germany; Germany made an alliance with Turkey to defend herself against the three; and the two unnatural and suicidal combinations fell on one another in a war that came nearer to being a war of extermination than any wars since those of Timur the Tartar; whilst the United States held aloof as long as they could, and the other States either did the same or joined in the fray through compulsion, bribery, or their judgment as to which side their bread was buttered. And at the present moment, though the main fighting has ceased through the surrender of Germany on terms which the victors have never dreamt of observing, the extermination by blockade and famine, which was what forced Germany to surrender, still continues, although it is certain that if the vanquished starve the victors will starve too, and Europe will liquidate its affairs by going, not into bankruptcy, but into chaos.

Now all this, it will be noticed, was fundamentally nothing but an idiotic attempt on the part of each belligerent State to secure for itself the advantage of the survival of the fittest through Circumstantial Selection. If the Western Powers had selected their allies in the Lamarckian manner intelligently, purposely, and vitally, *ad majorem Dei gloriam*, as what Nietzsche called good Europeans, there would have been a League of Nations and no war. But because the selection relied on was purely circumstantial opportunist selection, so that the alliances were mere marriages of convenience, they have turned out, not merely as badly as might have been expected, but far worse than the blackest pessimist had ever imagined possible.

CIRCUMSTANTIAL SELECTION IN FINANCE

How it will all end we do not yet know. When wolves combine to kill a horse, the death of the horse only sets them fighting one another for the choicest morsels. Men are no better than wolves if they have no better principles: accordingly, we find that the Armistice and the Treaty have not extricated us from the war. A handful of Serbian regicides flung us into it as a sporting navvy throws a bull pup at a cat; but the Supreme Council, with all its victorious legions and all its prestige, cannot get us out of it, though we are heartily sick and tired of the whole business, and know now very well that it should never have been allowed to happen. But we are helpless before a slate scrawled with figures of National Debts. As there is no money to pay them because it was all spent on the war (wars have to be paid for on the nail) the sensible thing to do is to wipe the slate and let the wrangling States distribute what they can spare, on the sound communist principle of from each according to his ability, to each according to his need. But no: we have no principles left, not even commercial ones; for what sane commercialist would decree that France must not pay for her failure to defend her own soil; that Germany must pay for her success in carrying the war into the enemy's country; and that as Germany has not the money to pay, and under our commercial system can make it only by becoming once more a commercial competitor of England and France, which neither of them will allow, she must borrow the money from England or America, or even from France: an arrangement by which the victorious creditors will pay one another, and wait to get their money back until Germany is either strong enough to refuse to pay or ruined beyond the possibility of paying? Meanwhile Russia, reduced to a scrap of fish and a pint of cabbage soup a day, has fallen into the hands of rulers who perceive that Materialist Communism is at all events more effective than Materialist Nihilism, and are attempting to move in an intelligent and ordered manner, practising a very strenuous Intentional Selection of workers as fitter to survive than idlers; whilst the Western Powers are drifting and colliding and running on the rocks, in the hope that if they continue to do their worst they will get Naturally Selected for survival without the trouble of thinking about it.

THE HOMEOPATHIC REACTION AGAINST DARWINISM

When, like the Russians, our Nihilists have it urgently borne in on them, by the brute force of rising wages that never overtake rising prices, that they are being Naturally Selected for destruction, they will perhaps remember that 'Dont Care came to a bad end,' and begin to look round for a religion. And the whole purpose of this book is to shew them where to look. For, throughout all the godless welter of the infidel half-century, Darwinism has been acting not only directly but homeopathically, its poison rallying our vital forces not only to resist it and cast it out, but to achieve a new Reformation and put a credible and healthy religion in its place. Samuel Butler was the pioneer of the reaction as far as the casting out was concerned; but the issue was confused by the physiologists, who were divided on the question into Mechanists and Vitalists. The Mechanists said that life is nothing but physical and chemical action; that they have demonstrated this in many cases of so-called vital phenomena; and that there is no reason to doubt that with improved methods they will presently be able to demonstrate it in all of them. The Vitalists said that a dead body and a live one are physically and chemically identical, and that the difference can be accounted for only by the existence of a Vital Force. This seems simple; but the Anti-Mechanists objected to be called Vitalists (obviously the right name for them) on two contradictory grounds. First, that vitality is scientifically inadmissible, because it cannot be isolated and experimented with in the laboratory. Second, that force, being by definition anything that can alter the speed or direction of matter in motion (briefly, that can overcome inertia), is essentially a mechanistic conception. Here we had the New Vitalist only half extricated from the Old Mechanist, objecting to be called either, and unable to give a clear lead in the new direction. And there was a deeper antagonism. The Old Vitalists, in postulating a Vital Force, were setting up a comparatively mechanical conception as against the divine idea of the life breathed into the clay nostrils of Adam, whereby he became a living soul. The New Vitalists, filled by their laboratory researches with a sense of the miraculousness of life that went far beyond the comparatively uninformed imaginations of the authors of the Book of Genesis, regarded the Old Vitalists as Mechanists who had tried to fill up the gulf between life and death with an empty phrase denoting an imaginary physical force.

These professional faction fights are ephemeral, and need not trouble us here. The Old Vitalist, who was essentially a Materialist, has evolved into the New Vitalist, who is, as every genuine scientist must be, finally a metaphysician. And as the New Vitalist turns from the disputes of his youth to the future of his science, he will cease to boggle at the name Vitalist, or at the inevitable, ancient, popular, and quite correct use of the term Force to denote metaphysical as well as physical overcomers of inertia.

Since the discovery of Evolution as the method of the Life Force the religion of metaphysical Vitalism has been gaining the definiteness and concreteness needed to make it assimilable by the educated critical man. But it has always been with us. The popular religions, disgraced by their Opportunist cardinals and bishops, have been kept in credit by canonized saints whose secret was their conception of themselves as the instruments and vehicles of divine power and aspiration: a conception which at moments becomes an actual experience of ecstatic possession by that power. And above and below all have been millions of humble and obscure persons, sometimes totally illiterate, sometimes unconscious of having any religion at all, sometimes believing in their simplicity that the gods and temples and priests of their district stood for their instinctive righteousness, who have kept sweet the tradition that good people follow a light that shines within and above and ahead of them, that bad people care only for themselves, and that the good are saved and blessed and the bad damned and miserable. Protestantism was a movement towards the pursuit of a light called an inner light because every man must see it with his own eyes and not take any priest's word for it or any Church's account of it. In short, there is no question of a new religion, but rather of redistilling the eternal spirit of religion and thus extricating it from the sludgy residue of temporalities and legends that are making belief impossible, though they are the stock-in-trade of all the Churches and all the Schools.

RELIGION AND ROMANCE

It is the adulteration of religion by the romance of miracles and paradises and torture chambers that makes it reel at the impact of every advance in science, instead of being clarified by it. If you take an English village lad, and teach him that religion means believing that the stories of Noah's Ark and the Garden of Eden are literally true on the authority of God himself, and if that boy becomes an artisan and goes into the town among the sceptical city proletariat, then, when the jibes of his mates set him thinking, and he sees that these stories cannot be literally true, and learns that no candid prelate now pretends to believe them, he does not make any fine distinctions: he declares at once that religion is a fraud, and parsons and teachers hypocrites and liars. He becomes indifferent to religion if he has little conscience, and indignantly hostile to it if he has a good deal.

The same revolt against wantonly false teaching is happening daily in the professional classes whose recreation is reading and whose intellectual sport is controversy. They banish the Bible from their houses, and sometimes put into the hands of their unfortunate children Ethical and Rationalist tracts of the deadliest dullness, compelling these wretched infants to sit out the discourses of Secularist lecturers (I have delivered some of them myself), who bore them at a length now forbidden by custom in the established pulpit. Our minds have reacted so violently towards provable logical theorems and demonstrable mechanical or chemical facts that we have become incapable of metaphysical truth, and try to cast out incredible and silly lies by credible and clever ones, calling in Satan to cast out Satan, and getting more into his clutches than ever in the process. Thus the world is kept sane less by the saints than by the vast mass of the indifferent, who neither act nor react in the matter. Butler's preaching of the gospel of Laodicea was a piece of common sense founded on his observation of this.

But indifference will not guide nations through civilization to the establishment of the perfect city of God. An indifferent statesman is a contradiction in terms; and a statesman who is indifferent on principle, a Laisser-faire or Muddle-Through doctrinaire, plays the deuce with us in the long run. Our statesmen must get a religion by hook or crook; and as we are committed to Adult Suffrage it must be a religion capable of vulgarization. The thought first put into words by the Mills when they said 'There is no God; but this is a family secret,' and long held unspoken by aristocratic statesmen and diplomatists, will not serve now; for the revival of civilization after the war cannot be effected by artificial breathing: the driving force of an undeluded popular consent is indispensable, and will be impossible until the statesman can appeal to the vital instincts of the people in terms of a common religion. The success of the Hang the Kaiser cry at the last General Election shews us very terrifyingly how a common irreligion can be used by myopic demagogy; and common irreligion will destroy civilization unless it is countered by common religion.

THE DANGER OF REACTION

And here arises the danger that when we realize this we shall do just what we did half a century ago, and what Pliable did in The Pilgrim's Progress when Christian landed him in the Slough of Despond: that is, run back in terror to our old superstitions. We jumped out of the frying-pan into the fire; and we are just as likely to jump back again, now that we feel hotter than ever. History records very little in the way of mental activity on the part of the mass of mankind except a series of stampedes from affirmative errors into negative ones and back again. It must therefore be said very precisely and clearly that the bankruptcy of Darwinism does not mean that Nobodaddy was Somebodaddy *with* 'body, parts, and passions' after all; that the world was made in the year 4004 B.C.; that damnation means an eternity of blazing brimstone; that the Immaculate Conception means that sex is sinful and that Christ was parthenogenetically brought forth by a virgin descended in like manner from a line of virgins right back to Eve; that the Trinity is an anthropomorphic monster with three heads which are yet only one head; that in Rome the bread and wine on the altar become flesh and blood, and in England, in a still more mystical manner, they do and they do not; that the Bible is an infallible scientific manual, an accurate historical chronicle, and a complete guide to conduct; that we may lie and cheat and murder and then wash ourselves innocent in the blood of the lamb on Sunday at the cost of a *credo* and a penny in the plate, and so on and so forth. Civilization cannot be saved by people not only crude enough to believe these things, but irreligious enough to believe that such belief constitutes a religion. The education of children cannot safely be left in their hands. If dwindling sects like the Church of England, the Church of Rome, the Greek Church, and the rest, persist in trying to cramp the human mind within the limits of these grotesque perversions of natural truths and poetic metaphors, then they must be ruthlessly banished from the schools until they either perish in general contempt or discover the soul that is hidden in every dogma. The real Class War will be a war of intellectual classes; and its conquest will be the souls of the children.

A TOUCHSTONE FOR DOGMA

The test of a dogma is its universality. As long as the Church of England preaches a single doctrine that the Brahman, the Buddhist, the Mussulman, the Parsee, and all the other sectarians who are

British subjects cannot accept, it has no legitimate place in the counsels of the British Commonwealth, and will remain what it is at present, a corrupter of youth, a danger to the State, and an obstruction to the Fellowship of the Holy Ghost. This has never been more strongly felt than at present, after a war in which the Church failed grossly in the courage of its profession, and sold its lilies for the laurels of the soldiers of the Victoria Cross. All the cocks in Christendom have been crowing shame on it ever since; and it will not be spared for the sake of the two or three faithful who were found even among the bishops. Let the Church take it on authority, even my authority (as a professional legend maker) if it cannot see the truth by its own light: no dogma can be a legend. A legend can pass an ethnical frontier as a legend, but not as a truth; whilst the only frontier to the currency of a sound dogma as such is the frontier of capacity for understanding it.

This does not mean that we should throw away legend and parable and drama: they are the natural vehicles of dogma; but woe to the Churches and rulers who substitute the legend for the dogma, the parable for the history, the drama for the religion! Better by far declare the throne of God empty than set a liar and a fool on it. What are called wars of religion are always wars to destroy religion by affirming the historical truth or material substantiality of some legend, and killing those who refuse to accept it as historical or substantial. But who has ever refused to accept a good legend with delight *as* a legend? The legends, the parables, the dramas, are among the choicest treasures of mankind. No one is ever tired of stories of miracles. In vain did Mahomet repudiate the miracles ascribed to him: in vain did Christ furiously scold those who asked him to give them an exhibition as a conjurer: in vain did the saints declare that God chose them not for their powers but for their weaknesses; that the humble might be exalted, and the proud rebuked. People will have their miracles, their stories, their heroes and heroines and saints and martyrs and divinities to exercise their gifts of affection, admiration, wonder, and worship, and their Judases and devils to enable them to be angry and yet feel that they do well to be angry. Every one of these legends is the common heritage of the human race; and there is only one inexorable condition attached to their healthy enjoyment, which is that no one shall believe them literally. The reading of stories and delighting in them made Don Quixote a gentleman: the believing them literally made him a madman who slew lambs instead of feeding them. In England today good books of Eastern religious legends are read eagerly; and Pro-

testants and Atheists read Roman Catholic legends of the Saints with
pleasure. But such fare is shirked by Indians and Roman Catholics.
Freethinkers read the Bible: indeed they seem to be its only readers
now except the reluctant parsons at the church lecterns, who communicate their discomfort to the congregation by gargling the words
in their throats in an unnatural manner that is as repulsive as it is un-
intelligible. And this is because the imposition of the legends as
literal truths at once changes them from parables into falsehoods.
The feeling against the Bible has become so strong at last that
educated people not only refuse to outrage their intellectual con-
sciences by reading the legend of Noah's Ark, with its funny beginning about the animals and its exquisite end about the birds: they
will not read even the chronicles of King David, which may very
well be true, and are certainly more candid than the official biographies of our contemporary monarchs.

WHAT TO DO WITH THE LEGENDS

What we should do, then, is to pool our legends and make a delightful stock of religious folk-lore on an honest basis for all mankind.
With our minds freed from pretence and falsehood we could enter
into the heritage of all the faiths. China would share her sages with
Spain, and Spain her saints with China. The Ulster man who now
gives his son an unmerciful thrashing if the boy is so tactless as to ask
how the evening and the morning could be the first day before the
sun was created, or to betray an innocent calf-love for the Virgin
Mary, would buy him a bookful of legends of the creation and of
mothers of God from all parts of the world, and be very glad to find
his laddie as interested in such things as in marbles or Police and
Robbers. That would be better than beating all good feeling towards religion out of the child, and blackening his mind by teaching
him that the worshippers of the holy virgins, whether of the Parthe-
non or St Peter's, are fire-doomed heathens and idolaters. All the
sweetness of religion is conveyed to the world by the hands of story-
tellers and image-makers. Without their fictions the truths of religion
would for the multitude be neither intelligible nor even apprehensible; and the prophets would prophesy and the teachers teach
in vain. And nothing stands between the people and the fictions
except the silly falsehood that the fictions are literal truths, and that
there is nothing in religion but fiction.

A LESSON FROM SCIENCE TO THE CHURCHES

Let the Churches ask themselves why there is no revolt against the dogmas of mathematics though there is one against the dogmas of religion. It is not that the mathematical dogmas are more comprehensible. The law of inverse squares is as incomprehensible to the common man as the Athanasian creed. It is not that science is free from legends, witchcraft, miracles, biographic boostings of quacks as heroes and saints, and of barren scoundrels as explorers and discoverers. On the contrary, the iconography and hagiology of Scientism are as copious as they are mostly squalid. But no student of science has yet been taught that specific gravity consists in the belief that Archimedes jumped out of his bath and ran naked through the streets of Syracuse shouting Eureka, Eureka, or that the law of inverse squares must be discarded if anyone can prove that Newton was never in an orchard in his life. When some unusually conscientious or enterprising bacteriologist reads the pamphlets of Jenner, and discovers that they might have been written by an ignorant but curious and observant nurserymaid, and could not possibly have been written by any person with a scientifically trained mind, he does not feel that the whole edifice of science has collapsed and crumbled, and that there is no such thing as smallpox. It may come to that yet; for hygiene, as it forces its way into our schools, is being taught as falsely as religion is taught there; but in mathematics and physics the faith is still kept pure, and you may take the law and leave the legends without suspicion of heresy. Accordingly, the tower of the mathematician stands unshaken whilst the temple of the priest rocks to its foundation.

THE RELIGIOUS ART OF THE TWENTIETH CENTURY

Creative Evolution is already a religion, and is indeed now unmistakeably the religion of the twentieth century, newly arisen from the ashes of pseudo-Christianity, of mere scepticism, and of the soulless affirmations and blind negations of the Mechanists and Neo-Darwinians. But it cannot become a popular religion until it has its legends, its parables, its miracles. And when I say popular I do not mean apprehensible by villagers only. I mean apprehensible by Cabinet Ministers as well. It is unreasonable to look to the professional politician and administrator for light and leading in religion. He is neither a philosopher nor a prophet: if he were, he would be philosophizing and prophesying, and not neglecting both for the drudgery of practical government. Socrates and Coleridge did not remain soldiers, nor could John Stuart Mill remain the representative of Westminster in the House of Commons even when he was willing. The Westminster electors admired Mill for telling them that much of the difficulty of dealing with them arose from their being inveterate liars. But they would not vote a second time for the man who was not afraid to break the crust of mendacity on which they were all dancing; for it seemed to them that there was a volcanic abyss beneath, not having his philosophic conviction that the truth is the solidest standing ground in the end. Your front bench man will always be an exploiter of the popular religion or irreligion. Not being an expert, he must take it as he finds it; and before he can take it, he must have been told stories about it in his childhood and had before him all his life an elaborate iconography of it produced by writers, painters, sculptors, temple architects, and artists of all the higher sorts. Even if, as sometimes happens, he is a bit of an amateur in metaphysics as well as a professional politician, he must still govern according to the popular iconography, and not according to his own personal interpretations if these happen to be heterodox.

It will be seen then that the revival of religion on a scientific basis does not mean the death of art, but a glorious rebirth of it. Indeed art has never been great when it was not providing an iconography for a live religion. And it has never been quite contemptible except when imitating the iconography after the religion had become a superstition. Italian painting from Giotto to Carpaccio is all religious painting; and it moves us deeply and has real greatness. Compare with it the attempts of our painters a century ago to achieve the effects of the old masters by imitation when they should have been illustrating a faith of their own. Contemplate, if you can bear it, the dull daubs of Hilton and Haydon, who knew so much more about drawing and scumbling and glazing and perspective and anatomy and 'marvellous foreshortening' than Giotto, the latchet of whose shoe they were nevertheless not worthy to unloose. Compare Mozart's Magic Flute, Beethoven's Ninth Symphony, Wagner's Ring, all of them reachings-forward to the new Vitalist art, with the dreary pseudo-sacred oratorios and cantatas which were produced for no better reason than that Handel had formerly made splendid thunder in that way, and with the stale confectionery, mostly too would-be pious to be even cheerfully toothsome, of Spohr and Mendelssohn, Stainer and Parry, which spread indigestion at our musical festivals until I publicly told Parry the bludgeoning truth about his Job and woke him to conviction of sin. Compare Flaxman and Thorwaldsen and Gibson with Phidias and Praxiteles, Stevens with Michael Angelo, Bouguereau's Virgin with Cimabue's, or the best operatic Christs of Scheffer and Müller with the worst Christs that the worst painters could paint before the end of the fifteenth century, and you must feel that until we have a great religious movement we cannot hope for a great artistic one. The disillusioned Raphael could paint a mother and child, but not a queen of Heaven as much less skilful men had done in the days of his great-grandfather; yet he could reach forward to the twentieth century and paint a Transfiguration of the Son of Man as they could not. Also, please note, he could decorate a house of pleasure for a cardinal very beautifully with voluptuous pictures of Cupid and Psyche: for this simple sort of Vitalism is always with us, and, like portrait painting, keeps the artist supplied with subject-matter in the intervals between the ages of faith; so that your sceptical Rembrandts and Velasquezs are at least not compelled to paint shop fronts for want of anything else to paint in which they can really believe.

THE ARTIST-PROPHETS

And there are always certain rare but intensely interesting anticipations. Michael Angelo could not very well believe in Julius II or Leo X, or in much that they believed in; but he could paint the Superman three hundred years before Nietzsche wrote Also Sprach Zarathustra and Strauss set it to music. Michael Angelo won the primacy among all modern painters and sculptors solely by his power of shewing us superhuman persons. On the strength of his decoration and color alone he would hardly have survived his own death twenty years; and even his design would have had only an academic interest; but as a painter of prophets and sibyls he is greatest among the very greatest in his craft, because we aspire to a world of prophets and sibyls. Beethoven never heard of radio-activity nor of electrons dancing in vortices of inconceivable energy; but pray can anyone explain the last movement of his Hammer-klavier Sonata, Opus 106, otherwise than as a musical picture of these whirling electrons? His contemporaries said he was mad, partly perhaps because the movement was so hard to play; but we, who can make a pianola play it to us over and over until it is as familiar as Pop Goes the Weasel, know that it is sane and methodical. As such, it must represent something; and as all Beethoven's serious compositions represent some process within himself, some nerve storm or soul storm, and the storm here is clearly one of physical movement, I should much like to know what other storm than the atomic storm could have driven him to this oddest of all those many expressions of cyclonic energy which have given him the same distinction among musicians that Michael Angelo has among draughtsmen.

In Beethoven's day the business of art was held to be 'the sublime and beautiful.' In our day it has fallen to be the imitative and voluptuous. In both periods the word passionate has been freely employed; but in the eighteenth century passion meant irresistible impulse of the loftiest kind: for example, a passion for astronomy or for truth. For us it has come to mean concupiscence and nothing else. One might say to the art of Europe what Antony said to the corpse of Caesar: 'Are all thy conquests, glories, triumphs, spoils, shrunk to this little measure?' But in fact it is the mind of Europe that has shrunk, being, as we have seen, wholly preoccupied with a busy spring-cleaning to get rid of its superstitions before readjusting itself to the new conception of Evolution.

EVOLUTION IN THE THEATRE

On the stage (and here I come at last to my own particular function in the matter), Comedy, as a destructive, derisory, critical, negative art, kept the theatre open when sublime tragedy perished. From Molière to Oscar Wilde we had a line of comedic playwrights who, if they had nothing fundamentally positive to say, were at least in revolt against falsehood and imposture, and were not only, as they claimed, 'chastening morals by ridicule,' but, in Johnson's phrase, clearing our minds of cant, and thereby shewing an uneasiness in the presence of error which is the surest symptom of intellectual vitality. Meanwhile the name of Tragedy was assumed by plays in which everyone was killed in the last act, just as, in spite of Molière, plays in which everyone was married in the last act called themselves comedies. Now neither tragedies nor comedies can be produced according to a prescription which gives only the last moments of the last act. Shakespear did not make Hamlet out of its final butchery, nor Twelfth Night out of its final matrimony. And he could not become the conscious iconographer of a religion because he had no conscious religion. He had therefore to exercise his extra-ordinary natural gifts in the very entertaining art of mimicry, giving us the famous 'delineation of character' which makes his plays, like the novels of Scott, Dumas, and Dickens, so delightful. Also, he developed that curious and questionable art of building us a refuge from despair by disguising the cruelties of Nature as jokes. But with all his gifts, the fact remains that he never found the inspiration to write an original play. He furbished up old plays, and adapted popular stories, and chapters of history from Holinshed's Chronicle and Plutarch's biographies, to the stage. All this he did (or did not; for there are minus quantities in the algebra of art) with a recklessness which shewed that his trade lay far from his conscience. It is true that he never takes his characters from the borrowed story, because it was less trouble and more fun to him to create them afresh; but none the less he heaps the murders and villainies of the borrowed story on his own essentially gentle creations without scruple, no matter how incongruous they may be. And all the time his vital need for a philosophy drives him to seek one by the quaint professional method of introducing philosophers as characters into his plays, and even of making his heroes philosophers; but when they come on the stage they have no philosophy to expound: they are only pessimists and railers; and their occasional would-be philosophic speeches, such as The Seven Ages of Man and The Soliloquy on Suicide, shew how deeply in the dark Shakespear was as to what philosophy means. He forced himself in among the greatest of playwrights without having once entered that region in which Michael Angelo, Beethoven, Goethe, and the antique Athenian stage poets are great. He would really not be great at all if it were not that he had religion enough to be aware that his religionless condition was one of despair. His towering King Lear would be only a melodrama were it not for its express admission that if there is nothing more to be said of the universe than Hamlet has to say, then 'as flies to wanton boys are we to the gods: they kill us for their sport.'

Ever since Shakespear, playwrights have been struggling with the same lack of religion; and many of them were forced to become mere panders and sensation-mongers because, though they had higher ambitions, they could find no better subject-matter. From Congreve to Sheridan they were so sterile in spite of their wit that they did not achieve between them the output of Molière's single lifetime; and they were all (not without reason) ashamed of their profession, and preferred to be regarded as mere men of fashion with a rakish hobby. Goldsmith's was the only saved soul in that pandemonium.

The leaders among my own contemporaries (now veterans) snatched at minor social problems rather than write entirely without any wider purpose than to win money and fame. One of them expressed to me his envy of the ancient Greek playwrights because the Athenians asked them, not for some 'new and original' disguise of the half-dozen threadbare plots of the modern theatre, but for the deepest lesson they could draw from the familiar and sacred legends of their country. 'Let us all,' he said, 'write an Electra, an Antigone, an Agamemnon, and shew what we can do with it.' But he did not write any of them, because these legends are no longer religious: Aphrodite and Artemis and Poseidon are deader than their statues. Another, with a commanding position and every trick of British farce and Parisian drama at his fingers' ends, finally could not write without a sermon to preach, and yet could not find texts more fundamental than the hypocrisies of sham Puritanism, or the matrimonial speculation which makes our young actresses as careful of their reputations as of their complexions. A third, too tender-hearted to break our spirits with the realities of a bitter experience, coaxed a wistful pathos and a dainty fun out of the fairy cloudland that lay between him and the empty heavens. The giants of the theatre of our time, Ibsen and Strindberg, had no greater comfort for the world than we: indeed much less; for they refused us even the Shakespearian-Dickensian consolation of laughter at mischief, accurately called comic relief. Our emancipated young successors scorn us, very properly. But they will be able to do no better whilst the drama remains pre-Evolutionist. Let them consider the great exception of Goethe. He, no richer than Shakespear, Ibsen, or Strindberg in specific talent as a playwright, is in the empyrean whilst they are gnashing their teeth in impotent fury in the mud, or at best finding an acid enjoyment in the irony of their predicament. Goethe is Olympian: the other giants are infernal in everything but their veracity and their repudiation of the irreligion of their time: that is, they are bitter and hopeless. It is not a question of mere dates. Goethe was an Evolutionist in 1830: many playwrights, even young ones, are still untouched by Creative Evolution in 1920. Ibsen was Darwinized to the extent of exploiting heredity on the stage much as the ancient Athenian playwrights exploited the Eumenides; but there is no trace in his plays of any faith in or knowledge of Creative Evolution as a modern scientific fact. True, the poetic aspiration is plain enough in his Emperor or Galilean; but it is one of Ibsen's distinctions that nothing was valid for him but science; and he left that vision of the future which his Roman seer calls 'the third Empire' behind him as a Utopian dream when he settled down to his serious grapple with realities in those plays of modern life with which he overcame Europe, and broke the dusty windows of every dry-rotten theatre in it from Moscow to Manchester.

MY OWN PART IN THE MATTER

In my own activities as a playwright I found this state of things intolerable. The fashionable theatre prescribed one serious subject: clandestine adultery: the dullest of all subjects for a serious author, whatever it may be for audiences who read the police intelligence and skip the reviews and leading articles. I tried slum-landlordism, doctrinaire Free Love (pseudo-Ibsenism), prostitution, militarism, marriage, history, current politics, natural Christianity, national and individual character, paradoxes of conventional society, husband hunting, questions of conscience, professional delusions and impostures, all worked into a series of comedies of manners in the classic fashion, which was then very much out of fashion, the mechanical tricks of Parisian 'construction' being de rigueur in the theatre. But this, though it occupied me and established me professionally, did not constitute me an iconographer of the religion of my time, and thus fulfil my natural function as an artist. I was quite conscious of this; for I had always known that civilization needs a religion as a matter of life or death; and as the conception of Creative Evolution developed I saw that we were at last within reach of a faith which complied with the first condition of all the religions that have ever taken hold of humanity: namely, that it must be, first and fundamentally, a science of metabiology. This was a crucial point with me; for I had seen Bible fetishism, after standing up to all the rationalistic batteries of Hume, Voltaire, and the rest, collapse before the onslaught of much less gifted Evolutionists, solely because they discredited it as a biological document; so that from that moment it lost its hold, and left literate Christendom faithless. My own Irish eighteenth-centuryism made it impossible for me to believe anything until I could conceive it as a scientific hypothesis, even though the abominations, quackeries, impostures, venalities, credulities, and delusions of the camp followers of science, and the brazen lies and priestly pretensions of the pseudo-scientific curemongers, all sedulously inculcated by modern 'secondary education,' were so monstrous that I was sometimes forced to make a verbal distinction between science and knowledge lest I should mislead my readers. But I never forgot that without knowledge even wisdom is more dangerous than mere opportunist ignorance, and that somebody must take the Garden of Eden in hand and weed it properly.

Accordingly, in 1901, I took the legend of Don Juan in its Mozartian form and made it a dramatic parable of Creative Evolution. But being then at the height of my invention and comedic talent, I decorated it too brilliantly and lavishly. I surrounded it with a comedy of which it formed only one act, and that act was so completely episodical (it was a dream which did not affect the action of the piece) that the comedy could be detached and played by itself: indeed it could hardly be played at full length owing to the enormous length of the entire work, though that feat has been performed a few times in Scotland by Mr Esme Percy, who led one of the forlorn hopes of the advanced drama at that time. Also I supplied the published work with an imposing framework consisting of a preface, an appendix called The Revolutionist's Handbook, and a final display of aphoristic fireworks. The effect was so vertiginous, apparently, that nobody noticed the new religion in the centre of the intellectual whirlpool. Now I protest I did not cut these cerebral capers in mere inconsiderate exuberance. I did it because the worst convention of the criticism of the theatre current at that time was that intellectual seriousness is out of place on the stage; that the theatre is a place of shallow amusement; that people go there to be soothed after the enormous intellectual strain of a day in the city: in short, that a playwright is a person whose business it is to make unwholesome confectionery out of cheap emotions. My answer to this was to put all my intellectual goods in the shop window under the sign of Man and Superman. That part of my design succeeded. By good luck and acting, the comedy triumphed on the stage; and the book was a good deal discussed. Since then the sweet-shop view of the theatre has been out of countenance; and its critical exponents have been driven to take an intellectual pose which, though often more trying than their old intellectually nihilistic vulgarity, at least concedes the dignity of the theatre, not to mention the usefulness of those who live by criticizing it. And the younger playwrights are not only taking their art seriously, but being taken seriously themselves. The critic who ought to be a newsboy is now comparatively rare.

I now find myself inspired to make a second legend of Creative Evolution without distractions and embellishments. My sands are running out; the exuberance of 1901 has aged into the garrulity of 1920; and the war has been a stern intimation that the matter is not one to be trifled with. I abandon the legend of Don Juan with its erotic associations, and go back to the legend of the Garden of Eden.

I exploit the eternal interest of the philosopher's stone which enables men to live for ever. I am not, I hope, under more illusion than is humanly inevitable as to the crudity of this my beginning of a Bible for Creative Evolution. I am doing the best I can at my age. My powers are waning; but so much the better for those who found me unbearably brilliant when I was in my prime. It is my hope that a hundred apter and more elegant parables by younger hands will soon leave mine as far behind as the religious pictures of the fifteenth century left behind the first attempts of the early Christians at iconography. In that hope I withdraw and ring up the curtain.

BACK TO METHUSELAH

PART I

In the Beginning

ACT I

The Garden of Eden. Afternoon. An immense serpent is sleeping with her head buried in a thick bed of Johnswort, and her body coiled in apparently endless rings through the branches of a tree, which is already well grown; for the days of creation have been longer than our reckoning. She is not yet visible to anyone unaware of her presence, as her colors of green and brown make a perfect camouflage. Near her head a low rock shews above the Johnswort.

The rock and tree are on the border of a glade in which lies a dead fawn all awry, its neck being broken. Adam, crouching with one hand on the rock, is staring in consternation at the dead body. He has not noticed the serpent on his left hand. He turns his face to his right and calls excitedly.

ADAM. Eve! Eve!

EVE'S VOICE. What is it, Adam?

ADAM. Come here. Quick. Something has happened.

EVE [*running in*] What? Where? [*Adam points to the fawn*]. Oh! [*She goes to it; and he is emboldened to go with her*]. What is the matter with its eyes?

ADAM. It is not only its eyes. Look. [*He kicks it.*]

EVE. Oh dont! Why doesnt it wake?

ADAM. I dont know. It is not asleep.

EVE. Not asleep?

ADAM. Try.

EVE [*trying to shake it and roll it over*] It is stiff and cold.

ADAM. Nothing will wake it.

EVE. It has a queer smell. Pah! [*She dusts her hands, and draws away from it*]. Did you find it like that?

ADAM. No. It was playing about; and it tripped and went head over heels. It never stirred again. Its neck is wrong [*he stoops to lift the neck and shew her*].

EVE. Dont touch it. Come away from it.

They both retreat, and contemplate it from a few steps' distance with growing repulsion.

EVE. Adam.

ADAM. Yes?

EVE. Suppose you were to trip and fall, would you go like that?

ADAM. Ugh! [*He shudders and sits down on the rock*].

EVE [*throwing herself on the ground beside him, and grasping his knee*] You must be careful. Promise me you will be careful.

ADAM. What is the good of being careful? We have to live here for ever. Think of what for ever means! Sooner or later I shall trip and fall. It may be tomorrow; it may be after as many days as there are leaves in the garden and grains of sand by the river. No matter: some day I shall forget and stumble.

EVE. I too.

ADAM [*horrified*] Oh no, no. I should be alone. Alone for ever. You must never put yourself in danger of stumbling. You must not move about. You must sit still. I will take care of you and bring you what you want.

EVE [*turning away from him with a shrug, and hugging her ankles*] I should soon get tired of that. Besides, if it happened to you, *I* should be alone. I could not sit still then. And at last it would happen to me too.

ADAM. And then?

EVE. Then we should be no more. There would be only the things on all fours, and the birds, and the snakes.

ADAM. That must not be.

EVE. Yes: that must not be. But it might be.

ADAM. No. I tell you it must not be. I know that it must not be.

EVE. We both know it. How do we know it?

EDAM. There is a voice in the garden that tells me things.

AVE. The garden is full of voices sometimes. They put all sorts of thoughts into my head.

ADAM. To me there is only one voice. It is very low; but it is so near that it is like a whisper from within myself. There is no mistaking it for any voice of the birds or beasts, or for your voice.

EVE. It is strange that I should hear voices from all sides and you only one from within. But I have some thoughts that come from within me and not from the voices. The thought that we must not cease to be comes from within.

ADAM [*despairingly*] But we *shall* cease to be. We shall fall like the fawn and be broken. [*Rising and moving about in his agitation*]. I cannot bear this knowledge. I will not have it. It must not be, I tell you. Yet I do not know how to prevent it.

EVE. That is just what I feel; but it is very strange that you should say so: there is no pleasing you. You change your mind so often.

ADAM [*scolding her*] Why do you say that? How have I changed my mind?

EVE. You say we must not cease to exist. But you used to complain of having to exist always and for ever. You sometimes sit for hours brooding and silent, hating me in your heart. When I ask you what I have done to you, you say you are not thinking of me, but of the horror of having to be here for ever. But I know very well that what you mean is the horror of having to be here with me for ever.

ADAM. Oh! That is what you think, is it? Well, you are wrong. [*He sits down again, sulkily*]. It is the horror of having to be with myself for ever. I like you; but I do not like myself. I want to be different; to be better, to begin again and again; to shed myself as a snake sheds its skin. I am tired of myself. And yet I must endure myself, not for a day or for many days, but for ever. That is a dreadful thought. That is what makes me sit brooding and silent and hateful. Do you never think of that?

EVE. No: I do not think about myself: what is the use? I am what I am: nothing can alter that. I think about you.

ADAM. You should not. You are always spying on me. I can never be alone. You always want to know what I have been doing. It is a burden. You should try to have an existence of your own, instead of occupying yourself with my existence.

EVE. I *have* to think about you. You are lazy: you are dirty: you neglect yourself: you are always dreaming: you would eat bad food and become disgusting if I did not watch you and occupy myself with you. And now some day, in spite of all my care, you will fall on your head and become dead.

ADAM. Dead? What word is that?

EVE [*pointing to the fawn*] Like that. I call it dead.

ADAM [*rising and approaching it slowly*] There is something uncanny about it.

EVE [*joining him*] Oh! It is changing into little white worms.

ADAM. Throw it into the river. It is unbearable.

EVE. I dare not touch it.

ADAM. Then I must, though I loathe it. It is poisoning the air. [*He gathers its hooves in his hand and carries it away in the direction from which Eve came, holding it as far from him as possible*].

 Eve looks after them for a moment; then, with a shiver of disgust, sits down on the rock brooding. The body of the serpent becomes visible, glowing with wonderful new colors. She rears her head slowly from the bed of Johnswort, and speaks into Eve's ear in a strange seductively musical whisper.

THE SERPENT. Eve.

EVE [*startled*] Who is that?

THE SERPENT. It is I. I have come to shew you my beautiful new hood. See [*she spreads a magnificent amethystine hood*]!

EVE [*admiring it*] Oh! But who taught you to speak?

THE SERPENT. You and Adam. I have crept through the grass, and hidden, and listened to you.

EVE. That was wonderfully clever of you.

THE SERPENT. I am the most subtle of all the creatures of the field.

EVE. Your hood is most lovely. [*She strokes it and pets the serpent*]. Pretty thing! Do you love your godmother Eve?

THE SERPENT. I adore her. [*She licks Eve's neck with her double tongue*].

EVE [*petting her*] Eve's wonderful darling snake. Eve will never be lonely now that her snake can talk to her.

THE SNAKE. I can talk of many things. I am very wise. It was I who whispered the word to you that you did not know. Dead. Death. Die.

EVE [*shuddering*] Why do you remind me of it? I forgot it when I saw your beautiful hood. You must not remind me of unhappy things.

THE SERPENT. Death is not an unhappy thing when you have learnt how to conquer it.

EVE. How can I conquer it?

THE SERPENT. By another thing, called birth.

EVE. What? [*Trying to pronounce it*] B-birth?

THE SERPENT. Yes, birth.

EVE. What is birth?

THE SERPENT. The serpent never dies. Some day you shall see me come out of this beautiful skin, a new snake with a new and lovelier skin. That is birth.

EVE. I have seen that. It is wonderful.

THE SERPENT. If I can do that, what can I not do? I tell you I am very subtle. When you and Adam talk, I hear you say 'Why?' Always 'Why?' You see things; and you say 'Why?' But I dream things that never were; and I say 'Why not?' I made the word dead to describe my old skin that I cast when I am renewed. I call that renewal being born.

EVE. Born is a beautiful word.

THE SERPENT. Why not be born again and again as I am, new and beautiful every time?

EVE. I! It does not happen: that is why.

THE SERPENT. That is how; but it is not why. Why not?

EVE. But I should not like it. It would be nice to be new again; but my old skin would lie on the ground looking just like me; and Adam would see it shrivel up and –

THE SERPENT. No. He need not. There is a second birth.

EVE. A second birth?

THE SERPENT. Listen. I will tell you a great secret. I am very subtle; and I have thought and thought and thought.

And I am very wilful, and must have what I want; and I have willed and willed and willed. And I have eaten strange things: stones and apples that you are afraid to eat.

EVE. You dared!

THE SERPENT. I dared everything. And at last I found a way of gathering together a part of the life in my body –

EVE. What is the life?

THE SERPENT. That which makes the difference between the dead fawn and the live one.

EVE. What a beautiful word! And what a wonderful thing! Life is the loveliest of all the new words.

THE SERPENT. Yes: it was by meditating on Life that I gained the power to do miracles.

EVE. Miracles? Another new word.

THE SERPENT. A miracle is an impossible thing that is nevertheless possible. Something that never could happen, and yet does happen.

EVE. Tell me some miracle that you have done.

THE SERPENT. I gathered a part of the life in my body, and shut it into a tiny white case made of the stones I had eaten.

EVE. And what good was that?

THE SERPENT. I shewed the little case to the sun, and left it in its warmth. And it burst; and a little snake came out; and it became bigger and bigger from day to day until it was as big as I. That was the second birth.

EVE. Oh! That is too wonderful. It stirs inside me. It hurts.

THE SERPENT. It nearly tore me asunder. Yet I am alive, and can burst my skin and renew myself as before. Soon there will be as many snakes in Eden as there are scales on my body. Then death will not matter: this snake and that snake will die; but the snakes will live.

EVE. But the rest of us will die sooner or later, like the fawn. And then there will be nothing but snakes, snakes, snakes everywhere.

THE SERPENT. That must not be. I worship you, Eve. I must have something to worship. Something quite different to myself, like you. There must be something greater than the snake.

EVE. Yes: it must not be. Adam must not perish. You are very subtle: tell me what to do.

THE SERPENT. Think. Will. Eat the dust. Lick the white stone: bite the apple you dread. The sun will give life.

EVE. I do not trust the sun. I will give life myself. I will tear another Adam from my body if I tear my body to pieces in the act.

THE SERPENT. Do. Dare it. Everything is possible: everything. Listen. I am old. I am the old serpent, older than Adam, older than Eve. I remember Lilith, who came before Adam and Eve. I was her darling as I am yours. She was alone: there was no man with her. She saw death as you saw it when the fawn fell; and she knew then that she must find out how to renew herself and cast the skin like me. She had a mighty will: she strove and strove and willed and willed for more moons than there are leaves on all the trees of the garden. Her pangs were terrible: her groans drove sleep from Eden. She said it must never be again: that the burden of renewing life was past bearing: that it was too much for one. And when she cast the skin, lo! there was not one new Lilith but two: one like herself, the other like Adam. You were the one: Adam was the other.

EVE. But why did she divide into two, and make us different?

THE SERPENT. I tell you the labor is too much for one. Two must share it.

EVE. Do you mean that Adam must share it with me? He will not. He cannot bear pain, nor take trouble with his body.

THE SERPENT. He need not. There will be no pain for him. He will implore you to let him do his share. He will be in your power through his desire.

EVE. Then I will do it. But how? How did Lilith work this miracle?

THE SERPENT. She imagined it.

EVE. What is imagined?

THE SERPENT. She told it to me as a marvellous story of

something that never happened to a Lilith that never was. She did not know then that imagination is the beginning of creation. You imagine what you desire; you will what you imagine; and at last you create what you will.

EVE. How can I create out of nothing?

THE SERPENT. Everything must have been created out of nothing. Look at that thick roll of hard flesh on your strong arm! That was not always there: you could not climb a tree when I first saw you. But you willed and tried and willed and tried; and your will created out of nothing the roll on your arm until you had your desire, and could draw yourself up with one hand and seat yourself on the bough that was above your head.

EVE. That was practice.

THE SERPENT. Things wear out by practice: they do not grow by it. Your hair streams in the wind as if it were trying to stretch itself further and further. But it does not grow longer for all its practice in streaming, because you have not willed it so. When Lilith told me what she had imagined in our silent language (for there were no words then) I bade her desire it and will it; and then, to our great wonder, the thing she had desired and willed created itself in her under the urging of her will. Then I too willed to renew myself as two instead of one; and after many days the miracle happened, and I burst from my skin another snake interlaced with me; and now there are two imaginations, two desires, two wills to create with.

EVE. To desire, to imagine, to will, to create. That is too long a story. Find me one word for it all: you, who are so clever at words.

THE SERPENT. In one word, to conceive. That is the word that means both the beginning in imagination and the end in creation.

EVE. Find me a word for the story Lilith imagined and told you in your silent language: the story that was too wonderful to be true, and yet came true.

THE SERPENT. A poem.

EVE. Find me another word for what Lilith was to me.

THE SERPENT. She was your mother.

EVE. And Adam's mother?

THE SERPENT. Yes.

EVE [*about to rise*] I will go and tell Adam to conceive.

THE SERPENT [*laughs*]!!!

EVE [*jarred and startled*] What a hateful noise! What is the matter with you? No one has ever uttered such a sound before.

THE SERPENT. Adam cannot conceive.

EVE. Why?

THE SERPENT. Lilith did not imagine him so. He can imagine: he can will: he can desire: he can gather his life together for a great spring towards creation: he can create all things except one; and that one is his own kind.

EVE. Why did Lilith keep this from him?

THE SERPENT. Because if he could do that he could do without Eve.

EVE. That is true. It is I who must conceive.

THE SERPENT. Yes. By that he is tied to you.

EVE. And I to him!

THE SERPENT. Yes, until you create another Adam.

EVE. I had not thought of that. You are very subtle. But if I create another Eve he may turn to her and do without me. I will not create any Eves, only Adams.

THE SERPENT. They cannot renew themselves without Eves. Sooner or later you will die like the fawn; and the new Adams will be unable to create without new Eves. You can imagine such an end; but you cannot desire it, therefore cannot will it, therefore cannot create Adams only.

EVE. If I am to die like the fawn, why should not the rest die too? What do I care?

THE SERPENT. Life must not cease. That comes before everything. It is silly to say you do not care. You do care. It is that care that will prompt your imagination; inflame your desires; make your will irresistible; and create out of nothing.

EVE [*thoughtfully*] There can be no such thing as nothing. The garden is full, not empty.

THE SERPENT. I had not thought of that. That is a great thought. Yes: there is no such thing as nothing, only things we cannot see. The chameleon eats the air.

EVE. I have another thought: I must tell it to Adam. [*Calling*] Adam! Adam! Coo-ee!

ADAM'S VOICE. Coo-ee!

EVE. This will please him, and cure his fits of melancholy.

THE SERPENT. Do not tell him yet. I have not told you the great secret.

EVE. What more is there to tell? It is I who have to do the miracle.

THE SERPENT. No: he, too, must desire and will. But he must give his desire and his will to you.

EVE. How?

THE SERPENT. That is the great secret. Hush! he is coming.

ADAM [*returning*] Is there another voice in the garden besides our voices and the Voice? I heard a new voice.

EVE [*rising and running to him*] Only think, Adam! Our snake has learnt to speak by listening to us.

ADAM [*delighted*] Is it so? [*He goes past her to the stone, and fondles the serpent*].

THE SERPENT [*responding affectionately*] It is so, dear Adam.

EVE. But I have more wonderful news than that. Adam: we need not live for ever.

ADAM [*dropping the snake's head in his excitement*] What! Eve: do not play with me about this. If only there may be an end some day, and yet no end! If only I can be relieved of the horror of having to endure myself for ever! If only the care of this terrible garden may pass on to some other gardener! If only the sentinel set by the Voice can be relieved! If only the rest and sleep that enable me to bear it from day to day could grow after many days into an eternal rest, an eternal sleep, then I could face my days, however long they may last. Only, there must be some end, some end: I am not strong enough to bear eternity.

THE SERPENT. You need not live to see another summer; and yet there shall be no end.

ADAM. That cannot be.

THE SERPENT. It can be.

EVE. It shall be.

THE SERPENT. It is. Kill me; and you will find another snake in the garden tomorrow. You will find more snakes than there are fingers on your hands.

EVE. I will make other Adams, other Eves.

ADAM. I tell you you must not make up stories about this. It cannot happen.

THE SERPENT. I can remember when you were yourself a thing that could not happen. Yet you are.

ADAM [struck] That must be true. [He sits down on the stone].

THE SERPENT. I will tell Eve the secret; and she will tell it to you.

ADAM. The secret! [He turns quickly towards the serpent, and in doing so puts his foot on something sharp]. Oh!

EVE. What is it?

ADAM [rubbing his foot] A thistle. And there, next to it, a briar. And nettles, too! I am tired of pulling these things up to keep the garden pleasant for us for ever.

THE SERPENT. They do not grow very fast. They will not overrun the whole garden for a long time: not until you have laid down your burden and gone to sleep for ever. Why should you trouble yourself? Let the new Adams clear a place for themselves.

ADAM. That is very true. You must tell us your secret. You see, Eve, what a splendid thing it is not to have to live for ever.

EVE [throwing herself down discontentedly and plucking at the grass] That is so like a man. The moment you find we need not last for ever, you talk as if we were going to end today. You must clear away some of those horrid things, or we shall be scratched and stung whenever we forget to look where we are stepping.

ADAM. Oh yes, some of them, of course. But only some. I will clear them away tomorrow.

THE SERPENT [laughs] !!!

ADAM. That is a funny noise to make. I like it.

EVE. I do not. Why do you make it again?

THE SERPENT. Adam has invented something new. He has invented tomorrow. You will invent things every day now that the burden of immortality is lifted from you.

EVE. Immortality? What is that?

THE SERPENT. My new word for having to live for ever.

EVE. The serpent has made a beautiful word for being. Living.

ADAM. Make me a beautiful word for doing things tomorrow; for that surely is a great and blessed invention.

THE SERPENT. Procrastination.

EVE. That is a sweet word. I wish I had a serpent's tongue.

THE SERPENT. That may come too. Everything is possible.

ADAM [*springing up in sudden terror*] Oh!

EVE. What is the matter now?

ADAM. My rest! My escape from life!

THE SERPENT. Death. That is the word.

ADAM. There is a terrible danger in this procrastination.

EVE. What danger?

ADAM. If I put off death until tomorrow, I shall never die. There is no such day as tomorrow, and never can be.

THE SERPENT. I am very subtle; but Man is deeper in his thought than I am. The woman knows that there is no such thing as nothing: the man knows that there is no such day as tomorrow. I do well to worship them.

ADAM. If I am to overtake death, I must appoint a real day, not a tomorrow. When shall I die?

EVE. You may die when I have made another Adam. Not before. But then, as soon as you like. [*She rises, and passing behind him, strolls off carelessly to the tree and leans against it, stroking a ring of the snake*].

ADAM. There need be no hurry even then.

EVE. I see you will put it off until tomorrow.

ADAM. And you? Will you die the moment you have made a new Eve?

EVE. Why should I? Are you eager to be rid of me? Only just now you wanted me to sit still and never move lest I should stumble and die like the fawn. Now you no longer care.

ADAM. It does not matter so much now.

EVE [*angrily to the snake*] This death that you have brought into the garden is an evil thing. He wants me to die.

THE SERPENT [*to Adam*] Do you want her to die?

ADAM. No. It is I who am to die. Eve must not die before me. I should be lonely.

EVE. You could get one of the new Eves.

ADAM. That is true. But they might not be quite the same. They could not: I feel sure of that. They would not have the same memories. They would be – I want a word for them.

THE SERPENT. Strangers.

ADAM. Yes: that is a good hard word. Strangers.

EVE. When there are new Adams and new Eves we shall live in a garden of strangers. We shall need each other. [*She comes quickly behind him and turns up his face to her*]. Do not forget that, Adam. Never forget it.

ADAM. Why should I forget it? It is I who have thought of it.

EVE. I, too, have thought of something. The fawn stumbled and fell and died. But you could come softly up behind me and [*she suddenly pounces on his shoulders and throws him forward on his face*] throw me down so that I should die. I should not dare to sleep if there were no reason why you should not make me die.

ADAM [*scrambling up in horror*] Make you die!!! What a frightful thought!

THE SERPENT. Kill, kill, kill, kill. That is the word.

EVE. The new Adams and Eves might kill us. I shall not make them. [*She sits on the rock and pulls him down beside her, clasping him to her with her right arm*].

THE SERPENT. You must. For if you do not there will be an end.

ADAM. No: they will not kill us: they will feel as I do. There is something against it. The Voice in the garden will tell them that they must not kill, as it tells me.

THE SERPENT. The voice in the garden is your own voice.

ADAM. It is; and it is not. It is something greater than me: I am only a part of it.

EVE. The Voice does not tell me not to kill you. Yet I do not want you to die before me. No voice is needed to make me feel that.

ADAM [*throwing his arm round her shoulder with an expression of anguish*] Oh no: that is plain without any voice. There is something that holds us together, something that has no word —

THE SERPENT. Love. Love. Love.

ADAM. That is too short a word for so long a thing.

THE SERPENT [*laughs*]!!!

EVE [*turning impatiently to the snake*] That heart-biting sound again! Do not do it. Why do you do it?

THE SERPENT. Love may be too long a word for so short a thing soon. But when it is short it will be very sweet.

ADAM [*ruminating*] You puzzle me. My old trouble was heavy; but it was simple. These wonders that you promise to do may tangle up my being before they bring me the gift of death. I was troubled with the burden of eternal being; but I was not confused in my mind. If I did not know that I loved Eve, at least I did not know that she might cease to love me, and come to love some other Adam and desire my death. Can you find a name for that knowledge?

THE SERPENT. Jealousy. Jealousy. Jealousy.

ADAM. A hideous word.

EVE [*shaking him*] Adam: you must not brood. You think too much.

ADAM [*angrily*] How can I help brooding when the future has become uncertain? Anything is better than uncertainty. Life has become uncertain. Love is uncertain. Have you a word for this new misery?

THE SERPENT. Fear. Fear. Fear.

ADAM. Have you a remedy for it?

THE SERPENT. Yes. Hope. Hope. Hope.

ADAM. What is hope?

THE SERPENT. As long as you do not know the future you do not know that it will not be happier than the past. That is hope.

ADAM. It does not console me. Fear is stronger in me than

hope. I must have certainty. [*He rises threateningly*]. Give it to me; or I will kill you when next I catch you asleep.

EVE [*throwing her arms round the serpent*] My beautiful snake. Oh no. How can you even think such a horror?

ADAM. Fear will drive me to anything. The serpent gave me fear. Let it now give me certainty or go in fear of me.

THE SERPENT. Bind the future by your will. Make a vow.

ADAM. What is a vow?

THE SERPENT. Choose a day for your death; and resolve to die on that day. Then death is no longer uncertain but certain. Let Eve vow to love you until your death. Then love will be no longer uncertain.

ADAM. Yes: that is splendid: that will bind the future.

EVE [*displeased, turning away from the serpent*] But it will destroy hope.

ADAM [*angrily*] Be silent, woman. Hope is wicked. Happiness is wicked. Certainty is blessed.

THE SERPENT. What is wicked? You have invented a word.

ADAM. Whatever I fear to do is wicked. Listen to me, Eve; and you, snake, listen too, that your memory may hold my vow. I will live a thousand sets of the four seasons –

THE SERPENT. Years. Years.

ADAM. I will live a thousand years; and then I will endure no more: I will die and take my rest. And I will love Eve all that time and no other woman.

EVE. And if Adam keeps his vow I will love no other man until he dies.

THE SERPENT. You have both invented marriage. And what he will be to you and not to any other woman is husband; and what you will be to him and not to any other man is wife.

ADAM [*instinctively moving his hand towards her*] Husband and wife.

EVE [*slipping her hand into his*] Wife and husband.

THE SERPENT [*laughs*] !!!

EVE [*snatching herself loose from Adam*] Do not make that odious noise, I tell you.

ADAM. Do not listen to her: the noise is good: it lightens my heart. You are a jolly snake. But you have not made a vow yet. What vow do you make?

THE SERPENT. I make no vows. I take my chance.

ADAM. Chance? What does that mean?

THE SERPENT. It means that I fear certainty as you fear uncertainty. It means that nothing is certain but uncertainty. If I bind the future I bind my will. If I bind my will I strangle creation.

EVE. Creation must not be strangled. I tell you I will create, though I tear myself to pieces in the act.

ADAM. Be silent, both of you. I *will* bind the future. I will be delivered from fear. [*To Eve*] We have made our vows; and if you must create, you shall create within the bounds of those vows. You shall not listen to that snake any more. Come [*he seizes her by the hair to drag her away*].

EVE. Let me go, you fool. It has not yet told me the secret.

ADAM [*releasing her*] That is true. What is a fool?

EVE. I do not know: the word came to me. It is what you are when you forget and brood and are filled with fear. Let us listen to the snake.

ADAM. No: I am afraid of it. I feel as if the ground were giving way under my feet when it speaks. Do you stay and listen to it.

THE SERPENT [*laughs*]!!!

ADAM [*brightening*] That noise takes away fear. Funny. The snake and the woman are going to whisper secrets. [*He chuckles and goes away slowly, laughing his first laugh*].

EVE. Now the secret. The secret. [*She sits on the rock and throws her arms round the serpent, who begins whispering to her*].

Eve's face lights up with intense interest, which increases until an expression of overwhelming repugnance takes its place. She buries her face in her hands.

ACT II

A few centuries later. Morning. An oasis in Mesopotamia. Close at hand the end of a log house abuts on a kitchen garden. Adam is digging in the middle of the garden. On his right, Eve sits on a stool in the shadow of a tree by the doorway, spinning flax. Her wheel, which she turns by hand, is a large disc of heavy wood, practically a fly-wheel. At the opposite side of the garden is a thorn brake with a passage through it barred by a hurdle.

The two are scantily and carelessly dressed in rough linen and leaves. They have lost their youth and grace; and Adam has an un-kempt beard and jaggedly cut hair; but they are strong and in the prime of life. Adam looks worried, like a farmer. Eve, better humored (having given up worrying), sits and spins and thinks.

A MAN'S VOICE. Hallo, mother!

EVE [*looking across the garden towards the hurdle*] Here is Cain.

ADAM [*uttering a grunt of disgust*]!!! [*He goes on digging without raising his head*].

Cain kicks the hurdle out of his way, and strides into the garden. In pose, voice, and dress he is insistently warlike. He is equipped with huge spear and broad brass-bound leather shield; his casque is a tiger's head with bull's horns; he wears a scarlet cloak with gold brooch over a lion's skin with the claws dangling; his feet are in sandals with brass ornaments; his shins are in brass greaves; and his bristling military moustache glistens with oil. To his parents he has the self-assertive, not-quite-at-ease manner of a re-volted son who knows that he is not forgiven nor approved of.

CAIN [*to Adam*] Still digging? Always dig, dig, dig. Sticking in the old furrow. No progress! no advanced ideas! no adventures! What should I be if I had stuck to the digging you taught me?

ADAM. What are you now, with your shield and spear, and your brother's blood crying from the ground against you?

CAIN. I am the first murderer: you are only the first man. Anybody could be the first man: it is as easy as to be the first cabbage. To be the first murderer one must be a man of spirit.

ADAM. Begone. Leave us in peace. The world is wide enough to keep us apart.

EVE. Why do you want to drive him away? He is mine. I made him out of my own body. I want to see my work sometimes.

ADAM. You made Abel also. He killed Abel. Can you bear
to look at him after that?

CAIN. Whose fault was it that I killed Abel? Who invented
killing? Did *I*? No: he invented it himself. I followed your
teaching. I dug and dug and dug. I cleared away the
thistles and briars. I ate the fruits of the earth. I lived in
the sweat of my brow, as you do. I was a fool. But Abel
was a discoverer, a man of ideas, of spirit: a true Progressive. He was the discoverer of blood. He was the inventor of killing. He found out that the fire of the sun
could be brought down by a dewdrop. He invented the
altar to keep the fire alive. He changed the beasts he
killed into meat by the fire on the altar. He kept himself
alive by eating meat. His meal cost him a day's glorious
health-giving sport and an hour's amusing play with the
fire. You learnt nothing from him: you drudged and
drudged and drudged, and dug and dug and dug, and
made me do the same. I envied his happiness, his freedom.
I despised myself for not doing as he did instead of what
you did. He became so happy that he shared his meal with
the Voice that had whispered all his inventions to him.
He said that the Voice was the voice of the fire that
cooked his food, and that the fire that could cook could
also eat. It was true: I saw the fire consume the food on his
altar. Then I, too, made an altar, and offered my food on
it, my grains, my roots, my fruit. Useless: nothing happened. He laughed at me; and then came my great idea:
why not kill him as he killed the beasts? I struck; and he
died, just as they did. Then I gave up your old silly
drudging ways, and lived as he had lived, by the chase,
by the killing, and by the fire. Am I not better than you?
stronger, happier, freer?

ADAM. You are not stronger: you are shorter in the wind:
you cannot endure. You have made the beasts afraid of
us; and the snake has invented poison to protect herself
against you. I fear you myself. If you take a step towards
your mother with that spear of yours I will strike you with
my spade as you struck Abel.

EVE. He will not strike me. He loves me.

ADAM. He loved his brother. But he killed him.

CAIN. I do not want to kill women. I do not want to kill my mother. And for her sake I will not kill you, though I could send this spear through you without coming within reach of your spade. But for her, I could not resist the sport of trying to kill you, in spite of my fear that you would kill me. I have striven with a boar and with a lion as to which of us should kill the other. I have striven with a man: spear to spear and shield to shield. It is terrible; but there is no joy like it. I call it fighting. He who has never fought has never lived. That is what has brought me to my mother today.

ADAM. What have you to do with one another now? She is the creator, you the destroyer.

CAIN. How can I destroy unless she creates? I want her to create more and more men: aye, and more and more women, that they may in turn create more men. I have imagined a glorious poem of many men, of more men than there are leaves on a thousand trees. I will divide them into two great hosts. One of them I will lead; and the other will be led by the man I fear most and desire to fight and kill most. And each host shall try to kill the other host. Think of that! all those multitudes of men fighting, fighting, killing, killing! The four rivers running with blood! The shouts of triumph! the howls of rage! the curses of despair! the shrieks of torment! That will be life indeed: life lived to the very marrow: burning, overwhelming life. Every man who has not seen it, heard it, felt it, risked it, will feel a humbled fool in the presence of the man who has.

EVE. And I! I am to be a mere convenience to make men for you to kill!

ADAM. Or to kill you, you fool.

CAIN. Mother: the making of men is your right, your risk, your agony, your glory, your triumph. You make my father here your mere convenience, as you call it, for that. He has to dig for you, sweat for you, plod for you, like the ox who helps him to tear up the ground or the ass who carries his burdens for him. No woman shall make me live my father's life. I will hunt: I will fight and strive to the very bursting of my sinews. When I have slain the boar at the risk of my life, I will throw it to my woman to cook, and give her a morsel of it for her pains. She shall have no other food; and that will make her my slave. And the man that slays me shall have her for his booty. Man shall be the master of Woman, not her baby and her drudge.

Adam throws down his spade, and stands looking darkly at Eve.

EVE. Are you tempted, Adam? Does this seem a better thing to you than love between us?

CAIN. What does he know of love? Only when he has fought, when he has faced terror and death, when he has striven to the spending of the last rally of his strength, can he know what it is to rest in love in the arms of a woman. Ask that woman whom you made, who is also my wife, whether she would have me as I was in the days when I followed the ways of Adam, and was a digger and a drudge?

EVE [*angrily throwing down her distaff*] What! You dare come here boasting about that good-for-nothing Lua, the worst of daughters and the worst of wives! You her master! You are more her slave than Adam's ox or your own sheepdog. Forsooth, when you have slain the boar at the risk of your life, you will throw her a morsel of it for her pains! Ha! Poor wretch: do you think I do not know her, and know you, better than that? Do you risk your life when you trap the ermine and the sable and the blue fox to hang on her lazy shoulders and make her look more like an animal than a woman? When you have to snare the little tender birds because it is too much trouble for her to chew honest food, how much of a great warrior do you feel then? You slay the tiger at the risk of your life; but who gets the striped skin you have run that risk for? She takes it to lie on, and flings you the carrion flesh you cannot eat. You fight because you think that your fighting makes her admire and desire you. Fool: she makes you fight because you bring her the ornaments and the treasures of those you have slain, and because she is courted and propitiated with power and gold by the people who fear you. You say that *I* make a mere convenience of Adam: I who spin and keep the house, and bear and rear children, and am a woman and not a pet animal to please men and prey on them! What are you, you poor slave of a painted face and a bundle of skunk's fur? You were a man-child when I bore you. Lua was a woman-child when I bore her. What have you made of yourselves?

CAIN [*letting his spear fall into the crook of his shield arm, and twirling his moustache*] There is something higher than man. There is hero and superman.

EVE. Superman! You are no superman: you are Anti-Man: you are to other men what the stoat is to the rabbit; and she is to you what the leech is to the stoat. You despise your father; but when he dies the world will be the richer because he lived. When you die, men will say, 'He was a great warrior; but it would have been better for the world if he had never been born.' And of Lua they will say nothing; but when they think of her they will spit.

CAIN. She is a better sort of woman to live with than you. If Lua nagged at me as you are nagging, and as you nag at Adam, I would beat her black and blue from head to foot. I have done it too, slave as you say I am.

EVE. Yes, because she looked at another man. And then you grovelled at her feet, and cried, and begged her to forgive you, and were ten times more her slave than ever; and she, when she had finished screaming and the pain went off a little, she forgave you, did she not?

CAIN. She loved me more than ever. That is the true nature of woman.

EVE [*now pitying him maternally*] Love! You call that love! You call that the nature of woman! My boy: this is neither man nor woman nor love nor life. You have no real strength in your bones nor sap in your flesh.

CAIN. Ha! [*he seizes his spear and swings it muscularly*].

EVE. Yes: you have to twirl a stick to feel your strength: you cannot taste life without making it bitter and boiling hot: you cannot love Lua until her face is painted, nor feel the natural warmth of her flesh until you have stuck a squirrel's fur on it. You can feel nothing but a torment, and believe nothing but a lie. You will not raise your head to look at all the miracles of life that surround you; but you will run ten miles to see a fight or a death.

ADAM. Enough said. Let the boy alone.

CAIN. Boy! Ha! ha!

EVE [*to Adam*] You think, perhaps, that his way of life may be better than yours after all. You are still tempted. Well, will you pamper me as he pampers his woman? Will you kill tigers and bears until I have a heap of their skins to lounge on? Shall I paint my face and let my arms waste into pretty softness, and eat partridges and doves, and the flesh of kids whose milk you will steal for me?

ADAM. You are hard enough to bear with as you are. Stay as you are; and I will stay as I am.

CAIN. You neither of you know anything about life. You are simple country folk. You are the nurses and valets of the oxen and dogs and asses you have tamed to work for you. I can raise you out of that. I have a plan. Why not tame men and women to work for us? Why not bring them up from childhood never to know any other lot, so that they may believe that we are gods, and that they are here only to make life glorious for us?

ADAM [*impressed*] That is a great thought, certainly.

EVE [*contemptuously*] Great thought!

ADAM. Well, as the serpent used to say, why not?

EVE. Because I would not have such wretches in my house. Because I hate creatures with two heads, or with withered limbs, or that are distorted and perverted and unnatural. I have told Cain already that he is not a man and that Lua is not a woman: they are monsters. And now you want to make still more unnatural monsters, so that you may be utterly lazy and worthless, and that your tamed human animals may find work a blasting curse. A fine dream, truly! [*To Cain*] Your father is a fool skin deep; but you are a fool to your very marrow; and your baggage of a wife is worse.

ADAM. Why am I a fool? How am I a greater fool than you?

EVE. You said there would be no killing because the Voice would tell our children that they must not kill. Why did it not tell Cain that?

CAIN. It did; but I am not a child to be afraid of a Voice. The Voice thought I was nothing but my brother's keeper. It found that I was myself, and that it was for Abel to be himself also, and look to himself. He was not my keeper any more than I was his: why did he not kill me? There was no more to prevent him than there was to prevent me: it was man to man; and I won. I was the first conqueror.

ADAM. What did the Voice say to you when you thought all that?

CAIN. Why, it gave me right. It said that my deed was as a mark on me, a burnt-in mark such as Abel put on his sheep, that no man should slay me. And here I stand unslain, whilst the cowards who have never slain, the men who are content to be their brothers' keepers instead of their masters, are despised and rejected, and slain like rabbits. He who bears the brand of Cain shall rule the earth. When he falls, he shall be avenged sevenfold: the Voice has said it; so beware how you plot against me, you and all the rest.

ADAM. Cease your boasting and bullying, and tell the truth. Does not the Voice tell you that as no man dare slay you for murdering your brother, you ought to slay yourself?

CAIN. No.

ADAM. Then there is no such thing as divine justice, unless you are lying.

CAIN. I am not lying: I dare all truths. There is divine justice. For the Voice tells me that I must offer myself to every man to be killed if he can kill me. Without danger I cannot be great. That is how I pay for Abel's blood. Danger and fear follow my steps everywhere. Without them courage would have no sense. And it is courage, courage, courage, that raises the blood of life to crimson splendor.

ADAM [*picking up his spade and preparing to dig again*] Take yourself off then. This splendid life of yours does not last for a thousand years; and I must last for a thousand years. When you fighters do not get killed in fighting one another or fighting the beasts, you die from mere evil in yourselves. Your flesh ceases to grow like man's flesh: it grows like a fungus on a tree. Instead of breathing you sneeze, or cough up your insides, and wither and perish. Your bowels become rotten; your hair falls from you; your teeth blacken and drop out; and you die before your time, not because you will, but because you must. I will dig, and live.

CAIN. And pray, what use is this thousand years of life to you, you old vegetable? Do you dig any better because you have been digging for hundreds of years? I have not lived as long as you; but I know all there is to be known of the craft of digging. By quitting it I have set myself free to learn nobler crafts of which you know nothing. I know the craft of fighting and of hunting: in a word, the craft of killing. What certainty have you of your thousand years? I could kill both of you; and you could no more defend yourselves than a couple of sheep. I spare you; but others may kill you. Why not live bravely, and die early and make room for others? Why, I – I! that know many more crafts than either of you, am tired of myself when I am not fighting or hunting. Sooner than face a thousand years of it I should kill myself, as the Voice sometimes tempts me to do already.

ADAM. Liar: you denied just now that it called on you to pay for Abel's life with your own.

CAIN. The Voice does not speak to me as it does to you. I am a man: you are only a grown-up child. One does not speak to a child as to a man. And a man does not listen and tremble in silence. He replies: he makes the Voice respect him: in the end he dictates what the Voice shall say.

ADAM. May your tongue be accurst for such blasphemy!

EVE. Keep a guard on your own tongue; and do not curse my son. It was Lilith who did wrong when she shared the labor of creation so unequally between man and wife. If you, Cain, had had the trouble of making Abel, or had had to make another man to replace him when he was gone, you would not have killed him: you would have risked your own life to save his. That is why all this empty talk of yours, which tempted Adam just now when he threw down his spade and listened to you for a while, went by me like foul wind that has passed over a dead body. That is why there is enmity between Woman the creator and Man the destroyer. I know you: I am your mother. You are idle: you are selfish. It is long and hard and painful to create life: it is short and easy to steal the life others have made. When you dug, you made the earth live and bring forth as I live and bring forth. It was for that that Lilith set you free from the travail of women, not for theft and murder.

CAIN. The Devil thank her for it! I can make better use of my time than to play the husband to the clay beneath my feet.

ADAM. Devil? What new word is that?

CAIN. Hearken to me, old fool. I have never in my soul listened willingly when you have told me of the Voice that whispers to you. There must be two Voices: one that gulls and despises you, and another that trusts and respects me. I call yours the Devil. Mine I call the Voice of God.

ADAM. Mine is the Voice of Life: yours the Voice of Death.

CAIN. Be it so. For it whispers to me that death is not really death: that it is the gate of another life: a life infinitely splendid and intense: a life of the soul alone: a life without clods or spades, hunger or fatigue —

EVE. Selfish and idle, Cain. I know.

CAIN. Selfish, yes: a life in which no man is his brother's keeper, because his brother can keep himself. But am I idle? In rejecting your drudgery, have I not embraced evils and agonies of which you know nothing? The arrow is lighter in the hand than the spade; but the energy that drives it through the breast of a fighter is as fire to water compared with the strength that drives the spade into the harmless dirty clay. My strength is as the strength of ten because my heart is pure.

ADAM. What is that word? What is pure?

CAIN. Turned from the clay. Turned upward to the sun, to the clear clean heavens.

ADAM. The heavens are empty, child. The earth is fruitful. The earth feeds us. It gives us the strength by which we made you and all mankind. Cut off from the clay which you despise, you would perish miserably.

CAIN. I revolt against the clay. I revolt against the food. You say it gives us strength: does it not also turn into filth and smite us with diseases? I revolt against these births that you and mother are so proud of. They drag us down to the level of the beasts. If that is to be the last thing as it has been the first, let mankind perish. If I am to eat like a bear, if Lua is to bring forth cubs like a bear, then I had rather be a bear than a man; for the bear is not ashamed: he knows no better. If you are content, like the bear, I am not. Stay with the woman who gives you children: I will go to the woman who gives me dreams. Grope in the ground for your food: I will bring it from the skies with my arrows, or strike it down as it roams the earth in the pride of its life. If I must have food or die, I will at least have it at as far a remove from the earth as I can. The ox shall make it something nobler than grass before it comes to me. And as the man is nobler than the ox, I shall some day let my enemy eat the ox; and then I will slay and eat him.

ADAM. Monster! You hear this, Eve?

EVE. So that is what comes of turning your face to the clean clear heavens! Man-eating! Child-eating! For that is what it would come to, just as it came to lambs and kids when Abel began with sheep and goats. You are a poor silly creature after all. Do you think I never have these thoughts: I! who have the labor of the child-bearing: I! who have the drudgery of preparing the food? I thought for a moment that perhaps this strong brave son of mine, who could imagine something better, and could desire what he imagined, might also be able to will what he desired until he created it. And all that comes of it is that he wants to be a bear and eat children. Even a bear would not eat a man if it could get honey instead.

CAIN. I do not want to be a bear. I do not want to eat children. I do not know what I want, except that I want to be something higher and nobler than this stupid old digger whom Lilith made to help you to bring me into the world, and whom you despise now that he has served your turn.

ADAM [*in sullen rage*] I have half a mind to shew you that my spade can split your undutiful head open, in spite of your spear.

CAIN. Undutiful! Ha! ha! [*Flourishing his spear*] Try it, old everybody's father. Try a taste of fighting.

EVE. Peace, peace, you two fools. Sit down and be quiet; and listen to me. [*Adam, with a weary shrug, throws down his spade. Cain, with a laughing one, throws down his shield and spear. Both sit on the ground*]. I hardly know which of you satisfies me least, you with your dirty digging, or he with his dirty killing. I cannot think it was for either of these cheap ways of life that Lilith set you free. [*To Adam*] You dig roots and coax grains out of the earth: why do you not draw down a divine sustenance from the skies? He steals and kills for his food; and makes up idle poems of life after death; and dresses up his terror-ridden life with fine words and his disease-ridden body with fine clothes, so that men may glorify and honor him instead of cursing him as murderer and thief. All you men, except only Adam, are my sons, or my sons' sons, or my sons' sons' sons: you all come to see me: you all shew off before me: all your little wisdoms and accomplishments are trotted out before mother Eve. The diggers come: the fighters and killers come: they are both very dull; for they either complain to me of the last harvest, or boast to me of the last fight; and one harvest is just like another, and the last fight only a repetition of the first. Oh, I have heard it all a thousand times. They tell me too of their last-born: the clever thing the darling child said yesterday, and how much more wonderful or witty or quaint it is than any child that ever was born before. And I have to pretend to be surprised, delighted, interested; though the last child is like the first, and has said and done nothing that did not delight Adam and me when you and Abel said it. For you were the first children in the world, and filled us with such wonder and delight as no couple can ever again feel while the world lasts. When I can bear no more, I go to our old garden, that is now a mass of nettles and thistles, in the hope of finding the serpent to talk to. But you have made the serpent our enemy: she has left the garden, or is dead: I never see her now. So I have to come back and listen to Adam saying the same thing for the ten-thousandth time, or to receive a visit from the last great-great-grandson who has grown up and wants to impress me with his importance. Oh, it is dreary, dreary! And there is yet nearly seven hundred years of it to endure.

CAIN. Poor mother! You see, life is too long. One tires of everything. There is nothing new under the sun.

ADAM [*to Eve, grumpily*] Why do you live on, if you can find nothing better to do than complain?

EVE. Because there is still hope.

CAIN. Of what?

EVE. Of the coming true of your dreams and mine. Of newly created things. Of better things. My sons and my sons' sons are not all diggers and fighters. Some of them will neither dig nor fight: they are more useless than either of you: they are weaklings and cowards: they are vain; yet they are dirty and will not take the trouble to cut their hair. They borrow and never pay; but one gives them what they want, because they tell beautiful lies in beautiful words. They can remember their dreams. They can dream without sleeping. They have not will enough to create instead of dreaming; but the serpent said that every dream could be willed into creation by those strong enough to believe in it. There are others who cut reeds of different lengths and blow through them, making lovely patterns of sound in the air; and some of them can weave the patterns together, sounding three reeds at the same time, and raising my soul to things for which I have no words. And others make little mammoths out of clay, or make faces appear on flat stones, and ask me to create women for them with such faces. I have watched those faces and willed; and then I have made a woman-child that has grown up quite like them. And others think of numbers without having to count on their fingers, and watch the sky at night, and give names to the stars, and can foretell when the sun will be covered with a black saucepan lid. And there is Tubal, who made this wheel for me which has saved me so much labor. And there is Enoch, who walks on the hills, and hears the Voice continually, and has given up his will to do the will of the Voice, and has some of the Voice's greatness. When they come, there is always some new wonder, or some new hope: something to live for. They never want to die, because they are always learning and always creating either things or wisdom, or at least dreaming of them. And then you, Cain, come to me with your stupid fighting and destroying, and your foolish boasting; and you want me to tell you that it is all splendid, and that you are heroic, and that nothing but death or the dread of death makes life worth living. Away with you, naughty child; and do you, Adam, go on with your work and not waste your time listening to him.

CAIN. I am not, perhaps, very clever; but –

EVE [*interrupting him*] Perhaps not; but do not begin to boast of that. It is no credit to you.

CAIN. For all that, mother, I have an instinct which tells me that death plays its part in life. Tell me this: who invented death?

Adam springs to his feet. Eve drops her distaff. Both shew the greatest consternation.

CAIN. What is the matter with you both?

ADAM. Boy: you have asked us a terrible question.

EVE. You invented murder. Let that be enough for you.

CAIN. Murder is not death. You know what I mean. Those

whom I slay would die if I spared them. If I am not slain, yet I shall die. Who put this upon me? I say, who invented death?

ADAM. Be reasonable, boy. Could you bear to live for ever? You think you could, because you know that you will never have to make your thought good. But I have known what it is to sit and brood under the terror of eternity, of immortality. Think of it, man: to have no escape! to be Adam, Adam, Adam through more days than there are grains of sand by the two rivers, and then be as far from the end as ever! I, who have so much in me that I hate and long to cast off! Be thankful to your parents, who enabled you to hand on your burden to new and better men, and won for you an eternal rest; for it was we who invented death.

CAIN [rising] You did well: I, too, do not want to live for ever. But if you invented death, why do you blame me, who am a minister of death?

ADAM. I do not blame you. Go in peace. Leave me to my digging, and your mother to her spinning.

CAIN. Well, I will leave you to it, though I have shewn you a better way. [He picks up his shield and spear]. I will go back to my brave warrior friends and their splendid women. [He strides to the thorn brake]. When Adam delved and Eve span, where was then the gentleman? [He goes away roaring with laughter, which ceases as he cries from the distance] Goodbye, mother.

ADAM [grumbling] He might have put the hurdle back, lazy hound! [He replaces the hurdle across the passage].

EVE. Through him and his like, death is gaining on life. Already most of our grandchildren die before they have sense enough to know how to live.

ADAM. No matter. [He spits on his hands, and takes up the spade again]. Life is still long enough to learn to dig, short as they are making it.

EVE [musing] Yes, to dig. And to fight. But is it long enough for the other things, the great things? Will they live long enough to eat manna?

ADAM. What is manna?

EVE. Food drawn down from heaven, made out of the air, not dug dirtily from the earth. Will they learn all the ways of all the stars in their little time? It took Enoch two hundred years to learn to interpret the will of the Voice. When he was a mere child of eighty, his babyish attempts to understand the Voice were more dangerous than the wrath of Cain. If they shorten their lives, they will dig and fight and kill and die; and their baby Enochs will tell them that it is the will of the Voice that they should dig and fight and kill and die for ever.

ADAM. If they are lazy and have a will towards death I cannot help it. I will live my thousand years: if they will not, let them die and be damned.

EVE. Damned? What is that?

ADAM. The state of them that love death more than life. Go on with your spinning; and do not sit there idle while I am straining my muscles for you.

EVE [*slowly taking up her distaff*] If you were not a fool you would find something better for both of us to live by than this spinning and digging.

ADAM. Go on with your work, I tell you; or you shall go without bread.

EVE. Man need not always live by bread alone. There is something else. We do not yet know what it is; but some day we shall find out; and then we will live on that alone; and there shall be no more digging nor spinning, nor fighting nor killing.

She spins resignedly; he digs impatiently.

PART II

The Gospel of the Brothers Barnabas

In the first years after the war an impressive-looking gentleman of 50 is seated writing in a well-furnished spacious study. He is dressed in black. His coat is a frock-coat; his tie is white; and his waistcoat, though it is not quite a clergyman's waistcoat, and his collar, though it buttons in front instead of behind, combine with the prosperity indicated by his surroundings, and his air of personal distinction, to suggest the clerical dignitary. Still, he is clearly neither dean nor bishop; he is rather too starkly intellectual for a popular Free Church enthusiast; and he is not careworn enough to be a great headmaster.

The study windows, which have broad comfortable window seats, overlook Hampstead Heath towards London. Consequently, it being a fine afternoon in spring, the room is sunny. As you face these windows, you have on your right the fireplace, with a few logs smouldering in it, and a couple of comfortable library chairs on the hearthrug; beyond it and beside it the door; before you the writing-table, at which the clerical gentleman sits a little to your left facing the door with his right profile presented to you; on your left a settee; and on your right a couple of Chippendale chairs. There is also an upholstered square stool in the middle of the room, against the writing-table. The walls are covered with bookshelves above and lockers beneath.

The door opens; and another gentleman, shorter than the clerical one, within a year or two of the same age, dressed in a well-worn tweed lounge suit, with a short beard and much less style in his bearing and carriage, looks in.

THE CLERICAL GENTLEMAN [*familiar and by no means cordial*] Hallo! I didnt expect you until the five o'clock train.

THE TWEEDED GENTLEMAN [*coming in very slowly*] I have something on my mind. I thought I'd come early.

THE CLERICAL GENTLEMAN [*throwing down his pen*] What is on your mind?

THE TWEEDED GENTLEMAN [*sitting down on the stool, heavily preoccupied with his thought*] I have made up my mind at last about the time. I make it three hundred years.

THE CLERICAL GENTLEMAN [*sitting up energetically*] Now that is extraordinary. Most extraordinary. The very last words I wrote when you interrupted me were 'at least three centuries.' [*He snatches up his manuscript, and points to it*]. Here it is: [*reading*] 'the term of human life must be extended to at least three centuries.'

THE TWEEDED GENTLEMAN. How did you arrive at it?

A parlor maid opens the door, ushering in a young clergyman.

THE PARLOR MAID. Mr Haslam. [*She withdraws*].

The visitor is so very unwelcome that his host forgets to rise; and the two brothers stare at the intruder, quite unable to conceal their dismay. Haslam, who has nothing clerical about him except his collar, and wears a snuff-colored suit, smiles with a frank school-boyishness that makes it impossible to be unkind to him, and explodes into obviously unpremeditated speech.

HASLAM. I'm afraid I'm an awful nuisance. I'm the rector; and I suppose one ought to call on people.

THE TWEEDED GENTLEMAN [*in ghostly tones*] We're not Church people, you know.

HASLAM. Oh, I dont mind that, if you dont. The Church people here are mostly as dull as ditch-water. I have heard such a lot about you; and there are so jolly few people to talk to. I thought you perhaps wouldnt mind. *Do* you mind? for of course I'll go like a shot if I'm in the way.

THE CLERICAL GENTLEMAN [*rising, disarmed*] Sit down, Mr–er?

HASLAM. Haslam.

THE CLERICAL GENTLEMAN. Mr Haslam.

THE TWEEDED GENTLEMAN [*rising and offering him the stool*] Sit down. [*He retreats towards the Chippendale chairs*].

HASLAM [*sitting down on the stool*] Thanks awfully.

THE CLERICAL GENTLEMAN [*resuming his seat*] This is my brother Conrad, Professor of Biology at Jarrowfields University: Dr Conrad Barnabas. My name is Franklyn:

Franklyn Barnabas. I was in the Church myself for some years.

HASLAM [*sympathizing*] Yes: one cant help it. If theres a living in the family, or one's Governor knows a patron, one gets shoved into the Church by one's parents.

CONRAD [*sitting down on the furthest Chippendale with a snort of amusement*] Mp!

FRANKLYN. One gets shoved out of it, sometimes, by one's conscience.

HASLAM. Oh yes; but where is a chap like me to go? I'm afraid I'm not intellectual enough to split straws when theres a job in front of me, and nothing better for me to do. I daresay the Church was a bit thick for you; but it's good enough for me. It will last my time, anyhow [*he laughs good-humoredly*].

FRANKLYN [*with renewed energy*] There again! You see, Con. It will last his time. Life is too short for men to take it seriously.

HASLAM. Thats a way of looking at it, certainly.

FRANKLYN. I was not shoved into the Church, Mr Haslam: I felt it to be my vocation to walk with God, like Enoch. After twenty years of it I realized that I was walking with my own ignorance and self-conceit, and that I was not within a hundred and fifty years of the experience and wisdom I was pretending to.

HASLAM. Now I come to think of it, old Methuselah must have had to think twice before he took on anything for life. If I thought I was going to live nine hundred and sixty years, I dont think I should stay in the Church.

FRANKLYN. If men lived even a third of that time, the Church would be very different from the thing it is.

CONRAD. If I could count on nine hundred and sixty years I could make myself a real biologist, instead of what I am now: a child trying to walk. Are you sure you might not become a good clergyman if you had a few centuries to do it in?

HASLAM. Oh, theres nothing much the matter with me; it's

quite easy to be a decent parson. It's the Church that chokes me off. I couldnt stick it for nine hundred years. I should chuck it. You know, sometimes, when the bishop, who is the most priceless of fossils, lets off something more than usually out-of-date, the bird starts in my garden.

FRANKLYN. The bird?

HASLAM. Oh yes. Theres a bird there that keeps on singing 'Stick it or chuck it: stick it or chuck it' – just like that – for an hour on end in the spring. I wish my father had found some other shop for me.

The parlor maid comes back.

THE PARLOR MAID. Any letters for the post, sir?

FRANKLYN. These [*He proffers a basket of letters. She comes to the table and takes them*].

HASLAM [*to the maid*] Have you told Mr Barnabas yet?

THE PARLOR MAID [*flinching a little*] No, sir.

FRANKLYN. Told me what?

HASLAM. She is going to leave you?

FRANKLYN. Indeed? I'm sorry. Is it our fault, Mr Haslam?

HASLAM. Not a bit. She is jolly well off here.

THE PARLOR MAID [*reddening*] I have never denied it, sir: I couldnt ask for a better place. But I have only one life to live; and I maynt get a second chance. Excuse me, sir; but the letters must go to catch the post. [*She goes out with the letters*].

The two brothers look inquiringly at Haslam.

HASLAM. Silly girl! Going to marry a village woodman and live in a hovel with him and a lot of kids tumbling over one another, just because the fellow has poetic-looking eyes and a moustache.

CONRAD [*demurring*] She said it was because she had only one life.

HASLAM. Same thing, poor girl! The fellow persuaded her to chuck it; and when she marries him she'll have to stick it. Rotten state of things, I call it.

CONRAD. You see, she hasnt time to find out what life really means. She has to die before she knows.

HASLAM [*agreeably*] Thats it.

FRANKLYN. She hasnt time to form a well-instructed conscience.

HASLAM [*still more cheerfully*] Quite.

FRANKLYN. It goes deeper. She hasnt time to form a genuine conscience at all. Some romantic points of honor and a few conventions. A world without conscience: that is the horror of our condition.

HASLAM [*beaming*] Simply fatuous. [*Rising*] Well, I suppose I'd better be going. It's most awfully good of you to put up with my calling.

CONRAD [*in his former low ghostly tone*] You neednt go, you know, if you are really interested.

HASLAM [*fed up*] Well, I'm afraid I ought to – I really must get back – I have something to do in the –

FRANKLYN [*smiling benignly and rising to proffer his hand*] Goodbye.

CONRAD [*gruffly, giving him up as a bad job*] Goodbye.

HASLAM. Goodbye. Sorry – er –

  As the rector moves to shake hands with Franklyn, feeling that he is making a frightful mess of his departure, a vigorous sunburnt young lady with hazel hair cut to the level of her neck, like an Italian youth in a Gozzoli picture, comes in impetuously. She seems to have nothing on but her short skirt, her blouse, her stockings and a pair of Norwegian shoes: in short, she is a Simple-Lifer.

THE SIMPLE-LIFER [*swooping on Conrad and kissing him*] Hallo, Nunk. Youre before your time.

CONRAD. Behave yourself. Theres a visitor.

  She turns quickly and sees the rector. She instinctively switches at her Gozzoli fringe with her fingers, but gives it up as hopeless.

FRANKLYN. Mr Haslam, our new rector. [*To Haslam*] My daughter Cynthia.

CONRAD. Usually called Savvy, short for Savage.

SAVVY. I usually call Mr Haslam Bill, short for William. [*She strolls to the hearthrug, and surveys them calmly from the commanding position*].

FRANKLYN. You know him?

SAVVY. Rather. Sit down, Bill.

FRANKLYN. Mr Haslam is going, Savvy. He has an engagement.

SAVVY. I know. I'm the engagement.

CONRAD. In that case, would you mind taking him into the garden while I talk to your father?

SAVVY [to Haslam] Tennis?

HASLAM. Rather!

SAVVY. Come on. [She dances out. He runs boyishly after her].

FRANKLYN [leaving his table and beginning to walk up and down the room discontentedly] Savvy's manners jar on me. They would have horrified her grandmother.

CONRAD [obstinately] They are happier manners than Mother's manners.

FRANKLYN. Yes: they are franker, wholesomer, better in a hundred ways. And yet I squirm at them. I cannot get it out of my head that Mother was a well-mannered woman, and that Savvy has no manners at all.

CONRAD. There wasnt any pleasure in Mother's fine manners. That makes a biological difference.

FRANKLYN. But there was beauty in Mother's manners, grace in them, style in them: above all, decision in them. Savvy is such a cub.

CONRAD. So she ought to be, at her age.

FRANKLYN. There it comes again! Her age! her age!

CONRAD. You want her to be fully grown at eighteen. You want to force her into a stuck-up, artificial, premature self-possession before she has any self to possess. You just let her alone: she is right enough for her years.

FRANKLYN. I have let her alone; and look at the result! Like all the other young people who have been let alone, she becomes a Socialist. That is, she becomes hopelessly demoralized.

CONRAD. Well, arnt you a Socialist?

FRANKLYN. Yes; but that is not the same thing. You and I were brought up in the old bourgeois morality. We were taught bourgeois manners and bourgeois points of honor. Bourgeois manners may be snobbish manners: there may be no pleasure in them, as you say; but they are better than no manners. Many bourgeois points of honor may be false; but at least they exist. The women know what to expect and what is expected of them. Savvy doesnt. She is a Bolshevist and nothing else. She has to improvise her manners and her conduct as she goes along. It's often charming, no doubt; but sometimes she puts her foot in it frightfully; and then I feel that she is blaming me for not teaching her better.

CONRAD. Well, you have something better to teach her now, at all events.

FRANKLYN. Yes: but it is too late. She doesnt trust me now. She doesnt talk about such things to me. She doesnt read anything I write. She never comes to hear me lecture. I am out of it as far as Savvy is concerned. [*He resumes his seat at the writing-table*].

CONRAD. I must have a talk to her.

FRANKLYN. Perhaps she will listen to you. You are not her father.

CONRAD. I sent her my last book. I can break the ice by asking her what she made of it.

FRANKLYN. When she heard you were coming, she asked me whether all the leaves were cut, in case it fell into your hands. She hasnt read a word of it.

CONRAD [*rising indignantly*] What!

FRANKLYN [*inexorably*] Not a word of it.

CONRAD [*beaten*] Well, I suppose it's only natural. Biology is a dry subject for a girl; and I am a pretty dry old codger. [*He sits down again resignedly*].

FRANKLYN. Brother: if that is so; if biology as you have worked at it, and religion as I have worked at it, are dry subjects like the old stuff they taught under these names, and we two are dry old codgers, like the old preachers and professors, then the Gospel of the Brothers Barnabas is a delusion. Unless this withered thing religion, and this dry thing science, have come alive in our hands, alive and intensely interesting, we may just as well go out and dig the garden until it is time to dig our graves. [*The parlor maid returns. Franklyn is impatient at the interruption*]. Well? what is it now?

THE PARLOR MAID. Mr Joyce Burge on the telephone, sir. He wants to speak to you.

FRANKLYN [*astonished*] Mr Joyce Burge!

THE PARLOR MAID. Yes, sir.

FRANKLYN [*to Conrad*] What on earth does this mean? I havnt heard from him nor exchanged a word with him for years. I resigned the chairmanship of the Liberal Association and shook the dust of party politics from my feet before he was Prime Minister in the Coalition. Of course, he dropped me like a hot potato.

CONRAD. Well, now that the Coalition has chucked him out, and he is only one of the half-dozen leaders of the Opposition, perhaps he wants to pick you up again.

THE PARLOR MAID [*warningly*] He is holding the line, sir.

FRANKLYN. Yes: all right [*he hurries out*].

The parlor maid goes to the hearthrug to make up the fire. Conrad rises and strolls to the middle of the room, where he stops and looks quizzically down at her.

CONRAD. So you have only one life to live, eh?

THE PARLOR MAID [*dropping on her knees in consternation*] I meant no offence, sir.

CONRAD. You didnt give any. But you know you could live a devil of a long life if you really wanted to.

THE PARLOR MAID [*sitting down on her heels*] Oh, dont say that, sir. It's so unsettling.

CONRAD. Why? Have you been thinking about it?

THE PARLOR MAID. It would never have come into my head if you hadnt put it there, sir. Me and cook had a look at your book.

CONRAD. What!

> You and cook
> Had a look
> At my book!

And my niece wouldnt open it! The prophet is without honor in his own family. Well, what do you think of living for several hundred years? Are you going to have a try for it?

THE PARLOR MAID. Well, of course youre not in earnest, sir. But it does set one thinking, especially when one is going to be married.

CONRAD. What has that to do with it? He may live as long as you, you know.

THE PARLOR MAID. Thats just it, sir. You see, he must take me for better for worse, til death do us part. Do you think he would be so ready to do that, sir, if he thought it might be for several hundred years?

CONRAD. Thats true. And what about yourself?

THE PARLOR MAID. Oh, I tell you straight out, sir, I'd never promise to live with the same man as long as that. I wouldnt put up with my own children as long as that. Why, cook figured it out, sir, that when you were only 200, you might marry your own great-great-great-great-great-great-grandson and not even know who he was.

CONRAD. Well, why not? For all you know, the man you are going to marry may be your great-great-great-great-great-great-grandmother's great-great-great-great-great-great-grandson.

THE PARLOR MAID. But do you think it would ever be thought respectable, sir?

CONRAD. My good girl, all biological necessities have to be made respectable whether we like it or not; so you neednt worry yourself about that.

Franklyn returns and crosses the room to his chair, but does not sit down. The parlor maid goes out.

CONRAD. Well, what does Joyce Burge want?

FRANKLYN. Oh, a silly misunderstanding. I have promised to address a meeting in Middlesborough; and some fool has put it into the papers that I am 'coming to Middlesborough,' without any explanation. Of course, now that we are on the eve of a general election, political people think I am coming there to contest the parliamentary seat. Burge knows that I have a following, and thinks I could get into the House of Commons and head a group there. So he insists on coming to see me. He is staying with some people at Dollis Hill, and can be here in five or ten minutes, he says.

CONRAD. But didnt you tell him that it's a false alarm?

FRANKLYN. Of course I did; but he wont believe me.

CONRAD. Called you a liar, in fact?

FRANKLYN. No: I wish he had: any sort of plain speaking is better than the nauseous sham good fellowship our democratic public men get up for shop use. He pretends to believe me, and assures me his visit is quite disinterested; but why should he come if he has no axe to grind? These chaps never believe anything they say themselves; and naturally they cannot believe anything anyone else says.

CONRAD [*rising*] Well, I shall clear out. It was hard enough to stand the party politicians before the war; but now that they have managed to half kill Europe between them, I cant be civil to them, and I dont see why I should be.

FRANKLYN. Wait a bit. We have to find out how the world will take our new gospel. [*Conrad sits down again*]. Party politicians are still unfortunately an important part of the world. Suppose we try it on Joyce Burge.

CONRAD. How can you? You can tell things only to people who can listen. Joyce Burge has talked so much that he has lost the power of listening. He doesnt listen even in the House of Commons.

Savvy rushes in breathless, followed by Haslam, who remains timidly just inside the door.

SAVVY [*running to Franklyn*] I say! Who do you think has just driven up in a big car?

FRANKLYN. Mr Joyce Burge, perhaps.

SAVVY [*disappointed*] Oh, they know, Bill. Why didnt you tell us he was coming? I have nothing on.

HASLAM. I'd better go, hadnt I?

CONRAD. You just wait here, both of you. When you start yawning, Joyce Burge will take the hint, perhaps.

SAVVY [*to Franklyn*] May we?

FRANKLYN. Yes, if you promise to behave yourself.

SAVVY [*making a wry face*] That will be a treat, wont it?

THE PARLOR MAID [*entering and announcing*] Mr Joyce Burge.

 Haslam hastily moves to the fireplace; and the parlor maid goes out and shuts the door when the visitor has passed in.

FRANKLYN [*hurrying past Savvy to his guest with the false cordiality he has just been denouncing*] Oh! Here you are. Delighted to see you. [*He shakes Burge's hand, and introduces Savvy*] My daughter.

SAVVY [*not daring to approach*] Very kind of you to come.

 Joyce Burge stands fast and says nothing; but he screws up his cheeks into a smile at each introduction, and makes his eyes shine in a very winning manner. He is a well-fed man turned fifty, with broad forehead, and grey hair which, his neck being short, falls almost to his collar.

FRANKLYN. Mr Haslam, our rector.

 Burge conveys an impression of shining like a church window; and Haslam seizes the nearest library chair on the hearth, and swings it round for Burge between the stool and Conrad. He then retires to the window seat at the other side of the room, and is joined by Savvy. They sit there, side by side, hunched up with their elbows on their knees and their chins on their hands, providing Burge with a sort of Stranger's Gallery during the ensuing sitting.

FRANKLYN. I forget whether you know my brother Conrad. He is a biologist.

BURGE [*suddenly bursting into energetic action and shaking hands heartily with Conrad*] By reputation only, but very well, of course. How I wish I could have devoted myself to biology! I have always been interested in rocks and strata and volcanoes and so forth: they throw such a light on the age of the earth. [*With conviction*] There is nothing like biology. 'The cloud-capped towers, the solemn binnacles, the gorgeous temples, the great globe itself: yea, all that it inherit shall dissolve, and, like this influential pageant faded, leave not a rack behind.' Thats biology, you know: good sound biology. [*He sits down. So do the others, Franklyn on the stool, and Conrad on his Chippendale*]. Well, my dear Barnabas, what do you think of the situation? Dont you think the time has come for us to make a move?

FRANKLYN. The time has always come to make a move.

BURGE. How true! But what is the move to be? You are a man of enormous influence. We know that. Weve always known it. We have to consult you whether we like it or not. We –

FRANKLYN [*interrupting firmly*] I never meddle in party politics now.

SAVVY. It's no use saying you have no influence, daddy. Heaps of people swear by you.

BURGE [*shining at her*] Of course they do. Come! let me prove to you what we think of you. Shall we find you a first-rate constituency to contest at the next election? One that wont cost you a penny. A metropolitan seat. What do you say to the Strand?

FRANKLYN. My dear Burge, I am not a child. Why do you go on wasting your party funds on the Strand? You know you cannot win it.

BURGE. We cannot win it; but you –

FRANKLYN. Oh, please!

SAVVY. The Strand's no use, Mr Burge. I once canvassed for a Socialist there. Cheese it.

BURGE. Cheese it!

HASLAM [*spluttering with suppressed laughter*] Priceless!

SAVVY. Well, I suppose I shouldnt say cheese it to a Right Honorable. But the Strand, you know! Do come off it.

FRANKLYN. You must excuse my daughter's shocking manners, Burge; but I agree with her that popular democratic statesmen soon come to believe that everyone they speak to is an ignorant dupe and a born fool into the bargain.

BURGE [*laughing genially*] You old aristocrat, you! But believe me, the instinct of the people is sound –

CONRAD [*cutting in sharply*] Then why are you in the Opposition instead of in the Government?

BURGE [*shewing signs of temper under this heckling*] I deny that I am in the Opposition *morally*. The Government does not represent the country. I was chucked out of the Coalition by a Tory conspiracy. The people want me back. I dont want to go back.

FRANKLYN [*gently remonstrant*] My dear Burge: of course you
do.

BURGE [*turning on him*] Not a bit of it. I want to cultivate my
garden. I am not interested in politics: I am interested in
roses. I havnt a scrap of ambition. I went into politics
because my wife shoved me into them, bless her! But I
want to serve my country. What else am I for? I want to
save my country from the Tories. They dont represent the
people. The man they have made Prime Minister has
never represented the people; and you know it. Lord Dunreen is the bitterest old Tory left alive. What has he to
offer to the people?

FRANKLYN [*cutting in before Burge can proceed – as he evidently
intends – to answer his own question*] I will tell you. He has
ascertainable beliefs and principles to offer. The people
know where they are with Lord Dunreen. They know
what he thinks right and what he thinks wrong. With your
followers they never know where they are. With you they
never know where they are.

BURGE [*amazed*] With me!

FRANKLYN. Well, where are you? What are you?

BURGE. Barnabas: you must be mad. You ask me what I
am?

FRANKLYN. I do.

BURGE. I am, if I mistake not, Joyce Burge, pretty well
known throughout Europe, and indeed throughout the
world, as the man who – unworthily perhaps, but not
quite unsuccessfully – held the helm when the ship of State
weathered the mightiest hurricane that has ever burst
with earth-shaking violence on the land of our fathers.

FRANKLYN. I know that. I know who you are. And the
earth-shaking part of it to me is that though you were
placed in that enormously responsible position, neither I
nor anyone else knows what your beliefs are, or even
whether you have either beliefs or principles. What we did
know was that your Government was formed largely of
men who regarded you as a robber of henroosts, and
whom you regarded as enemies of the people.

BURGE [*adroitly, as he thinks*] I agree with you. I agree with you absolutely. I dont believe in coalition governments.

FRANKLYN. Precisely. Yet you formed two.

BURGE. Why? Because we were at war. That is what you fellows never would realize. The Hun was at the gate. Our country, our lives, the honor of our wives and mothers and daughters, the tender flesh of our innocent babes, were at stake. Was that a time to argue about principles?

FRANKLYN. I should say it was the time of all others to confirm the resolution of our own men and gain the confidence and support of public opinion throughout the world by a declaration of principle. Do you think the Hun would ever have come to the gate if he had known that it would be shut in his face on principle? Did he not hold his own against you until America boldly affirmed the democratic principle and came to our rescue? Why did you let America snatch that honor from England?

BURGE. Barnabas: America was carried away by words, and had to eat them at the Peace Conference. Beware of eloquence: it is the bane of popular speakers like you.

FRANKLYN ⎫ [*exclaiming* ⎧ Well!!
SAVVY ⎬ *all* ⎨ I like that!
HASLAM ⎭ *together*] ⎩ Priceless!

BURGE [*continuing remorselessly*] Come down to facts. It wasnt principle that won the war: it was the British fleet and the blockade. America found the talk: I found the shells. You cannot win wars by principles; but you *can* win elections by them. There I am with you. You want the next election to be fought on principles: that is what it comes to, doesnt it?

FRANKLYN. I dont want it to be fought at all! An election is a moral horror, as bad as a battle except for the blood: a mud bath for every soul concerned in it. You know very well that it will not be fought on principle.

BURGE. On the contrary it will be fought on nothing else. I believe a program is a mistake. I agree with you that principle is what we want.

FRANKLYN. Principle without program, eh?

BURGE. Exactly. There it is in three words.

FRANKLYN. Why not in one word? Platitudes. That is what principle without program means.

BURGE [*puzzled but patient, trying to get at Franklyn's drift in order to ascertain his price*] I have not made myself clear. Listen. I am agreeing with you. I am on your side. I am accepting your proposal. There isnt going to be any more coalition. This time there wont be a Tory in the Cabinet. Every candidate will have to pledge himself to Free Trade, slightly modified by consideration for our Overseas Dominions; to Disestablishment; to Reform of the House of Lords; to a revised scheme of Taxation of Land Values; and to doing something or other to keep the Irish quiet. Does that satisfy you?

FRANKLYN. It does not even interest me. Suppose your friends do commit themselves to all this! What does it prove about them except that they are hopelessly out of date even in party politics? that they have learnt nothing and forgotten nothing since 1885? What is it to me that they hate the Church and hate the landed gentry; that they are jealous of the nobility, and have shipping shares instead of manufacturing businesses in the Midlands? I can find you hundreds of the most sordid rascals, or the most densely stupid reactionaries, with all these qualifications.

BURGE. Personal abuse proves nothing. Do you suppose the Tories are all angels because they are all members of the Church of England?

FRANKLYN. No; but they stand together as members of the Church of England, whereas your people, in attacking the Church, are all over the shop. The supporters of the Church are of one mind about religion: its enemies are of a dozen minds. The Churchmen are a phalanx: your people are a mob in which atheists are jostled by Plymouth Brethren, and Positivists by Pillars of Fire. You have with you all the crudest unbelievers and all the crudest fanatics.

BURGE. We stand, as Cromwell did, for liberty of conscience, if that is what you mean.

FRANKLYN. How can you talk such rubbish over the graves of your conscientious objectors? All law limits liberty of conscience: if a man's conscience allows him to steal your watch or to shirk military service, how much liberty do you allow it? Liberty of conscience is not my point.

BURGE [*testily*] I wish you would come to your point. Half the time you are saying that you must have principles; and when I offer you principles you say they wont work.

FRANKLYN. You have not offered me any principles. Your party shibboleths are not principles. If you get into power again you will find yourself at the head of a rabble of Socialists and anti-Socialists, of Jingo Imperialists and Little Englanders, of cast-iron Materialists and ecstatic Quakers, of Christian Scientists and Compulsory Inoculationists, of Syndicalists and Bureaucrats: in short, of men differing fiercely and irreconcilably on every principle that goes to the root of human society and destiny; and the impossibility of keeping such a team together will force you to sell the pass again to the solid Conservative Opposition.

BURGE [*rising in wrath*] Sell the pass again! You accuse me of having sold the pass!

FRANKLYN. When the terrible impact of real warfare swept your parliamentary sham warfare into the dustbin, you had to go behind the backs of your followers and make a secret agreement with the leaders of the Opposition to keep you in power on condition that you dropped all legislation of which they did not approve. And you could not even hold them to their bargain; for they presently betrayed the secret and forced the coalition on you.

BURGE. I solemnly declare that this is a false and monstrous accusation.

FRANKLYN. Do you deny that the thing occurred? Were the uncontradicted reports false? Were the published letters forgeries?

BURGE. Certainly not. But *I* did not do it. I was not Prime Minister then. It was that old dotard, that played-out old humbug Lubin. He was Prime Minister then, not I.

FRANKLYN. Do you mean to say you did not know?

BURGE [*sitting down again with a shrug*] Oh, I had to be told. But what could I do? If we had refused we might have had to go out of office.

FRANKLYN. Precisely.

BURGE. Well, could we desert the country at such a crisis? The Hun was at the gate. Everyone has to make sacrifices for the sake of the country at such moments. We had to rise above party; and I am proud to say we never gave party a second thought. We stuck to –

CONRAD. Office?

BURGE [*turning on him*] Yes, sir, to office: that is, to responsibility, to danger, to heart-sickening toil, to abuse and misunderstanding, to a martyrdom that made us envy the very soldiers in the trenches. If you had had to live for months on aspirin and bromide of potassium to get a wink of sleep, you wouldnt talk about office as if it were a catch.

FRANKLYN. Still, you admit that under our parliamentary system Lubin could not have helped himself?

BURGE. On that subject my lips are closed. Nothing will induce me to say one word against the old man. I never have; and I never will. Lubin is old: he has never been a real statesman: he is as lazy as a cat on a hearthrug: you cant get him to attend to anything: he is good for nothing but getting up and making speeches with a peroration that goes down with the back benches. But I say nothing against him. I gather that you do not think much of me as a statesman; but at all events I can get things done. I can hustle: even you will admit that. But Lubin? Oh my stars, Lubin!! If you only knew –

The parlor maid opens the door and announces a visitor.

THE PARLOR MAID. Mr Lubin.

BURGE [*bounding from his chair*] Lubin! Is this a conspiracy?

They all rise in amazement, staring at the door. Lubin enters: a man at the end of his sixties, a Yorkshireman with the last traces of Scandinavian flax still in his white hair, undistinguished in stature, unassuming in his manner, and taking his simple dignity for granted, but wonderfully comfortable and quite self-assured in contrast to the intellectual restlessness of Franklyn and the mesmeric self-assertiveness of Burge. His presence suddenly brings out the fact that they are unhappy men, ill at ease, square pegs in round holes, whilst he flourishes like a primrose.

The parlor maid withdraws.

LUBIN [*coming to Franklyn*] How do you do, Mr Barnabas? [*He speaks very comfortably and kindly, much as if he were the host, and Franklyn an embarrassed but welcome guest*]. I had the pleasure of meeting you once at the Mansion House. I think it was to celebrate the conclusion of the hundred years peace with America.

FRANKLYN [*shaking hands*] It was long before that: a meeting about Venezuela, when we were on the point of going to war with America.

LUBIN [*not at all put out*] Yes: you are quite right. I knew it was something about America. [*He pats Franklyn's hand*]. And how have you been all this time? Well, eh?

FRANKLYN [*smiling to soften the sarcasm*] A few vicissitudes of health naturally in so long a time.

LUBIN. Just so. Just so. [*Looking round at Savvy*] The young lady is– ?

FRANKLYN. My daughter, Savvy.

Savvy comes from the window between her father and Lubin.

LUBIN [*taking her hand affectionately in both his*] And why has she never come to see us?

BURGE. I dont know whether you have noticed, Lubin, that I am present.

Savvy takes advantage of this diversion to slip away to the settee, where she is stealthily joined by Haslam, who sits down on her left.

LUBIN [*seating himself in Burge's chair with ineffable comfortableness*] My dear Burge: if you imagine that it is possible to be within ten miles of your energetic presence without being acutely aware of it, you do yourself the greatest injustice. How are you? And how are your good newspaper friends? [*Burge makes an explosive movement; but Lubin goes on calmly and sweetly*] And what are you doing here with my old friend Barnabas, if I may ask?

BURGE [*sitting down in Conrad's chair, leaving him standing*

uneasily in the corner] Well, just what you are doing, if
you want to know. I am trying to enlist Mr Barnabas's
valuable support for my party.

LUBIN. Your party, eh? The newspaper party?

BURGE. The Liberal Party. The party of which I have the
honor to be leader.

LUBIN. Have you now? Thats very interesting; for I thought
I was the leader of the Liberal Party. However, it is very
kind of you to take it off my hands, if the party will let you.

BURGE. Do you suggest that I have not the support and
confidence of the party?

LUBIN. I dont suggest anything, my dear Burge. Mr Barnabas will tell you that we all think very highly of you. The
country owes you a great deal. During the war, you did
very creditably over the munitions; and if you were not
quite so successful with the peace, nobody doubted that
you meant well.

BURGE. Very kind of you, Lubin. Let me remark that you
cannot lead a progressive party without getting a move on.

LUBIN. You mean you cannot. I did it for ten years without
the least difficulty. And very comfortable, prosperous,
pleasant years they were.

BURGE. Yes; but what did they end in?

LUBIN. In you, Burge. You dont complain of that, do you?

BURGE [*fiercely*] In plague, pestilence, and famine; battle,
murder, and sudden death.

LUBIN [*with an appreciative chuckle*] The Nonconformist can
quote the prayer-book for his own purposes, I see. How
you enjoyed yourself over that business, Burge! Do you
remember the Knock-Out Blow?

BURGE. It came off: dont forget that. Do *you* remember
fighting to the last drop of your blood?

LUBIN [*unruffled, to Franklyn*] By the way, I remember your
brother Conrad – a wonderful brain and a dear good
fellow – explaining to me that I couldnt fight to the last
drop of my blood, because I should be dead long before
I came to it. Most interesting, and quite true. He was introduced to me at a meeting where the suffragettes kept

disturbing me. They had to be carried out kicking and making a horrid disturbance.

CONRAD. No: it was later, at a meeting to support the Franchise Bill which gave them the vote.

LUBIN [discovering Conrad's presence for the first time] Youre right: it was. I knew it had something to do with women. My memory never deceives me. Thank you. Will you introduce me to this gentleman, Barnabas?

CONRAD [not at all affably] I am the Conrad in question. [He sits down in dudgeon on the vacant Chippendale].

LUBIN. Are you? [Looking at him pleasantly] Yes: of course you are. I never forget a face. But [with an arch turn of his eyes to Savvy] your pretty niece engaged all my powers of vision.

BURGE. I wish youd be serious, Lubin. God knows we have passed through times terrible enough to make any man serious.

LUBIN. I do not think I need to be reminded of that. In peace time I used to keep myself fresh for my work by banishing all worldly considerations from my mind on Sundays; but war has no respect for the Sabbath; and there have been Sundays within the last few years on which I have had to play as many as sixty-six games of bridge to keep my mind off the news from the front.

BURGE [scandalized] Sixty-six games of bridge on Sunday!!!

LUBIN. You probably sang sixty-six hymns. But as I cannot boast either your admirable voice or your spiritual fervor, I had to fall back on bridge.

FRANKLYN. If I may go back to the subject of your visit, it seems to me that you may both be completely superseded by the Labor Party.

BURGE. But I am in the truest sense myself a Labor leader. I – [he stops, as Lubin has risen with a half-suppressed yawn, and is already talking calmly, but without a pretence of interest].

LUBIN. The Labor Party! Oh no, Mr Barnabas. No, no, no, no, no. [He moves in Savvy's direction]. There will be no trouble about that. Of course we must give them a few seats: more, I quite admit, than we should have dreamt of leaving to them before the war; but – [by this time he has

reached the sofa where Savvy and Haslam are seated. He sits down between them; takes her hand; and drops the subject of Labor].
Well, my dear young lady? What is the latest news? Whats going on? Have you seen Shoddy's new play? Tell me all about it, and all about the latest books, and all about everything.

SAVVY. You have not met Mr Haslam. Our Rector.

LUBIN [*who has quite overlooked Haslam*] Never heard of him. Is he any good?

FRANKLYN. I was introducing him. This is Mr Haslam.

HASLAM. How d'ye do?

LUBIN. I beg your pardon, Mr Haslam. Delighted to meet you. [*To Savvy*] Well, now, how many books have you written?

SAVVY [*rather overwhelmed but attracted*] None. I dont write.

LUBIN. You dont say so; Well, what do you do? Music? Skirt-dancing?

SAVVY. I dont do anything.

LUBIN. Thank God! You and I were born for one another. Who is your favorite poet, Sally?

SAVVY. Savvy.

LUBIN. Savvy! I never heard of him. Tell me all about him. Keep me up to date.

SAVVY. It's not a poet. *I* am Savvy, not Sally.

LUBIN. Savvy! Thats a funny name, and very pretty. Savvy. It sounds Chinese. What does it mean?

CONRAD. Short for Savage.

LUBIN [*patting her hand*] La belle Sauvage.

HASLAM [*rising and surrendering Savvy to Lubin by crossing to the fireplace*] I suppose the Church is out of it as far as progressive politics are concerned.

BURGE. Nonsense! That notion about the Church being unprogressive is one of those shibboleths that our party must drop. The Church is all right essentially. Get rid of the establishment; get rid of the bishops; get rid of the candlesticks; get rid of the 39 articles; and the Church of England is just as good as any other Church; and I dont care who hears me say so.

LUBIN. It doesnt matter a bit who hears you say so, my dear Burge. [*To Savvy*] Who did you say your favorite poet was?

SAVVY. I dont make pets of poets. Who's yours?

LUBIN. Horace.

SAVVY. Horace who?

LUBIN. Quintus Horatius Flaccus: the noblest Roman of them all, my dear.

SAVVY. Oh, if he is dead, that explains it. I have a theory that all the dead people we feel especially interested in must have been ourselves. You must be Horace's reincarnation.

LUBIN [*delighted*] That is the very most charming and penetrating and intelligent thing that has ever been said to me. Barnabas: will you exchange daughters with me? I can give you your choice of two.

FRANKLYN. Man proposes. Savvy disposes.

LUBIN. What does Savvy say?

BURGE. Lubin: I came here to talk politics.

LUBIN. Yes: you have only one subject, Burge. I came here to talk to Savvy. Take Burge into the next room, Barnabas; and let him rip.

BURGE [*half-angry, half-indulgent*] No; but really, Lubin, we are at a crisis –

LUBIN. My dear Burge, life is a disease; and the only difference between one man and another is the stage of the disease at which he lives. You are always at the crisis: I am always in the convalescent stage. I enjoy convalescence. It is the part that makes the illness worth while.

SAVVY [*half-rising*] Perhaps I'd better run away. I am distracting you.

LUBIN [*making her sit down again*] Not at all, my dear. You are only distracting Burge. Jolly good thing for him to be distracted by a pretty girl. Just what he needs.

BURGE. I sometimes envy you, Lubin. The great movement of mankind, the giant sweep of the ages, passes you by and leaves you standing.

LUBIN. It leaves me sitting, and quite comfortable, thank you. Go on sweeping. When you are tired of it, come

back; and you will find England where it was, and me in
my accustomed place, with Miss Savvy telling me all sorts
of interesting things.

SAVVY [*who has been growing more and more restless*] Dont let
him shut you up, Mr Burge. You know, Mr Lubin, I am
frightfully interested in the Labor movement, and in
Theosophy, and in reconstruction after the war, and all
sorts of things. I daresay the flappers in your smart set are
tremendously flattered when you sit beside them and are
nice to them as you are being nice to me; but I am not
smart; and I am no use as a flapper. I am dowdy and
serious. I want you to be serious. If you refuse, I shall go
and sit beside Mr Burge, and ask him to hold my hand.

LUBIN. He wouldnt know how to do it, my dear. Burge has
a reputation as a profligate –

BURGE [*starting*] Lubin: this is monstrous. I –

LUBIN [*continuing*] – but he is really a model of domesticity.
His name is coupled with all the most celebrated beauties;
but for him there is only one woman; and that is not you,
my dear, but his very charming wife.

BURGE. You are destroying my character in the act of pretending to save it. Have the goodness to confine yourself
to your own character and your own wife. Both of them
need all your attention.

LUBIN. I have the privilege of my age and of my transparent
innocence. I have not to struggle with your volcanic
energy.

BURGE [*with an immense sense of power*] No, by George!

FRANKLYN. I think I shall speak both for my brother and
myself, and possibly also for my daughter, if I say that
since the object of your visit and Mr Joyce Burge's is to
some extent political, we should hear with great interest
something about your political aims, Mr Lubin.

LUBIN [*assenting with complete good humor, and becoming attentive,
clear, and businesslike in his tone*] By all means, Mr Barnabas.
What we have to consider first, I take it, is what prospect
there is of our finding you beside us in the House after the
next election.

FRANKLYN. When I speak of politics, Mr Lubin, I am not thinking of elections, or available seats, or party funds, or the registers, or even, I am sorry to have to add, of parliament as it exists at present. I had much rather you talked about bridge than about electioneering: it is the more interesting game of the two.

BURGE. He wants to discuss principles, Lubin.

LUBIN [*very cool and clear*] I understand Mr Barnabas quite well. But elections are unsettled things; principles are settled things.

CONRAD [*impatiently*] Great Heavens! –

LUBIN [*interrupting him with quiet authority*] One moment, Dr Barnabas. The main principles on which modern civilized society is founded are pretty well understood among educated people. That is what our dangerously half-educated masses and their pet demagogues – if Burge will excuse that expression –

BURGE. Dont mind me. Go on. I shall have something to say presently.

LUBIN. – that is what our dangerously half-educated people do not realize. Take all this fuss about the Labor Party, with its imaginary new principles and new politics. The Labor members will find that the immutable laws of political economy take no more notice of their ambitions and aspirations than the law of gravitation. I speak, if I may say so, with knowledge; for I have made a special study of the Labor question.

FRANKLYN [*with interest and some surprise*] Indeed?

LUBIN. Yes. It occurred quite at the beginning of my career. I was asked to deliver an address to the students at the Working Men's College; and I was strongly advised to comply, as Gladstone and Morley and others were doing that sort of thing at the moment. It was rather a troublesome job, because I had not gone into political economy at the time. As you know, at the university I was a classical scholar; and my profession was the Law. But I looked up the text-books, and got up the case most carefully. I found that the correct view is that all this Trade Unionism and

Socialism and so forth is founded on the ignorant delusion that wages and the production and distribution of wealth can be controlled by legislation or by any human action whatever. They obey fixed scientific laws, which have been ascertained and settled finally by the highest economic authorities. Naturally I do not at this distance of time remember the exact process of reasoning; but I can get up the case again at any time in a couple of days; and you may rely on me absolutely, should the occasion arise, to deal with all these ignorant and unpractical people in a conclusive and convincing way, except, of course, as far as it may be advisable to indulge and flatter them a little so as to let them down without creating ill feeling in the working-class electorate. In short, I can get that lecture up again almost at a moment's notice.

SAVVY. But, Mr Lubin, I have had a university education too; and all this about wages and distribution being fixed by immutable laws of political economy is obsolete rot.

FRANKLYN [*shocked*] Oh, my dear! That is not polite.

LUBIN. No, no, no. Dont scold her. She mustnt be scolded. [*To Savvy*] I understand. You are a disciple of Karl Marx.

SAVVY. No, no. Karl Marx's economics are all rot.

LUBIN [*at last a little taken aback*] Dear me!

SAVVY. You must excuse me, Mr Lubin; but it's like hearing a man talk about the Garden of Eden.

CONRAD. Why shouldnt he talk about the Garden of Eden? It was a first attempt at biology anyhow.

LUBIN [*recovering his self-possession*] I am sound on the Garden of Eden. I have heard of Darwin.

SAVVY. But Darwin is all rot.

LUBIN. What! Already!

SAVVY. It's no good your smiling at me like a Cheshire cat, Mr Lubin; and I am not going to sit here mumchance like an old-fashioned goody goody wife while you men monopolize the conversation and pay out the very ghastliest exploded drivel as the latest thing in politics. I am not giving you my own ideas, Mr Lubin, but just the regular orthodox science of today. Only the most awful old fossils think that Socialism is bad economics and that Darwin invented Evolution. Ask Papa. Ask Uncle. Ask the first person you meet in the street. [*She rises and crosses to Haslam*]. Give me a cigaret, Bill, will you?

HASLAM. Priceless. [*He complies*].

FRANKLYN. Savvy has not lived long enough to have any manners, Mr Lubin; but that is where you stand with the younger generation. Dont smoke, dear.

Savvy, with a shrug of rather mutinous resignation, throws the cigaret into the fire. Haslam, on the point of lighting one for himself, changes his mind.

LUBIN [*shrewd and serious*] Mr Barnabas: I confess I am surprised; and I will not pretend that I am convinced. But I am open to conviction. I may be wrong.

BURGE [*in a burst of irony*] Oh no. Impossible! Impossible!

LUBIN. Yes, Mr Barnabas, though I do not possess Burge's genius for being always wrong, I have been in that position once or twice. I could not conceal from you, even if I wished to, that my time has been so completely filled by my professional work as a lawyer, and later on by my duties as leader of the House of Commons in the days when Prime Ministers were also leaders –

BURGE [*stung*] Not to mention bridge and smart society.

LUBIN. – not to mention the continual and trying effort to make Burge behave himself, that I have not been able to keep my academic reading up to date. I have kept my classics brushed up out of sheer love for them; but my economics and my science, such as they were, may possibly be a little rusty. Yet I think I may say that if you and your brother will be so good as to put me on the track of the necessary documents, I will undertake to put the case to the House or to the country to your entire satisfaction. You see, as long as you can shew these troublesome half-educated people who want to turn the world upside down that they are talking nonsense, it really does not matter very much whether you do it in terms of what Miss Barnabas calls obsolete rot or in terms of what her granddaughter will probably call unmitigated tosh. I have no objection whatever to denounce Karl Marx. Anything I can say against Darwin will please a large body of sincerely pious voters. If it will be easier to carry on the business of the country on the understanding that the present state of things is to be called Socialism, I have no objection in the world to call it Socialism. There is the precedent of the Emperor Constantine, who saved the society of his own day by agreeing to call his Imperialism Christianity. Mind: I must not go ahead of the electorate. You must not call a voter a Socialist until –

FRANKLYN. Until he is a Socialist. Agreed.

LUBIN. Oh, not at all. You need not wait for that. You must not call him a Socialist until he wishes to be called a Socialist: that is all. Surely you would not say that I must not address my constituents as gentlemen until they are gentlemen. I address them as gentlemen because they wish to be so addressed. [*He rises from the sofa and goes to Franklyn, placing a reassuring hand on his shoulder*]. Do not be afraid of Socialism, Mr Barnabas. You need not tremble for your property or your position or your dignity. England will remain what England is, no matter what new political names may come into vogue. I do not intend to resist the transition to Socialism. You may depend on me to guide it, to lead it, to give suitable expression to its aspirations, and to steer it clear of Utopian absurdities. I can honestly ask for your support on the most advanced Socialist grounds no less than on the soundest Liberal ones.

BURGE. In short, Lubin, youre incorrigible. You dont believe anything is going to change. The millions are still to toil – the people – my people – for I am a man of the people –.

LUBIN [*interrupting him contemptuously*] Dont be ridiculous, Burge. You are a country solicitor, further removed from the people, more foreign to them, more jealous of letting them up to your level, than any duke or any archbishop.

BURGE [*hotly*] I deny it. You think I have never been poor. You think I have never cleaned my own boots. You think my fingers have never come out through the soles when I was cleaning them. You think –

LUBIN. I think you fall into the very common mistake of supposing that it is poverty that makes the proletarian and money that makes the gentleman. You are quite wrong. You never belonged to the people: you belonged to the impecunious. Impecuniosity and broken boots are the lot of the unsuccessful middle class, and the commonplaces of the early struggles of the professional and younger son class. I defy you to find a farm laborer in England with broken boots. Call a mechanic one of the poor, and he'll punch your head. When you talk to your constituents about the toiling millions, they dont consider that you are referring to them. They are all third cousins of somebody with a title or a park. I am a Yorkshireman, my friend. I know England; and you dont. If you did you would know –

BURGE. What do you know that I dont know?

LUBIN. I know that we are taking up too much of Mr Barnabas's time. [*Franklyn rises*]. May I take it, my dear Barnabas, that I may count on your support if we succeed in forcing an election before the new register is in full working order?

BURGE [*rising also*] May the party count on your support? I say nothing about myself. Can the party depend on you? Is there any question of yours that I have left unanswered?

CONRAD. We havnt asked you any, you know.

BURGE. May I take that as a mark of confidence?

CONRAD. If I were a laborer in your constituency, I should ask you a biological question?

LUBIN. No you wouldnt, my dear Doctor. Laborers never ask questions.

BURGE. Ask it now. I have never flinched from being heckled. Out with it. Is it about the land?

CONRAD. No.

BURGE. Is it about the Church?

CONRAD. No.

BURGE. Is it about the House of Lords?

CONRAD. No.

BURGE. Is it about Proportional Representation?

CONRAD. No.

BURGE. Is it about Free Trade?

CONRAD. No.

BURGE. Is it about the priest in the school?

CONRAD. No.

BURGE. Is it about Ireland?

CONRAD. No.

BURGE. Is it about Germany?

CONRAD. No.

BURGE. Well, is it about Republicanism? Come! I wont flinch. Is it about the Monarchy?

CONRAD. No.

BURGE. Well, what the devil is it about, then?

CONRAD. You understand that I am asking the question in the character of a laborer who earned thirteen shillings a week before the war and earns thirty now, when he can get it?

BURGE. Yes: I understand that. I am ready for you. Out with it.

CONRAD. And whom you propose to represent in parliament?

BURGE. Yes, yes, yes. Come on.

CONRAD. The question is this. Would you allow your son to marry my daughter, or your daughter to marry my son?

BURGE [*taken aback*] Oh, come! Thats not a political question.

CONRAD. Then, as a biologist, I dont take the slightest interest in your politics; and I shall not walk across the street to vote for you or anyone else at the election. Good evening.

LUBIN. Serve you right, Burge! Dr Barnabas: you have my assurance that my daughter shall marry the man of her choice, whether he be lord or laborer. May *I* count on your support?

BURGE [*hurling the epithet at him*] Humbug!

SAVVY. Stop. [*They all stop short in the movement of leave-taking to look at her*]. Daddy: are you going to let them off like this? How are they to know anything if nobody ever tells them? If you dont, I will.

CONRAD. You cant. You didnt read my book; and you know nothing about it. You just hold your tongue.

SAVVY. I just wont, Nunk. I shall have a vote when I am thirty; and I ought to have it now. Why are these two ridiculous people to be allowed to come in and walk over us as if the world existed only to play their silly parliamentary game?

FRANKLYN [*severely*] Savvy: you really must not be uncivil to our guests.

SAVVY. I'm sorry. But Mr Lubin didnt stand on much ceremony with me, did he? And Mr Burge hasnt addressed a single word to me. I'm not going to stand it. You and Nunk have a much better program than either of them. It's the only one we are going to vote for; and they ought to be told about it for the credit of the family and the good of their own souls. You just tip them a chapter from the gospel of the brothers Barnabas, Daddy.

Lubin and Burge turn inquiringly to Franklyn, suspecting a move to form a new party.

FRANKLYN. It is quite true, Mr Lubin, that I and my brother have a little program of our own which –

CONRAD [*interrupting*] It's not a little program: it's an almighty big one. It's not our own: it's the program of the whole of civilization.

BURGE. Then why split the party before you have put it to us? For God's sake let us have no more splits. I am here to learn. I am here to gather your opinions and represent them. I invite you to put your views before me. I offer myself to be heckled. You have asked me only an absurd non-political question.

FRANKLYN. Candidly, I fear our program will be thrown away on you. It would not interest you.

BURGE [*with challenging audacity*] Try. Lubin can go if he likes; but I am still open to new ideas, if only I can find them.

FRANKLYN [*to Lubin*] Are you prepared to listen, Mr Lubin; or shall I thank you for your very kind and welcome visit, and say good evening?

LUBIN [*sitting down resignedly on the settee, but involuntarily making a movement which looks like the stifling of a yawn*] With pleasure, Mr Barnabas. Of course you know that before I can adopt any new plank in the party platform, it will have to reach me through the National Liberal Federation, which you can approach through your local Liberal and Radical Association.

FRANKLYN. I could recall to you several instances of the addition to your party program of measures of which no local branch of your Federation had ever dreamt. But I understand that you are not really interested. I will spare you, and drop the subject.

LUBIN [*waking up a little*] You quite misunderstand me. Please do not take it in that way. I only –

BURGE [*talking him down*] Never mind the Federation: *I* will answer for the Federation. Go on, Barnabas: go on. Never mind Lubin [*he sits down in the chair from which Lubin first displaced him*].

FRANKLYN. Our program is only that the term of human life shall be extended to three hundred years.

LUBIN [*softly*] Eh?

BURGE [*explosively*] What!

SAVVY. Our election cry is 'Back to Methuselah!'

HASLAM. Priceless!

   Lubin and Burge look at one another.

CONRAD. No. We are not mad.

SAVVY. Theyre not joking either. They mean it.

LUBIN [*cautiously*] Assuming that, in some sense which I am for the moment unable to fathom, you are in earnest, Mr Barnabas, may I ask what this has to do with politics?

FRANKLYN. The connection is very evident. You are now, Mr Lubin, within immediate reach of your seventieth year. Mr Joyce Burge is your junior by about eleven years. You will go down to posterity as one of a European group of immature statesmen and monarchs who, doing the very best for your respective countries of which you were capable, succeeded in all-but-wrecking the civilization of Europe, and did, in effect, wipe out of existence many millions of its inhabitants.

BURGE. Less than a million.

FRANKLYN. That was our loss alone.

BURGE. Oh, if you count foreigners – !

HASLAM. God counts foreigners, you know.

SAVVY [*with intense satisfaction*] Well said, Bill.

FRANKLYN. I am not blaming you. Your task was beyond human capacity. What with our huge armaments, our terrible engines of destruction, our systems of coercion manned by an irresistible police, you were called on to control powers so gigantic that one shudders at the thought of their being entrusted even to an infinitely experienced and benevolent God, much less to mortal men whose whole life does not last a hundred years.

BURGE. We won the war: dont forget that.

FRANKLYN. No: the soldiers and sailors won it, and left you to finish it. And you were so utterly incompetent that the multitudes of children slain by hunger in the first years of peace made us all wish we were at war again.

CONRAD. It's no use arguing about it. It is now absolutely certain that the political and social problems raised by our civilization cannot be solved by mere human mushrooms who decay and die when they are just beginning to have a glimmer of the wisdom and knowledge needed for their own government.

LUBIN. Quite an interesting idea, Doctor. Extravagant. Fantastic. But quite interesting. When I was young I used to feel my human limitations very acutely.

BURGE. God knows I have often felt that I could not go on if it had not been for the sense that I was only an instrument in the hands of a Power above us.

CONRAD. I'm glad you both agree with us, and with one another.

LUBIN. I have not gone so far as that, I think. After all, we have had many very able political leaders even within your recollection and mine.

FRANKLYN. Have you read the recent biographies – Dilke's, for instance – which revealed the truth about them?

LUBIN. I did not discover any new truth revealed in these books, Mr Barnabas.

FRANKLYN. What! Not the truth that England was governed all that time by a little woman who knew her own mind?

SAVVY. Hear, hear!

LUBIN. That often happens. Which woman do you mean?

FRANKLYN. Queen Victoria, to whom your Prime Ministers stood in the relation of naughty children whose heads she knocked together when their tempers and quarrels became intolerable. Within thirteen years of her death Europe became a hell.

BURGE. Quite true. That was because she was piously brought up, and regarded herself as an instrument. If a statesman remembers that he is only an instrument, and feels quite sure that he is rightly interpreting the divine purpose, he will come out all right, you know.

FRANKLYN. The Kaiser felt like that. Did he come out all right?

BURGE. Well, let us be fair, even to the Kaiser. Let us be fair.

FRANKLYN. Were you fair to him when you won an election on the program of hanging him?

BURGE. Stuff! I am the last man alive to hang anybody; but the people wouldnt listen to reason. Besides, I knew the Dutch wouldnt give him up.

SAVVY. Oh, dont start arguing about poor old Bill. Stick to our point. Let these two gentlemen settle the question for themselves. Mr Burge: do you think Mr Lubin is fit to govern England?

BURGE. No. Frankly, I dont.

LUBIN [remonstrant] Really!

CONRAD. Why?

BURGE. Because he has no conscience: thats why.

LUBIN [shocked and amazed] Oh!

FRANKLYN. Mr Lubin: do you consider Joyce Burge qualified to govern England?

LUBIN [with dignified emotion, wounded, but without bitterness] Excuse me, Mr Barnabas; but before I answer that question I want to say this. Burge: we have had differences of opinion; and your newspaper friends have said hard things of me. But we worked together for years; and I hope I have done nothing to justify you in the amazing accusation you have just brought against me. Do you realize that you said that I have no conscience?

BURGE. Lubin: I am very accessible to an appeal to my emotions; and you are very cunning in making such appeals. I will meet you to this extent. I dont mean that you are a bad man. I dont mean that I dislike you, in spite of your continual attempts to discourage and depress me. But you have a mind like a looking-glass. You are very clear and smooth and lucid as to what is standing in front of you. But you have no foresight and no hindsight. You have no vision and no memory. You have no continuity; and a man without continuity can have neither conscience nor honor from one day to another. The result is that you have always been a damned bad minister; and you have sometimes been a damned bad friend. Now you can answer Barnabas's question and take it out of me to your heart's content. He asked you was I fit to govern England.

LUBIN [*recovering himself*] After what has just passed I sincerely wish I could honestly say yes, Burge. But it seems to me that you have condemned yourself out of your own mouth. You represent something which has had far too much influence and popularity in this country since Joseph Chamberlain set the fashion; and that is mere energy without intellect and without knowledge. Your mind is not a trained mind: it has not been stored with the best information, nor cultivated by intercourse with educated minds at any of our great seats of learning. As I happen to have enjoyed that advantage, it follows that you do not understand my mind. Candidly, I think that disqualifies you. The peace found out your weaknesses.

BURGE. Oh! What did it find out in you?

LUBIN. You and your newspaper confederates took the peace out of my hands. The peace did not find me out because it did not find me in.

FRANKLYN. Come! Confess, both of you! You were only flies on the wheel. The war went England's way; but the peace went its own way, and not England's way nor any of the ways you had so glibly appointed for it. Your peace treaty was a scrap of paper before the ink dried on it. The statesmen of Europe were incapable of governing Europe. What they needed was a couple of hundred years training and experience: what they had actually had was a few years at the bar or in a counting-house or on the grouse moors and golf courses. And now we are waiting, with monster cannons trained on every city and seaport, and huge aeroplanes ready to spring into the air and drop bombs every one of which will obliterate a whole street, and poison gases that will strike multitudes dead with a breath, until one of you gentlemen rises in his helplessness to tell us, who are as helpless as himself, that we are at war again.

CONRAD. Aha! What consolation will it be for us then that you two are able to tell off one another's defects so cleverly in your afternoon chat?

BURGE [angrily] If you come to that, what consolation will it be that you two can sit there and tell both of us off? you, who have had no responsibility! you, who havnt lifted a finger, as far as I know, to help us through this awful crisis which has left me ten years older than my proper age! Can you tell me a single thing you did to help us during the whole infernal business?

CONRAD. We're not blaming you: you hadnt lived long enough. No more had we. Cant you see that three-score-and-ten, though it may be long enough for a very crude sort of village life, isnt long enough for a complicated civilization like ours? Flinders Petrie has counted nine attempts at civilization made by people exactly like us; and every one of them failed just as ours is failing. They failed because the citizens and statesmen died of old age or over-eating before they had grown out of schoolboy games and savage sports and cigars and champagne. The signs of the end are always the same: Democracy, Socialism, and

Votes for Women. We shall go to smash within the lifetime of men now living unless we recognize that we must live longer.

LUBIN. I am glad you agree with me that Socialism and Votes for Women are signs of decay.

FRANKLYN. Not at all: they are only the difficulties that overtax your capacity. If you cannot organize Socialism you cannot organize civilized life; and you will relapse into barbarism accordingly.

SAVVY. Hear, hear!

BURGE. A useful point. We cannot put back the clock.

HASLAM. *I* can. Ive often done it.

LUBIN. Tut tut! My dear Burge: what are you dreaming of? Mr Barnabas: I am a very patient man. But will you tell me what earthly use or interest there is in a conclusion that cannot be realized? I grant you that if we could live three hundred years we should all be, perhaps wiser, certainly older. You will grant me in return, I hope, that if the sky fell we should all catch larks.

FRANKLYN. Your turn now, Conrad. Go ahead.

CONRAD. I dont think it's any good. I dont think they want to live longer than usual.

LUBIN. Although I am a mere child of 69, I am old enough to have lost the habit of crying for the moon.

BURGE. Have you discovered the elixir of life or have you not? If not, I agree with Lubin that you are wasting our time.

CONRAD. Is your time of any value?

BURGE [*unable to believe his ears*] My time of any value! What do you mean?

LUBIN [*smiling comfortably*] From your high scientific point of view, I daresay, none whatever, Professor. In any case I think a little perfectly idle discussion would do Burge good. After all, we might as well hear about the elixir of life as read novels, or whatever Burge does when he is not playing golf on Walton Heath. What is your elixir, Dr Barnabas? Lemons? Sour milk? Or what is the latest?

BURGE. We were just beginning to talk seriously; and now

you snatch at the chance of talking rot. [*He rises*]. Good evening. [*He turns to the door*].

CONRAD [*rudely*] Die as soon as you like. Good evening.

BURGE [*hesitating*] Look here. I took sour milk twice a day until Metchnikoff died. He thought it would keep him alive for ever; and he died of it.

CONRAD. You might as well have taken sour beer.

BURGE. You believe in lemons?

CONRAD. I wouldnt eat a lemon for ten pounds.

BURGE [*sitting down again*] What do you recommend?

CONRAD [*rising with a gesture of despair*] Whats the use of going on, Frank? Because I am a doctor, and because they think I have a bottle to give them that will make them live for ever, they are listening to me for the first time with their mouths open and their eyes shut. Thats their notion of science.

SAVVY. Steady, Nunk! Hold the fort.

CONRAD [*growls and sits down*]!!!

LUBIN. You volunteered the consultation, Doctor. I may tell you that, far from sharing the credulity as to science which is now the fashion, I am prepared to demonstrate that during the last fifty years, though the Church has often been wrong, and even the Liberal Party has not been infallible, the men of science have always been wrong.

CONRAD. Yes: the fellows you call men of science. The people who make money by it, and their medical hangers-on. But has anybody been right?

LUBIN. The poets and story tellers, especially the classical poets and story tellers, have been, in the main, right. I will ask you not to repeat this as my opinion outside; for the vote of the medical profession and its worshippers is not to be trifled with.

FRANKLYN. You are quite right: the poem is our real clue to biological science. The most scientific document we possess at present is, as your grandmother would have told you quite truly, the story of the Garden of Eden.

BURGE [*pricking up his ears*] Whats that? If you can establish that, Barnabas, I am prepared to hear you out with my very best attention. I am listening. Go on.

FRANKLYN. Well, you remember, dont you, that in the Garden of Eden Adam and Eve were not created mortal, and that natural death, as we call it, was not a part of life, but a later and quite separate invention?

BURGE. Now you mention it, thats true. Death came afterwards.

LUBIN. What about accidental death? That was always possible.

FRANKLYN. Precisely. Adam and Eve were hung up between two frightful possibilities. One was the extinction of mankind by their accidental death. The other was the prospect of living for ever. They could bear neither. They decided that they would just take a short turn of a thousand years, and meanwhile hand on their work to a new pair. Consequently, they had to invent natural birth and natural death, which are, after all, only modes of perpetuating life without putting on any single creature the terrible burden of immortality.

LUBIN. I see. The old must make room for the new.

BURGE. Death is nothing but making room. Thats all there is in it or ever has been in it.

FRANKLYN. Yes; but the old must not desert their posts until the new are ripe for them. They desert them now two hundred years too soon.

SAVVY. I believe the old people are the new people reincarnated, Nunk. I suspect I am Eve. I am very fond of apples; and they always disagree with me.

CONRAD. You are Eve, in a sense. The Eternal Life persists; only It wears out Its bodies and minds and gets new ones, like new clothes. You are only a new hat and frock on Eve.

FRANKLYN. Yes. Bodies and minds ever better and better fitted to carry out Its eternal pursuit.

LUBIN [with quiet scepticism] What pursuit, may one ask, Mr Barnabas?

FRANKLYN. The pursuit of omnipotence and omniscience. Greater power and greater knowledge: these are what we are all pursuing even at the risk of our lives and the sacrifice of our pleasures. Evolution is that pursuit and nothing else. It is the path to godhead. A man differs from a microbe only in being further on the path.

LUBIN. And how soon do you expect this modest end to be reached?

FRANKLYN. Never, thank God! As there is no limit to power and knowledge there can be no end. 'The power and the glory, world without end': have those words meant nothing to you?

BURGE [*pulling out an old envelope*] I should like to make a note of that. [*He does so*].

CONRAD. There will always be something to live for.

BURGE [*pocketing his envelope and becoming more and more business-like*] Right: I have got that. Now what about sin? What about the Fall? How do you work them in?

CONRAD. I dont work in the Fall. The Fall is outside Science. But I daresay Frank can work it in for you.

BURGE [*to Franklyn*] I wish you would, you know. It's important. Very important.

FRANKLYN. Well, consider it this way. It is clear that when Adam and Eve were immortal it was necessary that they should make the earth an extremely comfortable place to live in.

BURGE. True. If you take a house on a ninety-nine years lease, you spend a good deal of money on it. If you take it for three months you generally have a bill for dilapidations to pay at the end of them.

FRANKLYN. Just so. Consequently, when Adam had the Garden of Eden on a lease for ever, he took care to make it what the house agents call a highly desirable country residence. But the moment he invented death, and became a tenant for life only, the place was no longer worth the trouble. It was then that he let the thistles grow. Life was so short that it was no longer worth his while to do anything thoroughly well.

BURGE. Do you think that is enough to constitute what an average elector would consider a Fall? Is it tragic enough?

FRANKLYN. That is only the first step of the Fall. Adam did not fall down that step only: he fell down a whole flight. For instance, before he invented birth he dared not have lost his temper; for if he had killed Eve he would have been lonely and barren to all eternity. But when he invented birth, and anyone who was killed could be replaced, he could afford to let himself go. He undoubtedly invented wife-beating; and that was another step down. One of his sons invented meat-eating. The other was horrified at the innovation. With the ferocity which is still characteristic of bulls and other vegetarians, he slew his beefsteak-eating brother, and thus invented murder. That was a very steep step. It was so exciting that all the others began to kill one another for sport, and thus invented war, the steepest step of all. They even took to killing animals as a means of killing time, and then, of course, ate them to save the long and difficult labor of agriculture. I ask you to contemplate our fathers as they came crashing down all the steps of this Jacob's ladder that reached from paradise to a hell on earth in which they had multiplied the chances of death from violence, accident, and disease until they could hardly count on three score and ten years of life, much less the thousand that Adam had been ready to face! With that picture before you, will you now ask me where was the Fall? You might as well stand at the foot of Snowdon and ask me where is the mountain. The very children see it so plainly that they compress its history into a two line epic:

Old Daddy Long Legs wouldnt say his prayers:
Take him by the hind legs and throw him downstairs.

LUBIN [*still immovably sceptical*] And what does Science say to this fairy tale, Doctor Barnabas? Surely Science knows nothing of Genesis, or of Adam and Eve.

CONRAD. Then it isnt Science: thats all. Science has to account for everything; and everything includes the Bible.

FRANKLYN. The Book of Genesis is a part of nature like any other part of nature. The fact that the tale of the Garden of Eden has survived and held the imagination of men spellbound for centuries, whilst hundreds of much more plausible and amusing stories have gone out of fashion and perished like last year's popular song, is a scientific fact; and Science is bound to explain it. You tell me that Science knows nothing of it. Then Science is more ignorant than the children at any village school.

CONRAD. Of course if you think it more scientific to say that what we are discussing is not Adam and Eve and Eden, but the phylogeny of the blastoderm –

SAVVY. You neednt swear, Nunk.

CONRAD. Shut up, you: I am not swearing. [*To Lubin*] If you want the professional humbug of rewriting the Bible in words of four syllables, and pretending it's something new, I can humbug you to your heart's content. I can call Genesis Phylogenesis. Let the Creator say, if you like, 'I will establish an antipathetic symbiosis between thee and the female, and between thy blastoderm and her blastoderm.' Nobody will understand you; and Savvy will think you are swearing. The meaning is the same.

HASLAM. Priceless. But it's quite simple. The one version is poetry: the other is science.

FRANKLYN. The one is classroom jargon: the other is inspired human language.

LUBIN [*calmly reminiscent*] One of the few modern authors into whom I have occasionally glanced is Rousseau, who was a sort of Deist like Burge –

BURGE [*interrupting him forcibly*] Lubin: has this stupendously important communication which Professor Barnabas has just made to us: a communication for which I shall be indebted to him all my life long: has this, I say, no deeper effect on you than to set you pulling my leg by trying to make out that I am an infidel?

LUBIN. It's very interesting and amusing, Burge; and I think I see a case in it. I think I could undertake to argue it in an ecclesiastical court. But important is hardly a word I should attach to it.

BURGE. Good God! Here is this professor: a man utterly

removed from the turmoil of our political life: devoted to pure learning in its most abstract phases; and I solemnly declare he is the greatest politician, the most inspired party leader, in the kingdom. I take off my hat to him. I, Joyce Burge, give him best. And you sit there purring like an Angora cat, and can see nothing in it!

CONRAD [*opening his eyes widely*] Hallo! What have I done to deserve this tribute?

BURGE. Done! You have put the Liberal Party into power for the next thirty years, Doctor: thats what youve done.

CONRAD. God forbid!

BURGE. It's all up with the Church now. Thanks to you, we go to the country with one cry and one only: Back to the Bible! Think of the effect on the Nonconformist vote. You gather that in with one hand; and you gather in the modern scientific sceptical professional vote with the other. The village atheist and the first cornet in the local Salvation Army band meet on the village green and shake hands. You take your school children, your Bible class under the Cowper-Temple clause, into the museum. You shew the kids the Piltdown skull; and you say, 'Thats Adam. Thats Eve's husband.' You take the spectacled science student from the laboratory in Owens College; and when he asks you for a truly scientific history of Evolution, you put into his hand The Pilgrim's Progress. You – [*Savvy and Haslam explode into shrieks of merriment*]. What are you two laughing at?

SAVVY. Oh, go on, Mr Burge. Dont stop.

HASLAM. Priceless!

FRANKLYN. Would thirty years of office for the Liberal Party seem so important to you, Mr Burge, if you had another two and a half centuries to live?

BURGE [*decisively*] No. You will have to drop that part of it. The constituencies wont swallow it.

LUBIN [*seriously*] I am not so sure of that, Burge. I am not sure that it may not prove the only point they will swallow.

BURGE. It will be no use to us even if they do. It's not a party point. It's as good for the other side as for us.

LUBIN. Not necessarily. If we get in first with it, it will be associated in the public mind with our party. Suppose I put it forward as a plank in our program that we advocate the extension of human life to three hundred years! Dunreen, as leader of the opposite party, will be bound to oppose me: to denounce me as a visionary and so forth. By doing so he will place himself in the position of wanting to rob the people of two hundred and thirty years of their natural life. The Unionists will become the party of Premature Death; and we shall become the Longevity party.

BURGE [shaken] You really think the electorate would swallow it?

LUBIN. My dear Burge: is there anything the electorate will not swallow if it is judiciously put to them? But we must make sure of our ground. We must have the support of the men of science. Is there serious agreement among them, Doctor, as to the possibility of such an evolution as you have described?

CONRAD. Yes. Ever since the reaction against Darwin set in at the beginning of the present century, all scientific opinion worth counting has been converging rapidly upon Creative Evolution.

FRANKLYN. Poetry has been converging on it: philosophy has been converging on it: religion has been converging on it. It is going to be the religion of the twentieth century: a religion that has its intellectual roots in philosophy and science just as medieval Christianity had its intellectual roots in Aristotle.

LUBIN. But surely any change would be so extremely gradual that —

CONRAD. Dont deceive yourself. It's only the politicians who improve the world so gradually that nobody can see the improvement. The notion that Nature does not proceed by jumps is only one of the budget of plausible lies that we call classical education. Nature always proceeds by jumps. She may spend twenty thousand years making up her mind to jump; but when she makes it up at last, the jump is big enough to take us into a new age.

LUBIN [*impressed*] Fancy my being leader of the party for the next three hundred years!

BURGE. What!!

LUBIN. Perhaps hard on some of the younger men. I think in fairness I shall have to step aside to make room after another century or so: that is, if Mimi can be persuaded to give up Downing Street.

BURGE. This is too much. Your colossal conceit blinds you to the most obvious necessity of the political situation.

LUBIN. You mean my retirement. I really cannot see that it is a necessity. I could not see it when I was almost an old man – or at least an elderly one. Now that it appears that I am a young man, the case for it breaks down completely. [*To Conrad*] May I ask are there any alternative theories? Is there a scientific Opposition?

CONRAD. Well, some authorities hold that the human race is a failure, and that a new form of life, better adapted to high civilization, will supersede us as we have superseded the ape and the elephant.

BURGE. The superman: eh!

CONRAD. No. Some being quite different from us.

LUBIN. Is that altogether desirable?

FRANKLYN. I fear so. However that may be, we may be quite sure of one thing. We shall not be let alone. The force behind evolution, call it what you will, is determined to solve the problem of civilization; and if it cannot do it through us, it will produce some more capable agents. Man is not God's last word: God can still create. If you cannot do His work He will produce some being who can.

BURGE [*with zealous reverence*] What do we know about Him, Barnabas? What does anyone know about Him?

CONRAD. We know this about Him with absolute certainty. The power my brother calls God proceeds by the method of Trial and Error; and if we turn out to be one of the errors, we shall go the way of the mastodon and the megatherium and all the other scrapped experiments.

LUBIN [*rising and beginning to walk up and down the room with his considering cap on*] I admit that I am impressed, gentlemen.

I will go so far as to say that your theory is likely to prove more interesting than ever Welsh Disestablishment was. But as a practical politician – hm! Eh, Burge?

CONRAD. We are not practical politicians. We are out to get something done. Practical politicians are people who have mastered the art of using parliament to prevent anything being done.

FRANKLYN. When we get matured statesmen and citizens –

LUBIN [stopping short] Citizens! Oh! Are the citizens to live three hundred years as well as the statesmen?

CONRAD. Of course.

LUBIN. I confess that had not occurred to me [he sits down abruptly, evidently very unfavorably affected by this new light].

Savvy and Haslam look at one another with unspeakable feelings.

BURGE. Do you think it would be wise to go quite so far at first? Surely it would be more prudent to begin with the best men.

FRANKLYN. You need not be anxious about that. It will begin with the best men.

LUBIN. I am glad to hear you say so. You see, we must put this into a practical parliamentary shape.

BURGE. We shall have to draft a Bill: that is the long and the short of it. Until you have your Bill drafted you dont know what you are really doing: that is my experience.

LUBIN. Quite so. My idea is that whilst we should interest the electorate in this as a sort of religious aspiration and personal hope, using it at the same time to remove their prejudices against those of us who are getting on in years, it would be in the last degree upsetting and even dangerous to enable everyone to live longer than usual. Take the mere question of the manufacture of the specific, whatever it may be! There are forty millions of people in the country. Let me assume for the sake of illustration that each person would have to consume, say, five ounces a day of the elixir. That would be – let me see – five times three hundred and sixty-five is – um – twenty-five – thirty-two – eighteen – eighteen hundred and twenty-five ounces a year: just two ounces over the hundredweight.

BURGE. Two million tons a year, in round numbers, of stuff that everyone would clamor for: that men would trample down women and children in the streets to get at. You couldnt produce it. There would be blue murder. It's out of the question. We must keep the actual secret to ourselves.

CONRAD [*staring at them*] The actual secret! What on earth is the man talking about?

BURGE. The stuff. The powder. The bottle. The tabloid. Whatever it is. You said it wasnt lemons.

CONRAD. My good sir: I have no powder, no bottle, no tabloid. I am not a quack: I am a biologist. This is a thing thats going to happen.

LUBIN [*completely let down*] Going to happen! Oh! Is that all? [*He looks at his watch*].

BURGE. Going to happen! What do you mean? Do you mean that you cant make it happen?

CONRAD. No more than I could have made you happen.

FRANKLYN. We can put it into men's heads that there is nothing to prevent its happening but their own will to die before their work is done, and their own ignorance of the splendid work there is for them to do.

CONRAD. Spread that knowledge and that conviction; and as surely as the sun will rise tomorrow, the thing will happen.

FRANKLYN. We dont know where or when or to whom it will happen. It may happen first to someone in this room.

HASLAM. It wont happen to me: thats jolly sure.

CONRAD. It might happen to anyone. It might happen to the parlor maid. How do we know?

SAVVY. The parlor maid! Oh, thats nonsense, Nunk.

LUBIN [*once more quite comfortable*] I think Miss Savvy has delivered the final verdict.

BURGE. Do you mean to say that you have nothing more practical to offer than the mere wish to live longer? Why, if people could live by merely wishing to, we should all be living for ever already! Everybody would like to live for ever. Why dont they?

CONRAD. Pshaw! Everybody would like to have a million of money. Why havnt they? Because the men who would like to be millionaires wont save sixpence even with the chance of starvation staring them in the face. The men who want to live for ever wont cut off a glass of beer or a pipe of tobacco, though they believe the teetotallers and non-smokers live longer. That sort of liking is not willing. See what they do when they know they must.

FRANKLYN. Do not mistake mere idle fancies for the tremendous miracle-working force of Will nerved to creation by a conviction of Necessity. I tell you men capable of such willing, and realizing its necessity, will do it reluctantly, under inner compulsion, as all great efforts are made. They will hide what they are doing from themselves: they will take care not to know what they are doing. They will live three hundred years, not because they would like to, but because the soul deep down in them will know that they must, if the world is to be saved.

LUBIN [*turning to Franklyn and patting him almost paternally*] Well, my dear Barnabas, for the last thirty years the post has brought me at least once a week a plan from some crank or other for the establishment of the millennium. I think you are the maddest of all the cranks; but you are much the most interesting. I am conscious of a very curious mixture of relief and disappointment in finding that your plan is all moonshine, and that you have nothing practical to offer us. But what a pity! It is such a fascinating idea! I think you are too hard on us practical men; but there are men in every Government, even on the Front Bench, who deserve all you say. And now, before dropping the subject, may I put just one question to you? An idle question, since nothing can come of it; but still –

FRANKLYN. Ask your question.

LUBIN. Why do you fix three hundred years as the exact figure?

FRANKLYN. Because we must fix some figure. Less would not be enough; and more would be more than we dare as yet face.

LUBIN. Pooh! I am quite prepared to face three thousand, not to say three million.

CONRAD. Yes, because you dont believe you will be called on to make good your word.

FRANKLYN [*gently*] Also, perhaps, because you have never been troubled much by vision of the future.

BURGE [*with intense conviction*] The future does not exist for Henry Hopkins Lubin.

LUBIN. If by the future you mean the millennial delusions which you use as a bunch of carrots to lure the uneducated British donkey to the polling booth to vote for you, it certainly does not.

BURGE. I can see the future not only because, if I may say so in all humility, I have been gifted with a certain power of spiritual vision, but because I have practised as a solicitor. A solicitor has to advise families. He has to think of the future and know the past. His office is the real modern confessional. Among other things he has to make people's wills for them. He has to shew them how to provide for their daughters after their deaths. Has it occurred to you, Lubin, that if you live three hundred years, your daughters will have to wait a devilish long time for their money?

FRANKLYN. The money may not wait for them. Few investments flourish for three hundred years.

SAVVY. And what about before your death? Suppose they didnt get married! Imagine a girl living at home with her mother and on her father for three hundred years! Theyd murder her if she didnt murder them first.

LUBIN. By the way, Barnabas, is your daughter to keep her good looks all the time?

FRANKLYN. Will it matter? Can you conceive the most hardened flirt going on flirting for three centuries? At the end of half the time we shall hardly notice whether it is a woman or a man we are speaking to.

LUBIN [*not quite relishing this ascetic prospect*] Hm! [*He rises*]. Ah, well: you must come and tell my wife and my young people all about it; and you will bring your daughter with you, of course. [*He shakes hands with Savvy*]. Goodbye. [*He shakes hands with Franklyn*]. Goodbye, Doctor. [*He shakes hands with Conrad*]. Come on, Burge: you must really tell me what line you are going to take about the Church at the election?

BURGE. Havnt you heard? Havnt you taken in the revelation that has been vouchsafed to us? The line I am going to take is Back to Methuselah.

LUBIN [*decisively*] Dont be ridiculous, Burge. You dont suppose, do you, that our friends here are in earnest, or that our very pleasant conversation has had anything to do with practical politics! They have just been pulling our legs very wittily. Come along. [*He goes out, Franklyn politely going with him, but shaking his head in mute protest*].

BURGE [*shaking Conrad's hand*] It's beyond the old man, Doctor. No spiritual side to him: only a sort of classical side that goes down with his own set. Besides, he's done, gone, past, burnt out, burst up; thinks he is our leader and is only our rag and bottle department. But you may depend on me. I will work this stunt of yours in. I see its value. [*He begins moving towards the door with Conrad*]. Of course I cant put it exactly in your way; but you are quite right about our needing something fresh; and I believe an election can be fought on the death rate and on Adam and Eve as scientific facts. It will take the Opposition right out of its depth. And if we win there will be an O.M. for somebody when the first honors list comes round [*by this time he has talked himself out of the room and out of earshot, Conrad accompanying him*].

Savvy and Haslam, left alone, seize each other in ecstasy of amusement, and jazz to the settee, where they sit down again side by side.

HASLAM [*caressing her*] Darling! what a priceless humbug old Lubin is!

SAVVY. Oh, sweet old thing! I love him. Burge is a flaming fraud if you like.

HASLAM. Did you notice one thing? It struck me as rather curious.

SAVVY. What?

HASLAM. Lubin and your father have both survived the war. But their sons were killed in it.

SAVVY [*sobered*] Yes. Jim's death killed mother.

HASLAM. And they never said a word about it!

SAVVY. Well, why should they? The subject didnt come up. *I* forgot about it too; and I was very fond of Jim.

HASLAM. *I* didnt forget it, because I'm of military age; and if I hadnt been a parson I'd have had to go out and be killed too. To me the awful thing about their political incompetence was that they had to kill their own sons. It was the war casualty lists and the starvation afterwards that finished me up with politics and the Church and everything else except you.

SAVVY. Oh, I was just as bad as any of them. I sold flags in the streets in my best clothes; and – hsh! [*she jumps up and pretends to be looking for a book on the shelves behind the settee*]. *Franklyn and Conrad return, looking weary and glum.*

CONRAD. Well, thats how the gospel of the brothers Barnabas is going to be received! [*He drops into Burge's chair*].

FRANKLYN [*going back to his seat at the table*] It's no use. Were you convinced, Mr Haslam?

HASLAM. About our being able to live three hundred years? Frankly no.

CONRAD [*to Savvy*] Nor you, I suppose?

SAVVY. Oh, I dont know. I thought I was for a moment. I can believe, in a sort of way, that people might live for three hundred years. But when you came down to tin tacks, and said that the parlor maid might, then I saw how absurd it was.

FRANKLYN. Just so. We had better hold our tongues about it, Con. We should only be laughed at, and lose the little credit we earned on false pretences in the days of our ignorance.

CONRAD. I daresay. But Creative Evolution doesnt stop while people are laughing. Laughing may even lubricate its job.

SAVVY. What does that mean?

CONRAD. It means that the first man to live three hundred years maynt have the slightest notion that he is going to do it, and may be the loudest laugher of the lot.

SAVVY. Or the first woman?

CONRAD [*assenting*] Or the first woman.

HASLAM. Well, it wont be one of us, anyhow.

FRANKLYN. How do you know?

This is unanswerable. None of them have anything more to say.

PART III

The Thing Happens

A summer afternoon in the year 2170 A.D. The official parlor of the President of the British Islands. A board table, long enough for three chairs at each side besides the presidential chair at the head and an ordinary chair at the foot, occupies the breadth of the room. On the table, opposite every chair, a small switchboard with a dial. There is no fireplace. The end wall is a silvery screen nearly as large as a pair of folding doors. The door is on your left as you face the screen; and there is a row of thick pegs, padded and covered with velvet, beside it.

A stoutish middle-aged man, good-looking and breezily genial, dressed in a silk smock, stockings, handsomely ornamented sandals, and a gold fillet round his brows, comes in. He is like Joyce Burge, yet also like Lubin, as if Nature had made a composite photograph of the two men. He takes off the fillet and hangs it on a peg; then sits down in the presidential chair at the head of the table, which is at the end farthest from the door. He puts a peg into his switchboard; turns the pointer on the dial; puts another peg in; and presses a button. Immediately the silvery screen vanishes; and in its place appears, in reverse from right to left, another office similarly furnished, with a thin, unamiable man similarly dressed, but in duller colors, turning over some documents at the table. His gold fillet is hanging up on a similar peg beside the door. He is rather like Conrad Barnabas, but younger, and much more commonplace.

BURGE-LUBIN. Hallo, Barnabas!

BARNABAS [*without looking round*] What number?

BURGE-LUBIN. Five double x three two gamma. Burge-Lubin.

Barnabas puts a plug in number five; turns his pointer to double x; and another plug in 32; presses a button and looks round at Burge-Lubin, who is now visible to him as well as audible.

BARNABAS [*curtly*] Oh! That you, President?

BURGE-LUBIN. Yes. They told me you wanted me to ring you up. Anything wrong?

BARNABAS [*harsh and querulous*] I wish to make a protest.

BURGE-LUBIN [*good-humored and mocking*] What! Another protest! Whats wrong now?

BARNABAS. If you only knew all the protests I havnt made, you would be surprised at my patience. It is you who are always treating me with the grossest want of consideration.

BURGE-LUBIN. What have I done now?

BARNABAS. You have put me down to go to the Record Office today to receive that American fellow, and do the honors of a ridiculous cinema show. That is not the business of the Accountant General: it is the business of the President. It is an outrageous waste of my time, and an unjustifiable shirking of your duty at my expense. I refuse to go. You must go.

BURGE-LUBIN. My dear boy, nothing would give me greater pleasure than to take the job off your hands –

BARNABAS. Then do it. Thats all I want [*he is about to switch off*].

BURGE-LUBIN. Dont switch off. Listen. This American has invented a method of breathing under water.

BARNABAS. What do I care? I dont want to breathe under water.

BURGE-LUBIN. You may, my dear Barnabas, at any time. You know you never look where you are going when you are immersed in your calculations. Some day you will walk into the Serpentine. This man's invention may save your life.

BARNABAS [*angrily*] Will you tell me what that has to do with your putting your ceremonial duties on to my shoulders? I will not be trifled [*he vanishes and is replaced by the blank screen*] –

BURGE-LUBIN [*indignantly holding down his button*] Dont cut us off, please: we have not finished. I am the President, speaking to the Accountant General. What are you dreaming of?

A WOMAN'S VOICE. Sorry. [*The screen shews Barnabas as before*].

BURGE-LUBIN. Since you take it that way, I will go in your place. It's a pity, because, you see, this American thinks you are the greatest living authority on the duration of human life; and –

BARNABAS [*interrupting*] The American thinks! What do you mean? I am the greatest living authority on the duration of human life. Who dares dispute it?

BURGE-LUBIN. Nobody, dear lad, nobody. Dont fly out at me. It is evident that you have not read the American's book.

BARNABAS. Dont tell me that you have, or that you have read any book except a novel for the last twenty years; for I wont believe you.

BURGE-LUBIN. Quite right, dear old fellow: I havnt read it. But I have read what The Times Literary Supplement says about it.

BARNABAS. I dont care two straws what it says about it. Does it say anything about me?

BURGE-LUBIN. Yes.

BARNABAS. Oh, does it? What?

BURGE-LUBIN. It points out that an extraordinary number of first-rate persons like you and me have died by drowning during the last two centuries, and that when this invention of breathing under water takes effect, your estimate of the average duration of human life will be upset.

BARNABAS [*alarmed*] Upset my estimate! Gracious Heavens! Does the fool realize what that means? Do you realize what that means?

BURGE-LUBIN. I suppose it means that we shall have to amend the Act.

BARNABAS. Amend my Act! Monstrous!

BURGE-LUBIN. But we must. We cant ask people to go on working until they are forty-three unless our figures are unchallengeable. You know what a row there was over those last three years, and how nearly the too-old-at-forty people won.

BARNABAS. They would have made the British Islands bankrupt if theyd won. But you dont care for that; you care for nothing but being popular.

BURGE-LUBIN. Oh, well: I shouldnt worry if I were you;

for most people complain that there is not enough work for them, and would be only too glad to stick on instead of retiring at forty-three, if only they were asked as a favor instead of having to.

BARNABAS. Thank you: I need no consolation. [*He rises determinedly and puts on his fillet*].

BURGE-LUBIN. Are you off? Where are you going to?

BARNABAS. To that cinema tomfoolery, of course. I shall put this American impostor in his place. [*He goes out*].

BURGE-LUBIN [*calling after him*] God bless you, dear old chap! [*With a chuckle, he switches off; and the screen becomes blank. He presses a button and holds it down while he calls*] Hallo!

A WOMAN'S VOICE. Hallo!

BURGE-LUBIN [*formally*] The President respectfully solicits the privilege of an interview with the Chief Secretary, and holds himself entirely at his honor's august disposal.

A CHINESE VOICE. He is coming.

BURGE-LUBIN. Oh! That you, Confucius? So good of you. Come along [*he releases the button*].

A man in a yellow gown, presenting the general appearance of a Chinese sage, enters.

BURGE-LUBIN [*jocularly*] Well, illustrious Sage-&-Onions, how are your poor sore feet?

CONFUCIUS [*gravely*] I thank you for your kind inquiries. I am well.

BURGE-LUBIN. Thats right. Sit down and make yourself comfortable. Any business for me today?

CONFUCIUS [*sitting down on the first chair round the corner of the table to the President's right*] None.

BURGE-LUBIN. Have you heard the result of the bye-election?

CONFUCIUS. A walk-over. Only one candidate.

BURGE-LUBIN. Any good?

CONFUCIUS. He was released from the County Lunatic Asylum a fortnight ago. Not mad enough for the lethal chamber: not sane enough for any place but the division lobby. A very popular speaker.

BURGE-LUBIN. I wish the people would take a serious interest in politics.

CONFUCIUS. I do not agree. The Englishman is not fitted by nature to understand politics. Ever since the public services have been manned by Chinese, the country has been well and honestly governed. What more is needed?

BURGE-LUBIN. What I cant make out is that China is one of the worst governed countries on earth.

CONFUCIUS. No. It was badly governed twenty years ago; but since we forbade any Chinaman to take part in our public services, and imported natives of Scotland for that purpose, we have done well. Your information here is always twenty years out of date.

BURGE-LUBIN. People dont seem to be able to govern themselves. I cant understand it. Why should it be so?

CONFUCIUS. Justice is impartiality. Only strangers are impartial.

BURGE-LUBIN. It ends in the public services being so good that the Government has nothing to do but think.

CONFUCIUS. Were it otherwise, the Government would have too much to do to think.

BURGE-LUBIN. Is that any excuse for the English people electing a parliament of lunatics?

CONFUCIUS. The English people always did elect parliaments of lunatics. What does it matter if your permanent officials are honest and competent?

BURGE-LUBIN. You do not know the history of this country. What would my ancestors have said to the menagerie of degenerates that is still called the House of Commons? Confucius: you will not believe me; and I do not blame you for it; but England once saved the liberties of the world by inventing parliamentary government, which was her peculiar and supreme glory.

CONFUCIUS. I know the history of your country perfectly well. It proves the exact contrary.

BURGE-LUBIN. How do you make that out?

CONFUCIUS. The only power your parliament ever had was the power of withholding supplies from the king.

BURGE-LUBIN. Precisely. That great Englishman Simon de Montfort —

CONFUCIUS. He was not an Englishman: he was a Frenchman. He imported parliaments from France.

BURGE-LUBIN [*surprised*] You dont say so!

CONFUCIUS. The king and his loyal subjects killed Simon for forcing his French parliament on them. The first thing British parliaments always did was to grant supplies to the king for life with enthusiastic expressions of loyalty, lest they should have any real power, and be expected to do something.

BURGE-LUBIN. Look here, Confucius: you know more history than I do, of course; but democracy —

CONFUCIUS. An institution peculiar to China. And it was never really a success there.

BURGE-LUBIN. But the Habeas Corpus Act!

CONFUCIUS. The English always suspended it when it threatened to be of the slightest use.

BURGE-LUBIN. Well, trial by jury: you cant deny that we established that?

CONFUCIUS. All cases that were dangerous to the governing classes were tried in the Star Chamber or by Court Martial, except when the prisoner was not tried at all, but executed after calling him names enough to make him unpopular.

BURGE-LUBIN. Oh, bother! You may be right in these little details; but in the large we have managed to hold our own as a great race. Well, people who could do nothing couldnt have done that, you know.

CONFUCIUS. I did not say you could do nothing. You could fight. You could eat. You could drink. Until the twentieth century you could produce children. You could play games. You could work when you were forced to. But you could not govern yourselves.

BURGE-LUBIN. Then how did we get our reputation as the pioneers of liberty?

CONFUCIUS. By your steadfast refusal to be governed at all. A horse that kicks everyone who tries to harness and guide him may be a pioneer of liberty; but he is not a pioneer of government. In China he would be shot.

BURGE-LUBIN. Stuff! Do you imply that the administration of which I am president is no Government?

CONFUCIUS. I do. *I* am the Government.

BURGE-LUBIN. You! You!! You fat yellow lump of conceit!

CONFUCIUS. Only an Englishman could be so ignorant of the nature of government as to suppose that a capable statesman cannot be fat, yellow, and conceited. Many Englishmen are slim, red-nosed, and modest. Put them in my place, and within a year you will be back in the anarchy and chaos of the nineteenth and twentieth centuries.

BURGE-LUBIN. Oh, if you go back to the dark ages, I have nothing more to say. But we did not perish. We extricated ourselves from that chaos. We are now the best governed country in the world. How did we manage that if we are such fools as you pretend?

CONFUCIUS. You did not do it until the slaughter and ruin produced by your anarchy forced you at last to recognize two inexorable facts. First, that government is absolutely necessary to civilization, and that you could not maintain civilization by merely doing down your neighbor, as you called it, and cutting off the head of your king whenever he happened to be a logical Scot and tried to take his position seriously. Second, that government is an art of which you are congenitally incapable. Accordingly, you imported educated negresses and Chinese to govern you. Since then you have done very well.

BURGE-LUBIN. So have you, you old humbug. All the same, I dont know how you stand the work you do. You seem to me positively to like public business. Why wont you let me take you down to the coast some week-end and teach you marine golf?

CONFUCIUS. It does not interest me. I am not a barbarian.

BURGE-LUBIN. You mean that I am?

CONFUCIUS. That is evident.

BURGE-LUBIN. How?

T–F

CONFUCIUS. People like you. They like cheerful good-natured barbarians. They have elected you President five times in succession. They will elect you five times more. I like you. You are better company than a dog or a horse because you can speak.

BURGE-LUBIN. Am I a barbarian because you like me?

CONFUCIUS. Surely. Nobody likes me: I am held in awe. Capable persons are never liked. I am not likeable; but I am indispensable.

BURGE-LUBIN. Oh, cheer up, old man: theres nothing so disagreeable about you as all that. I dont dislike you; and if you think I'm afraid of you, you jolly well dont know Burge-Lubin: thats all.

CONFUCIUS. You are brave: yes. It is a form of stupidity.

BURGE-LUBIN. You may not be brave: one doesnt expect it from a Chink. But you have the devil's own cheek.

CONFUCIUS. I have the assured certainty of the man who sees and knows. Your genial bluster, your cheery self-confidence, are pleasant, like the open air. But they are blind: they are vain. I seem to see a great dog wag his tail and bark joyously. But if he leaves my heel he is lost.

BURGE-LUBIN. Thank you for a handsome compliment. I have a big dog; and he is the best fellow I know. If you knew how much uglier you are than a chow, you wouldnt start those comparisons, though. [*Rising*] Well, if you have nothing for me to do, I am going to leave your heel for the rest of the day and enjoy myself. What would you recommend me to do with myself?

CONFUCIUS. Give yourself up to contemplation; and great thoughts will come to you.

BURGE-LUBIN. Will they? If you think I am going to sit here on a fine day like this with my legs crossed waiting for great thoughts, you exaggerate my taste for them. I prefer marine golf. [*Stopping short*] Oh, by the way, I forgot something. I have a word or two to say to the Minister of health. [*He goes back to his chair*].

CONFUCIUS. Her number is –

BURGE-LUBIN. I know it.

CONFUCIUS [*rising*] I cannot understand her attraction for you. For me a woman who is not yellow does not exist, save as an official. [*He goes out*].

Burge-Lubin operates his switchboard as before. The screen vanishes; and a dainty room with a bed, a wardrobe, and a dressing-table with a mirror and a switch on it, appears. Seated at it a handsome negress is trying on a brilliant head scarf. Her dressing-gown is thrown back from her shoulders to her chair. She is in corset, knickers, and silk stockings.

BURGE-LUBIN [*horrified*] I beg your pardon a thousand times – [*The startled negress snatches the peg out of her switch-board and vanishes*].

THE NEGRESS'S VOICE. Who is it?

BURGE-LUBIN. Me. The President. Burge-Lubin. I had no idea your bedroom switch was in. I beg your pardon.

The negress reappears. She has pulled the dressing-gown per-functorily over her shoulders, and continues her experiments with the scarf, not at all put out, and rather amused by Burge's prudery.

THE NEGRESS. Stupid of me. I was talking to another lady this morning; and I left the peg in.

BURGE-LUBIN. But I am so sorry.

THE NEGRESS [*sunnily: still busy with the scarf*] Why? It was my fault.

BURGE-LUBIN [*embarrassed*] Well – er – But I suppose you were used to it in Africa.

THE NEGRESS. Your delicacy is very touching, Mr President. It would be funny if it were not so unpleasant, because, like all white delicacy, it is in the wrong place. How do you think this suits my complexion?

BURGE-LUBIN. How can any really vivid color go wrong with a black satin skin? It is our women's wretched pale faces that have to be matched and lighted. Yours is always right.

THE NEGRESS. Yes: it is a pity your white beauties have all the same ashy faces, the same colorless drab, the same age. But look at their beautiful noses and little lips! They are physically insipid: they have no beauty: you cannot love them; but how elegant!

BURGE-LUBIN. Cant you find an official pretext for coming to see me? Isnt it ridiculous that we have never met? It's so tantalizing to see you and talk to you, and to know all the time that you are two hundred miles away, and that I cant touch you?

THE NEGRESS. I cannot live on the East Coast: it is hard enough to keep my blood warm here. Besides, my friend, it would not be safe. These distant flirtations are very charming; and they teach self-control.

BURGE-LUBIN. Damn self-control! I want to hold you in my arms – to – [*the negress snatches out the peg from the switchboard and vanishes. She is still heard laughing*]. Black devil! [*He snatches out his peg furiously: her laugh is no longer heard*]. Oh, these sex episodes! Why can I not resist them? Disgraceful!

Confucius returns.

CONFUCIUS. I forgot. There is something for you to do this morning. You have to go to the Record Office to receive the American barbarian.

BURGE-LUBIN. Confucius: once for all, I object to this Chinese habit of describing white men as barbarians.

CONFUCIUS [*standing formally at the end of the table with his hands palm to palm*] I make a mental note that you do not wish the Americans to be described as barbarians.

BURGE-LUBIN. Not at all. The Americans are barbarians. But we are not. I suppose the particular barbarian you are speaking of is the American who has invented a means of breathing under water.

CONFUCIUS. He says he has invented such a method. For some reason which is not intelligible in China, Englishmen always believe any statement made by an American inventor, especially one who has never invented anything. Therefore you believe this person and have given him a public reception. Today the Record Office is entertaining him with a display of the cinematographic records of all the eminent Englishmen who have lost their lives by drowning since the cinema was invented. Why not go to see it if you are at a loss for something to do?

BURGE-LUBIN. What earthly interest is there in looking at a moving picture of a lot of people merely because they were drowned? If they had had any sense, they would not have been drowned, probably.

CONFUCIUS. That is not so. It has never been noticed before; but the Record Office has just made two remarkable discoveries about the public men and women who have displayed extraordinary ability during the past century. One is that they retained unusual youthfulness up to an advanced age. The other is that they all met their death by drowning.

BURGE-LUBIN. Yes: I know. Can you explain it?

CONFUCIUS. It cannot be explained. It is not reasonable. Therefore I do not believe it.

The Accountant General rushes in, looking ghastly. He staggers to the middle of the table.

BURGE-LUBIN. Whats the matter? Are you ill?

BARNABAS [*choking*] No. I – [*he collapses into the middle chair*]. I must speak to you in private.

Confucius calmly withdraws.

BURGE-LUBIN. What on earth is it? Have some oxygen.

BARNABAS. I have had some. Go to the Record Office. You will see men fainting there again and again, and being revived with oxygen, as I have been. They have seen with their own eyes as I have.

BURGE-LUBIN. Seen what?

BARNABAS. Seen the Archbishop of York.

BURGE-LUBIN. Well, why shouldnt they see the Archbishop of York? What are they fainting for? Has he been murdered?

BARNABAS. No: he has been drowned.

BURGE-LUBIN. Good God! Where? When? How? Poor fellow!

BARNABAS. Poor fellow! Poor thief! Poor swindler! Poor robber of his country's Exchequer! Poor fellow indeed! Wait til I catch him.

BURGE-LUBIN. How can you catch him when he is dead? Youre mad.

BARNABAS. Dead! Who said he was dead?

BURGE-LUBIN. You did. Drowned.

BARNABAS [*exasperated*] Will you listen to me? Was old Archbishop Haslam, the present man's last predecessor but four, drowned or not?

BURGE-LUBIN. I dont know. Look him up in the Encyclopedia Britannica.

BARNABAS. Yah! Was Archbishop Stickit, who wrote Stickit on the Psalms, drowned or not?

BURGE-LUBIN. Yes, mercifully. He deserved it.

BARNABAS. Was President Dickenson drowned? Was General Bullyboy drowned?

BURGE-LUBIN. Who is denying it?

BARNABAS. Well, weve had moving pictures of all four put on the screen today for this American; and they and the Archbishop are the same man. Now tell me I am mad.

BURGE-LUBIN. I do tell you you are mad. Stark raving mad.

BARNABAS. Am I to believe my own eyes or am I not?

BURGE-LUBIN. You can do as you please. All I can tell you is that *I* dont believe your eyes if they cant see any difference between a live archbishop and two dead ones. [*The apparatus rings, he holds the button down*]. Yes?

THE WOMAN'S VOICE. The Archbishop of York, to see the President.

BARNABAS [*hoarse with rage*] Have him in. I'll talk to the scoundrel.

BURGE-LUBIN [*releasing the button*] Not while you are in this state.

BARNABAS [*reaching furiously for his button and holding it down*] Send the Archbishop in at once.

BURGE-LUBIN. If you lose your temper, Barnabas, remember that we shall be two to one.

The Archbishop enters. He has a white band round his throat, set in a black stock. He wears a sort of kilt of black ribbons, and soft black boots that button high up on his calves. His costume does not differ otherwise from that of the President and the Accountant General; but its color scheme is black and white. He is older than the Reverend Bill Haslam was when he wooed Miss Savvy

Barnabas; but he is recognizably the same man. He does not look a day over fifty, and is very well preserved even at that; but his boyishness of manner is quite gone: he now has complete authority and self-possession: in fact the President is a little afraid of him; and it seems quite natural and inevitable that he should speak first.

THE ARCHBISHOP. Good day, Mr President.

BURGE-LUBIN. Good day, Mr Archbishop. Be seated.

THE ARCHBISHOP [*sitting down between them*] Good day, Mr Accountant General.

BARNABAS [*malevolently*] Good day to you. I have a question to put to you, if you dont mind.

THE ARCHBISHOP [*looking curiously at him, jarred by his uncivil tone*] Certainly. What is it?

BARNABAS. What is your definition of a thief?

THE ARCHBISHOP. Rather an old-fashioned word, is it not?

BARNABAS. It survives officially in my department.

THE ARCHBISHOP. Our departments are full of survivals. Look at my tie! my apron! my boots! They are all mere survivals; yet it seems that without them I cannot be a proper Archbishop.

BARNABAS. Indeed! Well, in my department the word thief survives, because in the community the thing thief survives. And a very despicable and dishonorable thing he is, too.

THE ARCHBISHOP [*coolly*] I daresay.

BARNABAS. In my department, sir, a thief is a person who lives longer than the statutory expectation of life entitles him to, and goes on drawing public money when, if he were an honest man, he would be dead.

THE ARCHBISHOP. Then let me say, sir, that your department does not understand its own business. If you have miscalculated the duration of human life, that is not the fault of the persons whose longevity you have miscalculated. And if they continue to work and produce, they pay their way, even if they live two or three centuries.

BARNABAS. I know nothing about their working and producing. That is not the business of my department. I am concerned with their expectation of life; and I say that no

man has any right to go on living and drawing money
when he ought to be dead.

THE ARCHBISHOP. You do not comprehend the relation
between income and production.

BARNABAS. I understand my own department.

THE ARCHBISHOP. That is not enough. Your department
is part of a synthesis which embraces all the departments.

BURGE-LUBIN. Synthesis! This is an intellectual difficulty.
This is a job for Confucius. I heard him use that very word
the other day; and I wondered what the devil he meant.
[*Switching on*] Hallo! Put me through to the Chief
Secretary.

CONFUCIUS'S VOICE. You are speaking to him.

BURGE-LUBIN. An intellectual difficulty, old man. Something we dont understand. Come and help us out.

THE ARCHBISHOP. May I ask how the question has arisen?

BARNABAS. Ah! You begin to smell a rat, do you? You
thought yourself pretty safe. You –

BURGE-LUBIN. Steady, Barnabas. Dont be in a hurry.
    Confucius enters.

THE ARCHBISHOP [*rising*] Good morning, Mr Chief Secretary.

BURGE-LUBIN [*rising in instinctive imitation of the Archbishop*]
Honor us by taking a seat, O sage.

CONFUCIUS. Ceremony is needless. [*He bows to the company,
and takes the chair at the foot of the table*].
    The President and the Archbishop resume their seats.

BURGE-LUBIN. We wish to put a case to you, Confucius.
Suppose a man, instead of conforming to the official
estimate of his expectation of life, were to live for more
than two centuries and a half, would the Accountant
General be justified in calling him a thief?

CONFUCIUS. No. He would be justified in calling him a liar.

THE ARCHBISHOP. I think not, Mr Chief Secretary. What
do you suppose my age is?

CONFUCIUS. Fifty.

BURGE-LUBIN. You dont look it. Forty-five; and young for
your age.

THE ARCHBISHOP. My age is two hundred and eighty-three.

BARNABAS [*morosely triumphant*] Hmp! Mad, am I?

BURGE-LUBIN. Youre both mad. Excuse me, Archbishop; but this is getting a bit – well –

THE ARCHBISHOP [*to Confucius*] Mr Chief Secretary: will you, to oblige me, assume that I have lived nearly three centuries? As a hypothesis?

BURGE-LUBIN. What is a hypothesis?

CONFUCIUS. It does not matter. I understand. [*To the Archbishop*] Am I to assume that you have lived in your ancestors, or by metempsychosis –

BURGE-LUBIN. Met – Emp – Sy – Good Lord! What a brain, Confucius! What a brain!

THE ARCHBISHOP. Nothing of that kind. Assume in the ordinary sense that I was born in the year 1887, and that I have worked continuously in one profession or another since the year 1910. Am I a thief?

CONFUCIUS. I do not know. Was that one of your professions?

THE ARCHBISHOP. No. I have been nothing worse than an Archbishop, a President, and a General.

BARNABAS. Has he or has he not robbed the Exchequer by drawing five or six incomes when he was only entitled to one? Answer me that.

CONFUCIUS. Certainly not. The hypothesis is that he has worked continuously since 1910. We are now in the year 2170. What is the official lifetime?

BARNABAS. Seventy-eight. Of course it's an average; and we dont mind a man here and there going on to ninety, or even, as a curiosity, becoming a centenarian. But I say that a man who goes beyond that is a swindler.

CONFUCIUS. Seventy-eight into two hundred and eighty-three goes more than three and a half times. Your department owes the Archbishop two and a half educations and three and a half retiring pensions.

BARNABAS. Stuff! How can that be?

CONFUCIUS. At what age do your people begin to work for the community?

BURGE-LUBIN. Three. They do certain things every day when they are three. Just to break them in, you know. But they become self-supporting, or nearly so, at thirteen.

CONFUCIUS. And at what age do they retire?

BARNABAS. Forty-three.

CONFUCIUS. That is, they do thirty years' work; and they receive maintenance and education, without working, for thirteen years of childhood and thirty-five years of superannuation, forty-eight years in all, for each thirty years' work. The Archbishop has given you 260 years' work, and has received only one education and no superannuation. You therefore owe him over 300 years of leisure and nearly eight educations. You are thus heavily in his debt. In other words, he has effected an enormous national economy by living so long; and you, by living only seventy-eight years, are profiting at his expense. He is the benefactor: you are the thief. [*Half rising*] May I now withdraw and return to my serious business, as my own span is comparatively short?

BURGE-LUBIN. Dont be in a hurry, old chap. [*Confucius sits down again*]. This hypothecary, or whatever you call it, is put up seriously. I dont believe it; but if the Archbishop and the Accountant General are going to insist that it's true, we shall have either to lock them up or to see the thing through.

BARNABAS. It's no use trying these Chinese subtleties on me. I'm a plain man; and though I dont understand metaphysics, and dont believe in them, I understand figures; and if the Archbishop is only entitled to seventy-eight years, and he takes 283, I say he takes more than he is entitled to. Get over that if you can.

THE ARCHBISHOP. I have not taken 283 years: I have taken 23 and given 260.

CONFUCIUS. Do your accounts shew a deficiency or a surplus?

BARNABAS. A surplus. Thats what I cant make out. Thats the artfulness of these people.

BURGE-LUBIN. That settles it. Whats the use of arguing? The Chink says you are wrong; and theres an end of it.

BARNABAS. I say nothing against the Chink's arguments. But what about my facts?

CONFUCIUS. If your facts include a case of a man living 283 years, I advise you to take a few weeks at the seaside.

BARNABAS. Let there be an end of this hinting that I am out of my mind. Come and look at the cinema record. I tell you this man is Archbishop Haslam, Archbishop Stickit, President Dickenson, General Bullyboy and himself into the bargain; all five of them.

THE ARCHBISHOP. I do not deny it. I never have denied it. Nobody has ever asked me.

BURGE-LUBIN. But damn it, man – I beg your pardon, Archbishop; but really, really –

THE ARCHBISHOP. Dont mention it. What were you going to say?

BURGE-LUBIN. Well, you were drowned four times over. You are not a cat, you know.

THE ARCHBISHOP. That is very easy to understand. Consider my situation when I first made the amazing discovery that I was destined to live three hundred years! I –

CONFUCIUS [interrupting him] Pardon me. Such a discovery was impossible. You have not made it yet. You may live a million years if you have already lived two hundred. There is no question of three hundred years. You have made a slip at the very beginning of your fairy tale, Mr Archbishop.

BURGE-LUBIN. Good, Confucius! [To the Archbishop] He has you there. I dont see how you can get over that.

THE ARCHBISHOP. Yes: it is quite a good point. But if the Accountant General will go to the British Museum library, and search the catalogue, he will find under his own name a curious and now forgotten book, dated 1924, entitled The Gospel of the Brothers Barnabas. That gospel was that men must live three hundred years if civilization is to be saved. It shewed that this extension of individual human life was possible, and how it was likely to come about. I married the daughter of one of the brothers.

BARNABAS. Do you mean to say you claim to be a connection of mine?

THE ARCHBISHOP. I claim nothing. As I have by this time perhaps three or four million cousins of one degree or another, I have ceased to call on the family.

BURGE-LUBIN. Gracious heavens! Four million relatives! Is that calculation correct, Confucius?

CONFUCIUS. In China it might be forty millions if there were no checks on population.

BURGE-LUBIN. This is a staggerer. It brings home to one – but [recovering] it isnt true, you know. Let us keep sane.

CONFUCIUS [to the Archbishop] You wish us to understand that the illustrious ancestors of the Accountant General communicated to you a secret by which you could attain the age of three hundred years.

THE ARCHBISHOP. No. Nothing of the kind. They simply believed that mankind could live any length of time it knew to be absolutely necessary to save civilization from extinction. I did not share their belief: at least I was not conscious of sharing it: I thought I was only amused by it. To me my father-in-law and his brother were a pair of clever cranks who had talked one another into a fixed idea which had become a monomania with them. It was not until I got into serious difficulties with the pension authorities after turning seventy that I began to suspect the truth.

CONFUCIUS. The truth?

THE ARCHBISHOP. Yes, Mr Chief Secretary: the truth. Like all revolutionary truths, it began as a joke. As I shewed no signs of ageing after forty-five, my wife used to make fun of me by saying that I was certainly going to live three hundred years. She was sixty-eight when she died; and the last thing she said to me, as I sat by her bedside holding her hand, was 'Bill: you really dont look fifty. I wonder –' She broke off, and fell asleep wondering, and never awoke. Then I began to wonder too. That is the explanation of the three hundred years, Mr Secretary.

CONFUCIUS. It is very ingenious, Mr Archbishop. And very well told.

BURGE-LUBIN. Of course you understand that *I* dont for a moment suggest the very faintest doubt of your absolute veracity, Archbishop. You know that, dont you?

THE ARCHBISHOP. Quite, Mr President. Only you dont believe me: that is all. I do not expect you to. In your place I should not believe. You had better have a look at the films. [*Pointing to the Accountant General*] He believes.

BURGE-LUBIN. But the drowning? What about the drowning? A man might get drowned once, or even twice if he was exceptionally careless. But he couldnt be drowned four times. He would run away from water like a mad dog.

THE ARCHBISHOP. Perhaps Mr Chief Secretary can guess the explanation of that.

CONFUCIUS. To keep your secret, you had to die.

BURGE-LUBIN. But dash it all, man, he isnt dead.

CONFUCIUS. It is socially impossible not to do what everybody else does. One must die at the usual time.

BARNABAS. Of course. A simple point of honor.

CONFUCIUS. Not at all. A simple necessity.

BURGE-LUBIN. Well, I'm hanged if I see it. I should jolly well live for ever if I could.

THE ARCHBISHOP. It is not so easy as you think. You, Mr Chief Secretary, have grasped the difficulties of the position. Let me remind you, Mr President, that I was over eighty before the 1969 Act for the Redistribution of Income entitled me to a handsome retiring pension. Owing to my youthful appearance I was prosecuted for attempting to obtain public money on false pretences when I claimed it. I could prove nothing; for the register of my birth had been blown to pieces by a bomb dropped on a village church years before in the first of the big modern wars. I was ordered back to work as a man of forty, and had to work for fifteen years more, the retiring age being then fifty-five.

BURGE-LUBIN. As late as fifty-five! How did people stand it?

THE ARCHBISHOP. They made difficulties about letting me go even then, I still looked so young. For some years I was in continual trouble. The industrial police rounded me up again and again, refusing to believe that I was over age. They began to call me The Wandering Jew. You see how impossible my position was. I foresaw that in twenty years more my official record would prove me to be seventy-five; my appearance would make it impossible to believe that I was more than forty-five; and my real age would be one hundred and seventeen. What was I to do? Bleach my hair? Hobble about on two sticks? Mimic the voice of a centenarian? Better have killed myself.

BARNABAS. You ought to have killed yourself. As an honest man you were entitled to no more than an honest man's expectation of life.

THE ARCHBISHOP. I did kill myself. It was quite easy. I left a suit of clothes by the seashore during the bathing season, with documents in the pockets to identify me. I then turned up in a strange place, pretending that I had lost my memory, and did not know my name or my age or anything about myself. Under treatment I recovered my health, but not my memory. I have had several careers since I began this routine of life and death. I have been an archbishop three times. When I persuaded the authorities to knock down all our towns and rebuild them from the foundations, or move them, I went into the artillery, and became a general. I have been President.

BURGE-LUBIN. Dickenson?

THE ARCHBISHOP. Yes.

BURGE-LUBIN. But they found Dickenson's body: its ashes are buried in St Paul's.

THE ARCHBISHOP. They almost always found the body. During the bathing season there are plenty of bodies. I have been cremated again and again. At first I used to attend my own funeral in disguise, because I had read about a man doing that in an old romance by an author named Bennett, from whom I remember borrowing five pounds in 1912. But I got tired of that. I would not cross the street now to read my latest epitaph.

The Chief Secretary and the President look very glum. Their incredulity is vanquished at last.

BURGE-LUBIN. Look here. Do you chaps realize how awful this is? Here we are sitting calmly in the presence of a man whose death is overdue by two centuries. He may crumble into dust before our eyes at any moment.

BARNABAS. Not he. He'll go on drawing his pension until the end of the world.

THE ARCHBISHOP. Not quite that. My expectation of life is only three hundred years.

BARNABAS. You will last out my time anyhow: thats enough for me.

THE ARCHBISHOP [*coolly*] How do you know?

BARNABAS [*taken aback*] How do I know!

THE ARCHBISHOP. Yes: how do you know? I did not begin even to suspect until I was nearly seventy. I was only vain of my youthful appearance. I was not quite serious about it until I was ninety. Even now I am not sure from one moment to another, though I have given you my reason for thinking that I have quite unintentionally committed myself to a lifetime of three hundred years.

BURGE-LUBIN. But how do you do it? Is it lemons? Is it Soya beans? Is it –

THE ARCHBISHOP. I do not do it. It happens. It may happen to anyone. It may happen to you.

BURGE-LUBIN [*the full significance of this for himself dawning on him*] Then we three may be in the same boat with you, for all we know?

THE ARCHBISHOP. You may. Therefore I advise you to be very careful how you take any step that will make my position uncomfortable.

BURGE-LUBIN. Well, I'm dashed! One of my secretaries was remarking only this morning how well and young I am looking. Barnabas: I have an absolute conviction that I am one of the – the – shall I say one of the victims? – of this strange destiny.

THE ARCHBISHOP. Your great-great-great-great-great-great-grandfather formed the same conviction when he was between sixty and seventy. I knew him.

BURGE-LUBIN [*depressed*] Ah! But he died.

THE ARCHBISHOP. No.

BURGE-LUBIN [*hopefully*] Do you mean to say he is still alive?

THE ARCHBISHOP. No. He was shot. Under the influence of his belief that he was going to live three hundred years he became a changed man. He began to tell people the truth; and they disliked it so much that they took advantage of certain clauses of an Act of Parliament he had himself passed during the Four Years War, and had purposely forgotten to repeal afterwards. They took him to the Tower of London and shot him.

The apparatus rings.

CONFUCIUS [*answering*] Yes? [*He listens*].

A WOMAN'S VOICE. The Domestic Minister has called.

BURGE-LUBIN [*not quite catching the answer*] Who does she say has called?

CONFUCIUS. The Domestic Minister.

BARNABAS. Oh, dash it! That awful woman!

BURGE-LUBIN. She is certainly a bit of a terror. I dont exactly know why; for she is not at all bad-looking.

BARNABAS [*out of patience*] For Heaven's sake, dont be frivolous.

THE ARCHBISHOP. He cannot help it, Mr Accountant General. Three of his sixteen great-great-great-grandfathers married Lubins.

BURGE-LUBIN. Tut tut! I am not frivolling. *I* did not ask the lady here. Which of you did?

CONFUCIUS. It is her official duty to report personally to the President once a quarter.

BURGE-LUBIN. Oh, that. Then I suppose it's my official duty to receive her. Theyd better send her in. You dont mind, do you? She will bring us back to real life. I dont know how you fellows feel; but I'm just going dotty.

CONFUCIUS [*into the telephone*] The President will receive the Domestic Minister at once.

They watch the door in silence for the entrance of the Domestic Minister.

BURGE-LUBIN [*suddenly, to the Archbishop*] I suppose you have been married over and over again.

THE ARCHBISHOP. Once. You do not make vows until death when death is three hundred years off.

> *They relapse into uneasy silence. The Domestic Minister enters. She is a handsome woman, apparently in the prime of life, with elegant, tense, well held-up figure, and the walk of a goddess. Her expression and deportment are grave, swift, decisive, awful, unanswerable. She wears a Dianesque tunic instead of a blouse, and a silver coronet instead of a gold fillet. Her dress otherwise is not markedly different from that of the men, who rise as she enters, and incline their heads with instinctive awe. She comes to the vacant chair between Barnabas and Confucius.*

BURGE-LUBIN [*resolutely genial and gallant*] Delighted to see you, Mrs Lutestring.

CONFUCIUS. We are honored by your celestial presence.

BARNABAS. Good day, madam.

THE ARCHBISHOP. I have not had the pleasure of meeting you before. I am the Archbishop of York.

MRS LUTESTRING. Surely we have met, Mr Archbishop. I remember your face. We – [*she checks herself suddenly*] Ah, no: I remember now: it was someone else. [*She sits down*].

> *They all sit down.*

THE ARCHBISHOP [*also puzzled*] Are you sure you are mistaken? I also have some association with your face, Mrs Lutestring. Something like a door opening continually and revealing you. And a smile of welcome when you recognized me. Did you ever open a door for me, I wonder?

MRS LUTESTRING. I often opened a door for the person you have just reminded me of. But he has been dead many years.

> *The rest, except the Archbishop, look at one another quickly.*

CONFUCIUS. May I ask how many years?

MRS LUTESTRING [*struck by his tone, looks at him for a moment with some displeasure; then replies*] It does not matter. A long time.

BURGE-LUBIN. You mustnt rush to conclusions about the Archbishop, Mrs Lutestring. He is an older bird than you think. Older than you, at all events.

MRS LUTESTRING [*with a melancholy smile*] I think not, Mr President. But the subject is a delicate one. I had rather not pursue it.

CONFUCIUS. There is a question which has not been asked.

MRS LUTESTRING [*very decisively*] If it is a question about my age, Mr Chief Secretary, it had better not be asked. All that concerns you about my personal affairs can be found in the books of the Accountant General.

CONFUCIUS. The question I was thinking of will not be addressed to you. But let me say that your sensitiveness on the point is very strange, coming from a woman so superior to all common weaknesses as we know you to be.

MRS LUTESTRING. I may have reasons which have nothing to do with common weaknesses, Mr Chief Secretary. I hope you will respect them.

CONFUCIUS [*after bowing to her in assent*] I will now put my question. Have you, Mr Archbishop, any ground for assuming, as you seem to do, that what has happened to you has not happened to other people as well?

BURGE-LUBIN. Yes, by George! I never thought of that.

THE ARCHBISHOP. I have never met any case but my own.

CONFUCIUS. How do you know?

THE ARCHBISHOP. Well, no one has ever told me that they were in this extraordinary position.

CONFUCIUS. That proves nothing. Did you ever tell any-body that you were in it? You never told us. Why did you never tell us?

THE ARCHBISHOP. I am surprised at the question, coming from so astute a mind as yours, Mr Secretary. When you reach the age I reached before I discovered what was happening to me, I was old enough to know and fear the ferocious hatred with which human animals, like all other animals, turn upon any unhappy individual who has the misfortune to be unlike themselves in every respect: to be unnatural, as they call it. You will still find, among the tales of that twentieth-century classic, Wells, a story of a race of men who grew twice as big as their fellows, and another story of a man who fell into the hands of a race of blind men. The big people had to fight the little people for their lives; and the man with eyes would have had his eyes put out by the blind had he not fled to the desert, where he perished miserably. Wells's teaching, on that and other matters, was not lost on me. By the way, he lent me five pounds once which I never repaid; and it still troubles my conscience.

CONFUCIUS. And were you the only reader of Wells? If there were others like you, had they not the same reason for keeping the secret?

THE ARCHBISHOP. That is true. But I should know. You short-lived people are so childish. If I met a man of my own age I should recognize him at once. I have never done so.

MRS LUTESTRING. Would you recognize a woman of your age, do you think?

THE ARCHBISHOP. I – [*He stops and turns upon her with a searching look, startled by the suggestion and the suspicion it rouses*].

MRS LUTESTRING. What is your age, Mr Archbishop?

BURGE-LUBIN. Two hundred and eighty-three, he says. That is his little joke. Do you know, Mrs Lutestring, he had almost talked us into believing him when you came in and cleared the air with your robust common sense.

MRS LUTESTRING. Do you really feel that, Mr President? I hear the note of breezy assertion in your voice. I miss the note of conviction.

BURGE-LUBIN [*jumping up*] Look here. Let us stop talking damned nonsense. I dont wish to be disagreeable; but it's getting on my nerves. The best joke wont bear being pushed beyond a certain point. That point has been reached. I – I'm rather busy this morning. We all have our hands pretty full. Confucius here will tell you that I have a heavy day before me.

BARNABAS. Have you anything more important than this thing, if it's true?

BURGE-LUBIN. Oh, if if, if it's true! But it isnt true.

BARNABAS. Have you anything at all to do?

BURGE-LUBIN. Anything to do! Have you forgotten,

Barnabas, that I happen to be President, and that the weight of the entire public business of this country is on my shoulders?

BARNABAS. Has he anything to do, Confucius?

CONFUCIUS. He has to be President.

BARNABAS. That means that he has nothing to do.

BURGE-LUBIN [*sulkily*] Very well, Barnabas. Go on making a fool of yourself. [*He sits down*]. Go on.

BARNABAS. I am not going to leave this room until we get to the bottom of this swindle.

MRS LUTESTRING [*turning with deadly gravity on the Accountant General*] This what, did you say?

CONFUCIUS. These expressions cannot be sustained. You obscure the discussion in using them.

BARNABAS [*glad to escape from her gaze by addressing Confucius*] Well, this unnatural horror. Will that satisfy you?

CONFUCIUS. That is in order. But we do not commit ourselves to the implications of the word horror.

THE ARCHBISHOP. By the word horror the Accountant General means only something unusual.

CONFUCIUS. I notice that the honorable Domestic Minister, on learning the advanced age of the venerable prelate, shews no sign of surprise or incredulity.

BURGE-LUBIN. She doesnt take it seriously. Who would? Eh, Mrs Lutestring?

MRS LUTESTRING. I take it very seriously indeed, Mr President. I see now that I was not mistaken at first. I have met the Archbishop before.

THE ARCHBISHOP. I felt sure of it. This vision of a door opening to me, and a woman's face welcoming me, must be a reminiscence of something that really happened; though I see it now as an angel opening the gate of heaven.

MRS LUTESTRING. Or a parlor maid opening the door of the house of the young woman you were in love with?

THE ARCHBISHOP [*making a wry face*] Is that the reality? How these things grow in our imagination! But may I say, Mrs Lutestring, that the transfiguration of a parlor maid to an angel is not more amazing than her transfiguration to the very dignified and able Domestic Minister I am addressing. I recognize the angel in you. Frankly, I do not recognize the parlor maid.

BURGE-LUBIN. Whats a parlor maid?

MRS LUTESTRING. An extinct species. A woman in a black dress and white apron, who opened the house door when people knocked or rang, and was either your tyrant or your slave. I was a parlor maid in the house of one of the Accountant General's remote ancestors. [*To Confucius*] You asked me my age, Mr Chief Secretary, I am two hundred and seventy-four.

BURGE-LUBIN [*gallantly*] You dont look it. You really dont look it.

MRS LUTESTRING [*turning her face gravely towards him*] Look again, Mr President.

BURGE-LUBIN [*looking at her bravely until the smile fades from his face, and he suddenly covers his eyes with his hands*] Yes: you do look it. I am convinced. It's true. Now call up the Lunatic Asylum, Confucius; and tell them to send an ambulance for me.

MRS LUTESTRING [*to the Archbishop*] Why have you given away your secret? our secret?

THE ARCHBISHOP. They found it out. The cinema records betrayed me. But I never dreamt that there were others. Did you?

MRS LUTESTRING. I knew one other. She was a cook. She grew tired, and killed herself.

THE ARCHBISHOP. Dear me! However, her death simplifies the situation, as I have been able to convince these gentlemen that the matter had better go no further.

MRS LUTESTRING. What! When the President knows! It will be all over the place before the end of the week.

BURGE-LUBIN [*injured*] Really, Mrs Lutestring! You speak as if I were a notoriously indiscreet person. Barnabas: have I such a reputation?

BARNABAS [*resignedly*] It cant be helped. It's constitutional.

CONFUCIUS. It is utterly unconstitutional. But, as you say, it cannot be helped.

BURGE-LUBIN [*solemnly*] I deny that a secret of State has ever passed my lips – except perhaps to the Minister of Health, who is discretion personified. People think, because she is a negress –

MRS LUTESTRING. It does not matter much now. Once, it would have mattered a great deal. But my children are all dead.

THE ARCHBISHOP. Yes: the children must have been a terrible difficulty. Fortunately for me, I had none.

MRS LUTESTRING. There was one daughter who was the child of my very heart. Some years after my first drowning I learnt that she had lost her sight. I went to her. She was an old woman of ninety-six, blind. She asked me to sit and talk with her because my voice was like the voice of her dead mother.

BURGE-LUBIN. The complications must be frightful. Really I hardly know whether I do want to live much longer than other people.

MRS LUTESTRING. You can always kill yourself, as cook did; but that was influenza. Long life is complicated, and even terrible; but it is glorious all the same. I would no more change places with an ordinary woman than with a mayfly that lives only an hour.

THE ARCHBISHOP. What set you thinking of it first?

MRS LUTESTRING. Conrad Barnabas's book. Your wife told me it was more wonderful than Napoleon's Book of Fate and Old Moore's Almanac, which cook and I used to read. I was very ignorant: it did not seem so impossible to me as to an educated woman. Yet I forgot all about it, and married and drudged as a poor man's wife, and brought up children, and looked twenty years older than I really was, until one day, long after my husband died and my children were out in the world working for themselves, I noticed that I looked twenty years younger than I really was. The truth came to me in a flash.

BURGE-LUBIN. An amazing moment. Your feelings must have been beyond description. What was your first thought?

MRS LUTESTRING. Pure terror. I saw that the little money I had laid up would not last, and that I must go out and work again. They had things called Old Age Pensions then: miserable pittances for worn-out old laborers to die on. I thought I should be found out if I went on drawing it too long. The horror of facing another lifetime of drudgery, of missing my hard-earned rest and losing my poor little savings, drove everything else out of my mind. You people nowadays can have no conception of the dread of poverty that hung over us then, or of the utter tiredness of forty years' unending overwork and striving to make a shilling do the work of a pound.

THE ARCHBISHOP. I wonder you did not kill yourself. I often wonder why the poor in those evil old times did not kill themselves. They did not even kill other people.

MRS LUTESTRING. You never kill yourself, because you always may as well wait until tomorrow. And you have not energy or conviction enough to kill the others. Besides, how can you blame them when you would do as they do if you were in their place?

BURGE-LUBIN. Devilish poor consolation, that.

MRS LUTESTRING. There were other consolations in those days for people like me. We drank preparations of alcohol to relieve the strain of living and give us an artificial happiness.

BURGE-LUBIN   ⎧ [all together, ⎤ Alcohol!
CONFUCIUS   ⎨   making   ⎬ Pfff. . . .!
BARNABAS   ⎩   wry faces]   ⎦ Disgusting.

MRS LUTESTRING. A little alcohol would improve your temper and manners, and make you much easier to live with, Mr Accountant General.

BURGE-LUBIN [laughing] By George, I believe you! Try it, Barnabas.

CONFUCIUS. No. Try tea. It is the more civilized poison of the two.

MRS LUTESTRING. You, Mr President, were born intoxicated with your own well-fed natural exuberance. You cannot imagine what alcohol was to an underfed poor woman. I had carefully arranged my little savings so that I could get drunk, as we called it, once a week; and my only pleasure was looking forward to that poor little debauch. That is what saved me from suicide. I could not bear to miss my next carouse. But when I stopped working, and lived on my pension, the fatigue of my life's drudgery began to wear off, because, you see, I was not really old. I recuperated. I looked younger and younger. And at last I was rested enough to have courage and strength to begin life again. Besides, political changes were making it easier: life was a little better worth living for the nine-tenths of the people who used to be mere drudges. After that, I never turned back or faltered. My only regret now is that I shall die when I am three hundred or thereabouts. There was only one thing that made life hard; and that is gone now.

CONFUCIUS. May we ask what that was?

MRS LUTESTRING. Perhaps you will be offended if I tell you.

BURGE-LUBIN. Offended! My dear lady, do you suppose, after such a stupendous revelation, that anything short of a blow from a sledge-hammer could produce the smallest impression on any of us?

MRS LUTESTRING. Well, you see, it has been so hard on me never to meet a grown-up person. You are all such children. And I never was very fond of children, except that one girl who woke up the mother passion in me. I have been very lonely sometimes.

BURGE-LUBIN [again gallant] But surely, Mrs Lutestring, that has been your own fault. If I may say so, a lady of your attractions need never have been lonely.

MRS LUTESTRING. Why?

BURGE-LUBIN. Why! Well –. Well, er –. Well, er er –. Well! [he gives it up].

THE ARCHBISHOP. He means that you might have married. Curious, how little they understand our position.

MRS LUTESTRING. I did marry. I married again on my hundred and first birthday. But of course I had to marry an elderly man: a man over sixty. He was a great painter. On his deathbed he said to me 'It has taken me fifty years to learn my trade, and to paint all the foolish pictures a man must paint and get rid of before he comes through them to the great things he ought to paint. And now that my foot is at last on the threshold of the temple I find that it is also the threshold of my tomb.' That man would have been the greatest painter of all time if he could have lived as long as I. I saw him die of old age whilst he was still as he said himself, a gentleman amateur, like all modern painters.

BURGE-LUBIN. But why had you to marry an elderly man? Why not marry a young one? or shall I say a middle-aged one? If my own affections were not already engaged; and if, to tell the truth, I were not a little afraid of you – for you are a very superior woman, as we all acknowledge – I should esteem myself happy in – er – er –

MRS LUTESTRING. Mr President: have you ever tried to take advantage of the innocence of a little child for the gratification of your senses?

BURGE-LUBIN. Good Heavens, madam, what do you take me for? What right have you to ask me such a question?

MRS LUTESTRING. I am at present in my two hundred and seventy-fifth year. You suggest that I should take advantage of the innocence of a child of thirty, and marry it.

THE ARCHBISHOP. Can you shortlived people not understand that as the confusion and immaturity and primitive animalism in which we live for the first hundred years of our life is worse in this matter of sex than in any other, you are intolerable to us in that relation?

BURGE-LUBIN. Do you mean to say, Mrs Lutestring, that you regard me as a child?

MRS LUTESTRING. Do you expect me to regard you as a completed soul? Oh, you may well be afraid of me. There are moments when your levity, your ingratitude, your shallow jollity, make my gorge rise so against you that if I could not remind myself that you are a child I should be tempted to doubt your right to live at all.

CONFUCIUS. Do you grudge us the few years we have? you who have three hundred!

BURGE-LUBIN. You accuse me of levity! Must I remind you, madam, that I am the President, and that you are only the head of a department?

BARNABAS. Ingratitude too! You draw a pension for three hundred years when we owe you only seventy-eight; and you call us ungrateful!

MRS LUTESTRING. I do. When I think of the blessings that have been showered on you, and contrast them with the poverty! the humiliations! the anxieties! the heartbreak! the insolence and tyranny that were the daily lot of mankind when I was learning to suffer instead of learning to live! when I see how lightly you take it all! how you quarrel over the crumpled leaves in your beds of roses! how you are so dainty about your work that unless it is made either interesting or delightful to you you leave it to negresses and Chinamen, I ask myself whether even three hundred years of thought and experience can save you from being superseded by the Power that created you and put you on your trial.

BURGE-LUBIN. My dear lady: our Chinese and colored friends are perfectly happy. They are twenty times better off here than they would be in China or Liberia. They do their work admirably; and in doing it they set us free for higher employments.

THE ARCHBISHOP [*who has caught the infection of her indignation*] What higher employments are you capable of? you that are superannuated at seventy and dead at eighty!

MRS LUTESTRING. You are not really doing higher work. You are supposed to make the decisions and give the orders; but the negresses and the Chinese make up your minds for you and tell you what orders to give, just as my brother, who was a sergeant in the Guards, used to prompt his officers in the old days. When I want to get anything done at the Health Ministry I do not come to you: I go to the black lady who has been the real president during your present term of office, or to Confucius who goes on for ever while presidents come and presidents go.

BURGE-LUBIN. This is outrageous. This is treason to the white race. And let me tell you, madam, that I have never in my life met the Minister of Health, and that I protest against the vulgar color prejudice which disparages her great ability and her eminent services to the State. My relations with her are purely telephonic, gramophonic, photophonic, and, may I add, platonic.

THE ARCHBISHOP. There is no reason why you should be ashamed of them in any case, Mr President. But let us look at the position impersonally. Can you deny that what is happening is that the English people have become a Joint Stock Company admitting Asiatics and Africans as shareholders?

BARNABAS. Nothing like it. I know all about the old joint stock companies. The shareholders did no work.

THE ARCHBISHOP. That is true; but we, like them, get our dividends whether we work or not. We work partly because we know there would be no dividends if we did not, and partly because if we refuse we are regarded as mentally deficient and put into a lethal chamber. But what do we work at? Before the few changes we were forced to make by the revolutions that followed the Four Years War, our governing classes had been so rich, as it was called, that they had become the most intellectually lazy and fat-headed people on the face of the earth. There is a good deal of that fat still clinging to us.

BURGE-LUBIN. As President, I must not listen to unpatriotic criticisms of our national character, Mr Archbishop.

THE ARCHBISHOP. As Archbishop, Mr President, it is my official duty to criticize the national character unsparingly. At the canonization of Saint Henrik Ibsen, you yourself unveiled the monument to him which bears on its pedestal the noble inscription, 'I came not to call sinners, but the righteous, to repentance.' The proof of what I say is that our routine work, and what may be called our ornamental and figure-head work, is being more and more sought after by the English; whilst the thinking, organizing, calculating, directing work is done by yellow brains, brown brains, and black brains, just as it was done in my early days by Jewish brains, Scottish brains, Italian brains, German brains. The only white men who still do serious work are those who, like the Accountant General, have no capacity for enjoyment, and no social gifts to make them welcome outside their offices.

BARNABAS. Confound your impudence! I had gifts enough to find you out, anyhow.

THE ARCHBISHOP [*disregarding this outburst*] If you were to kill me as I stand here, you would have to appoint an Indian to succeed me. I take precedence today not as an Englishman, but as a man with more than a century and a half of fully adult experience. We are letting all the power slip into the hands of the colored people. In another hundred years we shall be simply their household pets.

BURGE-LUBIN [*reacting buoyantly*] Not the least danger of it. I grant you we leave the most troublesome part of the labor of the nation to them. And a good job too: why should we drudge at it? But think of the activities of our leisure! Is there a jollier place on earth to live in than England out of office hours? And to whom do we owe that? To ourselves, not to the niggers. The nigger and the Chink are all right from Tuesday to Friday; but from Friday to Tuesday they are simply nowhere; and the real life of England is from Friday to Tuesday.

THE ARCHBISHOP. That is terribly true. In devising brainless amusements; in pursuing them with enormous vigor, and taking them with eager seriousness, our English people are the wonder of the world. They always were. And it is just as well; for otherwise their sensuality would become morbid and destroy them. What appals me is that their amusements should amuse them. They are the amusements of boys and girls. They are pardonable up to the age of fifty or sixty: after that they are ridiculous. I tell you, what is wrong with us is that we are a non-adult race; and the Irish and the Scots, and the niggers and Chinks, as you call them, though their lifetime is as short as ours, or shorter, yet do somehow contrive to grow up a little before they die. We die in boyhood: the maturity that should make us the greatest of all the nations lies beyond the grave for us. Either we shall go under as greybeards with golf clubs in our hands, or we must will to live longer.

MRS LUTESTRING. Yes: that is it. I could not have expressed it in words; but you have expressed it for me. I felt, even when I was an ignorant domestic slave, that we had the possibility of becoming a great nation within us; but our faults and follies drove me to cynical hopelessness. We all ended then like that. It is the highest creatures who take the longest to mature, and are the most helpless during their immaturity. I know now that it took me a whole century to grow up. I began my serious life when I was a hundred and twenty. Asiatics cannot control me: I am not a child in their hands, as you are, Mr President. Neither, I am sure, is the Archbishop. They respect me. You are not grown up enough even for that, though you were kind enough to say that I frighten you.

BURGE-LUBIN. Honestly, you do. And will you think me very rude if I say that if I must choose between a white woman old enough to be my great-grandmother and a black woman of my own age, I shall probably find the black woman more sympathetic?

MRS LUTESTRING. And more attractive in color, perhaps?

BURGE-LUBIN. Yes. Since you ask me, more – well, not more attractive: I do not deny that you have an excellent appearance – but I will say, richer. More Venetian. Tropical. 'The shadowed livery of the burnished sun.'

MRS LUTESTRING. Our women, and their favorite story writers, begin already to talk about men with golden complexions.

CONFUCIUS [*expanding into a smile all across both face and body*] A-a-a-a-a – h!

BURGE-LUBIN. Well, what of it, madam? Have you read a

very interesting book by the librarian of the Biological Society suggesting that the future of the world lies with the Mulatto?

MRS LUTESTRING [*rising*] Mr Archbishop: if the white race is to be saved, our destiny is apparent.

THE ARCHBISHOP. Yes: our duty is pretty clear.

MRS LUTESTRING. Have you time to come home with me and discuss the matter?

THE ARCHBISHOP [*rising*] With pleasure.

BARNABAS [*rising also and rushing past Mrs Lutestring to the door, where he turns to bar her way*] No you dont. Burge: you understand, dont you?

BURGE-LUBIN. No. What is it?

BARNABAS. These two are going to marry.

BURGE-LUBIN. Why shouldnt they, if they want to?

BARNABAS. They dont want to. They will do it in cold blood because their children will live three hundred years. It mustnt be allowed.

CONFUCIUS. You cannot prevent it. There is no law that gives you power to interfere with them.

BARNABAS. If they force me to it I will obtain legislation against marriages above the age of seventy-eight.

THE ARCHBISHOP. There is not time for that before we are married, Mr Accountant General. Be good enough to get out of the lady's way.

BARNABAS. There is time to send the lady to the lethal chamber before anything comes of your marriage. Dont forget that.

MRS LUTESTRING. What nonsense, Mr Accountant General! Good afternoon, Mr President. Good afternoon, Mr Chief Secretary. [*They rise and acknowledge her salutation with bows. She walks straight at the Accountant General, who instinctively shrinks out of her way as she leaves the room*].

THE ARCHBISHOP. I am surprised at you, Mr Barnabas. Your tone was like an echo from the Dark Ages. [*He follows the Domestic Minister*].

Confucius, shaking his head and clucking with his tongue in deprecation of this painful episode, moves to the chair just vacated

by the Archbishop and stands behind it with folded palms, looking
at the President. The Accountant General shakes his fist after the
departed visitors, and bursts into savage abuse of them.

BARNABAS. Thieves! Cursed thieves! Vampires! What are
you going to do, Burge?

BURGE-LUBIN. Do?

BARNABAS. Yes, do. There must be dozens of these people
in existence. Are you going to let them do what the two
who have just left us mean to do, and crowd us off the face
of the earth?

BURGE-LUBIN [*sitting down*] Oh, come, Barnabas! What
harm are they doing? Arnt you interested in them? Dont
you like them?

BARNABAS. Like them! I hate them. They are monsters,
unnatural monsters. They are poison to me.

BURGE-LUBIN. What possible objection can there be to
their living as long as they can? It does not shorten our
lives, does it?

BARNABAS. If I have to die when I am seventy-eight, I
dont see why another man should be privileged to live to
be two hundred and seventy-eight. It does shorten my
life, relatively. It makes us ridiculous. If they grew to be
twelve feet high they would make us all dwarfs. They
talked to us as if we were children. There is no love lost
between us: their hatred of us came out soon enough. You
heard what the woman said, and how the Archbishop
backed her up?

BURGE-LUBIN. But what can we do to them?

BARNABAS. Kill them.

BURGE-LUBIN. Nonsense!

BARNABAS. Lock them up. Sterilize them somehow, anyhow.

BURGE-LUBIN. But what reason could we give?

BARNABAS. What reason can you give for killing a snake?
Nature tells you to do it.

BURGE-LUBIN. My dear Barnabas, you are out of your
mind.

BARNABAS. Havnt you said that once too often already this
morning?

BURGE-LUBIN. I dont believe you will carry a single soul with you.

BARNABAS. I understand. I know you. You think you are one of them.

CONFUCIUS. Mr Accountant General: you may be one of them.

BARNABAS. How dare you accuse me of such a thing? I am an honest man, not a monster. I won my place in public life by demonstrating that the true expectation of human life is seventy-eight point six. And I will resist any attempt to alter or upset it to the last drop of my blood if need be.

BURGE-LUBIN. Oh, tut tut! Come, come! Pull yourself together. How can you, a descendant of the great Conrad Barnabas, the man who is still remembered by his masterly Biography of a Black Beetle, be so absurd?

BARNABAS. You had better go and write the autobiography of a jackass. I am going to raise the country against this horror, and against you, if you shew the slightest sign of weakness about it.

CONFUCIUS [*very impressively*] You will regret it if you do.

BARNABAS. What is to make me regret it?

CONFUCIUS. Every mortal man and woman in the community will begin to count on living for three centuries. Things will happen which you do not foresee: terrible things. The family will dissolve: parents and children will be no longer the old and the young: brothers and sisters will meet as strangers after a hundred years separation: the ties of blood will lose their innocence. The imaginations of men, let loose over the possibilities of three centuries of life, will drive them mad and wreck human society. This discovery must be kept a dead secret. [*He sits down*].

BARNABAS. And if I refuse to keep the secret?

CONFUCIUS. I shall have you safe in a lunatic asylum the day after you blab.

BARNABAS. You forget that I can produce the Archbishop to prove my statement.

CONFUCIUS. So can I. Which of us do you think he will

support when I explain to him that your object in revealing his age is to get him killed?

BARNABAS [*desperate*] Burge: are you going to back up this yellow abomination against me? Are we public men and members of the Government? or are we damned blackguards?

CONFUCIUS [*unmoved*] Have you ever known a public man who was not what vituperative people called a damned blackguard when some inconsiderate person wanted to tell the public more than was good for it?

BARNABAS. Hold your tongue, you insolent heathen. Burge: I spoke to you.

BURGE-LUBIN. Well, you know, my dear Barnabas, Confucius is a very long-headed chap. I see his point.

BARNABAS. Do you? Then let me tell you that, except officially, I will never speak to you again. Do you hear?

BURGE-LUBIN [*cheerfully*] You will. You will.

BARNABAS. And dont you ever dare speak to me again. Do you hear? [*He turns to the door*].

BURGE-LUBIN. I will. I will. Goodbye, Barnabas. God bless you.

BARNABAS. May you live forever, and be the laughing-stock of the whole world! [*he dashes out in a fury*].

BURGE-LUBIN [*laughing indulgently*] He will keep the secret all right. I know Barnabas. You neednt worry.

CONFUCIUS [*troubled and grave*] There are no secrets except the secrets that keep themselves. Consider. There are those films at the Record Office. We have no power to prevent the Master of the Records from publishing this discovery made in his department. We cannot silence the American – who can silence an American? – nor the people who were there today to receive him. Fortunately, a film can prove nothing but a resemblance.

BURGE-LUBIN. Thats very true. After all, the whole thing is confounded nonsense, isnt it?

CONFUCIUS [*raising his head to look at him*] You have decided not to believe it now that you realize its inconveniences. That is the English method. It may not work in this case.

BURGE-LUBIN. English be hanged! It's common sense. You know, those two people got us hypnotized: not a doubt of it. They must have been kidding us. They were, werent they?

CONFUCIUS. You looked into that woman's face; and you believed.

BURGE-LUBIN. Just so. Thats where she had me. I shouldnt have believed her a bit if she'd turned her back to me.

CONFUCIUS [shakes his head slowly and repeatedly] ???

BURGE-LUBIN. You really think — ? [he hesitates].

CONFUCIUS. The Archbishop has always been a puzzle to me. Ever since I learnt to distinguish between one English face and another I have noticed what the woman pointed out: that the English face is not an adult face, just as the English mind is not an adult mind.

BURGE-LUBIN. Stow it, John Chinaman. If ever there was a race divinely appointed to take charge of the non-adult races and guide them and train them and keep them out of mischief until they grow up to be capable of adopting our institutions, that race is the English race. It is the only race in the world that has that characteristic. Now!

CONFUCIUS. That is the fancy of a child nursing a doll. But it is ten times more childish of you to dispute the highest compliment ever paid you.

BURGE-LUBIN. You call it a compliment to class us as grown-up children.

CONFUCIUS. Not grown-up children, children at fifty, sixty, seventy. Your maturity is so late that you never attain to it. You have to be governed by races which are mature at forty. That means that you are potentially the most highly developed race on earth, and would be actually the greatest if you could live long enough to attain to maturity.

BURGE-LUBIN [grasping the idea at last] By George, Confucius, youre right! I never thought of that. That explains everything. We are just a lot of schoolboys: theres no denying it. Talk to an Englishman about anything serious, and he listens to you curiously for a moment just as he listens to a chap playing classical music. Then he goes back to his marine golf, or motoring, or flying, or women, just like a bit of stretched elastic when you let it go. [*Soaring to the height of his theme*] Oh, youre quite right. We are only in our infancy. I ought to be in a perambulator, with a nurse shoving me along. It's true: it's absolutely true. But some day we'll grow up; and then, by Jingo, we'll shew em.

CONFUCIUS. The Archbishop is an adult. When I was a child I was dominated and intimidated by people whom I now know to have been weaker and sillier than I, because there was some mysterious quality in their mere age that overawed me. I confess that, though I have kept up appearances, I have always been afraid of the Archbishop.

BURGE-LUBIN. Between ourselves, Confucius, so have I.

CONFUCIUS. It is this that convinced me. It was this in the woman's face that convinced you. Their new departure in the history of the race is no fraud. It does not even surprise me.

BURGE-LUBIN. Oh, come! Not surprise you! It's your pose never to be surprised at anything; but if you are not surprised at this you are not human.

CONFUCIUS. I am staggered, just as a man may be staggered by an explosion for which he has himself laid the charge and lighted the fuse. But I am not surprised, because, as a philosopher and a student of evolutionary biology, I have come to regard some such development as this as inevitable. If I had not thus prepared myself to be credulous, no mere evidence of films and well-told tales would have persuaded me to believe. As it is, I do believe.

BURGE-LUBIN. Well, that being settled, what the devil is to happen next? Whats the next move for us?

CONFUCIUS. We do not make the next move. The next move will be made by the Archbishop and the woman.

BURGE-LUBIN. Their marriage?

CONFUCIUS. More than that. They have made the momentous discovery that they are not alone in the world.

BURGE-LUBIN. You think there are others?

CONFUCIUS. There must be many others. Each of them believes that he or she is the only one to whom the miracle has happened. But the Archbishop knows better now. He

will advertise in terms which only the longlived people
will understand. He will bring them together and organize
them. They will hasten from all parts of the earth. They
will become a great Power.

BURGE-LUBIN [*a little alarmed*] I say, will they? I suppose
they will. I wonder is Barnabas right after all? Ought we
to allow it?

CONFUCIUS. Nothing that we can do will stop it. We cannot in our souls really want to stop it: the vital force that
has produced this change would paralyze our opposition
to it, if we were mad enough to oppose. But we will not
oppose. You and I may be of the elect, too.

BURGE-LUBIN. Yes: thats what gets us every time. What
the deuce ought we to do? Something must be done
about it, you know.

CONFUCIUS. Let us sit still, and meditate in silence on the
vistas before us.

BURGE-LUBIN. By George, I believe youre right. Let us.

*They sit meditating, the Chinaman naturally, the President with
visible effort and intensity. He is positively glaring into the future
when the voice of the Negress is heard.*

THE NEGRESS. Mr President.

BURGE-LUBIN [*joyfully*] Yes. [*Taking up a peg*] Are you at
home?

THE NEGRESS. No. Omega, zero, x squared.

*The President rapidly puts the peg in the switchboard; works the
dial; and presses the button. The screen becomes transparent; and
the Negress, brilliantly dressed, appears on what looks like the
bridge of a steam yacht in glorious sea weather. The installation
with which she is communicating is beside the binnacle.*

CONFUCIUS [*looking round, and recoiling with a shriek of disgust*]
Ach! Avaunt! Avaunt! [*He rushes from the room*].

BURGE-LUBIN. What part of the coast is that?

THE NEGRESS. Fishguard Bay. Why not run over and join
me for the afternoon? I am disposed to be approachable at
last.

BURGE-LUBIN. But Fishguard! Two hundred and seventy
miles!

THE NEGRESS. There is a lightning express on the Irish Air
Service at half-past sixteen. They will drop you by a parachute in the bay. The dip will do you good. I will pick you
up and dry you and give you a first-rate time.

BURGE-LUBIN. Delightful. But a little risky, isnt it?

THE NEGRESS. Risky! I thought you were afraid of nothing.

BURGE-LUBIN. I am not exactly afraid; but –

THE NEGRESS [*offended*] But you think it is not good enough.
Very well [*she raises her hand to take the peg out of her switchboard*].

BURGE-LUBIN [*imploringly*] No: stop: let me explain: hold
the line just one moment. Oh, please.

THE NEGRESS [*waiting with her hand poised over the peg*] Well?

BURGE-LUBIN. The fact is, I have been behaving very
recklessly for some time past under the impression that my
life would be so short that it was not worth bothering
about. But I have just learnt that I may live – well, much
longer than I expected. I am sure your good sense will tell
you that this alters the case. I –

THE NEGRESS [*with suppressed rage*] Oh, quite. Pray dont risk
your precious life on my account. Sorry for troubling you.
Goodbye [*She snatches out her peg and vanishes*].

BURGE-LUBIN [*urgently*] No: please hold on. I can convince
you – [*a loud buzz-uzz-uzz*]. Engaged! Who is she calling
up now? [*He presses the button and calls*] The Chief Secretary.
Say I want to see him again, just for a moment.

CONFUCIUS'S VOICE. Is the woman gone.

BURGE-LUBIN. Yes, yes: it's all right. Just a moment, if –
[*Confucius returns*] Confucius: I have some important business at Fishguard. The Irish Air Service can drop me in
the bay by parachute. I suppose it's quite safe, isnt it?

CONFUCIUS. Nothing is quite safe. The air service is as safe
as any other travelling service. The parachute is safe. But
the water is not safe.

BURGE-LUBIN. Why? They will give me an unsinkable
tunic, wont they?

CONFUCIUS. You will not sink; but the sea is very cold. You
may get rheumatism for life.

BURGE-LUBIN. For life! That settles it: I wont risk it.

CONFUCIUS. Good. You have at last become prudent: you are no longer what you call a sportsman: you are a sensible coward, almost a grown-up man. I congratulate you.

BURGE-LUBIN [*resolutely*] Coward or no coward, I will not face an eternity of rheumatism for any woman that ever was born. [*He rises and goes to the rack for his fillet*] I have changed my mind: I am going home. [*He cocks the fillet rakishly*] Good evening.

CONFUCIUS. So early? If the Minister of Health rings you up, what shall I tell her?

BURGE-LUBIN. Tell her to go to the devil. [*He goes out*].

CONFUCIUS [*shaking his head, shocked at the President's impoliteness*] No. No, no, no, no, no. Oh, these English! these crude young civilizations! Their manners! Hogs. Hogs.

PART IV

Tragedy of an Elderly Gentleman

ACT I

Burrin pier on the south shore of Galway Bay in Ireland, a region of stone-capped hills and granite fields. It is a fine summer day in the year 3000 A.D. On an ancient stone stump, about three feet thick and three feet high, used for securing ships by ropes to the shore, and called a bollard or holdfast, an elderly gentleman sits facing the land with his head bowed and his face in his hands, sobbing. His sunburnt skin contrasts with his white whiskers and eyebrows. He wears a black frock-coat, a white waistcoat, lavender trousers, a brilliant silk cravat with a jewelled pin stuck in it, a tall hat of grey felt, and patent leather boots with white spats. His starched linen cuffs protrude from his coat sleeves; and his collar, also of starched white linen, is Gladstonian. On his right, three or four full sacks, lying side by side on the flags, suggest that the pier, unlike many remote Irish piers, is occasionally useful as well as romantic. On his left, behind him, a flight of stone steps descends out of sight to the sea level.

A woman in a silk tunic and sandals, wearing little else except a cap with the number 2 on it in gold, comes up the steps from the sea, and stares in astonishment at the sobbing man. Her age cannot be guessed: her face is firm and chiselled like a young face; but her expression is unyouthful in its severity and determination.

THE WOMAN. What is the matter?

> *The elderly gentleman looks up; hastily pulls himself together; takes out a silk handkerchief and dries his tears lightly with a brave attempt to smile through them; and tries to rise gallantly, but sinks back.*

THE WOMAN. Do you need assistance?

THE ELDERLY GENTLEMAN. No. Thank you very much. No. Nothing. The heat. [*He punctuates with sniffs, and dabs with his handkerchief at his eyes and nose.*] Hay fever.

THE WOMAN. You are a foreigner, are you not?

THE ELDERLY GENTLEMAN. No. You must not regard me as a foreigner. I am a Briton.

THE WOMAN. You come from some part of the British Commonwealth?

THE ELDERLY GENTLEMAN [*amiably pompous*] From its capital, madam.

THE WOMAN. From Baghdad?

THE ELDERLY GENTLEMAN. Yes. You may not be aware, madam, that these islands were once the centre of the British Commonwealth, during a period now known as The Exile. They were its headquarters a thousand years ago. Few people know this interesting circumstance now; but I assure you it is true. I have come here on a pious pilgrimage to one of the numerous lands of my fathers. We are of the same stock, you and I. Blood is thicker than water. We are cousins.

THE WOMAN. I do not understand. You say you have come here on a pious pilgrimage. Is that some new means of transport?

THE ELDERLY GENTLEMAN [*again shewing signs of distress*] I find it very difficult to make myself understood here. I was not referring to a machine, but to a – a – a sentimental journey.

THE WOMAN. I am afraid I am as much in the dark as before. You said also that blood is thicker than water. No doubt it is; but what of it?

THE ELDERLY GENTLEMAN. Its meaning is obvious.

THE WOMAN. Perfectly. But I assure you I am quite aware that blood is thicker than water.

THE ELDERLY GENTLEMAN [*sniffing: almost in tears again*] We will leave it at that, madam.

THE WOMAN [*going nearer to him and scrutinizing him with some concern*] I am afraid you are not well. Were you not warned that it is dangerous for shortlived people to come to this country? There is a deadly disease called discouragement, against which short-lived people have to take very strict precautions. Intercourse with us puts too great a strain on them.

THE ELDERLY GENTLEMAN [*pulling himself together huffily*] It has no effect on me, madam. I fear my conversation does not interest you. If not, the remedy is in your own hands.

THE WOMAN [*looking at her hands, and then looking inquiringly at him*] Where?

THE ELDERLY GENTLEMAN [*breaking down*] Oh, this is dreadful. No understanding, no intelligence, no sympathy – [*his sobs choke him*].

THE WOMAN. You see, you are ill.

THE ELDERLY GENTLEMAN [*nerved by indignation*] I am not ill. I have never had a day's illness in my life.

THE WOMAN. May I advise you?

THE ELDERLY GENTLEMAN. I have no need of a lady doctor, thank you, madam.

THE WOMAN [*shaking her head*] I am afraid I do not understand. I said nothing about a butterfly.

THE ELDERLY GENTLEMAN. Well, *I* said nothing about a butterfly.

THE WOMAN. You spoke of a lady doctor. The word is known here only as the name of a butterfly.

THE ELDERLY GENTLEMAN [*insanely*] I give up. I can bear this no longer. It is easier to go out of my mind at once. [*He rises and dances about, singing*]

> I'd be a butterfly, born in a bower,
> Making apple dumplings without any flour.

THE WOMAN [*smiling gravely*] It must be at least a hundred and fifty years since I last laughed. But if you do that any more I shall certainly break out like a primary of sixty. Your dress is so extraordinarily ridiculous.

THE ELDERLY GENTLEMAN [*halting abruptly in his antics*] My dress ridiculous! I may not be dressed like a Foreign Office clerk; but my clothes are perfectly in fashion in my native metropolis, where yours – pardon my saying so – would be considered extremely unusual and hardly decent.

THE WOMAN. Decent? There is no such word in our language. What does it mean?

THE ELDERLY GENTLEMAN. It would not be decent for

me to explain. Decency cannot be discussed without in-
decency.

THE WOMAN. I cannot understand you at all. I fear you
have not been observing the rules laid down for shortlived
visitors.

THE ELDERLY GENTLEMAN. Surely, madam, they do not
apply to persons of my age and standing. I am not a child,
nor an agricultural laborer.

THE WOMAN [*severely*] They apply to you very strictly. You
are expected to confine yourself to the society of children
under sixty. You are absolutely forbidden to approach
fully adult natives under any circumstances. You cannot
converse with persons of my age for long without bringing
on a dangerous attack of discouragement. Do you realize
that you are already shewing grave symptoms of that very
distressing and usually fatal complaint?

THE ELDERLY GENTLEMAN. Certainly not, madam. I am
fortunately in no danger of contracting it. I am quite accustomed to converse intimately and at the greatest length
with the most distinguished persons. If you cannot dis-
criminate between hay fever and imbecility, I can only say
that your advanced years carry with them the inevitable
penalty of dotage.

THE WOMAN. I am one of the guardians of this district; and
I am responsible for your welfare –

THE ELDERLY GENTLEMAN. The Guardians! Do you take
me for a pauper?

THE WOMAN. I do not know what a pauper is. You must
tell me who you are, if it is possible for you to express yourself intelligibly –

THE ELDERLY GENTLEMAN [*snorts indignantly*]!

THE WOMAN [*continuing*] – and why you are wandering here
alone without a nurse.

THE ELDERLY GENTLEMAN [*outraged*] Nurse!

THE WOMAN. Shortlived visitors are not allowed to go
about here without nurses. Do you not know that rules are
meant to be kept?

THE ELDERLY GENTLEMAN. By the lower classes, no

doubt. But to persons in my position there are certain courtesies which are never denied by well-bred people; and –

THE WOMAN. There are only two human classes here: the shortlived and the normal. The rules apply to the shortlived, and are for their own protection. Now tell me at once who you are.

THE ELDERLY GENTLEMAN [*impressively*] Madam, I am a retired gentleman, formerly Chairman of the All-British Synthetic Egg and Vegetable Cheese Trust in Baghdad, and now President of the British Historical and Archaeological Society, and a Vice-President of the Travellers' Club.

THE WOMAN. All that does not matter.

THE ELDERLY GENTLEMAN [*again snorting*] Hm! Indeed!

THE WOMAN. Have you been sent here to make your mind flexible?

THE ELDERLY GENTLEMAN. What an extraordinary question! Pray do you find my mind noticeably stiff?

THE WOMAN. Perhaps you do not know that you are on the west coast of Ireland, and that it is the practice among natives of the Eastern Island to spend some years here to acquire mental flexibility. The climate has that effect.

THE ELDERLY GENTLEMAN [*haughtily*] I was born, not in the Eastern Island, but, thank God, in dear old British Baghdad; and I am not in need of a mental health resort.

THE WOMAN. Then why are you here?

THE ELDERLY GENTLEMAN. Am I trespassing? I was not aware of it.

THE WOMAN. Trespassing? I do not understand the word.

THE ELDERLY GENTLEMAN. Is this land private property? If so, I make no claim. I proffer a shilling in satisfaction of damage (if any), and am ready to withdraw if you will be good enough to shew me the nearest way. [*He offers her a shilling*].

THE WOMAN [*taking it and examining it without much interest*] I do not understand a single word of what you have just said.

THE ELDERLY GENTLEMAN. I am speaking the plainest English. Are you the landlord?

THE WOMAN [*shaking her head*] There is a tradition in this part of the country of an animal with a name like that. It used to be hunted and shot in the barbarous ages. It is quite extinct now.

THE ELDERLY GENTLEMAN [*breaking down again*] It is a dreadful thing to be in a country where nobody understands civilized institutions. [*He collapses on the bollard, struggling with his rising sobs*]. Excuse me. Hay fever.

THE WOMAN [*taking a tuning-fork from her girdle and holding it to her ear; then speaking into space on one note, like a chorister intoning a psalm*] Burrin Pier Galway please send someone to take charge of a discouraged shortliver who has escaped from his nurse male harmless babbles unintelligibly with moments of sense distressed hysterical foreign dress very funny has curious fringe of white sea-weed under his chin.

THE ELDERLY GENTLEMAN. This is a gross impertinence. An insult.

THE WOMAN [*replacing her tuning-fork and addressing the elderly gentleman*] These words mean nothing to me. In what capacity are you here? How did you obtain permission to visit us?

THE ELDERLY GENTLEMAN [*importantly*] Our Prime Minister, Mr Badger Bluebin, has come to consult the oracle. He is my son-in-law. We are accompanied by his wife and daughter: my daughter and granddaughter. I may mention that General Aufsteig, who is one of our party, is really the Emperor of Turania travelling incognito. I understand he has a question to put to the oracle informally. I have come solely to visit the country.

THE WOMAN. Why should you come to a place where you have no business?

THE ELDERLY GENTLEMAN. Great Heavens, madam, can anything be more natural? I shall be the only member of the Travellers' Club who has set foot on these shores. Think of that! My position will be unique.

THE WOMAN. Is that an advantage? We have a person here who has lost both legs in an accident. His position is unique. But he would much rather be like everyone else.

THE ELDERLY GENTLEMAN. This is maddening. There is no analogy whatever between the two cases.

THE WOMAN. They are both unique.

THE ELDERLY GENTLEMAN. Conversation in this place seems to consist of ridiculous quibbles. I am heartily tired of them.

THE WOMAN. I conclude that your Travellers' Club is an assembly of persons who wish to be able to say that they have been in some place where nobody else has been.

THE ELDERLY GENTLEMAN. Of course if you wish to sneer at us –

THE WOMAN. What is sneer?

THE ELDERLY GENTLEMAN [*with a wild sob*] I shall drown myself.

He makes desperately for the edge of the pier, but is confronted by a man with the number one on his cap, who comes up the steps and intercepts him. He is dressed like the woman, but a slight moustache proclaims his sex.

THE MAN [*to the elderly gentleman*] Ah, here you are. I shall really have to put a collar and lead on you if you persist in giving me the slip like this.

THE WOMAN. Are you this stranger's nurse?

THE MAN. Yes. I am very tired of him. If I take my eyes off him for a moment, he runs away and talks to everybody.

THE WOMAN [*after taking out her tuning-fork and sounding it, intones as before*] Burrin Pier. Wash out. [*She puts up the fork, and addresses the man*]. I sent a call for someone to take care of him. I have been trying to talk to him; but I can understand very little of what he says. You must take better care of him: he is badly discouraged already. If I can be of any further use, Fusima, Gort, will find me. [*She goes away*].

THE ELDERLY GENTLEMAN. Any further use! She has been of no use to me. She spoke to me without any introduction, like any improper female. And she has made off with my shilling.

THE MAN. Please speak slowly: I cannot follow. What is a shilling? What is an introduction? Improper female doesnt make sense.

THE ELDERLY GENTLEMAN. Nothing seems to make sense here. All I can tell you is that she was the most impenetrably stupid woman I have ever met in the whole course of my life.

THE MAN. That cannot be. She cannot appear stupid to you. She is a secondary, and getting on for a tertiary at that.

THE ELDERLY GENTLEMAN. What is a tertiary? Everybody here keeps talking to me about primaries and secondaries and tertiaries as if people were geological strata.

THE MAN. The primaries are in their first century. The secondaries are in their second century. I am still classed as a primary [*he points to his number*]; but I may almost call myself a secondary, as I shall be ninety-five next January. The tertiaries are in their third century. Did you not see the number two on her badge? She is an advanced secondary.

THE ELDERLY GENTLEMAN. That accounts for it. She is in her second childhood.

THE MAN. Her second childhood! She is in her fifth childhood.

THE ELDERLY GENTLEMAN [*again resorting to the bollard*] Oh! I cannot bear these unnatural arrangements.

THE MAN [*impatient and helpless*] You shouldnt have come among us. This is no place for you.

THE ELDERLY GENTLEMAN [*nerved by indignation*] May I ask why? I am a Vice-President of the Travellers' Club. I have been everywhere: I hold the record in the Club for civilized countries.

THE MAN. What is a civilized country?

THE ELDERLY GENTLEMAN. It is – well, it is a civilized country. [*Desperately*] I dont know: I – I – I – I shall go mad if you keep on asking me to tell you things that everybody knows. Countries where you can travel comfortably. Where there are good hotels. Excuse me; but, though you say you are ninety-four, you are worse company than a child of five with your eternal questions. Why not call me Daddy at once?

THE MAN. I did not know your name was Daddy.

THE ELDERLY GENTLEMAN. My name is Joseph Popham Bolge Bluebin Barlow, O.M.

THE MAN. That is five men's names. Daddy is shorter. And O.M. will not do here. It is our name for certain wild creatures, descendants of the aboriginal inhabitants of this coast. They used to be called the O'Mulligans. We will stick to Daddy.

THE ELDERLY GENTLEMAN. People will think I am your father.

THE MAN [shocked] Sh-sh! People here never allude to such relationships. It is not quite delicate, is it? What does it matter whether you are my father or not?

THE ELDERLY GENTLEMAN. My worthy nonagenarian friend: your faculties are totally decayed. Could you not find me a guide of my own age?

THE MAN. A young person?

THE ELDERLY GENTLEMAN. Certainly not. I cannot go about with a young person.

THE MAN. Why?

THE ELDERLY GENTLEMAN. Why! Why!! Why!!! Have you no moral sense?

THE MAN. I shall have to give you up. I cannot understand you.

THE ELDERLY GENTLEMAN. But you meant a young woman, didnt you?

THE MAN. I meant simply somebody of your own age. What difference does it make whether the person is a man or a woman?

THE ELDERLY GENTLEMAN. I could not have believed in the existence of such scandalous insensibility to the elementary decencies of human intercourse.

THE MAN. What are decencies?

THE ELDERLY GENTLEMAN [shrieking] Everyone asks me that.

THE MAN [taking out a tuning-fork and using it as the woman did] Zozim on Burrin Pier to Zoo Ennistymon I have found the discouraged shortliver he has been talking to a secondary

and is much worse I am too old he is asking for someone
of his own age or younger come if you can. [*He puts up his
fork and turns to the Elderly Gentleman*]. Zoo is a girl of fifty,
and rather childish at that. So perhaps she may make you
happy.

THE ELDERLY GENTLEMAN. Make me happy! A bluestocking of fifty! Thank you.

THE MAN. Bluestocking? The effort to make out your meaning is fatiguing. Besides, you are talking too much to me:
I am old enough to discourage you. Let us be silent
until Zoo comes. [*He turns his back on the Elderly Gentleman,
and sits down on the edge of the pier, with his legs dangling over
the water*].

THE ELDERLY GENTLEMAN. Certainly. I have no wish to
force my conversation on any man who does not desire it.
Perhaps you would like to take a nap. If so, pray do not
stand on ceremony.

THE MAN. What is a nap?

THE ELDERLY GENTLEMAN [*exasperated, going to him and
speaking with great precision and distinctness*] A nap, my
friend, is a brief period of sleep which overtakes superannuated persons when they endeavor to entertain unwelcome visitors or to listen to scientific lectures. Sleep.
Sleep. [*Bawling into his ear*] Sleep.

THE MAN. I tell you I am nearly a secondary. I never sleep.

THE ELDERLY GENTLEMAN [*awestruck*] Good Heavens!

*A young woman with the number one on her cap arrives by
land. She looks no older than Savvy Barnabas, whom she some-
what resembles, looked a thousand years before. Younger, if
anything.*

THE YOUNG WOMAN. Is this the patient?

THE MAN [*scrambling up*] This is Zoo. [*To Zoo*] Call him Daddy.

THE ELDERLY GENTLEMAN [*vehemently*] No.

THE MAN [*ignoring the interruption*] Bless you for taking him off
my hands! I have had as much of him as I can bear. [*He
goes down the steps and disappears*].

THE ELDERLY GENTLEMAN [*ironically taking off his hat and
making a sweeping bow from the edge of the pier in the direction of*

the Atlantic Ocean] Good afternoon, sir; and thank you very much for your extraordinary politeness, your exquisite consideration for my feelings, your courtly manners. Thank you from the bottom of my heart. [*Clapping his hat on again*] Pig! Ass!

ZOO [*laughs very heartily at him*]!!!

THE ELDERLY GENTLEMAN [*turning sharply on her*] Good afternoon, madam. I am sorry to have had to put your friend in his place; but I find that here as elsewhere it is necessary to assert myself if I am to be treated with proper consideration. I had hoped that my position as a guest would protect me from insult.

ZOO. Putting my friend in his place. That is some poetic expression, is it not? What does it mean?

THE ELDERLY GENTLEMAN. Pray, is there no one in these islands who understands plain English?

ZOO. Well, nobody except the oracles. They have to make a special historical study of what we call the dead thought.

THE ELDERLY GENTLEMAN. Dead thought! I have heard of the dead languages, but never of the dead thought.

ZOO. Well, thoughts die sooner than languages. I understand your language; but I do not always understand your thought. The oracles will understand you perfectly. Have you had your consultation yet?

THE ELDERLY GENTLEMAN. I did not come to consult the oracle, madam. I am here simply as a gentleman travelling for pleasure in the company of my daughter, who is the wife of the British Prime Minister, and of General Aufsteig, who, I may tell you in confidence, is really the Emperor of Turania, the greatest military genius of the age.

ZOO. Why should you travel for pleasure! Can you not enjoy yourself at home?

THE ELDERLY GENTLEMAN. I wish to see the world.

ZOO. It is too big. You can see a bit of it anywhere.

THE ELDERLY GENTLEMAN [*out of patience*] Damn it, madam, you dont want to spend your life looking at the same bit of it! [*Checking himself*] I beg your pardon for swearing in your presence.

zoo. Oh! That is swearing, is it? I have read about that. It
sounds quite pretty. Dammitmaddam, dammitmaddam,
dammitmaddam, dammitmaddam. Say it as often as you
please: I like it.

THE ELDERLY GENTLEMAN [*expanding with intense relief*]
Bless you for those profane but familiar words! Thank
you, thank you. For the first time since I landed in this
terrible country I begin to feel at home. The strain which
was driving me mad relaxes: I feel almost as if I were at
the club. Excuse my taking the only available seat: I am
not so young as I was. [*He sits on the bollard*]. Promise me
that you will not hand me over to one of these dreadful
tertiaries or secondaries or whatever you call them.

zoo. Never fear. They had no business to give you in charge
to Zozim. You see he is just on the verge of becoming
a secondary; and these adolescents will give themselves
the airs of tertiaries. You naturally feel more at home
with a flapper like me. [*She makes herself comfortable on the
sacks*].

THE ELDERLY GENTLEMAN. Flapper? What does that
mean?

zoo. It is an archaic word which we still use to describe
a female who is no longer a girl and is not yet quite
adult.

THE ELDERLY GENTLEMAN. A very agreeable age to as-
sociate with, I find. I am recovering rapidly. I have a
sense of blossoming like a flower. May I ask your name?

zoo. Zoo.

THE ELDERLY GENTLEMAN. Miss Zoo.

zoo. Not Miss Zoo. Zoo.

THE ELDERLY GENTLEMAN. Precisely. Er – Zoo what?

zoo. No. Not Zoo What. Zoo. Nothing but Zoo.

THE ELDERLY GENTLEMAN [*puzzled*] Mrs Zoo, perhaps.

zoo. No. Zoo. Cant you catch it? Zoo.

THE ELDERLY GENTLEMAN. Of course. Believe me, I did
not really think you were married: you are obviously too
young; but here it is so hard to feel sure – er –

zoo [*hopelessly puzzled*] What?

THE ELDERLY GENTLEMAN. Marriage makes a difference, you know. One can say things to a married lady that would perhaps be in questionable taste to anyone without that experience.

ZOO. You are getting out of my depth: I dont understand a word you are saying. Married and questionable taste convey nothing to me. Stop, though. Is married an old form of the word mothered?

THE ELDERLY GENTLEMAN. Very likely. Let us drop the subject. Pardon me for embarrassing you. I should not have mentioned it.

ZOO. What does embarrassing mean?

THE ELDERLY GENTLEMAN. Well, really! I should have thought that so natural and common a condition would be understood as long as human nature lasted. To embarrass is to bring a blush to the cheek.

ZOO. What is a blush?

THE ELDERLY GENTLEMAN [amazed] Dont you blush???

ZOO. Never heard of it. We have a word flush, meaning a rush of blood to the skin. I have noticed it in my babies, but not after the age of two.

THE ELDERLY GENTLEMAN. Your babies!!! I fear I am treading on very delicate ground; but your appearance is extremely youthful; and if I may ask how many – ?

ZOO. Only four as yet. It is a long business with us. I specialize in babies. My first was such a success that they made me go on. I –

THE ELDERLY GENTLEMAN [reeling on the bollard] Oh! dear!

ZOO. Whats the matter? Anything wrong?

THE ELDERLY GENTLEMAN. In Heaven's name, madam, how old are you?

ZOO. Fifty-six.

THE ELDERLY GENTLEMAN. My knees are trembling. I fear I am really ill. Not so young as I was.

ZOO. I noticed that you are not strong on your legs yet. You have many of the ways and weaknesses of a baby. No doubt that is why I feel called on to mother you. You certainly are a very silly little Daddy.

THE ELDERLY GENTLEMAN [*stimulated by indignation*] My
name, I repeat, is Joseph Popham Bolge Bluebin Barlow, O.M.

ZOO. What a ridiculously long name! I cant call you all
that. What did your mother call you?

THE ELDERLY GENTLEMAN. You recall the bitterest struggles of my childhood. I was sensitive on the point. Children
suffer greatly from absurd nicknames. My mother thoughtlessly called me Iddy Toodles. I was called Iddy until I
went to school, when I made my first stand for children's
rights by insisting on being called at least Joe. At fifteen I
refused to answer to anything shorter than Joseph. At
eighteen I discovered that the name Joseph was supposed to indicate an unmanly prudery because of some
old story about a Joseph who rejected the advances of his
employer's wife: very properly in my opinion. I then
became Popham to my family and intimate friends, and
Mister Barlow to the rest of the world. My mother slipped
back into Iddy when her faculties began to fail her, poor
woman; but I could not resent that, at her age.

ZOO. Do you mean to say that your mother bothered about
you after you were ten?

THE ELDERLY GENTLEMAN. Naturally, madam. She was
my mother. What would you have had her do?

ZOO. Go on to the next, of course. After eight or nine
children become quite uninteresting, except to themselves. I shouldnt know my two eldest if I met them.

THE ELDERLY GENTLEMAN [*again drooping*] I am dying.
Let me die. I wish to die.

ZOO [*going to him quickly and supporting him*] Hold up. Sit up
straight. Whats the matter?

THE ELDERLY GENTLEMAN [*faintly*] My spine, I think.
Shock. Concussion.

ZOO [*maternally*] Pow wow wow! What is there to shock you?
[*Shaking him playfully*] There! Sit up; and be good.

THE ELDERLY GENTLEMAN [*still feebly*] Thank you. I am
better now.

ZOO [*resuming her seat on the sacks*] But what was all the rest of that long name for? There was a lot more of it. Blops Booby or something.

THE ELDERLY GENTLEMAN [*impressively*] Bolge Bluebin, madam: a historical name. Let me inform you that I can trace my family back for more than a thousand years, from the Eastern Empire to its ancient seat in these islands, to a time when two of my ancestors, Joyce Bolge and Hengist Horsa Bluebin, wrestled with one another for the prime ministership of the British Empire, and occupied that position successively with a glory of which we can in these degenerate days form but a faint conception. When I think of these mighty men, lions in war, sages in peace, not babblers and charlatans like the pigmies who now occupy their places in Baghdad, but strong silent men, ruling an empire on which the sun never set, my eyes fill with tears: my heart bursts with emotion: I feel that to have lived but to the dawn of manhood in their day, and then died for them, would have been a nobler and happier lot than the ignominious ease of my present longevity.

ZOO. Longevity! [*she laughs*].

THE ELDERLY GENTLEMAN. Yes, madam, relative longevity. As it is, I have to be content and proud to know that I am descended from both those heroes.

ZOO. You must be descended from every Briton who was alive in their time. Dont you know that?

THE ELDERLY GENTLEMAN. Do not quibble, madam. I bear their names, Bolge and Bluebin; and I hope I have inherited something of their majestic spirit. Well, they were born in these islands. I repeat, these islands were then, incredible as it now seems, the centre of the British Empire. When that centre shifted to Baghdad, and the Englishman at last returned to the true cradle of his race in Mesopotamia, the western islands were cast off, as they had been before by the Roman Empire. But it was to the British race, and in these islands, that the greatest miracle in history occurred.

ZOO. Miracle?

THE ELDERLY GENTLEMAN. Yes: the first man to live

three hundred years was an Englishman. The first, at this, since the contemporaries of Methuselah.

ZOO. Oh, that!

THE ELDERLY GENTLEMAN. Yes, that, as you call it so flippantly. Are you aware, madam, that at that immortal moment the English race had lost intellectual credit to such an extent that they habitually spoke of one another as fatheads? Yet England is now a sacred grove to which statesmen from all over the earth come to consult English sages who speak with the experience of two and a half centuries of life. The land that once exported cotton shirts and hardware now exports nothing but wisdom. You see before you, madam, a man utterly weary of the week-end riverside hotels of the Euphrates, the minstrels and pierrots on the sands of the Persian Gulf, the toboggans and funiculars of the Hindoo Koosh. Can you wonder that I turn, with a hungry heart, to the mystery and beauty of these haunted islands, thronged with spectres from a magic past, made holy by the footsteps of the wise men of the West. Consider this island on which we stand, the last foothold of man on this side of the Atlantic: this Ireland, described by the earliest bards as an emerald gem set in a silver sea! Can I, a scion of the illustrious British race, ever forget that when the Empire transferred its seat to the East, and said to the turbulent Irish race which it had oppressed but never conquered, 'At last we leave you to yourselves; and much good may it do you,' the Irish as one man uttered the historic shout 'No: we'll be damned if you do,' and emigrated to the countries where there was still a Nationalist question, to India, Persia, and Corea, to Morocco, Tunis, and Tripoli. In these countries they were ever foremost in the struggle for national independence; and the world rang continually with the story of their sufferings and wrongs. And what poem can do justice to the end, when it came at last? Hardly two hundred years had elapsed when the claims of nationality were so universally conceded that there was no longer a single country on the face of the earth with a national grievance or a national movement. Think of the position of the Irish, who had lost all their political faculties by disuse except that of nationalist agitation, and who owed their position as the most interesting race on earth solely to their sufferings! The very countries they had helped to set free boycotted them as intolerable bores. The communities which had once idolized them as the incarnation of all that is adorable in the warm heart and witty brain, fled from them as from a pestilence. To regain their lost prestige, the Irish claimed the city of Jerusalem, on the ground that they were the lost tribes of Israel; but on their approach the Jews abandoned the city and redistributed themselves throughout Europe. It was then that these devoted Irishmen, not one of whom had ever seen Ireland, were counselled by an English Archbishop, the father of the oracles, to go back to their own country. This had never once occurred to them, because there was nothing to prevent them and nobody to forbid them. They jumped at the suggestion. They landed here: here in Galway Bay, on this very ground. When they reached the shore the older men and women flung themselves down and passionately kissed the soil of Ireland, calling on the young to embrace the earth that had borne their ancestors. But the young looked gloomily on, and said 'There is no earth, only stone.' You will see by looking round you why they said that: the fields here are of stone: the hills are capped with granite. They all left for England next day; and no Irishman ever again confessed to being Irish, even to his own children; so that when that generation passed away the Irish race vanished from human knowledge. And the dispersed Jews did the same lest they should be sent back to Palestine. Since then the world, bereft of its Jews and its Irish, has been a tame dull place. Is there no pathos for you in this story? Can you not understand now why I am come to visit the scene of this tragic effacement of a race of heroes and poets?

zoo. We still tell our little children stories like that, to help them to understand. But such things do not happen really.

That scene of the Irish landing here and kissing the ground might have happened to a hundred people. It couldnt have happened to a hundred thousand: you know that as well as I do. And what a ridiculous thing to call people Irish because they live in Ireland! you might as well call them Airish because they live in air. They must be just the same as other people. Why do you shortlivers persist in making up silly stories about the world and trying to act as if they were true? Contact with truth hurts and frightens you: you escape from it into an imaginary vacuum in which you can indulge your desires and hopes and loves and hates without any obstruction from the solid facts of life. You love to throw dust in your own eyes.

THE ELDERLY GENTLEMAN. It is my turn now, madam, to inform you that I do not understand a single word you are saying. I should have thought that the use of a vacuum for removing dust was a mark of civilization rather than of savagery.

ZOO [*giving him up as hopeless*] Oh, Daddy, Daddy: I can hardly believe that you are human, you are so stupid. It was well said of your people in the olden days, 'Dust thou art; and to dust thou shalt return.'

THE ELDERLY GENTLEMAN [*nobly*] My body is dust, madam: not my soul. What does it matter what my body is made of? the dust of the ground, the particles of the air, or even the slime of the ditch? The important thing is that when my Creator took it, whatever it was, He breathed into its nostrils the breath of life; and Man became a living soul. Yes, madam, a living soul. I am not the dust of the ground: I am a living soul. That is an exalting, a magnificent thought. It is also a great scientific fact. I am not interested in the chemicals and the microbes: I leave them to the chumps and noodles, to the blockheads and the muckrakers who are incapable of their own glorious destiny, and unconscious of their own divinity. They tell me there are leucocytes in my blood, and sodium and carbon in my flesh. I thank them for the information, and tell them that there are blackbeetles in my kitchen, washing

soda in my laundry, and coal in my cellar. I do not deny
their existence; but I keep them in their proper place,
which is not, if I may be allowed to use an antiquated
form of expression, the temple of the Holy Ghost. No
doubt you think me behind the times; but I rejoice in my
enlightenment; and I recoil from your ignorance, your
blindness, your imbecility. Humanly I pity you. Intellectually I despise you.

ZOO. Bravo, Daddy! You have the root of the matter in you.
You will not die of discouragement after all.

THE ELDERLY GENTLEMAN. I have not the smallest intention of doing so, madam. I am no longer young; and I
have moments of weakness; but when I approach this
subject the divine spark in me kindles and glows, the cor-
ruptible becomes incorruptible, and the mortal Bolge Bluebin Barlow puts on immortality. On this ground I am your
equal, even if you survive me by ten thousand years.

ZOO. Yes; but what do we know about the breath of life
that puffs you up so exaltedly? Just nothing. So let us
shake hands as cultivated Agnostics, and change the
subject.

THE ELDERLY GENTLEMAN. Cultivated fiddlesticks, madam! You cannot change this subject until the heavens
and the earth pass away. I am not an Agnostic: I am a
gentleman. When I believe a thing I say I believe it: when
I dont believe it I say I dont believe it. I do not shirk my
responsibilities by pretending that I know nothing and
therefore can believe nothing. We cannot disclaim knowledge and shirk responsibility. We must proceed on assumptions of some sort or we cannot form a human society.

ZOO. The assumptions must be scientific, Daddy. We must
live by science in the long run.

THE ELDERLY GENTLEMAN. I have the utmost respect,
madam, for the magnificent discoveries which we owe to
science. But any fool can make a discovery. Every baby
has to discover more in the first years of its life than Roger
Bacon ever discovered in his laboratory. When I was seven
years old I discovered the sting of the wasp. But I do not

ask you to worship me on that account. I assure you, madam, the merest mediocrities can discover the most surprising facts about the physical universe as soon as they are civilized enough to have time to study these things, and to invent instruments and apparatus for research. But what is the consequence? Their discoveries discredit the simple stories of our religion. At first we had no idea of astronomical space. We believed the sky to be only the ceiling of a room as large as the earth, with another room on top of it. Death was to us a going upstairs into that room, or, if we did not obey the priests, going downstairs into the coal cellar. We founded our religion, our morality, our laws, our lessons, our poems, our prayers, on that simple belief. Well, the moment men became astronomers and made telescopes, their belief perished. When they could no longer believe in the sky, they found that they could no longer believe in their Deity, because they had always thought of him as living in the sky. When the priests themselves ceased to believe in their Deity and began to believe in astronomy, they changed their name and their dress, and called themselves doctors and men of science. They set up a new religion in which there was no Deity, but only wonders and miracles, with scientific instruments and apparatus as the wonder workers. Instead of worshipping the greatness and wisdom of the Deity, men gaped foolishly at the million billion miles of space and worshipped the astronomer as infallible and omniscient. They built temples for his telescopes. Then they looked into their own bodies with microscopes, and found there, not the soul they had formerly believed in, but millions of micro-organisms; so they gaped at these as foolishly as at the millions of miles, and built microscope temples in which horrible sacrifices were offered. They even gave their own bodies to be sacrificed by the microscope man, who was worshipped, like the astronomer, as infallible and omniscient. Thus our discoveries instead of increasing our wisdom, only destroyed the little childish wisdom we had. All I can grant you is that they increased our knowledge.

zoo. Nonsense! Consciousness of a fact is not knowledge of it: if it were, the fish would know more of the sea than the geographers and the naturalists.

THE ELDERLY GENTLEMAN. That is an extremely acute remark, madam. The dullest fish could not possibly know less of the majesty of the ocean than many geographers and naturalists of my acquaintance.

zoo. Just so. And the greatest fool on earth, by merely looking at a mariners' compass, may become conscious of the fact that the needle turns always to the pole. Is he any the less a fool with that consciousness than he was without it?

THE ELDERLY GENTLEMAN. Only a more conceited one, madam, no doubt. Still, I do not quite see how you can be aware of the existence of a thing without knowing it.

zoo. Well, you can see a man without knowing him, can you not?

THE ELDERLY GENTLEMAN [*illuminated*] Oh how true! Of course, of course. There is a member of the Travellers' Club who has questioned the veracity of an experience of mine at the South Pole. I see that man almost every day when I am at home. But I refuse to know him.

zoo. If you could see him much more distinctly through a magnifying glass, or examine a drop of his blood through a microscope, or dissect out all his organs and analyze them chemically, would you know him then?

THE ELDERLY GENTLEMAN. Certainly not. Any such investigation could only increase the disgust with which he inspires me, and make me more determined than ever not to know him on any terms.

zoo. Yet you would be much more conscious of him, would you not?

THE ELDERLY GENTLEMAN. I should not allow that to commit me to any familiarity with the fellow. I have been twice at the Summer Sports at the South Pole; and this man pretended he had been to the North Pole, which can hardly be said to exist, as it is in the middle of the sea. He declared he had hung his hat on it.

zoo [*laughing*] He knew that travellers are amusing only

when they are telling lies. Perhaps if you looked at that man through a microscope you would find some good in him.

THE ELDERLY GENTLEMAN. I do not want to find any good in him. Besides, madam, what you have just said encourages me to utter an opinion of mine which is so advanced! so intellectually daring! that I have never ventured to confess to it before, lest I should be imprisoned for blasphemy, or even burnt alive.

zoo. Indeed! What opinion is that?

THE ELDERLY GENTLEMAN [after looking cautiously round] I do not approve of microscopes. I never have.

zoo. You call that advanced! Oh, Daddy, that is pure obscurantism.

THE ELDERLY GENTLEMAN. Call it so if you will, madam; but I maintain that it is dangerous to shew too much to people who do not know what they are looking at. I think that a man who is sane as long as he looks at the world through his own eyes is very likely to become a dangerous madman if he takes to looking at the world through telescopes and microscopes. Even when he is telling fairy stories about giants and dwarfs, the giants had better not be too big nor the dwarfs too small and too malicious. Before the microscope came, our fairy stories only made the children's flesh creep pleasantly, and did not frighten grown-up persons at all. But the microscope men terrified themselves and everyone else out of their wits with the invisible monsters they saw: poor harmless little things that die at the touch of a ray of sunshine, and are themselves the victims of all the diseases they are supposed to produce! Whatever the scientific people may say, imagination without microscopes was kindly and often courageous, because it worked on things of which it had some real knowledge. But imagination with microscopes, working on a terrifying spectacle of millions of grotesque creatures of whose nature it had no knowledge, became a cruel, terrorstricken, persecuting delirium. Are you aware, madam, that a general massacre of men of science took place in the twenty-first century of the pseudo-Christian era, when all their laboratories were demolished, and all their apparatus destroyed?

ZOO. Yes: the shortlived are as savage in their advances as in their relapses. But when Science crept back, it had been taught its place. The mere collectors of anatomical or chemical facts were not supposed to know more about Science than the collector of used postage stamps about international trade or literature. The scientific terrorist who was afraid to use a spoon or a tumbler until he had dipt it in some poisonous acid to kill the microbes, was no longer given titles, pensions, and monstrous powers over the bodies of other people: he was sent to an asylum, and treated there until his recovery. But all that is an old story: the extension of life to three hundred years has provided the human race with capable leaders, and made short work of such childish stuff.

THE ELDERLY GENTLEMAN [*pettishly*] You seem to credit every advance in civilization to your inordinately long lives. Do you not know that this question was familiar to men who died before they had reached my own age?

ZOO. Oh yes: one or two of them hinted at it in a feeble way. An ancient writer whose name has come down to us in several forms, such as Shakespear, Shelley, Sheridan, and Shoddy, has a remarkable passage about your dispositions being horridly shaken by thoughts beyond the reaches of your souls. That does not come to much, does it?

THE ELDERLY GENTLEMAN. At all events, madam, I may remind you, if you come to capping ages, that whatever your secondaries and tertiaries may be, you are younger than I am.

ZOO. Yes, Daddy; but it is not the number of years we have behind us, but the number we have before us, that makes us careful and responsible and determined to find out the truth about everything. What does it matter to you whether anything is true or not? your flesh is as grass: you come up like a flower, and wither in your second childhood. A lie will last your time: it will not last mine. If I knew I had to die in twenty years it would not be worth my while to educate myself: I should not bother about anything but having a little pleasure while I lasted.

THE ELDERLY GENTLEMAN. Young woman: you are mistaken. Shortlived as we are, we – the best of us, I mean – regard civilization and learning, art and science, as an ever-burning torch, which passes from the hand of one generation to the hand of the next, each generation kindling it to a brighter, prouder flame. Thus each lifetime, however short, contributes a brick to a vast and growing edifice, a page to a sacred volume, a chapter to a Bible, a Bible to a literature. We may be insects; but like the coral insect we build islands which become continents: like the bee we store sustenance for future communities. The individual perishes; but the race is immortal. The acorn of today is the oak of the next millennium. I throw my stone on the cairn and die; but later comers add another stone and yet another; and lo! a mountain. I –

zoo [*interrupts him by laughing heartily at him*] !!!!!!

THE ELDERLY GENTLEMAN [*with offended dignity*] May I ask what I have said that calls for this merriment?

zoo. Oh, Daddy, Daddy, Daddy, you are a funny little man, with your torches, and your flames, and your bricks and edifices and pages and volumes and chapters and coral insects and bees and acorns and stones and mountains.

THE ELDERLY GENTLEMAN. Metaphors, madam. Metaphors merely.

zoo. Images, images, images. I was talking about men, not about images.

THE ELDERLY GENTLEMAN. I was illustrating – not, I hope, quite infelicitously – the great march of Progress. I was shewing you how, shortlived as we orientals are, mankind gains in stature from generation to generation, from epoch to epoch, from barbarism to civilization, from civilization to perfection.

zoo. I see. The father grows to be six feet high, and hands on his six feet to his son, who adds another six feet and becomes twelve feet high, and hands his twelve feet on to his son, who is full-grown at eighteen feet, and so on. In a thousand years you would all be three or four miles high. At that rate your ancestors Bilge and Bluebeard, whom you call giants, must have been about quarter of an inch high.

THE ELDERLY GENTLEMAN. I am not here to bandy quibbles and paradoxes with a girl who blunders over the greatest names in history. I am in earnest. I am treating a solemn theme seriously. I never said that the son of a man six feet high would be twelve feet high.

ZOO. You didnt mean that?

THE ELDERLY GENTLEMAN. Most certainly not.

ZOO. Then you didnt mean anything. Now listen to me, you little ephemeral thing. I knew quite well what you meant by your torch handed on from generation to generation. But every time that torch is handed on, it dies down to the tiniest spark; and the man who gets it can rekindle it only by his own light. You are no taller than Bilge or Bluebeard; and you are no wiser. Their wisdom, such as it was, perished with them: so did their strength, if their strength ever existed outside your imagination. I do not know how old you are: you look about five hundred –

THE ELDERLY GENTLEMAN. Five hundred! Really, madam –

ZOO [continuing]; but I know, of course, that you are an ordinary shortliver. Well, your wisdom is only such wisdom as a man can have before he has had experience enough to distinguish his wisdom from his folly, his destiny from his delusions, his –

THE ELDERLY GENTLEMAN. In short, such wisdom as your own.

ZOO. No, no, no, no. How often must I tell you that we are made wise not by the recollections of our past, but by the responsibilities of our future. I shall be more reckless when I am a tertiary than I am today. If you cannot understand that, at least you must admit that I have learnt from tertiaries. I have seen their work and lived under their institutions. Like all young things I rebelled against them;

and in their hunger for new lights and new ideas they listened to me and encouraged me to rebel. But my ways did not work; and theirs did; and they were able to tell me why. They have no power over me except that power: they refuse all other power; and the consequence is that there are no limits to their power except the limits they set themselves. You are a child governed by children, who make so many mistakes and are so naughty that you are in continual rebellion against them; and as they can never convince you that they are right: they can govern you only by beating you, imprisoning you, torturing you, killing you if you disobey them without being strong enough to kill or torture them.

THE ELDERLY GENTLEMAN. That may be an unfortunate fact. I condemn it and deplore it. But our minds are greater than the facts. We know better. The greatest ancient teachers, followed by the galaxy of Christs who arose in the twentieth century, not to mention such comparatively modern spiritual leaders as Blitherinjam, Tosh, and Spiffkins, all taught that punishment and revenge, coercion and militarism, are mistakes, and that the golden rule –

ZOO [*interrupting*] Yes, yes, yes, Daddy: we longlived people know that quite well. But did any of their disciples ever succeed in governing you for a single day on their Christlike principles? It is not enough to know what is good: you must be able to do it. They couldnt do it because they did not live long enough to find out how to do it, or to outlive the childish passions that prevented them from really wanting to do it. You know very well that they could only keep order – such as it was – by the very coercion and militarism they were denouncing and deploring. They had actually to kill one another for preaching their own gospel, or be killed themselves.

THE ELDERLY GENTLEMAN. The blood of the martyrs, madam, is the seed of the Church.

ZOO. More images, Daddy! The blood of the shortlived falls on stony ground.

THE ELDERLY GENTLEMAN [*rising, very testy*] You are simply mad on the subject of longevity. I wish you would change it. It is rather personal and in bad taste. Human nature is human nature, longlived or shortlived, and always will be.

ZOO. Then you give up the idea of progress? You cry off the torch, and the brick, and the acorn, and all the rest of it?

THE ELDERLY GENTLEMAN. I do nothing of the sort. I stand for progress and for freedom broadening down from precedent to precedent.

ZOO. You are certainly a true Briton.

THE ELDERLY GENTLEMAN. I am proud of it. But in your mouth I feel that the compliment hides some insult; so I do not thank you for it.

ZOO. All I meant was that though Britons sometimes say quite clever things and deep things as well as silly and shallow things, they always forget them ten minutes after they have uttered them.

THE ELDERLY GENTLEMAN. Leave it at that, madam: leave it at that. [*He sits down again*]. Even a Pope is not expected to be continually pontificating. Our flashes of inspiration shew that our hearts are in the right place.

ZOO. Of course. You cannot keep your heart in any place but the right place.

THE ELDERLY GENTLEMAN. Tcha!

ZOO. But you can keep your hands in the wrong place. In your neighbor's pockets, for example. So, you see, it is your hands that really matter.

THE ELDERLY GENTLEMAN [*exhausted*] Well, a woman must have the last word. I will not dispute it with you.

ZOO. Good. Now let us go back to the really interesting subject of our discussion. You remember? The slavery of the shortlived to images and metaphors.

THE ELDERLY GENTLEMAN [*aghast*] Do you mean to say, madam, that after having talked my head off, and reduced me to despair and silence by your intolerable loquacity, you actually propose to begin all over again? I shall leave you at once.

ZOO. You must not. I am your nurse; and you must stay with me.

THE ELDERLY GENTLEMAN. I absolutely decline to do anything of the sort [*he rises and walks away with marked dignity*].

ZOO [*using her tuning-fork*] Zoo on Burrin Pier to Oracle Police at Ennistymon have you got me?... What?... I am picking you up now but you are flat to my pitch.... Just a shade sharper.... Thats better: still a little more.... Got you: right. Isolate Burrin Pier quick.

THE ELDERLY GENTLEMAN [*is heard to yell*] Oh!

ZOO [*still intoning*] Thanks.... Oh nothing serious I am nursing a shortliver and the silly creature has run away he has discouraged himself very badly by gadding about and talking to secondaries and I must keep him strictly to heel. *The Elderly Gentleman returns, indignant.*

ZOO. Here he is you can release the Pier thanks. Goodbye. [*She puts up her tuning-fork*].

THE ELDERLY GENTLEMAN. This is outrageous. When I tried to step off the pier on to the road, I received a shock, followed by an attack of pins and needles which ceased only when I stepped back on to the stones.

ZOO. Yes: there is an electric hedge there. It is a very old and very crude method of keeping animals from straying.

THE ELDERLY GENTLEMAN. We are perfectly familiar with it in Baghdad, madam; but I little thought I should live to have it ignominiously applied to myself. You have actually Kiplingized me.

ZOO. Kiplingized! What is that?

THE ELDERLY GENTLEMAN. About a thousand years ago there were two authors named Kipling. One was an eastern and a writer of merit: the other, being a western, was of course only an amusing barbarian. He is said to have invented the electric hedge. I consider that in using it on me you have taken a very great liberty.

ZOO. What is a liberty?

THE ELDERLY GENTLEMAN [*exasperated*] I shall not explain, madam. I believe you know as well as I do. [*He sits down on the bollard in dudgeon*].

ZOO. No: even you can tell me things I do not know. Havnt you noticed that all the time you have been here we have been asking you questions?

THE ELDERLY GENTLEMAN. Noticed it! It has almost driven me mad. Do you see my white hair? It was hardly grey when I landed: there were patches of its original auburn still distinctly discernible.

ZOO. That is one of the symptoms of discouragement. But have you noticed something much more important to yourself: that is, that you have never asked us any questions, although we know so much more than you do?

THE ELDERLY GENTLEMAN. I am not a child, madam. I believe I have had occasion to say that before. And I am an experienced traveller. I know that what the traveller observes must really exist, or he could not observe it. But what the natives tell him is invariably pure fiction.

ZOO. Not here, Daddy. With us life is too long for telling lies. They all get found out. Youd better ask me questions while you have the chance.

THE ELDERLY GENTLEMAN. If I have occasion to consult the oracle I shall address myself to a proper one: to a tertiary: not to a primary flapper playing at being an oracle. If you are a nurserymaid, attend to your duties; and do not presume to ape your elders.

ZOO [*rising ominously and reddening*] You silly –

THE ELDERLY GENTLEMAN [*thundering*] Silence! Do you hear! Hold your tongue.

ZOO. Something very disagreeable is happening to me. I feel hot all over. I have a horrible impulse to injure you. What have you done to me?

THE ELDERLY GENTLEMAN [*triumphant*] Aha! I have made you blush. Now you know what blushing means. Blushing with shame!

ZOO. Whatever you are doing, it is something so utterly evil that if you do not stop I will kill you.

THE ELDERLY GENTLEMAN [*apprehending his danger*] Doubtless you think it safe to threaten an old man –

zoo [*fiercely*] Old! You are a child: an evil child. We kill evil
children here. We do it even against our own wills by
instinct. Take care.

THE ELDERLY GENTLEMAN [*rising with crestfallen courtesy*] I
did not mean to hurt your feelings. I – [*swallowing the
apology with an effort*] I beg your pardon. [*He takes off his hat,
and bows*].

zoo. What does that mean?

THE ELDERLY GENTLEMAN. I withdraw what I said.

zoo. How can you withdraw what you said?

THE ELDERLY GENTLEMAN. I can say no more than that I
am sorry.

zoo. You have reason to be. That hideous sensation you
gave me is subsiding; but you have had a very narrow
escape. Do not attempt to kill me again; for at the first
sign in your voice or face I shall strike you dead.

THE ELDERLY GENTLEMAN. *I* attempt to kill you! What a
monstrous accusation!

zoo [*frowns*]!

THE ELDERLY GENTLEMAN [*prudently correcting himself*] I
mean misunderstanding. I never dreamt of such a thing.
Surely you cannot believe that I am a murderer.

zoo. I know you are a murderer. It is not merely that you
threw words at me as if they were stones, meaning to hurt
me. It was the instinct to kill that you roused in me. I did
not know it was in my nature: never before has it wakened
and sprung out at me, warning me to kill or be killed. I
must now reconsider my whole political position. I am no
longer a Conservative.

THE ELDERLY GENTLEMAN [*dropping his hat*] Gracious
Heavens! you have lost your senses. I am at the mercy of a
madwoman: I might have known it from the beginning. I
can bear no more of this. [*Offering his chest for the sacrifice*]
Kill me at once; and much good may my death do you!

zoo. It would be useless unless all the other shortlivers were
killed at the same time. Besides, it is a measure which
should be taken politically and constitutionally, not
privately. However, I am prepared to discuss it with you.

THE ELDERLY GENTLEMAN. No, no, no. I had much rather discuss your intention of withdrawing from the Conservative party. How the Conservatives have tolerated your opinions so far is more than I can imagine: I can only conjecture that you have contributed very liberally to the party funds. [*He picks up his hat, and sits down again*].

ZOO. Do not babble so senselessly: our chief political controversy is the most momentous in the world for you and your life.

THE ELDERLY GENTLEMAN [*interested*] Indeed? Pray, may I ask what it is? I am a keen politician, and may perhaps be of some use. [*He puts on his hat, cocking it slightly*].

ZOO. We have two great parties: the Conservative party and the Colonization party. The Colonizers are of opinion that we should increase our numbers and colonize. The Conservatives hold that we should stay as we are, confined to these islands, a race apart, wrapped up in the majesty of our wisdom on a soil held as holy ground for us by an adoring world, with our sacred frontier traced beyond dispute by the sea. They contend that it is our destiny to rule the world, and that even when we were shortlived we did so. They say that our power and our peace depend on our remoteness, our exclusiveness, our separation, and the restriction of our numbers. Five minutes ago that was my political faith. Now I do not think there should be any shortlived people at all. [*She throws herself again carelessly on the sacks*].

THE ELDERLY GENTLEMAN. Am I to infer that you deny my right to live because I allowed myself – perhaps injudiciously – to give you a slight scolding?

ZOO. Is it worth living for so short a time? Are you any good to yourself?

THE ELDERLY GENTLEMAN [*stupent*] Well, upon my soul!

ZOO. It is such a very little soul. You only encourage the sin of pride in us, and keep us looking down at you instead of up to something higher than ourselves.

THE ELDERLY GENTLEMAN. Is not that a selfish view, madam? Think of the good you do us by your oracular counsels!

ZOO. What good have our counsels ever done you? You come to us for advice when you know you are in difficulties. But you never know you are in difficulties until twenty years after you have made the mistakes that led to them; and then it is too late. You cannot understand our advice: you often do more mischief by trying to act on it than if you had been left to your own childish devices. If you were not childish you would not come to us at all: you would learn from experience that your consultations of the oracle are never of any real help to you. You draw wonderful imaginary pictures of us, and write fictitious tales and poems about our beneficent operations in the past, our wisdom, our justice, our mercy: stories in which we often appear as sentimental dupes of your prayers and sacrifices; but you do it only to conceal from yourselves the truth that you are incapable of being helped by us. Your Prime Minister pretends that he has come to be guided by the oracle; but we are not deceived: we know quite well that he has come here so that when he goes back he may have the authority and dignity of one who has visited the holy islands and spoken face to face with the ineffable ones. He will pretend that all the measures he wishes to take for his own purposes have been enjoined on him by the oracle.

THE ELDERLY GENTLEMAN. But you forget that the answers of the oracle cannot be kept secret or misrepresented. They are written and promulgated. The Leader of the Opposition can obtain copies. All the nations know them. Secret diplomacy has been totally abolished.

ZOO. Yes: you publish documents; but they are garbled or forged. And even if you published our real answers it would make no difference, because the shortlived cannot interpret the plainest writings. Your scriptures command you in the plainest terms to do exactly the contrary of everything your own laws and chosen rulers command and execute. You cannot defy Nature. It is a law of Nature that there is a fixed relation between conduct and length of life.

THE ELDERLY GENTLEMAN. I have never heard of any such law, madam.

ZOO. Well, you are hearing of it now.

THE ELDERLY GENTLEMAN. Let me tell you that we short-livers, as you call us, have lengthened our lives very considerably.

ZOO. How?

THE ELDERLY GENTLEMAN. By saving time. By enabling men to cross the ocean in an afternoon, and to see and speak to one another when they are thousands of miles apart. We hope shortly to organize their labor, and press natural forces into their service, so scientifically that the burden of labor will cease to be perceptible, leaving common men more leisure than they will know what to do with.

ZOO. Daddy: the man whose life is lengthened in this way may be busier than a savage; but the difference between such men living seventy years and those living three hundred would be all the greater; for to a shortliver increase of years is only increase of sorrow; but to a long-liver every extra year is a prospect which forces him to stretch his faculties to the utmost to face it. Therefore I say that we who live three hundred years can be of no use to you who live less than a hundred, and that our true destiny is not to advise and govern you, but to supplant and supersede you. In that faith I now declare myself a Colonizer and an Exterminator.

THE ELDERLY GENTLEMAN. Oh, steady! steady! Pray! pray! Reflect, I implore you. It is possible to colonize without exterminating the natives. Would you treat us less mercifully than our barbarous forefathers treated the Redskin and the Negro? Are we not, as Britons, entitled at least to some reservations?

ZOO. What is the use of prolonging the agony? You would perish slowly in our presence, no matter what we did to preserve you. You were almost dead when I took charge of you today, merely because you had talked for a few minutes to a secondary. Besides, we have our own experience to go upon. Have you never heard that our children occasionally revert to the ancestral type, and are born shortlived?

THE ELDERLY GENTLEMAN [*eagerly*] Never. I hope you will not be offended if I say that it would be a great comfort to me if I could be placed in charge of one of those normal individuals.

ZOO. Abnormal, you mean. What you ask is impossible: we weed them all out.

THE ELDERLY GENTLEMAN. When you say that you weed them out, you send a cold shiver down my spine. I hope you dont mean that you – that you – that you assist Nature in any way?

ZOO. Why not? Have you not heard the saying of the Chinese sage Dee Ning, that a good garden needs weeding? But it is not necessary for us to interfere. We are naturally rather particular as to the conditions on which we consent to live. One does not mind the accidental loss of an arm or a leg or an eye: after all, no one with two legs is unhappy because he has not three; so why should a man with one be unhappy because he has not two? But infirmities of mind and temper are quite another matter. If one of us has no self-control, or is too weak to bear the strain of our truthful life without wincing, or is tormented by depraved appetites and superstitions, or is unable to keep free from pain and depression, he naturally becomes discouraged, and refuses to live.

THE ELDERLY GENTLEMAN. Good Lord! Cuts his throat, do you mean?

ZOO. No: why should he cut his throat? He simply dies. He wants to. He is out of countenance, as we call it.

THE ELDERLY GENTLEMAN. Well!!! But suppose he is depraved enough not to want to die, and to settle the difficulty by killing all the rest of you?

ZOO. Oh, he is one of the thoroughly degenerate shortlivers whom we occasionally produce. He emigrates.

THE ELDERLY GENTLEMAN. And what becomes of him then?

ZOO. You shortlived people always think very highly of him. You accept him as what you call a great man.

THE ELDERLY GENTLEMAN. You astonish me; and yet I must admit that what you tell me accounts for a great deal of the little I know of the private life of our great men. We must be very convenient to you as a dumping place for your failures.

ZOO. I admit that.

THE ELDERLY GENTLEMAN. Good. Then if you carry out your plan of colonization, and leave no shortlived countries in the world, what will you do with your undesirables?

ZOO. Kill them. Our tertiaries are not at all squeamish about killing.

THE ELDERLY GENTLEMAN. Gracious Powers!

ZOO [*glancing up at the sun*] Come. It is just sixteen o'clock; and you have to join your party at half-past in the temple in Galway.

THE ELDERLY GENTLEMAN [*rising*] Galway! Shall I at last be able to boast of having seen that magnificent city?

ZOO. You will be disappointed: we have no cities. There is a temple of the oracle: that is all.

THE ELDERLY GENTLEMAN. Alas! and I came here to fulfil two long-cherished dreams. One was to see Galway. It has been said, 'See Galway and die.' The other was to contemplate the ruins of London.

ZOO. Ruins! We do not tolerate ruins. Was London a place of any importance?

THE ELDERLY GENTLEMAN [*amazed*] What! London! It was the mightiest city of antiquity. [*Rhetorically*] Situate just where the Dover Road crosses the Thames, it –

ZOO [*curtly interrupting*] There is nothing there now. Why should anybody pitch on such a spot to live? The nearest houses are at a place called Strand-on-the-Green: it is very old. Come. We shall go across the water. [*She goes down the steps*].

THE ELDERLY GENTLEMAN. Sic transit gloria mundi!

ZOO [*from below*] What did you say?

THE ELDERLY GENTLEMAN [*despairingly*] Nothing. You would not understand. [*He goes down the steps*].

ACT II

A courtyard before the columned portico of a temple. The temple door is in the middle of the portico. A veiled and robed woman of majestic carriage passes along behind the columns towards the entrance. From the opposite direction a man of compact figure, clean-shaven, saturnine, and self-centred: in short, very like Napoleon I, and wearing a military uniform of Napoleonic cut, marches with measured steps: places his hand in his lapel in the traditional manner; and fixes the woman with his eye. She stops, her attitude expressing haughty amazement at his audacity. He is on her right: she on his left.

NAPOLEON [*impressively*] I am the Man of Destiny.

THE VEILED WOMAN [*unimpressed*] How did you get in here?

NAPOLEON. I walked in. I go on until I am stopped. I never am stopped. I tell you I am the Man of Destiny.

THE VEILED WOMAN. You will be a man of very short destiny if you wander about here without one of our children to guide you. I suppose you belong to the Baghdad envoy.

NAPOLEON. I came with him; but I do not belong to him. I belong to myself. Direct me to the oracle if you can. If not, do not waste my time.

THE VEILED WOMAN. Your time, poor creature, is short. I will not waste it. Your envoy and his party will be here presently. The consultation of the oracle is arranged for them, and will take place according to the prescribed ritual. You can wait here until they come [*she turns to go into the temple*].

NAPOLEON. I never wait. [*She stops*]. The prescribed ritual is, I believe, the classical one of the pythoness on her tripod, the intoxicating fumes arising from the abyss, the convulsions of the priestess as she delivers the message of the God, and so on. That sort of thing does not impose on me: I use it myself to impose on simpletons. I believe that what is, is. I know that what is not, is not. The antics of a woman sitting on a tripod and pretending to be drunk do not interest me. Her words are put into her mouth, not by a god, but by a man three hundred years old, who has had the capacity to profit by his experience. I wish to speak to that man face to face, without mummery or imposture.

THE VEILED WOMAN. You seem to be an unusually sensible person. But there is no old man. I am the oracle on duty today. I am on my way to take my place on the tripod, and go through the usual mummery, as you rightly call it, to impress your friend the envoy. As you are superior to that kind of thing, you may consult me now. [She leads the way into the middle of the courtyard]. What do you want to know?

NAPOLEON [following her] Madam: I have not come all this way to discuss matters of State with a woman. I must ask you to direct me to one of your oldest and ablest men.

THE ORACLE. None of our oldest and ablest men or women would dream of wasting their time on you. You would die of discouragement in their presence in less than three hours.

NAPOLEON. You can keep this idle fable of discouragement for people credulous enough to be intimidated by it, madam. I do not believe in metaphysical forces.

THE ORACLE. No one asks you to. A field is something physical, is it not. Well, I have a field.

NAPOLEON. I have several million fields. I am Emperor of Turania.

THE ORACLE. You do not understand. I am not speaking of an agricultural field. Do you not know that every mass of matter in motion carries with it an invisible gravitational field, every magnet an invisible magnetic field, and every living organism a mesmeric field? Even you have a perceptible mesmeric field. Feeble as it is, it is the strongest I have yet observed in a shortliver.

NAPOLEON. By no means feeble, madam. I understand you now; and I may tell you that the strongest characters blench in my presence, and submit to my domination. But I do not call that a physical force.

THE ORACLE. What else do you call it, pray? Our physicists deal with it. Our mathematicians express its measurements in algebraic equations.

NAPOLEON. Do you mean that they could measure mine?

THE ORACLE. Yes: by a figure infinitely near to zero. Even in us the force is negligible during our first century of life. In our second it develops quickly, and becomes dangerous to shortlivers who venture into its field. If I were not veiled and robed in insulating material you could not endure my presence; and I am still a young woman: one hundred and seventy if you wish to know exactly.

NAPOLEON [*folding his arms*] I am not intimidated: no woman alive, old or young, can put me out of countenance. Unveil, madam. Disrobe. You will move this temple as easily as shake me.

THE ORACLE. Very well [*she throws back her veil*].

NAPOLEON [*shrieking, staggering, and covering his eyes*] No. Stop. Hide your face again. [*Shutting his eyes and distractedly clutching at his throat and heart*] Let me go. Help! I am dying.

THE ORACLE. Do you still wish to consult an older person?

NAPOLEON. No, no. The veil, the veil, I beg you.

THE ORACLE [*replacing the veil*] So.

NAPOLEON. Ouf! One cannot always be at one's best. Twice before in my life I have lost my nerve and behaved like a poltroon. But I warn you not to judge my quality by these involuntary moments.

THE ORACLE. I have no occasion to judge of your quality. You want my advice. Speak quickly; or I shall go about my business.

NAPOLEON [*After a moment's hesitation, sinks respectfully on one knee*] I —

THE ORACLE. Oh, rise, rise. Are you so foolish as to offer me this mummery which even you despise?

NAPOLEON [*rising*] I knelt in spite of myself. I compliment you on your impressiveness, madam.

THE ORACLE [*impatiently*] Time! time! time! time!

NAPOLEON. You will not grudge me the necessary time, madam, when you know my case. I am a man gifted with a certain specific talent in a degree altogether extraordinary. I am not otherwise a very extraordinary person: my family is not influential; and without this talent I should cut no particular figure in the world.

THE ORACLE. Why cut a figure in the world?

NAPOLEON. Superiority will make itself felt, madam. But when I say I possess this talent I do not express myself accurately. The truth is that my talent possesses me. It is genius. It drives me to exercise it. I must exercise it. I am great when I exercise it. At other moments I am nobody.

THE ORACLE. Well, exercise it. Do you need an oracle to tell you that?

NAPOLEON. Wait. This talent involves the shedding of human blood.

THE ORACLE. Are you a surgeon, or a dentist?

NAPOLEON. Psha! You do not appreciate me, madam. I mean the shedding of oceans of blood, the death of millions of men.

THE ORACLE. They object, I suppose.

NAPOLEON. Not at all. They adore me.

THE ORACLE. Indeed!

NAPOLEON. I have never shed blood with my own hand. They kill each other: they die with shouts of triumph on their lips. Those who die cursing do not curse me. My talent is to organize this slaughter; to give mankind this terrible joy which they call glory; to let loose the devil in them that peace has bound in chains.

THE ORACLE. And you? Do you share their joy?

NAPOLEON. Not at all. What satisfaction is it to me to see one fool pierce the entrails of another with a bayonet? I am a man of princely character, but of simple personal tastes and habits. I have the virtues of a laborer: industry and indifference to personal comfort. But I must rule, because I am so superior to other men that it is intolerable to me to be misruled by them. Yet only as a slayer can I become a ruler. I cannot be great as a writer: I have tried and failed. I have no talent as a sculptor or painter; and as lawyer, preacher, doctor, or actor, scores of second-rate men can do as well as I, or better. I am not even a diplomatist: I can only play my trump card of force. What I can do is to organize war. Look at me! I seem a man like other men, because nine-tenths of me is common humanity.

But the other tenth is a faculty for seeing things as they are that no other man possesses.

THE ORACLE. You mean that you have no imagination?

NAPOLEON [*forcibly*] I mean that I have the only imagination worth having: the power of imagining things as they are, even when I cannot see them. You feel yourself my superior, I know: nay, you are my superior: have I not bowed my knee to you by instinct? Yet I challenge you to a test of our respective powers. Can you calculate what the mathematicians call vectors, without putting a single algebraic symbol on paper? Can you launch ten thousand men across a frontier and a chain of mountains and know to a mile exactly where they will be at the end of seven weeks? The rest is nothing: I got it all from the books at my military school. Now this great game of war, this playing with armies as other men play with bowls and skittles, is one which I must go on playing, partly because a man must do what he can and not what he would like to do, and partly because, if I stop, I immediately lose my power and become a beggar in the land where I now make men drunk with glory.

THE ORACLE. No doubt then you wish to know how to extricate yourself from this unfortunate position?

NAPOLEON. It is not generally considered unfortunate, madam. Supremely fortunate rather.

THE ORACLE. If you think so, go on making them drunk with glory. Why trouble me with their folly and your vectors?

NAPOLEON. Unluckily, madam, men are not only heroes: they are also cowards. They desire glory; but they dread death.

THE ORACLE. Why should they? Their lives are too short to be worth living. That is why they think your game of war worth playing.

NAPOLEON. They do not look at it quite in that way. The most worthless soldier wants to live for ever. To make him risk being killed by the enemy I have to convince him that if he hesitates he will inevitably be shot at dawn by his own comrades for cowardice.

THE ORACLE. And if his comrades refuse to shoot him?

NAPOLEON. They will be shot too, of course.

THE ORACLE. By whom?

NAPOLEON. By their comrades.

THE ORACLE. And if they refuse?

NAPOLEON. Up to a certain point they do not refuse.

THE ORACLE. But when that point is reached, you have to do the shooting yourself, eh?

NAPOLEON. Unfortunately, madam, when that point is reached, they shoot me.

THE ORACLE. Mf! It seems to me they might as well shoot you first as last. Why dont they?

NAPOLEON. Because their love of fighting, their desire for glory, their shame of being branded as dastards, their instinct to test themselves in terrible trials, their fear of being killed or enslaved by the enemy, their belief that they are defending their hearths and homes, overcome their natural cowardice, and make them willing not only to risk their own lives but to kill everyone who refuses to take that risk. But if war continues too long, there comes a time when the soldiers, and also the taxpayers who are supporting and munitioning them, reach a condition which they describe as being fed up. The troops have proved their courage, and want to go home and enjoy in peace the glory it has earned them. Besides, the risk of death for each soldier becomes a certainty if the fighting goes on for ever: he hopes to escape for six months, but knows he cannot escape for six years. The risk of bankruptcy for the citizen becomes a certainty in the same way. Now what does this mean for me?

THE ORACLE. Does that matter in the midst of such calamity?

NAPOLEON. Psha! madam: it is the only thing that matters: the value of human life is the value of the greatest living man. Cut off that infinitesimal layer of grey matter which distinguishes my brain from that of the common man, and you cut down the stature of humanity from that of a giant to that of a nobody. I matter supremely: my soldiers do not matter at all: there are plenty more where they came from. If you kill me, or put a stop to my activity (it is the same thing), the nobler part of human life perishes. You must save the world from that catastrophe, madam. War has made me popular, powerful, famous, historically immortal. But I foresee that if I go on to the end it will leave me execrated, dethroned, imprisoned, perhaps executed. Yet if I stop fighting I commit suicide as a great man and become a common one. How am I to escape the horns of this tragic dilemma? Victory I can guarantee: I am invincible. But the cost of victory is the demoralization, the depopulation, the ruin of the victors no less than of the vanquished. How am I to satisfy my genius by fighting until I die? that is my question to you.

THE ORACLE. Were you not rash to venture into these sacred islands with such a question on your lips? Warriors are not popular here, my friend.

NAPOLEON. If a soldier were restrained by such a consideration, madam, he would no longer be a soldier. Besides [he produces a pistol], I have not come unarmed.

THE ORACLE. What is that thing?

NAPOLEON. It is an instrument of my profession, madam. I raise this hammer; I point the barrel at you; I pull this trigger that is against my forefinger; and you fall dead.

THE ORACLE. Shew it to me [she puts out her hand to take it from him].

NAPOLEON [retreating a step] Pardon me, madam. I never trust my life in the hands of a person over whom I have no control.

THE ORACLE [sternly] Give it to me [she raises her hand to her veil].

NAPOLEON [dropping the pistol and covering his eyes] Quarter! Kamerad! Take it, madam [he kicks it towards her]: I surrender.

THE ORACLE. Give me that thing. Do you expect me to stoop for it?

NAPOLEON [taking his hands from his eyes with an effort] A poor victory, madam [he picks up the pistol and hands it to her]:

there was no vector strategy needed to win it. [*Making a pose of his humiliation*] But enjoy your triumph: you have made me – ME! Cain Adamson Charles Napoleon! Emperor of Turania! cry for quarter.

THE ORACLE. The way out of your difficulty, Cain Adamson, is very simple.

NAPOLEON [*eagerly*] Good. What is it?

THE ORACLE. To die before the tide of glory turns. Allow me [*she shoots him*].

He falls with a shriek. She throws the pistol away and goes haughtily into the temple.

NAPOLEON [*scrambling to his feet*] Murderess! Monster! She-devil! Unnatural, inhuman wretch! You deserve to be hanged, guillotined, broken on the wheel, burnt alive. No sense of the sacredness of human life! No thought for my wife and children! Bitch! Sow! Wanton! [*He picks up the pistol*]. And missed me at five yards! Thats a woman all over.

He is going away whence he came when Zoo arrives and confronts him at the head of a party consisting of the British Envoy, the Elderly Gentleman, the Envoy's wife and her daughter, aged about eighteen. The envoy, a typical politician, looks like an imperfectly reformed criminal disguised by a good tailor. The dress of the ladies is coeval with that of the Elderly Gentleman, and suitable for public official ceremonies in western capitals at the XVIII-XIX fin de siècle.

They file in under the portico. Zoo immediately comes out imperiously to Napoleon's right, whilst the Envoy's wife hurries effusively to his left. The Envoy meanwhile passes along behind the columns to the door, followed by his daughter. The Elderly Gentleman stops just where he entered, to see why Zoo has swooped so abruptly on the Emperor of Turania.

ZOO [*to Napoleon, severely*] What are you doing here by yourself? You have no business to go about here alone. What was that noise just now? What is that in your hand?

Napoleon glares at her in speechless fury; pockets the pistol; and produces a whistle.

THE ENVOY'S WIFE. Arnt you coming with us to the oracle, sire?

NAPOLEON. To hell with the oracle, and with you too [*he turns to go*]!

THE ENVOY'S WIFE } [*together*] { Oh, sire!!
ZOO } { Where are you going?

NAPOLEON. To fetch the police. [*He goes out past Zoo, almost jostling her, and blowing piercing blasts on his whistle*].

ZOO [*whipping out her tuning-fork and intoning*] Hallo Galway Central. [*The whistling continues*]. Stand by to isolate. [*To the Elderly Gentleman, who is staring after the whistling Emperor*] How far has he gone?

THE ELDERLY GENTLEMAN. To that curious statue of a fat old man.

ZOO [*quickly, intoning*] Isolate the Falstaff monument isolate hard. Paralyze – [*the whistling stops*]. Thank you. [*She puts up her tuning-fork*]. He shall not move a muscle until I come to fetch him.

THE ENVOY'S WIFE. Oh! he will be frightfully angry! Did you hear what he said to me?

ZOO. Much we care for his anger!

THE DAUGHTER [*coming forward between her mother and Zoo*]. Please, madam, whose statue is it? and where can I buy a picture postcard of it? It is so funny. I will take a snapshot when we are coming back; but they come out so badly sometimes.

ZOO. They will give you pictures and toys in the temple to take away with you. The story of the statue is too long. It would bore you [*she goes past them across the courtyard to get rid of them*].

THE WIFE [*gushing*] Oh no, I assure you.

THE DAUGHTER [*copying her mother*] We should be so interested.

ZOO. Nonsense! All I can tell you about it is that a thousand years ago, when the whole world was given over to you shortlived people, there was a war called the War to end War. In the war which followed it about ten years later, hardly any soldiers were killed; but seven of the capital cities of Europe were wiped out of existence. It seems to have been a great joke: for the statesmen who thought they had sent ten million common men to their deaths were themselves blown into fragments with their houses and families, while the ten million men lay snugly in the caves they had dug for themselves. Later on even the houses escaped; but their inhabitants were poisoned by gas that spared no living soul. Of course the soldiers starved and ran wild; and that was the end of pseudo-Christian civilization. The last civilized thing that happened was that the statesmen discovered that cowardice was a great patriotic virtue; and a public monument was erected to its first preacher, an ancient and very fat sage called Sir John Falstaff. Well [*pointing*], thats Falstaff.

THE ELDERLY GENTLEMAN [*coming from the portico to his granddaughter's right*] Great Heavens! And at the base of this monstrous poltroon's statue the War God of Turania is now gibbering impotently.

ZOO. Serve him right! War God indeed!

THE ENVOY [*coming between his wife and Zoo*] I dont know any history: a modern Prime Minister has something better to do than sit reading books; but –

THE ELDERLY GENTLEMAN [*interrupting him encouragingly*] You make history, Ambrose.

THE ENVOY. Well, perhaps I do; and perhaps history makes me. I hardly recognize myself in the newspapers sometimes, though I suppose leading articles are the materials of history, as you might say. But what I want to know is, how did war come back again? and how did they make those poisonous gases you speak of? We should be glad to know; for they might come in very handy if we have to fight Turania. Of course I am all for peace, and dont hold with the race of armaments in principle; still, we must keep ahead or be wiped out.

ZOO. You can make the gases for yourselves when your chemists find out how. Then you will do as you did before: poison each other until there are no chemists left, and no civilization. You will then begin all over again as half-starved ignorant savages, and fight with boomerangs and poisoned arrows until you work up to the poison gases and high explosives once more, with the same result. That is, unless we have sense enough to make an end of this ridiculous game by destroying you.

THE ENVOY [*aghast*] Destroying us!

THE ELDERLY GENTLEMAN. I told you, Ambrose. I warned you.

THE ENVOY. But —

ZOO [*impatiently*] I wonder what Zozim is doing. He ought to be here to receive you.

THE ELDERLY GENTLEMAN. Do you mean that rather insufferable young man whom you found boring me on the pier?

ZOO. Yes. He has to dress-up in a Druid's robe, and put on a wig and a long false beard, to impress you silly people. *I* have to put on a purple mantle. I have no patience with such mummery; but you expect it from us; so I suppose it must be kept up. Will you wait here until Zozim comes, please [*she turns to enter the temple*].

THE ENVOY. My good lady, is it worth while dressing-up and putting on false beards for us if you tell us beforehand that it is all humbug?

ZOO. One would not think so; but if you wont believe in anyone who is not dressed-up, why, we must dress-up for you. It was you who invented all this nonsense, not we.

THE ELDERLY GENTLEMAN. But do you expect us to be impressed after this?

ZOO. I dont expect anything. I know, as a matter of experience, that you will be impressed. The oracle will frighten you out of your wits. [*She goes into the temple*].

THE WIFE. These people treat us as if we were dirt beneath their feet. I wonder at you putting up with it, Amby. It would serve them right if we went home at once: wouldnt it, Eth?

THE DAUGHTER. Yes, mamma. But perhaps they wouldnt mind.

THE ENVOY. No use talking like that, Molly. Ive got to see this oracle. The folks at home wont know how we have been treated: all theyll know is that Ive stood face to face with the oracle and had the straight tip from her. I hope this Zozim chap is not going to keep us waiting much longer; for I feel far from comfortable about the approaching interview; and thats the honest truth.

THE ELDERLY GENTLEMAN. I never thought I should want to see that man again; but now I wish he would take charge of us instead of Zoo. She was charming at first: quite charming; but she turned into a fiend because I had a few words with her. You would not believe: she very nearly killed me. You heard what she said just now. She belongs to a party here which wants to have us all killed.

THE WIFE [*terrified*] Us! But we have done nothing: we have been as nice to them as nice could be. Oh, Amby, come away, come away: there is something dreadful about this place and these people.

THE ENVOY. There is, and no mistake. But youre safe with me: you ought to have sense enough to know that.

THE ELDERLY GENTLEMAN. I am sorry to say, Molly, that it is not merely us four poor weak creatures they want to kill, but the entire race of Man, except themselves.

THE ENVOY. Not so poor neither, Poppa. Nor so weak, if you are going to take in all the Powers. If it comes to killing, two can play at that game, longlived or shortlived.

THE ELDERLY GENTLEMAN. No, Ambrose: we should have no chance. We are worms beside these fearful people: mere worms.

Zozim comes from the temple, robed majestically, and wearing a wreath of mistletoe in his flowing white wig. His false beard reaches almost to his waist. He carries a staff with a curiously carved top.

ZOZIM [*in the doorway, impressively*] Hail, strangers!

ALL [*reverently*] Hail!

ZOZIM. Are ye prepared?

THE ENVOY. We are.

ZOZIM [*unexpectedly becoming conversational, and strolling down carelessly to the middle of the group between the two ladies*] Well, I'm sorry to say the oracle is not. She was delayed by some member of your party who got loose; and as the show takes a bit of arranging, you will have to wait a few minutes. The ladies can go inside and look round the entrance hall and get pictures and things if they want them.

THE WIFE
THE DAUGHTER } [together] { Thank you.
I should like to,
very much. } [They go into the temple].

THE ELDERLY GENTLEMAN [in dignified rebuke of Zozim's levity] Taken in this spirit, sir, the show, as you call it, becomes almost an insult to our common sense.

ZOZIM. Quite, I should say. You need not keep it up with me.

THE ENVOY [suddenly making himself very agreeable] Just so: just so. We can wait as long as you please. And now, if I may be allowed to seize the opportunity of a few minutes' friendly chat – ?

ZOZIM. By all means, if only you will talk about things I can understand.

THE ENVOY. Well, about this colonizing plan of yours. My father-in-law here has been telling me something about it; and he has just now let out that you want not only to colonize us, but to – to – to – well, shall we say to supersede us? Now why supersede us? Why not live and let live? Theres not a scrap of ill-feeling on our side. We should welcome a colony of immortals – we may almost call you that – in the British Middle East. No doubt the Turanian Empire, with its Mahometan traditions, overshadows us now. We have had to bring the Emperor with us on this expedition, though of course you know as well as I do that he has imposed himself on my party just to spy on me. I dont deny that he has the whip hand of us to some extent, because if it came to a war none of our generals could stand up against him. I give him best at that game: he is the finest soldier in the world. Besides, he is an emperor and an autocrat; and I am only an elected representative of the British democracy. Not that our British democrats wont fight: they will fight the heads off all the Turanians that ever walked; but then it takes so long to work them up to it, while he has only to say the word and march. But you people would never get on with him. Believe me, you would not be as comfortable in Turania as you would be with us. We understand you. We like you. We are easy-going people; and we are rich people. That will appeal to you. Turania is a poor place when all is said. Five-eighths of it is desert. They dont irrigate as we do. Besides – now I am sure this will appeal to you and to all right-minded men – we are Christians.

ZOZIM. The old uns prefer Mahometans.

THE ENVOY [*shocked*] What!

ZOZIM [*distinctly*] They prefer Mahometans. Whats wrong with that?

THE ENVOY. Well, of all the disgraceful –

THE ELDERLY GENTLEMAN [*diplomatically interrupting his scandalized son-in-law*] There can be no doubt, I am afraid, that by clinging too long to the obsolete features of the old pseudo-Christian Churches we allowed the Mahometans to get ahead of us at a very critical period of the development of the Eastern world. When the Mahometan Reformation took place, it left its followers with the enormous advantage of having the only established religion in the world in whose articles of faith any intelligent and educated person could believe.

THE ENVOY. But what about our Reformation? Dont give the show away, Poppa. We followed suit, didnt we?

THE ELDERLY GENTLEMAN. Unfortunately, Ambrose, we could not follow suit very rapidly. We had not only a religion to deal with, but a Church.

ZOZIM. What is a Church?

THE ENVOY. Not know what a Church is! Well!

THE ELDERLY GENTLEMAN. You must excuse me; but if I attempted to explain you would only ask me what a bishop is; and that is a question that no mortal man can answer. All I can tell you is that Mahomet was a truly wise man; for he founded a religion without a Church; consequently when the time came for a Reformation of the mosques there were no bishops and priests to obstruct it. Our bishops and priests prevented us for two hundred years from following suit; and we have never recovered the start

we lost then. I can only plead that we did reform our
Church at least. No doubt we had to make a few com-
promises as a matter of good taste; but there is now very
little in our Articles of Religion that is not accepted as at
least allegorically true by our Higher Criticism.

THE ENVOY [*encouragingly*] Besides, does it matter? Why, *I*
have never read the Articles in my life; and I am Prime
Minister! Come! if my services in arranging for the reception of a colonizing party would be acceptable, they are at
your disposal. And when I say a reception I mean a reception. Royal honors, mind you! A salute of a hundred
and one guns! The streets lined with troops! The Guards
turned out at the Palace! Dinner at the Guildhall!

ZOZIM. Discourage me if I know what youre talking about!
I wish Zoo would come: she understands these things. All
I can tell you is that the general opinion among the
Colonizers is in favor of beginning in a country where the
people are of a different color from us; so that we can make
short work without any risk of mistakes.

THE ENVOY. What do you mean by short work? I hope –

ZOZIM [*with obviously feigned geniality*] Oh, nothing, nothing,
nothing. We are thinking of trying North America: thats
all. You see, the Red Men of that country used to be
white. They passed through a period of sallow complexions, followed by a period of no complexions at all,
into the red characteristic of their climate. Besides, several
cases of long life have occurred in North America. They
joined us here; and their stock soon reverted to the
original white of these islands.

THE ELDERLY GENTLEMAN. But have you considered the
possibility of your colony turning red?

ZOZIM. That wont matter. We are not particular about our
pigmentation. The old books mention red-faced Englishmen: they appear to have been common objects at one
time.

THE ELDERLY GENTLEMAN [*very persuasively*] But do you
think you would be popular in North America? It seems
to me, if I may say so, that on your own shewing you need

a country in which society is organized in a series of highly
exclusive circles, in which the privacy of private life is very
jealously guarded, and in which no one presumes to speak
to anyone else without an introduction following a strict
examination of social credentials. It is only in such a
country that persons of special tastes and attainments can
form a little world of their own, and protect themselves
absolutely from intrusion by common persons. I think I
may claim that our British society has developed this exclusiveness to perfection. If you would pay us a visit and
see the working of our caste system, our club system, our
guild system, you would admit that nowhere else in the
world, least of all, perhaps in North America, which has a
regrettable tradition of social promiscuity, could you keep
yourselves so entirely to yourselves.

ZOZIM [*good-naturedly embarrassed*] Look here. There is no
good discussing this. I had rather not explain; but it wont
make any difference to our Colonizers what sort of shortlivers they come across. We shall arrange all that. Never
mind how. Let us join the ladies.

THE ELDERLY GENTLEMAN [*throwing off his diplomatic attitude and abandoning himself to despair*] We understand you
only too well, sir. Well, kill us. End the lives you have
made miserably unhappy by opening up to us the possibility that any of us may live three hundred years. I
solemnly curse that possibility. To you it may be a blessing,
because you do live three hundred years. To us, who live
less than a hundred, whose flesh is as grass, it is the most
unbearable burden our poor tortured humanity has ever
groaned under.

THE ENVOY. Hullo, Poppa! Steady! How do you make that
out?

ZOZIM. What is three hundred years? Short enough, if you
ask me. Why, in the old days you people lived on the assumption that you were going to last out for ever and ever
and ever. Immortal, you thought yourselves. Were you
any happier then?

THE ELDERLY GENTLEMAN. As President of the Baghdad

Historical Society I am in a position to inform you that the communities which took this monstrous pretension seriously were the most wretched of which we have any record. My Society has printed an editio princeps of the works of the father of history, Thucyderodotus Macollybuckle. Have you read his account of what was blasphemously called the Perfect City of God, and the attempt made to reproduce it in the northern part of these islands by Jonhobsnoxius, called the Leviathan? Those misguided people sacrificed the fragment of life that was granted to them to an imaginary immortality. They crucified the prophet who told them to take no thought for the morrow, and that here and now was their Australia: Australia being a term signifying paradise, or an eternity of bliss. They tried to produce a condition of death in life: to mortify the flesh, as they called it.

ZOZIM. Well, you are not suffering from that, are you? You have not a mortified air.

THE ELDERLY GENTLEMAN. Naturally we are not absolutely insane and suicidal. Nevertheless we impose on ourselves abstinences and disciplines and studies that are meant to prepare us for living three centuries. And we seldom live one. My childhood was made unnecessarily painful, my boyhood unnecessarily laborious, by ridiculous preparations for a length of days which the chances were fifty thousand to one against my ever attaining. I have been cheated out of the natural joys and freedoms of my life by this dream to which the existence of these islands and their oracles gives a delusive possibility of realization. I curse the day when long life was invented, just as the victims of Jonhobsnoxius cursed the day when eternal life was invented.

ZOZIM. Pooh! You could live three centuries if you chose.

THE ELDERLY GENTLEMAN. That is what the fortunate always say to the unfortunate. Well, I do not choose. I accept my three score and ten years. If they are filled with usefulness, with justice, with mercy, with good-will: if they are the lifetime of a soul that never loses its honor and a brain that never loses its eagerness, they are enough for me, because these things are infinite and eternal, and can make ten of my years as long as thirty of yours. I shall not conclude by saying live as long as you like and be damned to you, because I have risen for the moment far above any ill-will to you or to any fellow-creature; but I am your equal before that eternity in which the difference between your lifetime and mine is as the difference between one drop of water and three in the eyes of the Almighty Power from which we have both proceeded.

ZOZIM [*impressed*] You spoke that piece very well, Daddy. I couldnt talk like that if I tried. It sounded fine. Ah! here come the ladies.

To his relief, they have just appeared on the threshold of the temple.

THE ELDERLY GENTLEMAN [*passing from exaltation to distress*] It means nothing to him: in this land of discouragement the sublime has become the ridiculous. [*Turning on the hopelessly puzzled Zozim*] 'Behold, thou hast made my days as it were a span long; and mine age is even as nothing in respect of thee.'

THE WIFE ⎫ [*running* ⎧ Poppa, Poppa: dont look like
THE DAUGHTER ⎭ *to him*] ⎨   that.
                               ⎩ Oh, granpa, whats the matter?

ZOZIM [*with a shrug*] Discouragement!

THE ELDERLY GENTLEMAN [*throwing off the women with a superb gesture*] Liar! [*Recollecting himself, he adds, with noble courtesy, raising his hat and bowing*] I beg your pardon, sir; but I am NOT discouraged.

A burst of orchestral music, through which a powerful gong sounds, is heard from the temple. Zoo, in a purple robe, appears in the doorway.

ZOO. Come. The oracle is ready.

Zozim motions them to the threshold with a wave of his staff. The Envoy and the Elderly Gentleman take off their hats and go into the temple on tiptoe, Zoo leading the way. The Wife and Daughter, frightened as they are, raise their heads uppishly and follow flatfooted, sustained by a sense of their Sunday clothes and social consequence. Zozim remains in the portico, alone.

ZOZIM [*taking off his wig, beard, and robe, and bundling them under his arm*] Ouf! [*He goes home*].

ACT III

Inside the temple. A gallery overhanging an abyss. Dead silence. The gallery is brightly lighted; but beyond is a vast gloom, continually changing in intensity. A shaft of violet light shoots upward; and a very harmonious and silvery carillon chimes. When it ceases the violet ray vanishes.

Zoo comes along the gallery, followed by the Envoy's daughter, his wife, the Envoy himself, and the Elderly Gentleman. The two men are holding their hats with the brims near their noses, as if prepared to pray into them at a moment's notice. Zoo halts: they all follow her example. They contemplate the void with awe. Organ music of the kind called sacred in the nineteenth century begins. Their awe deepens. The violet ray, now a diffused mist, rises again from the abyss.

THE WIFE [*to Zoo, in a reverent whisper*] Shall we kneel?

ZOO [*loudly*] Yes, if you want to. You can stand on your head if you like. [*She sits down carelessly on the gallery railing, with her back to the abyss*].

THE ELDERLY GENTLEMAN [*jarred by her callousness*] We desire to behave in a becoming manner.

ZOO. Very well. Behave just as you feel. It doesnt matter how you behave. But keep your wits about you when the pythoness ascends, or you will forget the questions you have come to ask her.

THE ENVOY } [*simul-* } [*very nervous, takes out a paper to refresh his memory*] Ahem!

THE DAUGHTER } *taneously*] } [*alarmed*] The pythoness? Is she a snake?

THE ELDERLY GENTLEMAN. Tch-ch! The priestess of the oracle. A sybil. A prophetess. Not a snake.

THE WIFE. How awful!

ZOO. I'm glad you think so.

THE WIFE. Oh dear! Dont you think so?

ZOO. No. This sort of thing is got up to impress you, not to impress me.

THE ELDERLY GENTLEMAN. I wish you would let it impress us, then, madam. I am deeply impressed; but you are spoiling the effect.

ZOO. You just wait. All this business with colored lights and chords on that old organ is only tomfoolery. Wait til you see the pythoness.

The Envoy's wife falls on her knees, and takes refuge in prayer.

THE DAUGHTER [*trembling*] Are we really going to see a woman who has lived three hundred years?

ZOO. Stuff! Youd drop dead if a tertiary as much as looked at you. The oracle is only a hundred and seventy; and youll find it hard enough to stand her.

THE DAUGHTER [*piteously*] Oh! [*she falls on her knees*].

THE ENVOY. Whew! Stand by me, Poppa. This is a little more than I bargained for. Are you going to kneel; or how?

THE ELDERLY GENTLEMAN. Perhaps it would be in better taste.

The two men kneel.

The vapor of the abyss thickens; and a distant roll of thunder seems to come from its depths. The pythoness, seated on her tripod, rises slowly from it. She has discarded the insulating robe and veil in which she conversed with Napoleon, and is now draped and hooded in voluminous folds of a single piece of grey-white stuff. Something supernatural about her terrifies the beholders, who throw themselves on their faces. Her outline flows and waves: she is almost distinct at moments, and again vague and shadowy: above all, she is larger than life-size, not enough to be measured by the flustered congregation, but enough to affect them with a dreadful sense of her supernaturalness.

ZOO. Get up, get up. Do pull yourselves together, you people.

The Envoy and his family, by shuddering negatively, intimate that it is impossible. The Elderly Gentleman manages to get on his hands and knees.

ZOO. Come on, Daddy: you are not afraid. Speak to her. She wont wait here all day for you, you know.

THE ELDERLY GENTLEMAN [*rising very deferentially to his feet*] Madam: you will excuse my very natural nervousness in addressing, for the first time in my life, a – a – a – a goddess. My friend and relative the Envoy is unhinged. I throw myself upon your indulgence –

ZOO [*interrupting him intolerantly*] Dont throw yourself on anything belonging to her or you will go right through her and break your neck. She isnt solid, like you.

THE ELDERLY GENTLEMAN. I was speaking figuratively –

ZOO. You have been told not to do it. Ask her what you want to know; and be quick about it.

THE ELDERLY GENTLEMAN [*stooping and taking the prostrate Envoy by the shoulders*] Ambrose: you must make an effort. You cannot go back to Baghdad without the answers to your questions.

THE ENVOY [*rising to his knees*] I shall be only too glad to get back alive on any terms. If my legs would support me I'd just do a bunk straight for the ship.

THE ELDERLY GENTLEMAN. No, no. Remember: your dignity –

THE ENVOY. Dignity be damned! I'm terrified. Take me away, for God's sake.

THE ELDERLY GENTLEMAN [*producing a brandy flask and taking the cap off*] Try some of this. It is still nearly full, thank goodness!

THE ENVOY [*clutching it and drinking eagerly*] Ah! Thats better. [*He tries to drink again. Finding that he has emptied it, he hands it back to his father-in-law upside down*].

THE ELDERLY GENTLEMAN [*taking it*] Great heavens! He has swallowed half-a-pint of neat brandy. [*Much perturbed, he screws the cap on again, and pockets the flask*].

THE ENVOY [*staggering to his feet; pulling a paper from his pocket; and speaking with boisterous confidence*] Get up, Molly. Up with you, Eth.

   The two women rise to their knees.

THE ENVOY. What I want to ask is this. [*He refers to the*

paper]. Ahem! Civilization has reached a crisis. We are at the parting of the ways. We stand on the brink of the Rubicon. Shall we take the plunge? Already a leaf has been torn out of the book of the Sybil. Shall we wait until the whole volume is consumed? On our right is the crater of the volcano: on our left the precipice. One false step, and we go down to annihilation dragging the whole human race with us. [*He pauses for breath*].

THE ELDERLY GENTLEMAN [*recovering his spirits under the familiar stimulus of political oratory*] Hear, hear!

ZOO. What are you raving about? Ask your question while you have the chance. What is it you want to know?

THE ENVOY [*patronizing her in the manner of a Premier debating with a very young member of the Opposition*] A young woman asks me a question. I am always glad to see the young taking an interest in politics. It is an impatient question; but it is a practical question, an intelligent question. She asks why we seek to lift a corner of the veil that shrouds the future from our feeble vision.

ZOO. I dont. I ask you to tell the oracle what you want, and not keep her sitting there all day.

THE ELDERLY GENTLEMAN [*warmly*] Order, order!

ZOO. What does 'Order, order!' mean?

THE ENVOY. I ask the august oracle to listen to my voice –

ZOO. You people seem never to tire of listening to your voices; but it doesnt amuse us. What do you want?

THE ENVOY. I want, young woman, to be allowed to proceed without unseemly interruptions.

A low roll of thunder comes from the abyss.

THE ELDERLY GENTLEMAN. There! Even the oracle is indignant. [*To the Envoy*] Do not allow yourself to be put down by this lady's rude clamor, Ambrose. Take no notice. Proceed.

THE ENVOY'S WIFE. I cant bear this much longer, Amby. Remember: *I* havnt had any brandy.

HIS DAUGHTER [*trembling*] There are serpents curling in the vapor. I am afraid of the lightning. Finish it, Papa; or I shall die.

THE ENVOY [*sternly*] Silence. The destiny of British civilization is at stake. Trust me. I am not afraid. As I was saying – where was I?

ZOO. I dont know. Does anybody?

THE ELDERLY GENTLEMAN [*tactfully*] You were just coming to the election, I think.

THE ENVOY [*reassured*] Just so. The election. Now what we want to know is this: ought we to dissolve in August, or put it off until next spring?

ZOO. Dissolve? In what? [*Thunder*]. Oh! My fault this time. That means that the oracle understands you, and desires me to hold my tongue.

THE ENVOY [*fervently*] I thank the oracle.

THE WIFE [*to Zoo*] Serve you right!

THE ELDERLY GENTLEMAN. Before the oracle replies, I should like to be allowed to state a few of the reasons why, in my opinion, the Government should hold on until the spring. In the first –

> *Terrific lightning and thunder. The Elderly Gentleman is knocked flat; but as he immediately sits up again dazedly it is clear that he is none the worse for the shock. The ladies cower in terror. The Envoy's hat is blown off; but he seizes it just as it quits his temples, and holds it on with both hands. He is recklessly drunk, but quite articulate, as he seldom speaks in public without taking stimulants beforehand.*

THE ENVOY [*taking one hand from his hat to make a gesture of stilling the tempest*] Thats enough. We know how to take a hint. I'll put the case in three words. I am the leader of the Potterbill party. My party is in power. I am Prime Minister. The Opposition – the Rotterjacks – have won every bye-election for the last six months. They –

THE ELDERLY GENTLEMAN [*scrambling heatedly to his feet*] Not by fair means. By bribery, by misrepresentation, by pandering to the vilest prejudices [*muttered thunder*] – I beg your pardon [*he is silent*].

THE ENVOY. Never mind the bribery and lies. The oracle knows all about that. The point is that though our five years will not expire until the year after next, our majority will be eaten away at the bye-elections by about Easter. We cant wait: we must start some question that will excite the public, and go to the country on it. But some of us say do it now. Others say wait til the spring. We cant make up our minds one way or the other. Which would you advise?

zoo. But what is the question that is to excite your public?

THE ENVOY. That doesnt matter. I dont know yet. We will find a question all right enough. The oracle can foresee the future: we cannot. [*Thunder*]. What does that mean? What have I done now?

zoo [*severely*] How often must you be told that we cannot foresee the future? There is no such thing as the future until it is the present.

THE ELDERLY GENTLEMAN. Allow me to point out, madam, that when the Potterbill party sent to consult the oracle fifteen years ago, the oracle prophesied that the Potterbills would be victorious at the General Election; and they were. So it is evident that the oracle can foresee the future, and is sometimes willing to reveal it.

THE ENVOY. Quite true. Thank you, Poppa. I appeal now, over your head, young woman, direct to the August Oracle, to repeat the signal favor conferred on my illustrious predecessor, Sir Fuller Eastwind, and to answer me exactly as he was answered.

The oracle raises her hands to command silence.

ALL Sh-sh-sh!

Invisible trombones utter three solemn blasts in the manner of Die Zauberflöte.

THE ELDERLY GENTLEMAN. May I –

zoo [*quickly*] Hush. The oracle is going to speak.

THE ORACLE. Go home, poor fool.

She vanishes; and the atmosphere changes to prosaic daylight. Zoo comes off the railing; throws off her robe; makes a bundle of it; and tucks it under her arm. The magic and mystery are gone. The women rise to their feet. The Envoy's party stare at one another helplessly.

zoo. The same reply, word for word, that your illustrious

predecessor, as you call him, got fifteen years ago. You asked for it; and you got it. And just think of all the important questions you might have asked. She would have answered them, you know. It is always like that. I will go and arrange to have you sent home: you can wait for me in the entrance hall [*she goes out*].

THE ENVOY. What possessed me to ask for the same answer old Eastwind got?

THE ELDERLY GENTLEMAN. But it was not the same answer. The answer to Eastwind was an inspiration to our party for years. It won us the election.

THE ENVOY'S DAUGHTER. I learnt it at school, granpa. It wasnt the same at all. I can repeat it. [*She quotes*] 'When Britain was cradled in the west, the east wind hardened her and made her great. Whilst the east wind prevails Britain shall prosper. The east wind shall wither Britain's enemies in the day of contest. Let the Rotterjacks look to it.'

THE ENVOY. The old man invented that. I see it all. He was a doddering old ass when he came to consult the oracle. The oracle naturally said 'Go home, poor fool.' There was no sense in saying that to me; but as that girl said, I asked for it. What else could the poor old chap do but fake up an answer fit for publication? There were whispers about it; but nobody believed them. I believe them now.

THE ELDERLY GENTLEMAN. Oh, I cannot admit that Sir Fuller Eastwind was capable of such a fraud.

THE ENVOY. He was capable of anything: I knew his private secretary. And now what are we going to say? You dont suppose I am going back to Baghdad to tell the British Empire that the oracle called me a fool, do you?

THE ELDERLY GENTLEMAN. Surely we must tell the truth, however painful it may be to our feelings.

THE ENVOY. I am not thinking of my feelings: I am not so selfish as that, thank God. I am thinking of the country, of our party. The truth, as you call it, would put the Rotterjacks in for the next twenty years. It would be the end of me politically. Not that I care for that: I am only too

willing to retire if you can find a better man. Dont hesitate
on my account.

THE ELDERLY GENTLEMAN. No, Ambrose: you are indispensable. There is no one else.

THE ENVOY. Very well, then. What are you going to do?

THE ELDERLY GENTLEMAN. My dear Ambrose, you are
the leader of the party, not I. What are you going to do?

THE ENVOY. I am going to tell the exact truth; thats what
I'm going to do. Do you take me for a liar?

THE ELDERLY GENTLEMAN [*puzzled*] Oh. I beg your pardon. I understood you to say –

THE ENVOY [*cutting him short*] You understood me to say that
I am going back to Baghdad to tell the British electorate
that the oracle repeated to me, word for word, what it said
to Sir Fuller Eastwind fifteen years ago. Molly and Ethel can
bear me out. So must you, if you are an honest man. Come on.

He goes out, followed by his wife and daughter.

THE ELDERLY GENTLEMAN [*left alone and shrinking into an
old and desolate figure*] What am I to do? I am a most perplexed and wretched man. [*He falls on his knees, and stretches
his hands in entreaty over the abyss*]. I invoke the oracle. I cannot go back and connive at a blasphemous lie. I implore
guidance.

*The Pythoness walks in on the gallery behind him, and touches
him on the shoulder. Her size is now natural. Her face is hidden by
her hood. He flinches as if from an electric shock; turns to her;
and cowers, covering his eyes in terror.*

THE ELDERLY GENTLEMAN. No: not close to me. I'm afraid
I cant bear it.

THE ORACLE [*with grave pity*] Come: look at me. I am my
natural size now: what you saw there was only a foolish
picture of me thrown on a cloud by a lantern. How can I
help you?

THE ELDERLY GENTLEMAN. They have gone back to lie
about your answer. I cannot go with them. I cannot live
among people to whom nothing is real. I have become incapable of it through my stay here. I implore to be
allowed to stay.

THE ORACLE. My friend: if you stay with us you will die of discouragement.

THE ELDERLY GENTLEMAN. If I go back I shall die of disgust and despair. I take the nobler risk. I beg you, do not cast me out.

He catches her robe and holds her.

THE ORACLE. Take care. I have been here one hundred and seventy years. Your death does not mean to me what it means to you.

THE ELDERLY GENTLEMAN. It is the meaning of life, not of death, that makes banishment so terrible to me.

THE ORACLE. Be it so, then. You may stay.

She offers him her hands. He grasps them and raises himself a little by clinging to her. She looks steadily into his face. He stiffens; a little convulsion shakes him; his grasp relaxes; and he falls dead.

THE ORACLE [*looking down at the body*] Poor shortlived thing! What else could I do for you?

PART V

As Far as Thought can Reach

Summer afternoon in the year 31,920 A.D. A sunlit glade at the southern foot of a thickly wooded hill. On the west side of it, the steps and columned porch of a dainty little classic temple. Between it and the hill, a rising path to the wooded heights begins with rough steps of stones in the moss. On the opposite side, a grove. In the middle of the glade, an altar in the form of a low marble table as long as a man, set parallel to the temple steps and pointing to the hill. Curved marble benches radiate from it into the foreground; but they are not joined to it: there is plenty of space to pass between the altar and the benches.

A dance of youths and maidens is in progress. The music is provided by a few fluteplayers seated carelessly on the steps of the temple. There are no children; and none of the dancers seems younger than eighteen. Some of the youths have beards. Their dress, like the architecture of the theatre and the design of the altar and curved seats, resembles Grecian of the fourth century B.C., freely handled. They move with perfect balance and remarkable grace, racing through a figure like a farandole. They neither romp nor hug in our manner.

At the first full close they clap their hands to stop the musicians, who recommence with a saraband, during which a strange figure appears on the path beyond the temple. He is deep in thought, with his eyes closed and his feet feeling automatically for the rough irregular steps as he slowly descends them. Except for a sort of linen kilt consisting mainly of a girdle carrying a sporran and a few minor pockets, he is naked. In physical hardihood and uprightness he seems to be in the prime of life; and his eyes and mouth shew no signs of age; but his face, though fully and firmly fleshed, bears a network of lines, varying from furrows to hairbreadth reticulations, as if Time had worked over every inch of it incessantly through whole geologic periods. His head is finely domed and utterly bald. Except for his eyelashes he is quite hairless. He is unconscious of his surroundings, and walks right into one of the dancing couples, separating them. He wakes up and stares about him. The couple stop indignantly. The rest stop. The music stops. The youth whom he has jostled accosts him without malice, but without anything that we should call manners.

THE YOUTH. Now, then, ancient sleepwalker, why dont you keep your eyes open and mind where you are going?

THE ANCIENT [*mild, bland, and indulgent*] I did not know there was a nursery here, or I should not have turned my face in this direction. Such accidents cannot always be avoided. Go on with your play: I will turn back.

THE YOUTH. Why not stay with us and enjoy life for once in a way? We will teach you to dance.

THE ANCIENT. No, thank you. I danced when I was a child like you. Dancing is a very crude attempt to get into the rhythm of life. It would be painful to me to go back from that rhythm to your babyish gambols: in fact I could not do it if I tried. But at your age it is pleasant: and I am sorry I disturbed you.

THE YOUTH. Come! own up: arnt you very unhappy? It's dreadful to see you ancients going about by yourselves, never noticing anything, never dancing, never laughing, never singing, never getting anything out of life. None of us are going to be like that when we grow up. It's a dog's life.

THE ANCIENT. Not at all. You repeat that old phrase without knowing that there was once a creature on earth called a dog. Those who are interested in extinct forms of life will tell you that it loved the sound of its own voice and bounded about when it was happy, just as you are doing here. It is you, my children, who are living the dog's life.

THE YOUTH. The dog must have been a good sensible creature: it set you a very wise example. You should let yourself go occasionally and have a good time.

THE ANCIENT. My children: be content to let us ancients go our ways and enjoy ourselves in our own fashion.

He turns to go.

THE MAIDEN. But wait a moment. Why will you not tell us how you enjoy yourself? You must have secret pleasures that you hide from us, and that you never get tired of. I get tired of all our dances and all our tunes. I get tired of all my partners.

THE YOUTH [*suspiciously*] Do you? I shall bear that in mind.
They all look at one another as if there were some sinister significance in what she has said.

THE MAIDEN. We all do: what is the use of pretending we dont? It is natural.

SEVERAL YOUNG PEOPLE. No, no. We dont. It is not natural.

THE ANCIENT. You are older than he is, I see. You are growing up.

THE MAIDEN. How do you know? I do not look so much older, do I?

THE ANCIENT. Oh, I was not looking at you. Your looks do not interest me.

THE MAIDEN. Thank you.
They all laugh.

THE YOUTH. You old fish! I believe you dont know the difference between a man and a woman.

THE ANCIENT. It has long ceased to interest me in the way it interests you. And when anything no longer interests us we no longer know it.

THE MAIDEN. You havnt told me how I shew my age. That is what I want to know. As a matter of fact I am older than this boy here: older than he thinks. How did you find that out?

THE ANCIENT. Easily enough. You are ceasing to pretend that these childish games – this dancing and singing and mating – do not become tiresome and unsatisfying after a while. And you no longer care to pretend that you are younger than you are. These are the signs of adolescence. And then, see these fantastic rags with which you have draped yourself. [*He takes up a piece of her draperies in his hand*]. It is rather badly worn here. Why do you not get a new one?

THE MAIDEN. Oh, I did not notice it. Besides, it is too much trouble. Clothes are a nuisance. I think I shall do without them some day, as you ancients do.

THE ANCIENT. Signs of maturity. Soon you will give up all these toys and games and sweets.

THE YOUTH. What! And be as miserable as you?

THE ANCIENT. Infant: one moment of the ecstasy of life as we live it would strike you dead. [*He stalks gravely out through the grove*].

They stare after him, much damped.

THE YOUTH [*to the musicians*] Let us have another dance.

The musicians shake their heads; get up from their seats on the steps; and troop away into the temple. The others follow them, except the Maiden, who sits down on the altar.

A MAIDEN [*as she goes*] There! The ancient has put them out of countenance. It is your fault, Strephon, for provoking him. [*She leaves, much disappointed*].

A YOUTH. Why need you have cheeked him like that? [*He goes grumbling*].

STREPHON [*calling after him*] I thought it was understood that we are always to cheek the ancients on principle.

ANOTHER YOUTH. Quite right too! There would be no holding them if we didnt. [*He goes*].

THE MAIDEN. Why dont you really stand up to them? *I* did.

ANOTHER YOUTH. Sheer, abject, pusillanimous, dastardly cowardice. Thats why. Face the filthy truth. [*He goes*].

ANOTHER YOUTH [*turning on the steps as he goes out*] And dont you forget, infant, that one moment of the ecstasy of life as I live it would strike you dead. Haha!

STREPHON [*now the only one left, except the Maiden*] Arnt you coming, Chloe?

THE MAIDEN [*shakes her head*]!

THE YOUTH [*hurrying back to her*] What is the matter?

THE MAIDEN [*tragically pensive*] I dont know.

THE YOUTH. Then there is something the matter. Is that what you mean?

THE MAIDEN. Yes. Something is happening to me. I dont know what.

THE YOUTH. You no longer love me. I have seen it for a month past.

THE MAIDEN. Dont you think all that is rather silly? We

cannot go on as if this kind of thing, this dancing and sweethearting, were everything.

THE YOUTH. What is there better? What else is there worth living for?

THE MAIDEN Oh, stuff! Dont be frivolous.

THE YOUTH. Something horrible is happening to you. You are losing all heart, all feeling. [*He sits on the altar beside her and buries his face in his hands*]. I am bitterly unhappy.

THE MAIDEN. Unhappy! Really, you must have a very empty head if there is nothing in it but a dance with one girl who is no better than any of the other girls.

THE YOUTH. You did not always think so. You used to be vexed if I as much as looked at another girl.

THE MAIDEN. What does it matter what I did when I was a baby? Nothing existed for me then except what I tasted and touched and saw; and I wanted all that for myself, just as I wanted the moon to play with. Now the world is opening out for me. More than the world: the universe. Even little things are turning out to be great things, and becoming intensely interesting. Have you ever thought about the properties of numbers?

THE YOUTH [*sitting up, markedly disenchanted*] Numbers!!! I cannot imagine anything drier or more repulsive.

THE MAIDEN. They are fascinating, just fascinating. I want to get away from our eternal dancing and music, and just sit down by myself and think about numbers.

THE YOUTH [*rising indignantly*] Oh, this is too much. I have suspected you for some time past. We have all suspected you. All the girls say that you have deceived us as to your age: that you are getting flat-chested: that you are bored with us; that you talk to the ancients when you get the chance. Tell me the truth: how old are you?

THE MAIDEN. Just twice your age, my poor boy.

THE YOUTH. Twice my age! Do you mean to say you are four?

THE MAIDEN. Very nearly four.

THE YOUTH [*collapsing on the altar with a groan*] Oh!

THE MAIDEN. My poor Strephon: I pretended I was only two for your sake. I was two when you were born. I saw you break from your shell; and you were such a charming child! You ran round and talked to us all so prettily, and were so handsome and well grown, that I lost my heart to you at once. But now I seem to have lost it altogether: bigger things are taking possession of me. Still, we were very happy in our childish way for the first year, werent we?

STREPHON. I was happy until you began cooling towards me.

THE MAIDEN. Not towards you, but towards all the trivialities of our life here. Just think. I have hundreds of years to live: perhaps thousands. Do you suppose I can spend centuries dancing; listening to flutes ringing changes on a few tunes and a few notes; raving about the beauty of a few pillars and arches; making jingles with words; lying about with your arms round me, which is really neither comfortable nor convenient; everlastingly choosing colors for dresses, and putting them on, and washing; making a business of sitting together at fixed hours to absorb our nourishment; taking little poisons with it to make us delirious enough to imagine we are enjoying ourselves; and then having to pass the nights in shelters lying in cots and losing half our lives in a state of unconsciousness. Sleep is a shameful thing: I have not slept at all for weeks past. I have stolen out at night when you were all lying insensible – quite disgusting, I call it – and wandered about the woods, thinking, thinking, thinking; grasping the world; taking it to pieces; building it up again; devising methods; planning experiments to test the methods; and having a glorious time. Every morning I have come back here with greater and greater reluctance; and I know that the time will soon come – perhaps it has come already – when I shall not come back at all.

STREPHON. How horribly cold and uncomfortable!

THE MAIDEN. Oh, dont talk to me of comfort! Life is not worth living if you have to bother about comfort. Comfort makes winter a torture, spring an illness, summer an oppression, and autumn only a respite. The ancients could make life one long frowsty comfort if they chose. But they never lift a finger to make themselves comfortable. They will not sleep under a roof. They will not clothe themselves: a girdle with a few pockets hanging on it to carry things about in is all they wear: they will sit down on the wet moss or in a gorse bush when there is dry heather within two yards of them. Two years ago, when you were born, I did not understand this. Now I feel that I would not put myself to the trouble of walking two paces for all the comfort in the world.

STREPHON. But you dont know what this means to me. It means that you are dying to me: yes, just dying. Listen to me [*he puts his arm around her*].

THE MAIDEN [*extricating herself*] Dont. We can talk quite as well without touching one another.

STREPHON [*horrified*] Chloe! Oh, this is the worst symptom of all! The ancients never touch one another.

THE MAIDEN. Why should they?

STREPHON. Oh, I dont know. But dont you want to touch me? You used to.

THE MAIDEN. Yes: that is true: I used to. We used to think it would be nice to sleep in one another's arms; but we never could go to sleep because our weight stopped our circulations just above the elbows. Then somehow my feeling began to change bit by bit. I kept a sort of interest in your head and arms long after I lost interest in your whole body. And now that has gone.

STREPHON. You no longer care for me at all, then?

THE MAIDEN. Nonsense! I care for you much more seriously than before; though perhaps not so much for you in particular. I mean I care more for everybody. But I dont want to touch you unnecessarily; and I certainly dont want you to touch me.

STREPHON [*rising decisively*] That finishes it. You dislike me.

THE MAIDEN [*impatiently*] I tell you again, I do not dislike you; but you bore me when you cannot understand; and I think I shall be happier by myself in future. You had better get a new companion. What about the girl who is to be born today?

STREPHON. I do not want the girl who is to be born today. How do I know what she will be like? I want you.

THE MAIDEN. You cannot have me. You must recognize facts and face them. It is no use running after a woman twice your age. I cannot make my childhood last to please you. The age of love is sweet; but it is short; and I must pay nature's debt. You no longer attract me; and I no longer care to attract you. Growth is too rapid at my age: I am maturing from week to week.

STREPHON. You are maturing, as you call it – I call it ageing – from minute to minute. You are going much further than you did when we began this conversation.

THE MAIDEN. It is not the ageing that is so rapid. It is the realization of it when it has actually happened. Now that I have made up my mind to the fact that I have left childhood behind me, it comes home to me in leaps and bounds with every word you say.

STREPHON. But your vow. Have you forgotten that? We all swore together in that temple: the temple of love. You were more earnest than any of us.

THE MAIDEN [with a grim smile] Never to let our hearts grow cold! Never to become as the ancients! Never to let the sacred lamp be extinguished! Never to change or forget! To be remembered for ever as the first company of true lovers faithful to this vow so often made and broken by past generations! Ha! ha! Oh, dear!

STREPHON. Well, you need not laugh. It is a beautiful and holy compact; and I will keep it whilst I live. Are you going to break it?

THE MAIDEN. Dear child: it has broken itself. The change has come in spite of my childish vow. [She rises]. Do you mind if I go into the woods for a walk by myself? This chat of ours seems to me an unbearable waste of time. I have so much to think of.

STREPHON [again collapsing on the altar and covering his eyes with his hands] My heart is broken. [He weeps].

THE MAIDEN [with a shrug] I have luckily got through my childhood without that experience. It shews how wise I was to choose a lover half my age. [*She goes towards the grove, and is disappearing among the trees, when another youth, older and manlier than Strephon, with crisp hair and firm arms, comes from the temple, and calls to her from the threshold*].

THE TEMPLE YOUTH. I say, Chloe. Is there any sign of the Ancient yet? The hour of birth is overdue. The baby is kicking like mad. She will break her shell prematurely.

THE MAIDEN [*looks across to the hill path; then points up it, and says*] She is coming, Acis.

The Maiden turns away through the grove and is lost to sight among the trees.

ACIS [*coming to Strephon*] Whats the matter? Has Chloe been unkind?

STREPHON. She has grown up in spite of all her promises. She deceived us about her age. She is four.

ACIS. Four! I am sorry, Strephon. I am getting on for three myself; and I know what old age is. I hate to say 'I told you so'; but she was getting a little hard set and flat-chested and thin on the top, wasnt she?

STREPHON [*breaking down*] Dont.

ACIS. You must pull yourself together. This is going to be a busy day. First the birth. Then the Festival of the Artists.

STREPHON [*rising*] What is the use of being born if we have to decay into unnatural, heartless, loveless, joyless monsters in four short years? What use are the artists if they cannot bring their beautiful creations to life? I have a great mind to die and have done with it all. [*He moves away to the corner of the curved seat farthest from the theatre, and throws himself moodily into it*].

An Ancient Woman has descended the hill path during Strephon's lament, and has heard most of it. She is like the He-Ancient, equally bald, and equally without sexual charm, but intensely interesting and rather terrifying. Her sex is discoverable only by her voice, as her breasts are manly, and her figure otherwise not very different. She wears no clothes, but has draped herself rather perfunctorily with a ceremonial robe, and carries two implements like long slender saws. She comes to the altar between the two young men.

THE SHE-ANCIENT [*to Strephon*] Infant: you are only at the beginning of it all. [*To Acis*] Is the child ready to be born?

ACIS. More than ready, Ancient. Shouting and kicking and cursing. We have called to her to be quiet and wait until you come; but of course she only half understands, and is very impatient.

THE SHE-ANCIENT. Very well. Bring her out into the sun.

ACIS [*going quickly into the temple*] All ready. Come along.

Joyous processional music strikes up in the temple.

THE SHE-ANCIENT [*going close to Strephon*]. Look at me.

STREPHON [*sulkily keeping his face averted*] Thank you; but I dont want to be cured. I had rather be miserable in my own way than callous in yours.

THE SHE-ANCIENT. You like being miserable? You will soon grow out of that. [*She returns to the altar*].

The procession, headed by Acis, emerges from the temple. Six youths carry on their shoulders a burden covered with a gorgeous but light pall. Before them certain official maidens carry a new tunic, ewers of water, silver dishes pierced with holes, clothes, and immense sponges. The rest carry wands with ribbons, and strew flowers. The burden is deposited on the altar, and the pall removed. It is a huge egg.

THE SHE-ANCIENT [*freeing her arms from her robe, and placing her saws on the altar ready to her hand in a businesslike manner*] A girl, I think you said?

ACIS. Yes.

THE TUNIC BEARER. It is a shame. Why cant we have more boys?

SEVERAL YOUTHS [*protesting*] Not at all. More girls. We want new girls.

A GIRL'S VOICE FROM THE EGG. Let me out. Let me out. I want to be born. I want to be born. [*The egg rocks*].

ACIS [*snatching a wand from one of the others and whacking the egg with it*] Be quiet, I tell you. Wait. You will be born presently.

THE EGG. No, no: at once, at once. I want to be born: I want to be born. [*Violent kicking within the egg, which rocks so hard that it has to be held on the altar by the bearers*].

THE SHE-ANCIENT. Silence. [*The music stops; and the egg behaves itself*].

The She-Ancient takes her two saws, and with a couple of strokes rips the egg open. The Newly Born, a pretty girl who would have been guessed as seventeen in our day, sits up in the broken shell, exquisitely fresh and rosy, but with filaments of spare albumen clinging to her here and there.

THE NEWLY BORN [*as the world bursts on her vision*] Oh! Oh!! Oh!!! Oh!!!! [*She continues this ad libitum during the following remonstrances*].

ACIS. Hold your noise, will you?

The washing begins. The Newly Born shrieks and struggles.

A YOUTH. Lie quiet, you clammy little devil.

A MAIDEN. You must be washed, dear. Now quiet, quiet, quiet: be good.

ACIS. Shut your mouth, or I'll shove the sponge in it.

THE MAIDEN. Shut your eyes. Itll hurt if you dont.

ANOTHER MAIDEN. Dont be silly. One would think nobody had ever been born before.

THE NEWLY BORN [*yells*]!!!!!!

ACIS. Serve you right! You were told to shut your eyes.

THE YOUTH. Dry her off quick. I can hardly hold her. Shut it, will you; or I'll smack you into a pickled cabbage.

The dressing begins. The Newly Born chuckles with delight.

THE MAIDEN. Your arms go here, dear. Isnt it pretty? Youll look lovely.

THE NEWLY BORN [*rapturously*] Oh! Oh!! Oh!!! Oh!!!!

ANOTHER YOUTH. No: the other arm: youre putting it on back to front. You are a silly little beast.

ACIS. Here! Thats it. Now youre clean and decent. Up with you! Oopsh! [*He hauls her to her feet. She cannot walk at first, but masters it after a few steps*]. Now then: march. Here she is, Ancient: put her through the catechism.

THE SHE-ANCIENT. What name have you chosen for her?

ACIS. Amaryllis.

THE SHE-ANCIENT [*to the Newly Born*] Your name is Amaryllis.

THE NEWLY BORN. What does it mean?

A YOUTH. Love.

A MAIDEN. Mother.

ANOTHER YOUTH. Lilies.

THE NEWLY BORN [*to Acis*] What is your name?

ACIS. Acis.

THE NEWLY BORN. I love you, Acis. I must have you all to myself. Take me in your arms.

ACIS. Steady, young one. I am three years old.

THE NEWLY BORN. What has that to do with it? I love you; and I must have you or I will go back into my shell again.

ACIS. You cant. It's broken. Look here [*pointing to Strephon, who has remained in his seat without looking round at the birth, wrapped up in his sorrow*]! Look at this poor fellow!

THE NEWLY BORN. What is the matter with him?

ACIS. When he was born he chose a girl two years old for his sweetheart. He is two years old now himself; and already his heart is broken because she is four. That means that she has grown up like this Ancient here, and has left him. If you choose me, we shall have only a year's happiness before I break your heart by growing up. Better choose the youngest you can find.

THE NEWLY BORN. I will not choose anyone but you. You must not grow up. We will love one another for ever. [*They all laugh*]. What are you laughing at?

THE SHE-ANCIENT. Listen, child –

THE NEWLY BORN. Do not come near me, you dreadful old creature. You frighten me.

ACIS. Just give her another moment. She is not quite reasonable yet. What can you expect from a child less than five minutes old?

THE NEWLY BORN. I think I feel a little more reasonable now. Of course I was rather young when I said that; but the inside of my head is changing very rapidly. I should like to have things explained to me.

ACIS [*to the She-Ancient*] Is she all right, do you think?

The She-Ancient looks at the Newly Born critically; feels her bumps like a phrenologist; grips her muscles and shakes her limbs; examines her teeth; looks into her eyes for a moment; and finally relinquishes her with an air of having finished her job.

THE SHE-ANCIENT. She will do. She may live.

They all wave their hands and shout for joy.

THE NEWLY BORN [*indignant*] I may live! Suppose there had been anything wrong with me?

THE SHE-ANCIENT. Children with anything wrong do not live here, my child. Life is not cheap with us. But you would not have felt anything.

THE NEWLY BORN. You mean that you would have murdered me!

THE SHE-ANCIENT. That is one of the funny words the newly born bring with them out of the past. You will forget it tomorrow. Now listen. You have four years of childhood before you. You will not be very happy; but you will be interested and amused by the novelty of the world; and your companions here will teach you how to keep up an imitation of happiness during your four years by what they call arts and sports and pleasures. The worst of your troubles is already over.

THE NEWLY BORN. What! In five minutes?

THE SHE-ANCIENT. No: you have been growing for two years in the egg. You began by being several sorts of creatures that no longer exist, though we have fossils of them. Then you became human; and you passed in fifteen months through a development that once cost human beings twenty years of awkward stumbling immaturity after they were born. They had to spend fifty years more in the sort of childhood you will complete in four years. And then they died of decay. But you need not die until your accident comes.

THE NEWLY BORN. What is my accident?

THE SHE-ANCIENT. Sooner or later you will fall and break your neck; or a tree will fall on you; or you will be struck by lightning. Something or other must make an end of you some day.

THE NEWLY BORN. But why should any of these things happen to me?

THE SHE-ANCIENT. There is no why. They do. Everything happens to everybody sooner or later if there is time enough. And with us there is eternity.

THE NEWLY BORN. Nothing need happen. I never heard such nonsense in all my life. I shall know how to take care of myself.

THE SHE-ANCIENT. So you think.

THE NEWLY BORN. I dont think: I know. I shall enjoy life for ever and ever.

THE SHE-ANCIENT. If you should turn out to be a person of infinite capacity, you will no doubt find life infinitely interesting. However, all you have to do now is to play with your companions. They have many pretty toys, as you see: a playhouse, pictures, images, flowers, bright fabrics, music: above all, themselves; for the most amusing child's toy is another child. At the end of four years, your mind will change: you will become wise; and then you will be entrusted with power.

THE NEWLY BORN. But I want power now.

THE SHE-ANCIENT. No doubt you do; so that you could play with the world by tearing it to pieces.

THE NEWLY BORN. Only to see how it is made. I should put it all together again much better than before.

THE SHE-ANCIENT. There was a time when children were given the world to play with because they promised to improve it. They did not improve it; and they would have wrecked it had their power been as great as that which you will wield when you are no longer a child. Until then your young companions will instruct you in whatever is necessary. You are not forbidden to speak to the ancients; but you had better not do so, as most of them have long ago exhausted all the interest there is in observing children and conversing with them. [*She turns to go*].

THE NEWLY BORN. Wait. Tell me some things that I ought to do and ought not to do. I feel the need of education.

They all laugh at her, except the She-Ancient.

THE SHE-ANCIENT. You will have grown out of that by tomorrow. Do what you please. [*She goes away up the hill path*].

The officials take their paraphernalia and the fragments of the egg back into the temple.

ACIS. Just fancy: that old girl has been going for seven

hundred years and hasnt had her fatal accident yet; and she is not a bit tired of it all.

THE NEWLY BORN. How could anyone ever get tired of life?

ACIS. They do. That is, of the same life. They manage to change themselves in a wonderful way. You meet them sometimes with a lot of extra heads and arms and legs: they make you split laughing at them. Most of them have forgotten how to speak: the ones that attend to us have to brush up their knowledge of the language once a year or so. Nothing makes any difference to them that I can see. They never enjoy themselves. I dont know how they can stand it. They dont even come to our festivals of the arts. That old one who saw you out of your shell has gone off to moodle about doing nothing; though she knows that this is Festival Day.

THE NEWLY BORN. What is Festival Day?

ACIS. Two of our greatest sculptors are bringing us their latest masterpieces; and we are going to crown them with flowers and sing dithyrambs to them and dance round them.

THE NEWLY BORN. How jolly! What is a sculptor?

ACIS. Listen here, young one. You must find out things for yourself, and not ask questions. For the first day or two you must keep your eyes and ears open and your mouth shut. Children should be seen and not heard.

THE NEWLY BORN. Who are you calling a child? I am fully a quarter of an hour old [*She sits down on the curved bench near Strephon with her maturest air*].

VOICES IN THE TEMPLE [*all expressing protest, disappointment, disgust*] Oh! Oh! Scandalous. Shameful. Disgraceful. What filth! Is this a joke? Why, theyre ancients! Ss-s-s-sss! Are you mad, Arjillax? This is an outrage. An insult. Yah! etc. etc. etc. [*The malcontents appear on the steps, grumbling*].

ACIS. Hullo: whats the matter? [*He goes to the steps of the temple*].

The two sculptors issue from the temple. One has a beard two feet long: the other is beardless. Between them comes a handsome nymph with marked features, dark hair richly waved, and authoritative bearing.

THE AUTHORITATIVE NYMPH [*swooping down to the centre of the glade with the sculptors, between Acis and the Newly Born*] Do not try to browbeat me, Arjillax, merely because you are clever with your hands. Can you play the flute?

ARJILLAX [*the bearded sculptor on her right*] No, Ecrasia: I cannot. What has that to do with it? [*He is half derisive, half impatient, wholly resolved not to take her seriously in spite of her beauty and imposing tone*].

ECRASIA. Well, have you ever hesitated to criticize our best flute players, and to declare whether their music is good or bad? Pray have I not the same right to criticize your busts, though I cannot make images any more than you can play?

ARJILLAX. Any fool can play the flute, or play anything else, if he practises enough; but sculpture is a creative art, not a mere business of whistling into a pipe. The sculptor must have something of the god in him. From his hand comes a form which reflects a spirit. He does not make it to please you, nor even to please himself, but because he must. You must take what he gives you, or leave it if you are not worthy of it.

ECRASIA [*scornfully*] Not worthy of it! Ho! May I not leave it because it is not worthy of me?

ARJILLAX. Of you! Hold your silly tongue, you conceited humbug. What do you know about it?

ECRASIA. I know what every person of culture knows: that the business of the artist is to create beauty. Until today your works have been full of beauty; and I have been the first to point that out.

ARJILLAX. Thank you for nothing. People have eyes, havnt they, to see what is as plain as the sun in the heavens without your pointing it out?

ECRASIA. You were very glad to have it pointed out. You did not call me a conceited humbug then. You stifled me with caresses. You modelled me as the genius of art presiding over the infancy of your master here [*indicating the other sculptor*], Martellus.

MARTELLUS [*a silent and meditative listener, shudders and shakes his head, but says nothing*].

ARJILLAX [*quarrelsomely*] I was taken in by your talk.

ECRASIA. I discovered your genius before anyone else did. Is that true, or is it not?

ARJILLAX. Everybody knew I was an extraordinary person. When I was born my beard was three feet long.

ECRASIA. Yes; and it has shrunk from three feet to two. Your genius seems to have been in the last foot of your beard; for you have lost both.

MARTELLUS [*with a short sardonic cachinnation*] Ha! My beard was three and a half feet long when I was born; and a flash of lightning burnt it off and killed the ancient who was delivering me. Without a hair on my chin I became the greatest sculptor in ten generations.

ECRASIA. And yet you come to us today with empty hands. We shall actually have to crown Arjillax here because no other sculptor is exhibiting.

ACIS [*returning from the temple steps to behind the curved seat on the right of the three*] Whats the row, Ecrasia? Why have you fallen out with Arjillax?

ECRASIA. He has insulted us! outraged us! profaned his art! You know how much we hoped from the twelve busts he placed in the temple to be unveiled today. Well, go in and look at them. That is all I have to say. [*She sweeps to the curved seat, and sits down just where Acis is leaning over it*].

ACIS. I am no great judge of sculpture. Art is not my line. What is wrong with the busts?

ECRASIA. Wrong with them! Instead of being ideally beautiful nymphs and youths, they are horribly realistic studies of – but I really cannot bring my lips to utter it.

The Newly Born, full of curiosity, runs to the temple, and peeps in.

ACIS. Oh, stow it, Ecrasia. Your lips are not so squeamish as all that. Studies of what?

THE NEWLY BORN [*from the temple steps*] Ancients.

ACIS [*surprised but not scandalized*] Ancients!

ECRASIA. Yes, ancients. The one subject that is by the universal consent of all connoisseurs absolutely excluded from the fine arts. [*To Arjillax*] How can you defend such a proceeding?

ARJILLAX. If you come to that, what interest can you find in the statues of smirking nymphs and posturing youths you stick up all over the place?

ECRASIA. You did not ask that when your hand was still skilful enough to model them.

ARJILLAX. Skilful! You high-nosed idiot, I could turn such things out by the score with my eyes bandaged and one hand tied behind me. But what use would they be? They would bore me; and they would bore you if you had any sense. Go in and look at my busts. Look at them again and yet again until you receive the full impression of the intensity of mind that is stamped on them; and then go back to the pretty-pretty confectionery you call sculpture, and see whether you can endure its vapid emptiness. [*He mounts the altar impetuously*] Listen to me, all of you; and do you, Ecrasia, be silent if you are capable of silence.

ECRASIA. Silence is the most perfect expression of scorn. Scorn! That is what I feel for your revolting busts.

ARJILLAX. Fool: the busts are only the beginning of a mighty design. Listen.

ACIS. Go ahead, old sport. We are listening.

Martellus stretches himself on the sward beside the altar. The Newly Born sits on the temple steps with her chin on her hands, ready to devour the first oration she has ever heard. The rest sit or stand at ease.

ARJILLAX. In the records which generations of children have rescued from the stupid neglect of the ancients, there has come down to us a fable which, like many fables, is not a thing that was done in the past, but a thing that is to be done in the future. It is a legend of a supernatural being called the Archangel Michael.

THE NEWLY BORN. Is this a story? I want to hear a story. [*She runs down the steps and sits on the altar at Arjillax's feet*].

ARJILLAX. The Archangel Michael was a mighty sculptor

and painter. He found in the centre of the world a temple erected to the goddess of the centre, called Mediterranea. This temple was full of silly pictures of pretty children, such as Ecrasia approves.

ACIS. Fair play, Arjillax! If she is to keep silent, let her alone.

ECRASIA. I shall not interrupt, Acis. Why should I not prefer youth and beauty to age and ugliness?

ARJILLAX. Just so. Well, the Archangel Michael was of my opinion, not yours. He began by painting on the ceiling the newly born in all their childish beauty. But when he had done this he was not satisfied; for the temple was no more impressive than it had been before, except that there was a strength and promise of greater things about his newly born ones than any other artist had attained to. So he painted all round these newly born a company of ancients, who were in those days called prophets and sybils, whose majesty was that of the mind alone at its intensest. And this painting was acknowledged through ages and ages to be the summit and masterpiece of art. Of course we cannot believe such a tale literally. It is only a legend. We do not believe in archangels; and the notion that thirty thousand years ago sculpture and painting existed, and had even reached the glorious perfection they have reached with us, is absurd. But what men cannot realize they can at least aspire to. They please themselves by pretending that it was realized in a golden age of the past. This splendid legend endured because it lived as a desire in the hearts of the greatest artists. The temple of Mediterranea never was built in the past, nor did Michael the Archangel exist. But today the temple is here [*he points to the porch*]; and the man is here [*he slaps himself on the chest*]. I, Arjillax, am the man. I will place in your theatre such images of the newly born as must satisfy even Ecrasia's appetite for beauty; and I will surround them with ancients more august than any who walk through our woods.

MARTELLUS [*as before*] Ha!

ARJILLAX [*stung*] Why do you laugh, you who have come empty-handed, and, it seems, empty-headed?

ECRASIA [*rising indignantly*] Oh, shame! You dare disparage Martellus, twenty times your master.

ACIS. Be quiet, will you [*he seizes her shoulders and thrusts her back into her seat*].

MARTELLUS. Let him disparage his fill, Ecrasia. [*Sitting up*] My poor Arjillax. I too had this dream. I too found one day that my images of loveliness had become vapid, uninteresting, tedious, a waste of time and material. I too lost my desire to model limbs, and retained only my interest in heads and faces. I, too, made busts of ancients; but I had not your courage: I made them in secret, and hid them from you all.

ARJILLAX [*jumping down from the altar behind Martellus in his surprise and excitement*] You made busts of ancients! Where are they, man? Will you be talked out of your inspiration by Ecrasia and the fools who imagine she speaks with authority? Let us have them all set up beside mine in the theatre. I have opened the way for you; and you see I am none the worse.

MARTELLUS. Impossible. They are all smashed. [*He rises, laughing*].

ALL. Smashed!

ARJILLAX. Who smashed them?

MARTELLUS. I did. That is why I laughed at you just now. You will smash yours before you have completed a dozen of them. [*He goes to the end of the altar and sits down beside the Newly Born*].

ARJILLAX. But why?

MARTELLUS. Because you cannot give them life. A live ancient is better than a dead statue. [*He takes the Newly Born on his knee : she is flattered and voluptuously responsive*]. Anything alive is better than anything that is only pretending to be alive. [*To Arjillax*] Your disillusion with your works of beauty is only the beginning of your disillusion with images of all sorts. As your hand became more skilful and your chisel cut deeper, you strove to get nearer and nearer to truth and reality, discarding the fleeting fleshly lure, and making images of the mind that fascinates to the end.

But how can so noble an inspiration be satisfied with any image, even an image of the truth? In the end the intellectual conscience that tore you away from the fleeting in art to the eternal must tear you away from art altogether, because art is false and life alone is true.

THE NEWLY BORN [*flings her arms round his neck and kisses him enthusiastically*].

MARTELLUS [*rises; carries her to the curved bench on his left; deposits her beside Strephon as if she were his overcoat; and continues without the least change of tone*] Shape it as you will, marble remains marble, and the graven image an idol. As I have broken my idols, and cast away my chisel and modelling tools, so will you too break these busts of yours.

ARJILLAX. Never.

MARTELLUS. Wait, my friend. I do not come empty-handed today, as you imagined. On the contrary, I bring with me such a work of art as you have never seen, and an artist who has surpassed both you and me further than we have surpassed all our competitors.

ECRASIA. Impossible. The greatest things in art can never be surpassed.

ARJILLAX. Who is this paragon whom you declare greater than I?

MARTELLUS. I declare him greater than myself, Arjillax.

ARJILLAX [*frowning*] I understand. Sooner than not drown me, you are willing to clasp me round the waist and jump overboard with me.

ACIS. Oh, stop squabbling. That is the worst of you artists. You are always in little squabbling cliques; and the worst cliques are those which consist of one man. Who is this new fellow you are throwing in one another's teeth?

ARJILLAX. Ask Martellus: do not ask me. I know nothing of him. [*He leaves Martellus, and sits down beside Ecrasia, on her left.*]

MARTELLUS. You know him quite well. Pygmalion.

ECRASIA [*indignantly*] Pygmalion! That soulless creature! A scientist! A laboratory person!

ARJILLAX. Pygmalion produce a work of art! You have lost

your artistic senses. The man is utterly incapable of modelling a thumb nail, let alone a human figure.

MARTELLUS. That does not matter: I have done the modelling for him.

ARJILLAX. What on earth do you mean?

MARTELLUS [*calling*] Pygmalion: come forth.

*Pygmalion, a square-fingered youth with his face laid out in
horizontal blocks, and a perpetual smile of eager benevolent interest
in everything, and expectation of equal interest from everybody else,
comes from the temple to the centre of the group, who regard him for
the most part with dismay, as dreading that he will bore them.
Ecrasia is openly contemptuous.*

MARTELLUS. Friends: it is unfortunate that Pygmalion is
constitutionally incapable of exhibiting anything without
first giving a lecture about it to explain it; but I promise
you that if you will be patient he will shew you the two
most wonderful works of art in the world, and that they
will contain some of my own very best workmanship. Let
me add that they will inspire a loathing that will cure you
of the lunacy of art for ever. [*He sits down next to the Newly
Born, who pouts and turns a very cold right shoulder to him, a
demonstration utterly lost on him*].

*Pygmalion, with the smile of a simpleton, and the eager confid-
ence of a fanatical scientist, climbs awkwardly on to the altar.
They prepare for the worst.*

PYGMALION. My friends: I will omit the algebra –

ACIS. Thank God!

PYGMALION [*continuing*] – because Martellus has made me
promise to do so. To come to the point, I have succeeded
in making artificial human beings. Real live ones, I mean.

INCREDULOUS VOICES. Oh, come! Tell us another. Really,
Pyg! Get out. You havnt. What a lie!

PYGMALION. I tell you I have. I will shew them to you. It
has been done before. One of the very oldest documents
we possess mentions a tradition of a biologist who ex-
tracted certain unspecified minerals from the earth and,
as it quaintly expresses it, 'breathed into their nostrils the
breath of life.' This is the only tradition from the primitive

ages which we can regard as really scientific. There are later documents which specify the minerals with great precision, even to their atomic weights; but they are utterly unscientific, because they overlook the element of life which makes all the difference between a mere mixture of salts and gases and a living organism. These mixtures were made over and over again in the crude laboratories of the Silly-Clever Ages; but nothing came of them until the ingredient which the old chronicler called the breath of life was added by this very remarkable early experimenter. In my view he was the founder of biological science.

ARJILLAX. Is that all we know about him? It doesnt amount to very much, does it?

PYGMALION. There are some fragments of pictures and documents which represent him as walking in a garden and advising people to cultivate their gardens. His name has come down to us in several forms. One of them is Jove. Another is Voltaire.

ECRASIA. You are boring us to distraction with your Voltaire. What about your human beings?

ARJILLAX. Aye: come to them.

PYGMALION. I assure you that these details are intensely interesting. [*Cries of* No! They are not! Come to the human beings! Conspuez Voltaire! Cut it short, Pyg! *interrupt him from all sides*]. You will see their bearing presently. I promise you I will not detain you long. We know, we children of science, that the universe is full of forces and powers and energies of one kind and another. The sap rising in a tree, the stone holding together in a definite crystalline structure, the thought of a philosopher holding his brain in form and operation with an inconceivably powerful grip, the urge of evolution: all these forces can be used by us. For instance, I use the force of gravitation when I put a stone on my tunic to prevent it being blown away when I am bathing. By substituting appropriate machines for the stone we have made not only gravitation our slave, but also electricity and magnetism, atomic attraction, repulsion, polarization, and so forth. But hitherto the vital force has eluded us; so it has had to create machinery for itself. It has created and developed bony structures of the requisite strength, and clothed them with cellular tissue of such amazing sensitiveness that the organs it forms will adapt their action to all the normal variations in the air they breathe, the food they digest, and the circumstances about which they have to think. Yet, as these live bodies, as we call them, are only machines after all, it must be possible to construct them mechanically.

ARJILLAX. Everything is possible. Have you done it? that is the question.

PYGMALION. Yes. But that is a mere fact. What is interesting is the explanation of the fact. Forgive my saying so; but it is such a pity that you artists have no intellect.

ECRASIA [*sententiously*] I do not admit that. The artist divines by inspiration all the truths that the so-called scientist grubs up in his laboratory slowly and stupidly long afterwards.

ARJILLAX [*to Ecrasia, quarrelsomely*] What do you know about it? You are not an artist.

ACIS. Shut your heads, both of you. Let us have the artificial men. Trot them out, Pygmalion.

PYGMALION. It is a man and a woman. But I really must explain first.

ALL [*groaning*]!!!

PYGMALION. Yes: I –

ACIS. We want results, not explanations.

PYGMALION [*hurt*] I see I am boring you. Not one of you takes the least interest in science. Goodbye. [*He descends from the altar and makes for the temple*].

SEVERAL YOUTHS AND MAIDENS [*rising and rushing to him*] No, no. Dont go. Dont be offended. We want to see the artificial pair. We will listen. We are tremendously interested. Tell us all about it.

PYGMALION [*relenting*] I shall not detain you two minutes.

ALL. Half an hour if you like. Please go on, Pygmalion. [*They rush him back to the altar, and hoist him on to it*]. Up you go.

They return to their former places.

PYGMALION. As I told you, lots of attempts were made to produce protoplasm in the laboratory. Why were these synthetic plasms, as they called them, no use?

ECRASIA. We are waiting for you to tell us.

THE NEWLY BORN [*modelling herself on Ecrasia, and trying to outdo her intellectually*] Clearly because they were dead.

PYGMALION. Not bad for a baby, my pet. But dead and alive are very loose terms. You are not half as much alive as you will be in another month or so. What was wrong with the synthetic protoplasm was that it could not fix and conduct the Life Force. It was like a wooden magnet or a lightning conductor made of silk: it would not take the current.

ACIS. Nobody but a fool would make a wooden magnet, and expect it to attract anything.

PYGMALION. He might if he were so ignorant as not to be able to distinguish between wood and soft iron. In those days they were very ignorant of the differences between things, because their methods of analysis were crude. They mixed up messes that were so like protoplasm that they could not tell the difference. But the difference was there, though their analysis was too superficial and incomplete to detect it. You must remember that these poor devils were very little better than our idiots: we should never dream of letting one of them survive the day of its birth. Why, the Newly Born there already knows by instinct many things that their greatest physicists could hardly arrive at by forty years of strenuous study. Her simple direct sense of space-time and quantity unconsciously solves problems which cost their most famous mathematicians years of prolonged and laborious calculations requiring such intense mental application that they frequently forgot to breathe when engaged in them, and almost suffocated themselves in consequence.

ECRASIA. Leave these obscure prehistoric abortions; and come back to your synthetic man and woman.

PYGMALION. When I undertook the task of making synthetic men, I did not waste my time on protoplasm. It was evident to me that if it were possible to make protoplasm in the laboratory, it must be equally possible to begin higher up and make fully evolved muscular and nervous tissues, bone, and so forth. Why make the seed when the making of the flower would be no greater miracle? I tried thousands of combinations before I succeeded in producing anything that would fix high-potential Life Force.

ARJILLAX. High what?

PYGMALION. High-po-tential. The Life Force is not so simple as you think. A high-potential current of it will turn a bit of dead tissue into a philosopher's brain. A low-potential current will reduce the same bit of tissue to a mass of corruption. Will you believe me when I tell you that, even in man himself, the Life Force used to slip suddenly down from its human level to that of a fungus, so that men found their flesh no longer growing as flesh, but proliferating horribly in a lower form which was called cancer, until the lower form of life killed the higher, and both perished together miserably?

MARTELLUS. Keep off the primitive tribes, Pygmalion. They interest you; but they bore these young things.

PYGMALION. I am only trying to make you understand. There was the Life Force raging all round me: there was I, trying to make organs that would capture it as a battery captures electricity, and tissues that would conduct it and operate it. It was easy enough to make eyes more perfect than our own, and ears with a larger range of sound; but they could neither see nor hear, because they were not susceptible to the Life Force. But it was far worse when I discovered how to make them susceptible; for the first thing that happened was that they ceased to be eyes and ears and turned into heaps of maggots.

ECRASIA. Disgusting! Please stop.

ACIS. If you dont want to hear, go away. You go ahead, Pyg.

PYGMALION. I went ahead. You see, the lower potentials of the Life Force could make maggots, but not human eyes or ears. I improved the tissue until it was susceptible to a higher potential.

ARJILLAX [*intensely interested*] Yes; and then?

PYGMALION. Then the eyes and ears turned into cancers.

ECRASIA. Oh, hideous!

PYGMALION. Not at all. That was a great advance. It encouraged me so much that I put aside the eyes and ears,
and made a brain. It wouldnt take the Life Force at all
until I had altered its constitution a dozen times; but when
it did, it took a much higher potential, and did not dissolve; and neither did the eyes and ears when I connected
them up with the brain. I was able to make a sort of
monster: a thing without arms or legs; and it really and
truly lived for half-an-hour.

THE NEWLY BORN. Half-an-hour! What good was that?
Why did it die?

PYGMALION. Its blood went wrong. But I got that right;
and then I went ahead with a complete human body;
arms and legs and all. He was my first man.

ARJILLAX. Who modelled him?

PYGMALION. I did.

MARTELLUS. Do you mean to say you tried your own hand
before you sent for me?

PYGMALION. Bless you, yes, several times. My first man
was the ghastliest creature: a more dreadful mixture of
horror and absurdity than you who have not seen him can
conceive.

ARJILLAX. If you modelled him, he must indeed have been
a spectacle.

PYGMALION. Oh, it was not his shape. You see I did not
invent that. I took actual measurements and moulds from
my own body. Sculptors do that sometimes, you know;
though they pretend they dont.

MARTELLUS. Hm!

ARJILLAX. Hah!

PYGMALION. He was all right to look at, at first, or nearly
so. But he behaved in the most appalling manner; and the
subsequent developments were so disgusting that I really
cannot describe them to you. He seized all sorts of things
and swallowed them. He drank every fluid in the labora-

tory. I tried to explain to him that he must take nothing that he could not digest and assimilate completely; but of course he could not understand me. He assimilated a little of what he swallowed; but the process left horrible residues which he had no means of getting rid of. His blood turned to poison; and he perished in torments, howling. I then perceived that I had produced a prehistoric man; for there are certain traces in our own bodies of arrangements which enabled the earlier forms of mankind to renew their bodies by swallowing flesh and grains and vegetables and all sorts of unnatural and hideous foods, and getting rid of what they could not digest.

ECRASIA. But what a pity he died! What a glimpse of the past we have lost! He could have told us stories of the Golden Age.

PYGMALION. Not he. He was a most dangerous beast. He was afraid of me, and actually tried to kill me by snatching up things and striking at me with them. I had to give him two or three pretty severe shocks before I convinced him that he was at my mercy.

THE NEWLY BORN. Why did you not make a woman instead of a man? She would have known how to behave herself.

MARTELLUS Why did you not make a man and a woman? Their children would have been interesting.

PYGMALION. I intended to make a woman; but after my experience with the man it was out of the question.

ECRASIA. Pray why?

PYGMALION. Well, it is difficult to explain if you have not studied prehistoric methods of reproduction. You see the only sort of men and women I could make were men and women just like us as far as their bodies were concerned. That was how I killed the poor beast of a man. I hadnt provided for his horrible prehistoric methods of feeding himself. Suppose the woman had reproduced in some prehistoric way instead of being oviparous as we are? She couldnt have done it with a modern female body. Besides, the experiment might have been painful.

ECRASIA. Then you have nothing to shew us at all?

PYGMALION. Oh yes I have. I am not so easily beaten as that. I set to work again for months to find out how to make a digestive system that would deal with waste products and a reproductive system capable of internal nourishment and incubation.

ECRASIA. Why did you not find out how to make them like us?

STREPHON [*crying out in his grief for the first time*] Why did you not make a woman whom you could love? That was the secret you needed.

THE NEWLY BORN. Oh yes. How true! How great of you, darling Strephon! [*She kisses him impulsively*].

STREPHON [*passionately*] Let me alone.

MARTELLUS. Control your reflexes, child.

THE NEWLY BORN. My what!

MARTELLUS. Your reflexes. The things you do without thinking. Pygmalion is going to shew you a pair of human creatures who are all reflexes and nothing else. Take warning by them.

THE NEWLY BORN. But wont they be alive, like us?

PYGMALION. That is a very difficult question to answer, my dear. I confess I thought at first I had created living creatures; but Martellus declares they are only automata. But then Martellus is a mystic: *I* am a man of science. He draws a line between an automaton and a living organism. I cannot draw that line to my own satisfaction.

MARTELLUS. Your artificial men have no self-control. They only respond to stimuli from without.

PYGMALION. But they are conscious. I have taught them to talk and read; and now they tell lies. That is so very life-like.

MARTELLUS. Not at all. If they were alive they would tell the truth. You can provoke them to tell any silly lie; and you can foresee exactly the sort of lie they will tell. Give them a clip below the knee, and they will jerk their foot forward. Give them a clip in their appetites or vanities or any of their lusts and greeds, and they will boast and lie,

T-K

and affirm and deny, and hate and love without the slightest regard to the facts that are staring them in the face, or to their own obvious limitations. That proves that they are automata.

PYGMALION [*unconvinced*] I know, dear old chap; but there really is some evidence that we are descended from creatures quite as limited and absurd as these. After all, the baby there is three-quarters an automaton. Look at the way she has been going on!

THE NEWLY BORN [*indignantly*] What do you mean? How have I been going on?

ECRASIA. If they have no regard for truth, they can have no real vitality.

PYGMALION. Truth is sometimes so artificial: so relative, as we say in the scientific world, that it is very hard to feel quite sure that what is false and even ridiculous to us may not be true to them.

ECRASIA. I ask you again, why did you not make them like us? Would any true artist be content with less than the best?

PYGMALION. I couldnt. I tried. I failed. I am convinced that what I am about to shew you is the very highest living organism that can be produced in the laboratory. The best tissues we can manufacture will not take as high potentials as the natural product: that is where Nature beats us. You dont seem to understand, any of you, what an enormous triumph it was to produce consciousness at all.

ACIS. Cut the cackle; and come to the synthetic couple.

SEVERAL YOUTHS AND MAIDENS. Yes, yes. No more talking. Let us have them. Dry up, Pyg; and fetch them along. Come on: out with them! The synthetic couple.

PYGMALION [*waving his hands to appease them*] Very well, very well. Will you please whistle for them? They respond to the stimulus of a whistle.

All who can, whistle like streetboys.

ECRASIA [*makes a wry face and puts her fingers in her ears*]!

PYGMALION. Sh-sh-sh! Thats enough: thats enough: thats enough. [*Silence*]. Now let us have some music. A dance tune. Not too fast.

The flutists play a quiet dance.

MARTELLUS. Prepare yourselves for something ghastly.

Two figures, a man and woman of noble appearance, beautifully modelled and splendidly attired, emerge hand in hand from the temple. Seeing that all eyes are fixed on them, they halt on the steps, smiling with gratified vanity. The woman is on the man's left.

PYGMALION [*rubbing his hands with the purring satisfaction of a creator*] This way, please.

The Figures advance condescendingly and pose themselves centrally between the curved seats.

PYGMALION. Now if you will be so good as to oblige us with a little something. You dance so beautifully, you know. [*He sits down next Martellus, and whispers to him*] It is extraordinary how sensitive they are to the stimulus of flattery.

The Figures, with a gracious air, dance pompously, but very passably. At the close they bow to one another.

ON ALL HANDS [*clapping*] Bravo! Thank you. Wonderful! Splendid. Perfect.

The Figures acknowledge the applause in an obvious condition of swelled head.

THE NEWLY BORN. Can they make love?

PYGMALION. Yes: they can respond to every stimulus. They have all the reflexes. Put your arm round the man's neck, and he will put his arm round your body. He cannot help it.

THE FEMALE FIGURE [*frowning*] Round mine, you mean.

PYGMALION. Yours, too, of course, if the stimulus comes from you.

ECRASIA. Cannot he do anything original?

PYGMALION. No. But then, you know, I do not admit that any of us can do anything really original, though Martellus thinks we can.

ACIS. Can he answer a question?

PYGMALION. Oh yes. A question is a stimulus, you know. Ask him one.

ACIS [*to the Male Figure*] What do you think of what you see around you? Of us, for instance, and our ways and doings?

THE MALE FIGURE. I have not seen the newspaper today.

THE FEMALE FIGURE. How can you expect my husband to know what to think of you if you give him his breakfast without his paper?

MARTELLUS. You see. He is a mere automaton.

THE NEWLY BORN. I dont think I should like him to put his arm round my neck. I dont like them. [*The Male Figure looks offended, and the Female jealous*]. Oh, I thought they couldnt understand. Have they feelings?

PYGMALION. Of course they have. I tell you they have all the reflexes.

THE NEWLY BORN. But feelings are not reflexes.

PYGMALION. They are sensations. When the rays of light enter their eyes and make a picture on their retinas, their brains become conscious of the picture and they act accordingly. When the waves of sound started by your speaking enter their ears and record a disparaging remark on their keyboards, their brains become conscious of the disparagement and resent it accordingly. If you did not disparage them they would not resent it. They are merely responding to a stimulus.

THE MALE FIGURE. We are part of a cosmic system. Free will is an illusion. We are the children of Cause and Effect. We are the Unalterable, the Irresistible, the Irresponsible, the Inevitable.

My name is Ozymandias, king of kings:
Look on my works, ye mighty, and despair.

There is a general stir of curiosity at this.

ACIS. What the dickens does he mean?

THE MALE FIGURE. Silence, base accident of Nature. This [*taking the hand of the Female Figure and introducing her*] is Cleopatra-Semiramis, consort of the king of kings, and therefore queen of queens. Ye are things hatched from eggs by the brainless sun and the blind fire; but the king of kings and queen of queens are not accidents of the egg: they are thought-out and hand-made to receive the sacred Life Force. There is one person of the king and one of the queen; but the Life Force of the king and queen is all one: the glory equal, the majesty co-eternal. Such as the king is so is the queen, the king thought-out and hand-made, the queen thought-out and hand-made. The actions of the king are caused, and therefore determined, from the beginning of the world to the end; and the actions of the queen are likewise. The king logical and predetermined and inevitable, and the queen logical and predetermined and inevitable. And yet they are not two logical and predetermined and inevitable, but one logical and predetermined and inevitable. Therefore confound not the persons, nor divide the substance: but worship us twain as one throne, two in one and one in two, lest by error ye fall into irretrievable damnation.

THE FEMALE FIGURE. And if any say unto you 'Which one?' remember that though there is one person of the king and one of the queen, yet these two persons are not alike, but are woman and man, and that as woman was created after man, the skill and practice gained in making him were added to her, wherefore she is to be exalted above him in all personal respects, and –

THE MALE FIGURE. Peace, woman; for this is a damnable heresy. Both Man and Woman are what they are and must do what they must according to the eternal laws of Cause and Effect. Look to your words; for if they enter my ear and jar too repugnantly on my sensorium, who knows that the inevitable response to that stimulus may not be a message to my muscles to snatch up some heavy object and break you in pieces.

The Female Figure picks up a stone and is about to throw it at her consort.

ARJILLAX [*springing up and shouting to Pygmalion, who is fondly watching the Male Figure*] Look out, Pygmalion! Look at the woman!

Pygmalion, seeing what is happening, hurls himself on the Female Figure and wrenches the stone out of her hand.

All spring up in consternation.

ARJILLAX. She meant to kill him.

STREPHON. This is horrible.

THE FEMALE FIGURE [*wrestling with Pygmalion*] Let me go. Let me go, will you [*she bites his hand*].

PYGMALION [*releasing her and staggering*] Oh!

A general shriek of horror·echoes his exclamation. He turns deadly pale, and supports himself against the end of the curved seat.

THE FEMALE FIGURE [*to her consort*] You would stand there and let me be treated like this, you unmanly coward.

Pygmalion falls dead.

THE NEWLY BORN. Oh! Whats the matter? Why did he fall! What has happened to him?

They look on anxiously as Martellus kneels down and examines the body of Pygmalion.

MARTELLUS. She has bitten a piece out of his hand nearly as large as a finger nail: enough to kill ten men. There is no pulse, no breath.

ECRASIA. But his thumb is clinched.

MARTELLUS. No: it has just straightened out. See! He has gone. Poor Pygmalion!

THE NEWLY BORN. Oh! [*She weeps*].

STREPHON. Hush, dear: thats childish.

THE NEWLY BORN [*subsiding with a sniff*]!!

MARTELLUS [*rising*] Dead in his third year. What a loss to Science!

ARJILLAX. Who cares about Science? Serve him right for making that pair of horrors!

THE MALE FIGURE [*glaring*] Ha!

THE FEMALE FIGURE. Keep a civil tongue in your head, you.

THE NEWLY BORN. Oh, do not be so unkind, Arjillax. You will make water come out of my eyes again.

MARTELLUS [*contemplating the Figures*] Just look at these two devils. I modelled them out of the stuff Pygmalion made for them. They are masterpieces of art. And see what they have done! Does that convince you of the value of art, Arjillax!

STREPHON. They look dangerous. Keep away from them.

ECRASIA. No need to tell us that, Strephon. Pf! They poison the air.

THE MALE FIGURE. Beware, woman. The wrath of Ozymandias strikes like the lightning.

THE FEMALE FIGURE. You just say that again if you dare, you filthy creature.

ACIS. What are you going to do with them, Martellus? You are responsible for them, now that Pygmalion has gone.

MARTELLUS. If they were marble it would be simple enough: I could smash them. As it is, how am I to kill them without making a horrible mess?

THE MALE FIGURE [*posing heroically*] Ha! [*He declaims*]

> Come one: come all: this rock shall fly
> From its firm base as soon as I.

THE FEMALE FIGURE [*fondly*] My man! My hero husband! I am proud of you. I love you.

MARTELLUS. We must send out a message for an ancient.

ACIS. Need we bother an ancient about such a trifle? It will take less than half a second to reduce our poor Pygmalion to a pinch of dust. Why not calcine the two along with him?

MARTELLUS. No: the two automata are trifles; but the use of our powers of destruction is never a trifle. I had rather have the case judged.

The He-ancient emerges from the grove. The Figures are panic-stricken.

THE HE-ANCIENT [*mildly*] Am I wanted? I feel called. [*Seeing the body of Pygmalion, and immediately taking a sterner tone*] What! A child lost! A life wasted! How has this happened?

THE FEMALE FIGURE [*frantically*] I didnt do it. It was not me. May I be struck dead if I touched him! It was he [*pointing to the Male Figure*].

ALL [*amazed at the lie*] Oh!

THE MALE FIGURE. Liar. You bit him. Everyone here saw you do it.

THE HE-ANCIENT. Silence. [*Going between the Figures*] Who made these two loathsome dolls?

THE MALE FIGURE [*trying to assert himself with his knees knocking*] My name is Ozymandias, king of –

THE HE-ANCIENT [*with a contemptuous gesture*] Pooh!

THE MALE FIGURE [*falling on his knees*] Oh dont, sir. Dont. She did it, sir: indeed she did.

THE FEMALE FIGURE [*howling lamentably*] Boohoo! oo! ooh!

THE HE-ANCIENT. Silence, I say.

He knocks the Male Automaton upright by a very light flip under the chin. The Female Automaton hardly dares to sob. The immortals contemplate them with shame and loathing. The She-Ancient comes from the trees opposite the temple.

THE SHE-ANCIENT. Somebody wants me. What is the matter? [*She comes to the left hand of the Female Figure, not seeing the body of Pygmalion*]. Pf! [*Severely*] You have been making dolls. You must not: they are not only disgusting: they are dangerous.

THE FEMALE FIGURE [*snivelling piteously*] I'm not a doll, mam. I'm only poor Cleopatra-Semiramis, queen of queens. [*Covering her face with her hands*] Oh, dont look at me like that, mam. I meant no harm. He hurt me: indeed he did.

THE HE-ANCIENT. The creature has killed that poor youth.

THE SHE-ANCIENT [*seeing the body of Pygmalion*] What! This clever child, who promised so well!

THE FEMALE FIGURE. He made me. I had as much right to kill him as he had to make me. And how was I to know that a little thing like that would kill him? I shouldnt die if he cut off my arm or leg.

ECRASIA. What nonsense!

MARTELLUS. It may not be nonsense. I daresay if you cut off her leg she would grow another, like the lobsters and the little lizards.

THE HE-ANCIENT. Did this dead boy make these two things?

MARTELLUS. He made them in his laboratory. I moulded their limbs. I am sorry. I was thoughtless: I did not foresee that they would kill and pretend to be persons they were not, and declare things that were false, and wish evil. I thought they would be merely mechanical fools.

THE MALE FIGURE. Do you blame us for our human nature?

THE FEMALE FIGURE. We are flesh and blood and not angels.

THE MALE FIGURE. Have you no hearts?

ARJILLAX. They are mad as well as mischievous. May we not destroy them?

STREPHON. We abhor them.

THE NEWLY BORN. We loathe them.

ECRASIA. They are noisome.

ACIS. I dont want to be hard on the poor devils; but they are making me feel uneasy in my inside. I never had such a sensation before.

MARTELLUS. I took a lot of trouble with them. But as far as I am concerned, destroy them by all means. I loathed them from the beginning.

ALL. Yes, yes: we all loathe them. Let us calcine them.

THE FEMALE FIGURE. Oh, dont be so cruel. I'm not fit to die. I will never bite anyone again. I will tell the truth. I will do good. Is it my fault if I was not made properly? Kill him; but spare me.

THE MALE FIGURE. No! I have done no harm: she has. Kill her if you like: you have no right to kill me.

THE NEWLY BORN. Do you hear that? They want to have one another killed.

ARJILLAX. Monstrous! Kill them both.

THE HE-ANCIENT. Silence. These things are mere automata: they cannot help shrinking from death at any cost. You see that they have no self-control, and are merely shuddering through a series of reflexes. Let us see whether we cannot put a little more life into them. [*He takes the Male Figure by the hand, and places his disengaged hand on its head*]. Now listen. One of you two is to be destroyed. Which of you shall it be?

THE MALE FIGURE [*after a slight convulsion during which his eyes are fixed on the He-Ancient*] Spare her; and kill me.

STREPHON. Thats better.

THE NEWLY BORN. Much better.

THE SHE-ANCIENT [*handling the Female Automaton in the same manner*] Which of you shall we kill?

THE FEMALE FIGURE. Kill us both. How could either of us live without the other?

ECRASIA. The woman is more sensible than the man.

The Ancients release the Automata.

THE MALE FIGURE [*sinking to the ground*] I am discouraged. Life is too heavy a burden.

THE FEMALE FIGURE [*collapsing*] I am dying. I am glad. I am afraid to live.

THE NEWLY BORN. I think it would be nice to give the poor things a little music.

ARJILLAX. Why?

THE NEWLY BORN. I dont know. But it would.

The Musicians play.

THE FEMALE FIGURE. Ozymandias: do you hear that? [*She rises on her knees and looks raptly into space*] Queen of queens! [*She dies*].

THE MALE FIGURE [*crawling feebly towards her until he reaches her hand*] I knew I was really a king of kings. [*To the others*] Illusions, farewell: we are going to our thrones. [*He dies*].

The music stops. There is dead silence for a moment.

THE NEWLY BORN. That was funny.

STREPHON. It was. Even the Ancients are smiling.

THE NEWLY BORN. Just a little.

THE SHE-ANCIENT [*quickly recovering her grave and peremptory manner*] Take these two abominations away to Pygmalion's laboratory, and destroy them with the rest of the laboratory refuse. [*Some of them move to obey*]. Take care: do not touch their flesh: it is noxious: lift them by their robes. Carry Pygmalion into the temple; and dispose of his remains in the usual way.

The three bodies are carried out as directed, Pygmalion into the temple by his bare arms and legs, and the two Figures through the grove by their clothes. Martellus superintends the removal of the Figures, Acis that of Pygmalion. Ecrasia, Arjillax, Strephon, and the Newly Born sit down as before, but on contrary benches; so that Strephon and the Newly Born now face the grove, and Ecrasia and Arjillax the temple. The Ancients remain standing at the altar.

ECRASIA [*as she sits down*] Oh for a breeze from the hills!

STREPHON. Or the wind from the sea at the turn of the tide!

THE NEWLY BORN. I want some clean air.

THE HE-ANCIENT. The air will be clean in a moment. This doll flesh that children make decomposes quickly at best; but when it is shaken by such passions as the creatures are capable of, it breaks up at once and becomes horribly tainted.

THE SHE-ANCIENT. Let it be a lesson to you all to be content with lifeless toys, and not attempt to make living ones. What would you think of us ancients if we made toys of you children?

THE NEWLY BORN [*coaxingly*] Why do you not make toys of us? Then you would play with us; and that would be very nice.

THE SHE-ANCIENT. It would not amuse us. When you play with one another you play with your bodies, and that makes you supple and strong; but if we played with you we should play with your minds, and perhaps deform them.

STREPHON. You are a ghastly lot, you ancients. I shall kill myself when I am four years old. What do you live for?

THE HE-ANCIENT. You will find out when you grow up. You will not kill yourself.

STREPHON. If you make me believe that, I shall kill myself now.

THE NEWLY BORN. Oh no. I want you. I love you.

STREPHON. I love someone else. And she has gone old, old. Lost to me for ever.

THE HE-ANCIENT. How old?

STREPHON. You saw her when you barged into us as we were dancing. She is four.

THE NEWLY BORN. How I should have hated her twenty minutes ago! But I have grown out of that now.

THE HE-ANCIENT. Good. That hatred is called jealousy, the worst of our childish complaints.

Martellus, dusting his hands and puffing, returns from the grove.

MARTELLUS. Ouf! [*He sits down next the Newly Born*] That job's finished.

ARJILLAX. Ancients: I should like to make a few studies of you. Not portraits, of course: I shall idealize you a little. I have come to the conclusion that you ancients are the most interesting subjects after all.

MARTELLUS. What! Have those two horrors, whose ashes I have just deposited with peculiar pleasure in poor Pygmalion's dustbin, not cured you of this silly image-making!

ARJILLAX. Why did you model them as young things, you fool? If Pygmalion had come to me, I should have made ancients of them for him. Not that I should have modelled them any better. I have always said that no one can beat you at your best as far as handwork is concerned. But this job required brains. That is where I should have come in.

MARTELLUS. Well, my brainy boy, you are welcome to try your hand. There are two of Pygmalion's pupils at the laboratory who helped him to manufacture the bones and tissues and all the rest of it. They can turn out a couple of new automatons; and you can model them as ancients if this venerable pair will sit for you.

ECRASIA [decisively] No. No more automata. They are too disgusting.

ACIS [returning from the temple] Well, thats done. Poor old Pyg!

ECRASIA. Only fancy, Acis! Arjillax wants to make more of those abominable things, and to destroy even their artistic character by making ancients of them.

THE NEWLY BORN. You wont sit for them, will you? Please dont.

THE HE-ANCIENT. Children, listen.

ACIS [striding down the steps to the bench and seating himself next Ecrasia] What! Even the Ancient wants to make a speech! Give it mouth, O Sage.

STREPHON. For heaven's sake dont tell us that the earth was once inhabited by Ozymandiases and Cleopatras. Life is hard enough for us as it is.

THE HE-ANCIENT. Life is not meant to be easy, my child; but take courage: it can be delightful. What I wanted to tell you is that ever since men existed, children have played with dolls.

ECRASIA. You keep using that word. What are dolls, pray?

THE SHE-ANCIENT. What you call works of art. Images. We call them dolls.

ARJILLAX. Just so. You have no sense of art; and you instinctively insult it.

THE HE-ANCIENT. Children have been known to make dolls out of rags, and to caress them with the deepest fondness.

THE SHE-ANCIENT. Eight centuries ago, when I was a child, I made a rag doll. The rag doll is the dearest of all.

THE NEWLY BORN [eagerly interested] Oh! Have you got it still?

THE SHE-ANCIENT. I kept it a full week.

ECRASIA. Even in your childhood, then, you did not understand high art, and adored your own amateur crudities.

THE SHE-ANCIENT. How old are you?

ECRASIA. Eight months.

THE SHE-ANCIENT. When you have lived as long as I have –

ECRASIA [interrupting rudely] I shall worship rag dolls, perhaps. Thank heaven I am still in my prime.

THE HE-ANCIENT. You are still capable of thanking, though you do not know what you thank. You are a thanking little animal, a blaming little animal, a –

ACIS. A gushing little animal.

ARJILLAX. And, as she thinks, an artistic little animal.

ECRASIA [nettled] I am an animated being with a reasonable soul and human flesh subsisting. If your Automata had been properly animated, Martellus, they would have been more successful.

THE SHE-ANCIENT. That is where you are wrong, my child. If those two loathsome things had been rag dolls, they would have been amusing and lovable. The Newly Born here would have played with them; and you would all have laughed and played with them too until you had torn them to pieces; and then you would have laughed more than ever.

THE NEWLY BORN. Of course we should. Isnt that funny?

THE HE-ANCIENT. When a thing is funny, search it for a hidden truth.

STREPHON. Yes; and take all the fun out of it.

THE SHE-ANCIENT. Do not be so embittered because your sweetheart has outgrown her love for you. The Newly Born will make amends.

THE NEWLY BORN. Oh yes: I will be more than she could ever have been.

STREPHON. Psha! Jealous!

THE NEWLY BORN. Oh no. I have grown out of that. I love her now because she loved you, and because you love her.

THE HE-ANCIENT. That is the next stage. You are getting on very nicely, my child.

MARTELLUS. Come! what is the truth that was hidden in the rag doll?

THE HE-ANCIENT. Well, consider why you are not content with the rag doll, and must have something more closely resembling a real living creature. As you grow up you make images and paint pictures. Those of you who cannot do that make stories about imaginary dolls. Or you dress yourselves up as dolls and act plays about them.

THE SHE-ANCIENT. And, to deceive yourself the more completely, you take them so very very seriously that Ecrasia here declares that the making of dolls is the holiest work of creation, and the words you put into the mouths of dolls the sacredest of scriptures and the noblest of utterances.

ECRASIA. Tush!

ARJILLAX. Tosh!

THE SHE-ANCIENT. Yet the more beautiful they become the further they retreat from you. You cannot caress them as you caress the rag doll. You cannot cry for them when they are broken or lost, or when you pretend they have been unkind to you, as you could when you played with rag dolls.

THE HE-ANCIENT. At last, like Pygmalion, you demand from your dolls the final perfection of resemblance to life. They must move and speak.

THE SHE-ANCIENT. They must love and hate.

THE HE-ANCIENT. They must think that they think.

THE SHE-ANCIENT. They must have soft flesh and warm blood.

THE HE-ANCIENT. And then, when you have achieved this as Pygmalion did; when the marble masterpiece is dethroned by the automaton and the homo by the homunculus; when the body and the brain, the reasonable soul and human flesh subsisting, as Ecrasia says, stand before you unmasked as mere machinery, and your impulses are shewn to be nothing but reflexes, you are filled with horror and loathing, and would give worlds to be young enough to play with your rag doll again, since every step away from it has been a step away from love and happiness. Is it not true?

THE SHE-ANCIENT. Speak, Martellus: you who have travelled the whole path.

MARTELLUS. It is true. With fierce joy I turned a temperature of a million degrees on those two things I had modelled, and saw them vanish in an instant into inoffensive dust.

THE SHE-ANCIENT. Speak, Arjillax: you who have advanced from imitating the lightly living child to the intensely living ancient. Is it true, so far?

ARJILLAX. It is partly true: I cannot pretend to be satisfied now with modelling pretty children.

THE HE-ANCIENT. And you, Ecrasia: you cling to your highly artistic dolls as the noblest projections of the Life Force, do you not?

ECRASIA. Without art, the crudeness of reality would make the world unbearable.

THE NEWLY BORN [*anticipating the She-Ancient, who is evidently going to challenge her*] Now you are coming to me, because I am the latest arrival. But I dont understand your art and your dolls at all. I want to caress my darling Strephon, not to play with dolls.

ACIS. I am in my fourth year; and I have got on very well without your dolls. I had rather walk up a mountain and down again than look at all the statues Martellus and

Arjillax ever made. You prefer a statue to an automaton, and a rag doll to a statue. So do I; but I prefer a man to a rag doll. Give me friends, not dolls.

THE HE-ANCIENT. Yet I have seen you walking over the mountains alone. Have you not found your best friend in yourself?

ACIS. What are you driving at, old one? What does all this lead to?

THE HE-ANCIENT. It leads, young man, to the truth that you can create nothing but yourself.

ACIS [musing] I can create nothing but myself. Ecrasia: you are clever. Do you understand it? I dont.

ECRASIA. It is as easy to understand as any other ignorant error. What artist is as great as his own works? He can create masterpieces; but he cannot improve the shape of his own nose.

ACIS. There! What have you to say to that, old one?

THE HE-ANCIENT. He can alter the shape of his own soul. He could alter the shape of his nose if the difference between a turned-up nose and a turned-down one were worth the effort. One does not face the throes of creation for trifles.

ACIS. What have you to say to that, Ecrasia?

ECRASIA. I say that if the ancients had thoroughly grasped the theory of fine art they would understand that the difference between a beautiful nose and an ugly one is of supreme importance: that it is indeed the only thing that matters.

THE SHE-ANCIENT. That is, they would understand something they could not believe, and that you do not believe.

ACIS. Just so, mam. Art is not honest: that is why I never could stand much of it. It is all make-believe. Ecrasia never really says things: she only rattles her teeth in her mouth.

ECRASIA. Acis: you are rude.

ACIS. You mean that I wont play the game of make-believe. Well, I dont ask you to play it with me; so why should you expect me to play it with you?

ECRASIA. You have no right to say that I am not sincere. I have found a happiness in art that real life has never given me. I am intensely in earnest about art. There is a magic and mystery in art that you know nothing of.

THE SHE-ANCIENT. Yes, child: art is the magic mirror you make to reflect your invisible dreams in visible pictures. You use a glass mirror to see your face: you use works of art to see your soul. But we who are older use neither glass mirrors nor works of art. We have a direct sense of life. When you gain that you will put aside your mirrors and statues, your toys and your dolls.

THE HE-ANCIENT. Yet we too have our toys and our dolls. That is the trouble of the ancients.

ARJILLAX. What! The ancients have their troubles! It is the first time I ever heard one of them confess it.

THE HE-ANCIENT. Look at us. Look at me. This is my body, my blood, my brain; but it is not me. I am the eternal life, the perpetual resurrection; but [*striking his body*] this structure, this organism, this makeshift, can be made by a boy in a laboratory, and is held back from dissolution only by my use of it. Worse still, it can be broken by a slip of the foot, drowned by a cramp in the stomach, destroyed by a flash from the clouds. Sooner or later, its destruction is certain.

THE SHE-ANCIENT. Yes: this body is the last doll to be discarded. When I was a child, Ecrasia, I, too, was an artist, like your sculptor friends there, striving to create perfection in things outside myself. I made statues: I painted pictures: I tried to worship them.

THE HE-ANCIENT. I had no such skill; but I, like Acis, sought perfection in friends, in lovers, in nature, in things outside myself. Alas! I could not create it: I could only imagine it

THE SHE-ANCIENT. I, like Arjillax, found out that my statues of bodily beauty were no longer even beautiful to me; and I pressed on and made statues and pictures of men and women of genius, like those in the old fable of Michael Angelo. Like Martellus, I smashed them when I saw that there was no life in them: that they were so dead that they would not even dissolve as a dead body does.

THE HE-ANCIENT. And I, like Acis, ceased to walk over the mountains with my friends, and walked alone; for I found that I had creative power over myself but none over my friends. And then I ceased to walk on the mountains; for I saw that the mountains were dead.

ACIS [*protesting vehemently*] No. I grant you about the friends perhaps; but the mountains are still the mountains, each with its name, its individuality, its upstanding strength and majesty, its beauty –

ECRASIA. What! Acis among the rhapsodists!

THE HE-ANCIENT. Mere metaphor, my poor boy: the mountains are corpses.

ALL THE YOUNG [*repelled*] Oh!

THE HE-ANCIENT. Yes. In the hardpressed heart of the earth, where the inconceivable heat of the sun still glows, the stone lives in fierce atomic convulsion, as we live in our slower way. When it is cast out to the surface it dies like deep-sea fish: what you see is only its cold dead body. We have tapped that central heat as prehistoric man tapped water springs; but nothing has come up alive from those flaming depths: your landscapes, your mountains, are only the world's cast skins and decaying teeth on which we live like microbes.

ECRASIA. Ancient: you blaspheme against Nature and against Man.

THE SHE-ANCIENT. Child, child, how much enthusiasm will you have for man when you have endured eight centuries of him, as I have, and seen him perish by an empty mischance that is yet a certainty? When I discarded my dolls as he discarded his friends and his mountains, it was to myself I turned as to the final reality. Here, and here alone, I could shape and create. When my arm was weak and I willed it to be strong, I could create a roll of muscle on it; and when I understood that, I understood that I could without any greater miracle give myself ten arms and three heads.

THE HE-ANCIENT. I also came to understand such miracles. For fifty years I sat contemplating this power in myself and concentrating my will.

THE SHE-ANCIENT. So did I; and for five more years I made myself into all sorts of fantastic monsters. I walked upon a dozen legs: I worked with twenty hands and a hundred fingers: I looked to the four quarters of the compass with eight eyes out of four heads. Children fled in amazement from me until I had to hide myself from them; and the ancients, who had forgotten how to laugh, smiled grimly when they passed.

THE HE-ANCIENT. We have all committed these follies. You will all commit them.

THE NEWLY BORN. Oh, do grow a lot of arms and legs and heads for us. It would be so funny.

THE HE-ANCIENT. My child: I am just as well as I am. I would not lift my finger now to have a thousand heads.

THE SHE-ANCIENT. But what would I not give to have no head at all?

ALL THE YOUNG. Whats that? No head at all? Why? How?

THE HE-ANCIENT. Can you not understand?

ALL THE YOUNG [shaking their heads] No.

THE SHE-ANCIENT. One day, when I was tired of learning to walk forward with some of my feet and backwards with others and sideways with the rest all at once, I sat on a rock with my four chins resting on four of my palms, and four of my elbows resting on four of my knees. And suddenly it came into my mind that this monstrous machinery of heads and limbs was no more me than my statues had been me, and that it was only an automaton that I had enslaved.

MARTELLUS. Enslaved? What does that mean?

THE SHE-ANCIENT. A thing that must do what you command it is a slave; and its commander is its master. These are words you will learn when your turn comes.

THE HE-ANCIENT. You will also learn that when the master has come to do everything through the slave, the slave becomes his master, since he cannot live without him.

THE SHE-ANCIENT. And so I perceived that I had made myself the slave of a slave.

THE HE-ANCIENT. When we discovered that, we shed our superfluous heads and legs and arms until we had our old shapes again, and no longer startled the children.

THE SHE-ANCIENT. But still I am the slave of this slave, my body. How am I to be delivered from it?

THE HE-ANCIENT. That, children, is the trouble of the ancients. For whilst we are tied to this tyrannous body we are subject to its death, and our destiny is not achieved.

THE NEWLY BORN. What is your destiny?

THE HE-ANCIENT. To be immortal.

THE SHE-ANCIENT. The day will come when there will be no people, only thought.

THE HE-ANCIENT. And that will be life eternal.

ECRASIA. I trust I shall meet my fatal accident before that day dawns.

ARJILLAX. For once, Ecrasia, I agree with you. A world in which there were nothing plastic would be an utterly miserable one.

ECRASIA. No limbs, no contours, no exquisite lines and elegant shapes, no worship of beautiful bodies, no poetic embraces in which cultivated lovers pretend that their caressing hands are wandering over celestial hills and enchanted valleys, no –

ACIS [interrupting her disgustedly] What an inhuman mind you have, Ecrasia!

ECRASIA. Inhuman!

ACIS. Yes: inhuman. Why dont you fall in love with someone?

ECRASIA: I! I have been in love all my life. I burned with it even in the egg.

ACIS. Not a bit of it. You and Arjillax are just as hard as two stones.

ECRASIA. You did not always think so, Acis.

ACIS. Oh, I know. I offered you my love once, and asked for yours.

ECRASIA. And did I deny it to you, Acis?

ACIS. You didnt even know what love was.

ECRASIA. Oh! I adored you, you stupid oaf, until I found that you were a mere animal.

ACIS. And I made no end of a fool of myself about you until I discovered that you were a mere artist. You appreciated my contours! I was plastic, as Arjillax says. I wasnt a man to you: I was a masterpiece appealing to your tastes and your senses. Your tastes and senses had overlaid the direct impulse of life in you. And because I cared only for our life, and went straight to it, and was bored by your calling my limbs fancy names and mapping me into mountains and valleys and all the rest of it, you called me an animal. Well, I am an animal, if you call a live man an animal.

ECRASIA. You need not explain. You refused to be refined. I did my best to lift your prehistoric impulses on to the plane of beauty, of imagination, of romance, of poetry, of art, of –

ACIS. These things are all very well in their way and in their proper places. But they are not love. They are an unnatural adulteration of love. Love is a simple thing and a deep thing: it is an act of life and not an illusion. Art is an illusion.

ARJILLAX. That is false. The statue comes to life always. The statues of today are the men and women of the next incubation. I hold up the marble figure before the mother and say, 'This is the model you must copy.' We produce what we see. Let no man dare to create in art a thing that he would not have exist in life.

MARTELLUS. Yes: I have been through all that. But you yourself are making statues of ancients instead of beautiful nymphs and swains. And Ecrasia is right about the ancients being inartistic. They are damnably inartistic.

ECRASIA [*triumphant*] Ah! Our greatest artist vindicates me. Thanks, Martellus.

MARTELLUS. The body always ends by being a bore. Nothing remains beautiful and interesting except thought, because the thought is the life. Which is just what this old gentleman and this old lady seem to think too.

THE SHE-ANCIENT. Quite so.

THE HE-ANCIENT. Precisely.

THE NEWLY BORN [*to the He-Ancient*] But you cant be nothing. What do you want to be?

THE HE-ANCIENT. A vortex.

THE NEWLY BORN. A what?

THE SHE-ANCIENT. A vortex. I began as a vortex: why should I not end as one?

ECRASIA. Oh! That is what you old people are. Vorticists.

ACIS. But if life is thought, can you live without a head?

THE HE-ANCIENT. Not now perhaps. But prehistoric men thought they could not live without tails. I can live without a tail. Why should I not live without a head?

THE NEWLY BORN. What is a tail?

THE HE-ANCIENT. A habit of which your ancestors managed to cure themselves.

THE SHE-ANCIENT. None of us now believe that all this machinery of flesh and blood is necessary. It dies.

THE HE-ANCIENT. It imprisons us on this petty planet and forbids us to range through the stars.

ACIS. But even a vortex is a vortex in something. You cant have a whirlpool without water; and you cant have a vortex without gas, or molecules or atoms or ions or electrons or something, not nothing.

THE HE-ANCIENT. No: the vortex is not the water nor the gas nor the atoms: it is a power over these things.

THE SHE-ANCIENT. The body was the slave of the vortex; but the slave has become the master; and we must free ourselves from that tyranny. It is this stuff [*indicating her body*], this flesh and blood and bone and all the rest of it, that is intolerable. Even prehistoric man dreamed of what he called an astral body, and asked who would deliver him from the body of this death.

ACIS [*evidently out of his depth*] I shouldnt think too much about it if I were you. You have to keep sane, you know.

The two Ancients look at one another; shrug their shoulders; and address themselves to their departure.

THE HE-ANCIENT. We are staying too long with you, children. We must go.

All the young people rise rather eagerly.

ARJILLAX. Dont mention it.

THE SHE-ANCIENT. It is tiresome for us, too. You see, children, we have to put things very crudely to you to make ourselves intelligible.

THE HE-ANCIENT. And I am afraid we do not quite succeed.

STREPHON. Very kind of you to come at all and talk to us, I'm sure.

ECRASIA. Why do the other ancients never come and give us a turn?

THE SHE-ANCIENT. It is difficult for them. They have forgotten how to speak; how to read; even how to think in your fashion. We do not communicate with one another in that way or apprehend the world as you do.

THE HE-ANCIENT. I find it more and more difficult to keep up your language. Another century or two and it will be impossible. I shall have to be relieved by a younger shepherd.

ACIS. Of course we are always delighted to see you; but still, if it tries you very severely, we could manage pretty well by ourselves, you know.

THE SHE-ANCIENT. Tell me, Acis: do you ever think of yourself as having to live perhaps for thousands of years?

ACIS. Oh, dont talk about it. Why, I know very well that I have only four years of what any reasonable person would call living; and three and a half of them are already gone.

ECRASIA. You must not mind our saying so; but really you cannot call being an ancient living.

THE NEWLY BORN [*almost in tears*] Oh, this dreadful shortness of our lives! I cannot bear it.

STREPHON. I made up my mind on that subject long ago. When I am three years and fifty weeks old, I shall have my fatal accident. And it will not be an accident.

THE HE-ANCIENT. We are very tired of this subject. I must leave you.

THE NEWLY BORN. What is being tired?

THE SHE-ANCIENT. The penalty of attending to children. Farewell.

> *The two Ancients go away severally, she into the grove, he up to the hills behind the temple.*

ALL. Ouf! [*A great sigh of relief*].

ECRASIA. Dreadful people!

STREPHON. Bores!

MARTELLUS. Yet one would like to follow them; to enter into their life: to grasp their thought; to comprehend the universe as they must.

ARJILLAX. Getting old, Martellus?

MARTELLUS. Well, I have finished with the dolls; and I am no longer jealous of you. That looks like the end. Two hours sleep is enough for me. I am afraid I am beginning to find you all rather silly.

STREPHON. I know. My girl went off this morning. She hadnt slept for weeks. And she found mathematics more interesting than me.

MARTELLUS. There is a prehistoric saying that has come down to us from a famous woman teacher. She said: 'Leave women; and study mathematics.' It is the only remaining fragment of a lost scripture called The Confessions of St Augustin, the English Opium Eater. That primitive savage must have been a great woman, to say a thing that still lives after three hundred centuries. I too will leave women and study mathematics, which I have neglected too long. Farewell, children, my old playmates. I almost wish I could feel sentimental about parting from you; but the cold truth is that you bore me. Do not be angry with me: your turn will come. [*He passes away gravely into the grove*].

ARJILLAX. There goes a great spirit. What a sculptor he was! And now, nothing! It is as if he had cut off his hands.

THE NEWLY BORN. Oh, will you all leave me as he has left you?

ECRASIA. Never. We have sworn it.

STREPHON. What is the use of swearing? She swore. He swore. You have sworn. They have sworn.

ECRASIA. You speak like a grammar.

STREPHON. That is how one ought to speak, isnt it? We shall all be forsworn.

THE NEWLY BORN. Do not talk like that. You are saddening us; and you are chasing the light away. It is growing dark.

ACIS. Night is falling. The light will come back tomorrow.

THE NEWLY BORN. What is tomorrow?

ACIS. The day that never comes. [*He turns towards the temple*]. *All begin trooping into the temple.*

THE NEWLY BORN [*holding Acis back*] That is no answer. What –

ARJILLAX. Silence. Little children should be seen and not heard.

THE NEWLY BORN [*putting out her tongue at him*]!

ECRASIA. Ungraceful. You must not do that.

THE NEWLY BORN. I will do what I like. But there is something the matter with me. I want to lie down. I cannot keep my eyes open.

ECRASIA. You are falling asleep. You will wake up again.

THE NEWLY BORN [*drowsily*] What is sleep?

ACIS. Ask no questions; and you will be told no lies. [*He takes her by the ear, and leads her firmly towards the temple*].

THE NEWLY BORN. Ai! oi! ai! Dont. I want to be carried. [*She reels into the arms of Acis, who carries her into the temple*].

ECRASIA. Come, Arjillax: you at least are still an artist. I adore you.

ARJILLAX. Do you? Unfortunately for you, I am not still a child. I have grown out of cuddling. I can only appreciate your figure. Does that satisfy you?

ECRASIA. At what distance?

ARJILLAX. Arm's length or more.

ECRASIA. Thank you: not for me. [*She turns away from him*].

ARJILLAX. Ha! ha! [*He strides off into the temple*].

ECRASIA [*calling to Strephon, who is on the threshold of the temple, going in*] Strephon.

STREPHON. No. My heart is broken. [*He goes into the temple*].

ECRASIA. Must I pass the night alone? [*She looks round,*

seeking another partner; but they have all gone]. After all, I can imagine a lover nobler than any of you. [*She goes into the temple*].

It is now quite dark. A vague radiance appears near the temple and shapes itself into the ghost of Adam.

A WOMAN'S VOICE [*in the grove*] Who is that?

ADAM. The ghost of Adam, the first father of mankind. Who are you?

THE VOICE. The ghost of Eve, the first mother of mankind.

ADAM. Come forth, wife; and shew yourself to me.

EVE [*appearing near the grove*] Here I am, husband. You are very old.

A VOICE [*in the hills*] Ha! ha! ha!

ADAM. Who laughs? Who dares laugh at Adam?

EVE. Who has the heart to laugh at Eve?

THE VOICE. The ghost of Cain, the first child, and the first murderer. [*He appears between them; and as he does so there is a prolonged hiss*]. Who dares to hiss at Cain, the lord of death?

A VOICE. The ghost of the serpent, that lived before Adam and before Eve, and taught them how to bring forth Cain. [*She becomes visible, coiled in the trees*].

A VOICE. There is one that came before the serpent.

THE SERPENT. That is the voice of Lilith, in whom the father and mother were one. Hail, Lilith!

Lilith becomes visible between Cain and Adam.

LILITH. I suffered unspeakably; I tore myself asunder; I lost my life, to make of my one flesh these twain, man and woman. And this is what has come of it. What do you make of it, Adam, my son?

ADAM. I made the earth bring forth by my labor, and the woman bring forth by my love. And this is what has come of it. What do you make of it, Eve, my wife?

EVE. I nourished the egg in my body and fed it with my blood. And now they let it fall as the birds did, and suffer not at all. What do you make of it, Cain, my first-born?

CAIN. I invented killing and conquest and mastery and the winnowing out of the weak by the strong. And now the strong have slain one another; and the weak live for ever;

and their deeds do nothing for the doer more than for another. What do you make of it, snake?

THE SERPENT. I am justified. For I chose wisdom and the knowledge of good and evil; and now there is no evil; and wisdom and good are one. It is enough. [*She vanishes*].

CAIN. There is no place for me on earth any longer. You cannot deny that mine was a splendid game while it lasted. But now! Out, out, brief candle! [*He vanishes*].

EVE. The clever ones were always my favorites. The diggers and the fighters have dug themselves in with the worms. My clever ones have inherited the earth. All's well. [*She fades away*].

ADAM. I can make nothing of it, neither head nor tail. What is it all for? Why? Whither? Whence? We were well enough in the garden. And now the fools have killed all the animals; and they are dissatisfied because they cannot be bothered with their bodies! Foolishness, I call it. [*He disappears*].

LILITH. They have accepted the burden of eternal life. They have taken the agony from birth; and their life does not fail them even in the hour of their destruction. Their breasts are without milk: their bowels are gone: the very shapes of them are only ornaments for their children to admire and caress without understanding. Is this enough; or shall I labor again? Shall I bring forth something that will sweep them away and make an end of them as they have swept away the beasts of the garden, and made an end of the crawling things and the flying things and of all them that refuse to live for ever? I had patience with them for many ages: they tried me very sorely. They did terrible things: they embraced death, and said that eternal life was a fable. I stood amazed at the malice and destructiveness of the things I had made: Mars blushed as he looked down on the shame of his sister planet: cruelty and hypocrisy became so hideous that the face of the earth was pitted with the graves of little children among which living skeletons crawled in search of horrible food. The pangs of another birth were already upon me when one man repented and lived three hundred years; and I waited to see what would come of that. And so much came of it that the horrors of that time seem now but an evil dream. They have redeemed themselves from their vileness, and turned away from their sins. Best of all, they are still not satisfied: the impulse I gave them in that day when I sundered myself in twain and launched Man and Woman on the earth still urges them: after passing a million goals they press on to the goal of redemption from the flesh, to the vortex freed from matter, to the whirlpool in pure intelligence that, when the world began, was a whirlpool in pure force. And though all that they have done seems but the first hour of the infinite work of creation, yet I will not supersede them until they have forded this last stream that lies between flesh and spirit, and disentangled their life from the matter that has always mocked it. I can wait: waiting and patience mean nothing to the eternal. I gave the woman the greatest of gifts: curiosity. By that her seed has been saved from my wrath; for I also am curious; and I have waited always to see what they will do tomorrow. Let them feed that appetite well for me. I say, let them dread, of all things, stagnation; for from the moment I, Lilith, lose hope and faith in them, they are doomed. In that hope and faith I have let them live for a moment; and in that moment I have spared them many times. But mightier creatures than they have killed hope and faith, and perished from the earth; and I may not spare them for ever. I am Lilith: I brought life into the whirlpool of force, and compelled my enemy, Matter, to obey a living soul. But in enslaving Life's enemy I made him Life's master; for that is the end of all slavery; and now I shall see the slave set free and the enemy reconciled, the whirlpool become all life and no matter. And because these infants that call themselves ancients are reaching out towards that, I will have patience with them still; though I know well that when they attain it they shall become one with me and supersede me, and Lilith will be only a legend and a lay that has lost its meaning. Of Life only is there no end;

and though of its million starry mansions many are empty and many still unbuilt, and though its vast domain is as yet unbearably desert, my seed shall one day fill it and master its matter to its uttermost confines. And for what may be beyond, the eyesight of Lilith is too short. It is enough that there is a beyond. [*She vanishes*].

THE END

*Some other books published by Penguins
are described overleaf*

THE PENGUIN SHAW

ANDROCLES AND THE LION
(*Also available in the Shaw alphabet edition*)

THE APPLE CART

BACK TO METHUSELAH

THE DOCTOR'S DILEMMA

HEARTBREAK HOUSE

MAJOR BARBARA

MAN AND SUPERMAN

THE MILLIONAIRESS

PLAYS PLEASANT*
(*Arms and the Man, Candida, The Man of Destiny, You Never Can Tell*)

PLAYS UNPLEASANT
(*Widowers' Houses, The Philanderer, Mrs Warren's Profession*)

PYGMALION

SAINT JOAN

SELECTED ONE ACT PLAYS VOLS 1 & 2

SEVEN ONE ACT PLAYS
(*Available in the U.S.A.*)

THREE PLAYS FOR PURITANS*
(*The Devil's Disciple, Cæsar and Cleopatra, Captain Brassbound's Conversion*)

*Published as separate plays in the U.S.A.